Author: Teddy Baire
https://www.teddybaire.com/
Editor: Heather Williams
https://www.fiverr.com/heatherwealth
Cover Designer: Queen Mercedes
https://www.fiverr.com/Queenmercedes
ISBN: 978-1-7349516-4-6

I0582440

READER BEWARE

This novel MAY CONTAIN depictions of sex, assault, murder, blood, gore, horrors from the moon, multiple phobias, and other questionable acts.

Thank you for visiting this world of magic.

CHAPTER 1

The moon was full in the sky above Burlus as a chilled wind blew across the plains outside the city. Breaking the silence of the night were the sounds of horses cutting through the wind on their way towards its gates. They barreled down the dirt road that led to where two men stood guard at the entrance.

Hearing horses approaching the gate from the shadows, one guard peered out into the darkness, holding a torch in his hand. Suddenly they appeared out of the night, a group of mounted horses driven towards the gate.

"Halt!" shouted the guard, "Halt! Who goes there." He

waved the torch in an arc over his head before the closed gate.

The group of horses reared to a stop before the guard and a cloaked figure on horseback made his way ahead of them, trotting his steed up to the guard.

"Greetings Faylin," said Prince Saffron as he removed the cloak from his head to reveal his face. "I take it the nights have been easy on you while I've been away."

"Oh, I didn't realize it was you," said the guard. "Welcome back your highness. We'd all wondered where you'd gone off to. Not much happened here, just a random street fight here and there, nothing much else."

"Well, maybe one day you'll get the excitement of a full city under siege," said Saffron with a smirk on his lips, looking down at Faylin. "That way, you'll have some fun stories to tell those two kids of yours, rather than just moping about at night and having a few drinks."

"Hey now, don't say that. I've never heard of any stories where those guarding the gate survived things like that. I'm very thankful for the peace the king has," said the guard before whistling up to men above the gate. "Alright, open her up." He then turned back to Saffron. "I'll gladly lie to my children about the wars I've been in if that means I'm alive long enough to keep feeding 'em."

Soon came the sound of metal chains clanking against one another from behind the guard as the gate lurched upward, exposing the city's dark streets ahead of them.

"Be well, gentlemen," said Saffron as he and his guards trotted into the city.

The streets of Burlus were primarily empty at night, except for the occasional soldier or wandering peasant looking for a drink. Alongside the doors of some of the homes they passed, the flicker of torches sent shadows dancing throughout dimly lit streets. The wind nipped at the small flames, making the passageway seem as if the shadows were moving to surround them. The mixture of light and shadow swayed over the stone and marble build-ings as they moved forward. At every turn they made, there were metal fire bowls that spread throughout the streets.

"Has Saffron decided what he will tell king about not getting girl?" asked Frenka, trotting alongside Saffron and Dekol, with the rest of the prince's guards behind them.

Saffron smiled back at Frenka, "The truth. We quelled a minor rebellion of sorts out in the village of Nyril as well as some weird type of magic that Victor mentioned about crystals being implanted into people's bodies. Seems like more than enough reason to not have her. Plus, it seems as if he knows that Highland fella who has the girl. So, I'd say Father should clean up his own messes."

"Well, we did follow them to make sure they left the kingdom," said Dekol, looking up at the castle as they approached. "What will we do next?"

"What's that Dekol?" asked Saffron, patting Dekol on the back as he rode alongside him. "Are you ready for another adventure already? That shoulder of yours hasn't even healed properly yet."

"You both can have adventure. I just want bath in hot water and to soak hair," said Frenka.

"And I'd like to watch you do that, Frenka." Saffron laughed as Frenka glowered back at him. "Well, even with my advances tossed aside, I'd imagine we all could use a rest after all this time on the road."

The prince dismounted his horse at the castle steps as two more guards bowed to him.

"Welcome back your highness," said a guard as he approached.

Saffron dismounted, giving the reins of his horse to Dekol, "You all head home. I shall inform Father of the current circumstances we find ourselves in."

Frenka and the rest of the prince's guards rode off into the night while Dekol stayed behind, giving Saffron a knowing look.

"Would you like for me to accompany you, Saffron?"

"Don't worry about me, Dekol. We aren't children anymore. Come visit me on the morrow some time. And we'll have drinks as we find someone to properly tend to that shoulder of yours. You haven't been letting on, but I can tell it hasn't healed properly."

"Tomorrow, then," said Dekol as he tightened his hand on the reins of both horses and made his way off into the darkness of the city.

After watching Dekol leave, Saffron turned back to the castle and took a deep breath before staring up at it's cold walls in the darkness. *Home once again. And yet, I'd rather be sleeping on the ground in the woods than be here.* He thought before taking the steps up to the castle. *Right. Well, no use prolonging this I guess.* He passed the guards at the top of the steps.

"Welcome home your highness," spoke one of the guards to Saffron. "You're back from another trip I see."

"You know me Willard. It's hard for me to stay in one place," said Saffron, pressing his hand on the door, and pushing it open into the main hall.

Inside, there was a single guard who stood watch in a room that was lit by candle fire. The tiny ember did little to illuminate the room as only hints of the castle banners could be seen against the walls alongside suits of polished armor that gleamed, hidden in the darkness.

"Your highness," spoke the guard.

"I've returned, Humfrey. Has father been made aware?"

"Yes, Sir. He awaits you in his study."

"Of course he does," Saffron said as he walked past Humfrey, placing his hand on the guard's shoulder. "Wanna wish me luck?"

"You'll be fine, your highness. You've grown into a fine man. Even if the King never says it, I know he sees it."

"Well, it's nice to know one of us has faith in me," said Saffron as he released his hand from Humfrey's shoulder.

"Give it time, your highness. I've known your father a long time. He can be hard on you, I know. But he cares deeply for you."

"You've always been a good friend, Humfrey," said Saffron as he walked on ahead up the steps. Slowly, he made his way through the halls of the dark castle, gliding his hands along the cold stone walls as the torch lights flickered as he passed. He greeted every guard he met along the way by name until he finally reached his father's study. *And once again the charade must go on.* Saffron took a deep breath once again and gave two knocks on the door.

"Enter," came the deep voice of the king from inside.

Saffron opened the door to see the king sitting at a desk alight by candle flame. He held two pieces of parchment in his hands as his face glanced between the two. His father's face was half-hidden in shadow, and the other half revealed by candle-light, creating a visage far scarier than any ghost. He stepped inside the room, closing the door, letting his finger linger between the cracks in the wood.

"Hello again, Father," said Saffron as he turned around to face the king. "Don't you want to stand and greet your son in a warm embrace?"

The king narrowed his eyes at Saffron from above the parchment, "Seeing as I don't see a small girl beside you, I assume a failure has come to report his failure."

"Depends on which one of us is the failure," Saffron stepped towards his father, his footsteps sounding off his ears in the quiet room. "Is it me as a son, or you as a father? I'd imagine we both have plenty of stories to tell."

"Fine," said the king, as he placed the pieces of parchment on the desk, leaning back into his chair. "Why are you here and not the emissary?"

Saffron walked over to the candle atop his father's desk and began waving his hand over the flame. He watched the flame try to nip at his fingers as they danced over the burning wick. "That man Victor is quite the capable ally to have. He did indeed find the girl. Twice, in fact. Apparently, she had adopted the name Rana and was still hiding out in the city."

The king brought his hands together, intertwining his fingers and placing his thumbs against the bridge of his nose as he narrowed his eyes at his son.

"If the girl was found, then where is she?"

"Oscar Highland," said Saffron, turning his attention away from the flame and towards his father.

"What?" asked the king, raising a brow.

"He wanted me to tell you that he now claims the girl as his daughter and was quite adamant that you would understand. He was even willing to challenge me in a fight to keep her. I don't suppose you would like to share some info on that man. Frenka said you'd hired him before as a mercenary, but that was as much as she knew."

The king balled his fist, taking in a deep breath, closed his eyes, and began tapping his finger slowly onto his desk. "And where are Oscar and the girl now?"

"We followed them until they entered Latrusa. He warned me that if I were to try anything, that he would immediately take the girl to Queen Yasmine."

"The king sighed, "Of course that bastard did," shaking his head in disapproval.

"Who is this Oscar Highland father, and why was he so sure of himself?"

"An old fox that should have died a hundred battles ago." The king began tapping his finger on the table again. The sound thrummed through the silence of the room.

"And what of the girl? Are you going to inform me as to why she is so important?"

"The girl is of no importance to you, that is... Wait. Did you see her? Was she able to cast any magic?"

"I did see her. Her leg was bandaged, and she was walking with a crutch. But I never saw her use any magic."

"And what of the emissary? Where is he?"

"Apparently, he was Oscar's prisoner. He mentioned they would release him only after they were safely into Latrusa. But it didn't seem as if he was held captive," said Saffron as he began to pace around the dimly lit room. "He wanted me to inform you that he held up his end of the deal and found the girl. It's simply our fault for losing her."

The king drummed his fingers on the desk, "Fine; you can leave. I'll deal with the rest myself."

"And you will not inform me as to why this girl is so important to you. You know the magistrate down there assumed that she might be your daughter. A secret love child from a tawdry affair, perhaps."

"As if I would sire a female child," said the king with a chuckle. "The girl is of no concern to you. Instead, focus on your upcoming nuptials to house Dunblane. I imagine the simple act of plowing your wife wouldn't be too much of a task for you."

"No father," said Saffron as he stopped pacing the room, placed his back against the wall and folded his arms. He then gave a sigh and closed his eyes. "I shall endeavor through the act as any dutiful son might. I'm sure if I have trouble, I can ask one of the guards to give me some pointers. After all, a bit of fatherly advice doesn't exactly need to come from one's own father, now does it?"

"We do what we must for the line. Family sentiment is a luxury that gets in the way. Both you and I have a role to play. We're not common peasants, so thinking like one is a waste of time."

"How poetic. Such selfless dedication," said the prince with a tired expression on his face.

"Forget your childish mockery. Tell me about this mess in Nyril," remarked the king as he held up the crumpled parchment. "It says the city was ransacked by a pack of Sakari on horseback. They killed all the city's guards and took several women and men with them."

The prince gazed back at his father in wonderment, "I

was in Nyril, but when I left, the city was very much intact. A few guards were dead, but there was nothing like... Highland; his group had a Sakari in it. But why would he ransack the village?" The prince shook his head. "The girl... Frenka and Dekol said they rescued the girl from the village. But why would he do that after he had already gotten her back?"

The king sighed, "Nyril is around where we had gotten reports of people disappearing, wasn't it? Any info on that?"

"No, I was following the girl, and didn't look into it." *Just what the hell is happening? What aren't you telling me, dammit?*

"No matter then, I've already set out for a fresh garrison of men to be stationed there. They should arrive in a week's time. Things should calm down once they arrive."

"Do you still have plans to retrieve the girl, or will you just hand her off to Highland?"

The king opened a drawer in his desk and pulled out another piece of parchment, "You leave the girl's concern to me. As I have said, you have other matters to attend to. Now go on, I have preparations to make." Dipping the quill into the ink, the king began to write.

Saffron walked to the door before turning back to his father, "Fine, I shall leave you to scheme in the darkness as you seem to enjoy it." He then left the room before his father could respond to the comment.

Once outside the door, Saffron placed his back against the wall, bringing his hands over his eyes and sighed. *I'm sick of all of this. Must it really always be this way? Can I never do anything enough where he could acknowledge his own damn son for his efforts?* Wondered Saffron as he closed eyes. His lip began to twitch. *Of course not, acting like an actual father is beneath him.*

"Need a shoulder to cry on?"

Saffron turned to see Dekol emerge from a shadowy corner into the torch-lit corridor, and he sighed again, dropping his head, "Weren't you supposed to listen to your prince's orders and go home?"

Dekol shrugged, "I'm the son of a traitor. You're an idiot for expecting me to follow orders. My father didn't listen to your father, so what right do you have to expect me to listen to you?"

"Perhaps father and I have more in common than I assumed," said Saffron with a chuckle despite his feelings as he lifted his back from the wall to greet Dekol.

"Besides, I'm your friend. And what friend would leave you to wallow in self-pity for the rest of the night?"

Saffron shook his head, walking over to join Dekol, "You know, if you acted like this around others, perhaps you'd make more friends."

"Bah, you're enough of a friend. And besides, given your unrivaled mix of recklessness and stupidity, it just makes everyone else seem boring by comparison."

"I'm not sure if that was a compliment or not."

"Neither am I, but let's just say it was and go get you drunk," said Dekol, patting Saffron on the back and escorting him down the dark corridor.

CHAPTER 2

On a morning in the kingdom of Latrusa, high in a tree, birds chirped to the glow of the sun as it shone down upon a grassy meadow. The tree leaves were shaken free from their branch as a small brown-haired girl swung upside down from a rope that was tied around her ankles. A small distance away from her, sat a dark-haired woman on an old wooden log with a book in her hand.

"Okay, now focus, Rana. You need to push everything else away and learn how your body reacts to the motion and adjust accordingly."

Rana swung back and forth, her hair dangling in the

air from the motion. She wore bloomers that stopped at her knees. Tied to a string along her waist, there was an assortment of small blades. Across her chest was a tightly wrapped cloth to conceal her modesty.

Reaching upward to her waist, Rana grabbed one of the blades bringing it down to her face. It shimmered in the sunlight as she watched a twisted image of herself in its reflection. *Is this what I look like now?* She appeared to herself as some type of disfigured abomination as a bead of sweat dripped down her face to her eyes, which were turning red from the rush of blood to her brain. She blinked, sending the droplet falling to the grass beneath.

Shaking the distorted image from her mind, Rana narrowed her eyes. Focusing ahead, where three circular targets stood nailed to spokes sticking out of the ground. She threw one blade at the center post, but it missed, landing on the ground behind it alongside another dozen blades that had missed their targets.

"Oh, you got close that time," said Dessi as she flipped another page of her book.

Rana watched the upside-down world spin as the momentum from the throw sent her swinging back and forth through the air as the rope stretched under her weight. The tree limb waned from the momentum, its leaves having been shaken free and gliding down around Rana in a fluttery fashion, creating small shadows over her body in the sunlight.

"Try to use the momentum to predict when you're going to throw the blade," said Dessi, placing her thumb in between the pages of her book. "That will help you anticipate where your target will be. It's all about prediction."

Rana refocused her efforts, trying to swing her body back and forth again. The time upside down was getting to her. She could taste the blood in her mouth from the inversion and felt the pressure building in her head. *Just one more. Come on, I can do this.* She gripped the blade in between her fingers, tossing a few more, but none of them hit their mark as they all went sailing over and under each of their target posts. *Dammit, dammit. Why?* She breathed heavily as sweat dripped from her face as more frustration set in. She swung back and tried reaching up for another blade from her waist, when a sharp pain in her leg on that last swing caused her to lose focus, the metal slipping from her hand, landing in the blades of grass below her.

"Can I get down now? I... I think I'm done for a while."

Dessi rose up and walked over to a rope tied to the base of a spike in the ground. Releasing the rope, she slowly lowered Rana back down to the soil where she caught herself with her arms, cushioning her descent. Sitting up on the grass, Rana started rubbing at a scar on her leg while breathing deeply, enduring the pain until it subsided.

"I told you we should have waited to resume your training," said Dessi, walking over to her.

"No, it's fine. They said I needed to start exercising my leg now."

"I highly doubt this is the type of exercise they meant," commented Dessi, looking over at the slew of blades piercing the ground around the targets. "Why do you still want to train in knives, anyway? Isn't Oscar planning to have you trained in magic? I can't imagine those blades helping much when you're gonna be casting fireballs or gusts of wind everywhere."

"I might not be able to. Victor said some mages are healers or tracers. And I met a mage before and she still had a sword, even though she had fire magic. And if she and Jacob can do it, then I want to."

"Well, Jacob's isn't really meant for combat. But as stubborn as you are, I guess that would be the route you'd take."

"That stubbornness is probably the reason you're both still alive," said Victor, approaching from behind a tent.

"Every day you show up here. I wonder if Oscar's

recruited you," said Dessi, placing her hands on her hips.

"Hey, this is my long-awaited vacation," replied Victor with a smile. "Are you so eager to run me off after saving your lives? And here I thought ladies were supposed to be grateful to their heroes."

"Sorry, I'm not the type to bat my eyes or shake my tits at you unless I have plans to put a blade through your throat."

"Yeah, well..." Victor rubbed at his neck. "That seems to be a common thing around here, apparently."

Dessi raised a brow, giving Victor a curious look.

"Well, either way, since I'm enjoying your company, my goal is to continue training Rana until Oscar's finished making arrangements."

"I don't need training anymore. I'm fine now," said Rana, still rubbing at the scar on her leg.

"Oh, is that so?" asked Victor with a chuckle. "I'm glad you think so. Although that leg of yours might say something different. How's it feeling today?"

"She's working it too hard again," sighed Dessi, shaking her head.

"I'm not. It feels a lot better now."

"Well, you probably won't be running for a while." Victor noted, looking down at Rana's leg. "But still, it's been less than a month, and here you are swinging from trees with blades in your hand. That must be a sign of progress."

"Well, she hasn't managed to hit anything yet, so I think she just doesn't want to let on how bad it is," said Dessi as Rana frowned at her. "Don't pull that sour face with me. Just look at that mess over there." She pointed to the mass of blades lying on the ground. "You haven't been able to land not a one since we've started back training. So, something must be off, and it's gonna be off till you get better," expressed Dessi in an authoritative tone.

"And that would bring me back to why I'm here; you think that leg's good enough for our training now?"

"Yes, Sir," said Rana, sighing while standing up and

walking over, gathering up the blades from the ground, shaking the dirt from them, and placing them into a leather sleeve. *I'm fine. I don't need this silly training anymore. Why won't he believe I'm okay now?* She tried to hide that she favored her uninjured leg as she reached down and picked up a jewel-encrusted dagger and pouch tied to a belt. Tying the belt to her waist, she picked up the leather sleeve of blades.

"Bring me them blades, honey. I'll take 'em back to the tent while you have your training with Victor."

Rana did as Dessi instructed, handing her the bag before walking over to Victor and grabbing his hand. The two walked off through the campsite, leaving Dessi to finish pulling the rope down. She shook her head as she watched Rana walking off, trying to conceal her slight limp.

"You're still favoring your leg; you wanna swing by and get your crutches?" asked Victor, leading Rana by the hand.

"It's not that bad," assured Rana, dropping her head. "It just stings a little, is all. Audebe said that as long as I didn't try running, it should be okay."

"Did she now? But I'm sure she didn't expect you to be dangling from trees with your legs tied."

"I won't overdo it. I wanna get better."

"I hope not; you're gonna need to be happy and healthy if you're going to continue your training."

The two of them saw a Sakari man up ahead, waving at them. Victor waved back and approached him.

"Hello Victor and Rana."

"Hey Daypa," said Rana.

Daypa smiled down at Rana, "Here, I have brought you sweet cakes. You can take and eat them." He opened a bag and pulled out a warm bundle, handing it to Rana. She took the bundle, unwrapped it, and revealed a warm piece of bread. Its warmth and sweet scent instantly made her mouth water.

"Thank you, Daypa. Have Momo and Jomo made it back

yet?" asked Rana as she took a bite.

"No, they still off with Gregga somewhere, should be back soon. But I sure they be missing you too little one." Daypa slowly reached out his hand and placed it on Rana's head for a few seconds, before removing it. "Okay, now I go; I still got baking to do."

"Bye, Daypa." Rana waved to him as he headed back into the mass of tents uphill, where a few other Sakari were scattered about.

"I'm not sure I'll ever get used to a Sakari strutting around camp handing out muffins to people," said Victor as he watched the Sakari man enter one of the tents.

Rana stopped chewing the bread, her lips quivering slightly as she looked down to the ground, frowning. Taking a breath, she allowed Victor to guide her once again through the camp. It was filled with tents and smoke from the smothering of the night's fires. As they went forward through the grounds, they could see many soldiers walking about or training with the weapons.

Victor even spotted some of the men who had appeared that day on horseback with Molan. They were once again shirtless as they stood around watching an exhibition match, but still, the look about them seemed uneasy without their leader amongst them. A few of them even turned to see him and Rana, nodding as they passed. Reflexively, Rana squeezed Victor's hand as she caught them staring at her.

"No one here blames you for what you did," said Victor trying to comfort Rana as he slowed his pace, turning by a group of women washing clothes. They heard the sound of them splashing into buckets of water as they passed. "Oscar had a good chance to talk with them. A few of them even have daughters a bit younger than you. They may regret losing their leader, but they assuredly don't have any ill will against you."

"I know," said Rana, shaking her head. "They came and told me so. I just... I just don't know why he did that."

"I haven't asked since it happened but tell me. Have you been able to feel that magic anymore?" asked Victor, quickly trying to divert the subject of their conversation.

"No, but sometimes I feel hot though when I'm tired. But then it goes away."

"Hot? That's a weird way to put it, but I guess that makes sense. You burned everything around you that night. You still have that burned horse?"

"I still have it; I keep it in my bag."

"Well, no need to rush learning magical powers, I guess. Like most things in life, it's going to happen whether you want it to or not. Have you thought about what type of magic you want?"

"What do you mean?" asked Rana, looking up at him. "Do I get to pick?"

"No, just guessing on what you think you'd prefer. As for my take on it, I'd be guessing you'll be a fire mage. But who knows? Maybe you'll be able to move the soil beneath you or fly through the sky like a bird."

"Have you ever really seen people fly before?"

"I've seen the Queen do it. Well, the Queen of Mari. But apparently, it's hard to control, and you're likely to pass out from magic headaches and fall to your death. So, most mages don't even try."

"I don't think I want to fly then," said Rana as she scratched at her head, "Maybe I can make myself stronger and lift heavy stuff."

"That's called magical strengthening. Most trained mages can do that. I'm sure you'll be able to do the same."

"Then that's fine; I don't really care about the rest."

"What? And here I thought you had a grand scheme. That maybe you'd grow up and start talking to the trees and bunny rabbits."

"Can magic let me talk to bunny rabbits?" asked Rana excitedly.

"It seems you do have a dream," said Victor with a laugh.

"But I'm not sure. I do know that I've met a few mages who had pet owls and I think they were able to communicate with them. I don't see why rabbits would be any different."

"If I can, I'll talk to bunny rabbits over owls."

"I'm sure you would," said Victor as he gripped her hand.

Ahead of her, Rana saw a bare-chested Jacob swinging his sword in practice. The blade shone every time it caught the sunlight, looking as if it was a beacon in the daylight. She noticed how smooth and quick the steel cut through the air, creating an audible whooshing sound as he brought it down in an overhead slash.

She also paid attention to the muscles of his body as he twisted. A slash and then a strike, his chest tightening with every movement. Along the side of his belly was a large scar and Rana immediately wondered where it came from. Looking at him now as he swung his blade, he seemed so different from her when she tried wielding her wooden sword. Even with the lightly shaved lumber in her hand, she felt she was clunky and slow when compared with how he moved with his blade.

Jacob swung a few more times before a dark-haired man in a ponytail approached him, holding out a book in his hand. He stopped swinging his blade, taking a look in the book as the man held it out, opening it for him. Skimming it over, Jacob said a few words, and the man tore the parchment free from the book before handing it to Jacob, who took it as he noticed Victor and Rana approaching. Placing the parchment piece into his pocket, he then laid his blade on a cloth he had on the ground before walking over with the man to meet them.

"Hey there... you two," said Jacob as he pulled a small rag from the back of his trousers and began wiping the sweat from his face.

Rana stared at his upper body, noticing more of his muscles. His chest was big, and his arms looked strong. Jacob rubbed the sweaty cloth against the back of his neck.

Glancing down to his waist again, she could see so much sweat on his stomach.

"Don't stare too hard, or he'll catch you," whispered Victor.

Rana turned her face up to see Victor smiling back down at her. "I... ahh."

Victor raised a brow at her, and she just turned away from him, looking down at the ground as her face blushed.

"I take it Rana's training is going well," said Jacob, trying to catch his breath.

Victor turned back to Jacob, smiling, "Yeah, although you might have sped the training along a lot more than I could have expected."

"Really? How's that?" asked Jacob, rubbing the cloth across his face.

"Oh, well, let's just say that I think little Rana here has grown quite fond of you and Dessi. So, I imagine her getting to watch you out here training hard has inspired her to put forth some effort of her own," said Victor holding in a chuckle.

"Oh, is that right?" asked Jacob as he knelt to Rana, patting her on the head. "What about you, little lady? Would you say you've grown fond of us here?"

Rana kept her face turned, refusing to look at Jacob.

"Hey now, don't act sour with me. I'm just... hey, your face is all red," Jacob reached out and rubbed the side of Rana's cheek with his thumb. "That leg of your giving ya trouble again? I told Dessi she might need to wait a while before training you again."

Rana quickly slapped Jacob's hand away, "I'm fine. My leg is fine. Stop treating me like a baby."

"Woah," said Jacob, pulling his hand back, "where'd that come from?"

Victor started laughing, "I think we just witnessed her grow up a little."

"Is this the girl that Jasper rescued?" asked the

dark-haired man.

"Oh, sorry, I probably should have introduced you," said Jacob, gesturing to the fellow beside him. "This here's Rebby. Jasper picked him up a few years ago, and he travels around gathering information much the same as he did."

"So, you're a spy, then?" asked Victor with a smirk.

"Not unless I have to be," replied Rebby as he tapped the book to his side. "I mostly just write down interesting stories or rumors and pass them off to Oscar."

Rana noticed a deep scar on Rebby's neck before looking at his face and saw he was still staring back at her.

He stepped forward and squatted down in front of her looking her in her eyes. "I was told Jasper really liked you. Even asked Oscar to look after you."

Rana's leg began to shake. Her mouth feeling dry she tried to speak but the words wouldn't come out. But before anything else could happen. Jacob put his hands on Rebby's shoulders and pulled him back a bit.

"Yeah," said Jacob. "She doesn't really do well around strange men. Give her some time to warm up to you."

"Oh," replied Rebby, standing up and taking a step back. "I see. Well, explain it to me later. I still need to report to your father."

"Sure, I'll catch up with you."

Rebby took one final look down at Rana and turned, making his way back off into the camp.

"Seems like a nice enough fellow," said Victor, watching the man go, before turning back to Jacob. "And you seem to be having fun this morning. How goes the training?"

"Everything's going well," replied Jacob, rising back up to his feet. "Just practicing a few routines so I won't lose to you again."

"Goddess willing, I hope to never be in a situation like that again. After this whole ordeal is over, I have plans to run away to a nice quiet place and fill my life with books and rest, not bloody blades and war."

"Says the famous war general to a mercenary. I don't think our lives are destined to be that easy."

"Did he really beat you in a fight?" asked Rana, looking up at the size difference between the two men.

"Yeah, the bastard did," said Jacob, looking at Victor and biting his lip. "Usually, I'm fairly confident in my skills with a blade, but Victor here's fighting style has a questionable moral code to it, if I must say."

"But you're bigger, and you have magic," said Rana, continuing to glance between the two men.

Jacob frowned, looking down at Rana, before extending a finger and placing it on her head. "I think I remember saying something about how this was the best weapon you have when it comes to fighting." Jacob looked back at Victor, raised to his full height, looking him in the eye. "This bastard was kind enough to re-educate me on that lesson."

Rana noticed the tension in Jacob's posture change as he rubbed his thumb against the fingers of his sword hand.

"I merely got lucky is all," said Victor with his hand raised in submission. "The fight could have gone either way, really."

"It sure didn't seem that way when you had your knee in my back and whatever that was around my neck." Jacob smiled and gestured over to his blade, "Don't suppose you'd be interested in a friendly sparring match."

"Not as long as common sense is my companion," chuckled Victor as he took a small step back. "You seem a little too eager to whip my ass at the moment."

Jacob took a deep breath, "Alright, I get it. This will be a grudge I'll just have to let go." Jacob walked back over, picking up his blade. "You two off to see the old man then, I take it."

"Yeah, he asked for me to swing by and see him today. So, we're headed up that way." Victor looked around the camp at the small number of tents and a few people walking around. "Your group here really has shrunk since we entered Latrusa. I'm still not exactly sure how you all operate."

"Yeah, a lot of the men have families, so they've headed home until the old man calls for them again. Gregga and her Sakari pretty much do what they want, so even I'm not too sure what deal father has made out with them." Jacob stretched his arm, balancing the blade in his hand, then looked back down at Rana, who was still holding onto Victor's fingers. "But I imagine that they'll return soon enough. Those two Sakari girls seem to have gotten pretty attached to Rana now."

Victor turned to Rana shaking her hand, "Actually, why do those girls call you sister now? That surely can't be a normal thing for Sakari girls to go around making sisters of newly found kingdom girls."

"Now, that's something I've been wondering about myself," said Jacob. "I've asked father about it before, but he was being all tight-lipped. Be good to get an explanation on that little phenomenon."

Rana looked down at the blade at her hip and remembered that night in the tent with Oscar, Jomo, and Momo before biting her lip and looking back at the two men. "I don't wanna talk about it."

"And thus, the mystery continues. You really are a little bundle of secrets," said Jacob.

"From my experience with the fairer sex, I'm starting to believe almost any woman would fit into that category," spoke Victor shaking his head.

"Careful now, there's an old wives' tale that says, the more a man wishes for less women in his life, the more that shall appear."

"Between the blades at my neck, the fire on my ass, and one crazy queen. I fail to see how things could get worse."

"Suit yourself, but tales like that exist for a reason."

"I'll take my chances," said Victor as he looked ahead up the camp. "Well, come along little miss secrets. We still have to go see Oscar."

"Off with you two then. I'll be swinging by to see Dessi later if ya need me."

Saying bye to Jacob, Rana walked beside Victor to the northern part of the camp until they reached Oscar's tent and saw Amos standing guard outside. He waved at them as they approached.

"Hey, you two," said Amos. "You're here to see the commander; I take it?"

"Yeah, he asked for us to stop by today after training."

"What about you, little lady? That leg still giving you trouble? You seem to be walking well enough now." Amos squatted down in front of Rana, looking at her leg.

Rana was silent for a while as she clenched her fist at her side and the one around Victor's finger while swallowing the saliva in her mouth. She began to feel nervous as her breathing quickened ever so slightly. Her neck stiffened as her right leg started shaking the heel of her foot, tapping the ground over and over.

"Amos, have you ever dated a Sakari woman before?" asked Victor, "I heard that you've been making googly eyes at one of the girls before they left the camp."

"What? I wouldn't dare," said Amos, quickly rising back up to his feet. "That Gregga lady is scary. Who's been saying that?"

"Just some small talk from some of the boys in camp. You sure are a brave man, Amos. I didn't think you had it in you."

"That's because I don't have it in me. I've seen what they do to the men they capture."

Rana felt her body relax as Amos started talking to Victor. It felt to her as if someone was squeezing her entire body. She couldn't move. Everything just froze. *Dammit, it happened again. I'm not scared; I'm not scared. I can do this. I just need more time, is all. I'm fine.*

"If you say so, but perhaps you're the man who can tame

Gregga. I've heard she likes young men like yourself," said Victor as he quickly glanced down at Rana.

"Not a chance."

Victor laughed and squeezed Rana's hand, "Come on then, let's go see what Oscar wants."

The two walked past Amos, with Victor opening the tent's flap to see Oscar sitting in his chair looking over two pieces of parchment.

"You seem to be enjoying a leisurely morning here," said Victor as he stepped inside with Rana in hand.

Oscar placed the parchment pieces on a table beside him and stood up to greet them. Victor noticed the table was made out of what looked to be random pieces of aged lumber that had been gathered from the camp. It was a far cry from the handcrafted table that was utterly destroyed a month ago. *We make do with the tools we have.*

"Hardly, I'm looking over the arrangements for that munchkin beside you," said Oscar as he looked down at Rana. "And how are you today, daughter? Is that leg still giving you troubles?"

"No, father. It's better now."

"You're not Jasper," said Oscar with a brown raised at the girl trying to act tough. "Lying to me won't work. So, spit it out."

Rana sighed and slumped her shoulders, "It just hurts a little, but it's getting better. I can walk just fine, but I don't think I can run yet."

"Wow, a straight answer. Is that the power a father has over his daughter?"

Rana frowned back up at Victor.

"Now there's a better answer," said Oscar as he glanced at her leg. "Well, ya won't be doing any running for a while, anyway. Tomorrow we'll be heading off to Vontal to get everything squared away with you going to that magic school."

"How did you manage that, anyway? I'm no mage, but I know that getting a child into Sceana isn't easy. Most noble families would kill to get their children into that school. I'm sure a few even have."

"That headmaster of theirs is an old acquaintance of mine. I've fought in a lot of wars in my life, and a lot of people owe me a favor or two."

"You sure sending her away so soon is a good idea? King Nevander is probably looking for a way to get her back."

"Well, she sure as hell can't stay here crippling every mage in the camp every time she's put in danger."

"It's not like I tried to do that," said Rana, narrowing her eyes at Oscar.

"It's not about what ya tried or didn't try to do. It's about what ya did do. And what ya did was turn the brains of all the mages I have into mush. Now, given the situation ya were in, I don't blame ya one bit. Ya could have burned down half the camp, and none here would blame ya for it. But you're gonna go learn how to use that magic of yours so that I can get some proper use out of ya. The boy Jacob's magical core was already settled by the time I found 'em to get trained properly. But that little show ya put on was your first time using magic, which means ya can be trained."

"On this, I agree with Oscar," said Victor. "I'm sure you don't want what you did to Molan to happen to those Sakari girls either. So, learning to control whatever that was will protect them as well, Rana." *I just wish I had my own resources to figure out what exactly happened that night. Or why the king is after you.*

"I... I... Yes, Sir." Rana sighed.

"Speaking of that name of yours," said Oscar with a hand on his beard. "Rana, I think it's time you decide on your next name. That King Nevander might still be looking for ya, and I don't plan on making it easy for 'em. So have ya decided on a new name for yourself?"

"I guess…" Rana thought for a second. "I guess you can call me Isha."

"I remember you telling me that name. It's from those warrior sisters, right?"

"Mhmm, it was one of the stories Papa would always tell me."

"Well, it's a name I've never heard of," said Oscar rubbing at his beard. "So ya names Isha now, and I'll make sure everyone here calls ya that from now on. Ya gotta get used to people calling ya that."

"You," said Isha, looking back at Oscar.

"What?"

"You always say Ya, it should be you. You're not saying it right."

Oscar looked down at the little girl as she stared back up at him, her hands on her hips and a smirk came over his lips. "Alright then, you little know it all. Why don't you, little Isha," he said flipping his finger towards her, "go and see that Sakari doctor. Tomorrow we'll be heading into the city of Vontal for you to meet with Soulden. I want *you* making sure that *you'll* be okay on your feet."

"Yes, father. And remember to keep using your words," said the newly named Isha, before heading out of the tent.

"She's already starting to act like Dessi," said Oscar, the smirk on his face ever-present. "So, tell me, ambassador, what's your guess? Am I going to have to worry about her burning down a whole damn city tomorrow?"

"No," replied Victor as he watched Isha run out of the tent. "The therapy training has been working well enough. For the last two weeks, having her go around and greet different men has slowly been getting her to accept them."

"She's getting better then?"

"She's still jittery around the ones she doesn't trust yet, but yes, she's able to control herself for the most part. If she ever starts to get nervous, just hold her hand. She seems to have trust in you, so that physical contact will help calm her down if she ever finds herself jittery," said Victor looking at the tent flaps before turning back around to see Oscar staring back at him with narrowed eyes. "You seem to have another question you wish to ask me. What is it?"

"Well, I once knew a really good fighter. He used to fight in the pits over in Franval some years back. That fella never lost a fight; it was always as if he knew exactly where to hit. It was the most curious thing. He'd beat bigger people, faster people; didn't matter who they put him up against. He'd take 'em down soon enough. Even tried to recruit him once or twice, but he'd never bite. Well, sometime after that, one of my men was hurt in a scuffle a few towns over, so I took 'em to get patched up. And wouldn't ya know that the doctor was that same bastard who'd been knocking people out for months."

Victor smiled, "That's a fun story, but what's it got to do with me."

"Oh, nothing much. I just noticed how you seem really good at putting my daughter back together again. After what Molan did to her, she'd stay in her tent all day and start screaming if any man came close to her. But now you say she's going around camp meeting 'em. So ya just started reminding me of that doctor, is all. And I began thinking. If you're so good at putting people back together, it makes me wonder just how much time you spent breaking 'em down."

There was a moment of silence in the air as Victor narrowed his eyes back at Oscar. He slid his tongue against his cheek in contemplation.

"Who are you, old man? Besides the leader of this group of mercenaries? You command a group of Sakari, challenge kings for children, and apparently know the leader of the most prestigious school of magic in the land. And yet here you are lurking about in the countryside in a dirty tent. Is Oscar Highland even your real name?"

Oscar smiled while walking over and picking up the

makeshift-looking table, sliding the pieces of parchment off to the rug beneath, and placing it before Victor. He walked over and picked up a box from the corner and returned, placing it on the table in front of Victor. He then gave him a look which hinted at him to open it.

Victor twisted his lips in suspicion but gripped the lid of the box, opening it to reveal a board with four sets of different collared stones in glass jars. He then looked back to Oscar with a brow raised.

"Didn't realize you played."

"Not really anyone round here to play with. This group isn't much of the thinking type. But you seem up to the challenge. So, what ya say?"

"And what's the wager?"

"Loser is the one who's gonna be answering those questions we just asked," said Oscar with a smug smile on his face.

"I call the black and green pieces."

CHAPTER 3

Early in the morning, Isha, Victor, Dessi, and Oscar, along with a few others, arrived in Vontal. The city was massive, with stone buildings stretching off into the distance as men in fancy doublets and women in colorful dresses littered the street. The entire city had stone roads and colorful sheets of fabrics that hung from the sides of many buildings. Isha stepped out into the crowd beside Oscar. She felt a humid breeze flow over her body that came from the city's assortment of fountains littered throughout the streets where people would stop to drink or just take a rest. All the nearby water gave the surrounding area a cool feeling, even in the heat from the day's sun.

"You seem to be enjoying yourself, little Isha," said Victor with a smile on his face.

"Everything is so pretty here."

"A lot of the bigger cities of Latrusa are like this. They specialize in commerce, and everything here is accented by magic for appeal. So, from the people to the flowers, it all is enhanced by magic to make it visually appealing to the eye. Even the water from the fountains is set to keep the air around the city cool. That's why you see so many watering holes scattered throughout the city."

Oscar looked around the area, "Humm, looks as if my acquaintance is late to arrive, so I guess we have some time. What about you? Is this where we say goodbye?"

"Are you going to go now?" asked Isha, looking up at Victor with doe-eyes.

"Depends," said Victor, ruffling Isha's hair. "I'll be in the city till I find travel back to Mari. So, I'll be around till then if you guys plan to stay here for a bit. First, I'm going over to a communication post we have here to contact my kingdom and tell them I require passage back. Perhaps they could speed the process along."

Oscar noticed Isha looking up at him with the same sad eyes she gave Victor and sighed, "Fine, we'll be here when ya get back, not like my acquaintance has shown up anyway, and I told 'em to find me between the three fountains. So, I'm stuck here. But I'll expect ya not to share any of the information about my daughter with that Queen of yours."

"Now that's an easy promise to keep," said Victor with a smirk. "Alright, you two, I'll meet up with you later." He waved to them and walked off into the crowd of people, leaving Oscar, Isha, and Dessi along with the few guards that had followed them.

"I guess we wait then," said Oscar.

Victor made his way through the city, reaching the far north side, and stood in front of an herbal shop. Green vines covered most of the stone wall as plants in buckets hung from hooks attached to the building's wooden awning. The smell of fresh forestry lingered in the air as if it was perfume. He opened the door to the shop and saw a bald man holding a small pot with a plant in his hand.

"Hey there, what ya looking for? We got a good selection of herbs in, so you're sure to find what ya need."

Victor walked in, looking around the shop. The windows were set to each side of the building to catch light through-out each time of day. He even noticed a sunroof above him that was currently covered with a board.

"Nothing too special. Tell me, have you ever seen what happens when a rose catches fire?"

"No, tell me what happens when a rose catches fire," said the bald man, narrowing his eyes.

"It's simple. Another rose will be born from its ashes."

"Alright, what ya really be looking for?"

"I need communication with the capital. Do you have a mage nearby that can grant that to me?"

"Aye, she'll be upstairs tending to the day plants," said the man as he turned around and yelled. "Hey Marrin, ya got a visitor."

Victor heard the sound of footsteps, and soon a woman covered in fine cloth appeared from the steps behind the bald man. She was short with a slim face and had soft-look-ing clothing wrapped around her head and neck. But Victor couldn't help but stare at her eyes. They had a milky white-ness to them, with only a hint of the blackness that surely had once been there.

"Hello there," said the woman as she seemed to stare directly at him. "How may I help you?"

"Ahh yes," replied Victor, catching himself staring, "I'd like a conversation with the kingdom of Mari."

"Is that so?" asked the woman with suspicion in her tone.

"It's fine. He knew the words," said the bald man.

"Ahh, well then. Follow me, will you? And we can get started." Marrin then turned around and headed back upstairs with Victor following behind her.

The building's second floor was much like the downstairs; plants hanging down from hooks and greenery spread throughout the walls with sunlight coming in from two of the windows. Above him, a second sunroof, presumably to share its light with the first on days that needed it. He watched as Marrin walked over, poured a bucket of water into a small pail, and brought it over to Victor. She set it down on the floor in front of him and dropped to her knees, crossing her feet in front of her.

"Sit stranger and place your hands into the water with mine."

Victor sat on the floor with legs crossed, placing his hands into the lukewarm water, "Never seen it done with water before; usually, they just clasp my hands, and away we go."

Marrin smiled and giggled, "Yes, that used to be the case. But Ianwall, the man downstairs, is my husband and doesn't take kindly to me touching other men, unless necessary. So, this is our little compromise. Water will suit our purposes just fine. Are you ready to go?"

"Of course, take me away." Victor closed his eyes, and seconds after opening them again, he found himself inside of a lush garden of roses sitting at an ornate white table with Marrin. He gazed around the scenery at the thousands of roses that spread out around them in the middle of the countryside that they were now in. Victor noticed that he could even smell the scent of roses in the air. It was beautiful, but the colors of everything were oddly off. The reds were duller, and the grass lacked a lushness that seemed like it would have in an environment like this. "Wow, this is a wonderful place you've sculpted here. How long did it take you?"

Marrin gazed around with a loving smile on her face, "Ianwall and I come here almost every night and trim roses."

"I feel honored to be allowed in your mind then. Your husband is lucky to have you. Tell me, does that little water ritual apply to the women who come here?"

Marrin chuckled, "That's a good question; no woman ever has. Perhaps one day I'll be able to find out."

Victor stared at the milky smoke in her eyes, "You're blind, aren't you?"

"Yes, was it my eyes that gave me away? I've been told I can give off quite the visage."

"It is certainly a striking image you have," said Victor as he gazed around the scenery once again. "Tell me, how does a woman with no vision manage to create such a detailed vision in her head?"

Marrin stretched out her hand as the image of a rose appeared in her palm. She wrapped her fingers around the stem and rubbed her fingers over the petals of the rose. "It was hard at first, but Ianwall would describe everything to me over and over until finally, a person with no vision was able to imagine a world like this."

"Love does seem to have its advantages if it can do something like this," said Victor waving his hand around. Taking another look around, the scenery, while beautiful, still felt as if something was missing. Even though he felt a breeze against his face, the truth was that nothing here moved. With the shift in the air, the petals of the roses didn't move in the breeze and the blades of grass around them were unwavering. Instead of a vibrant world, he felt as if he were in a still painting.

"Do you not have anyone you…"

Suddenly a small area before them began to glow white. And as the light faded away, a door appeared in its place. The knob on the door turned, then it swung open as a man in the uniform of the Kingdom of Mari appeared.

"Hello there, what business do you have with the capital?"

"I am Victor Krill; I would like to inform—"

"Oh, Victor, yes. I was told to inform the Queen, if you tried to contact us. She's actually in the main hall at the moment. I shall go and inform her," said the man as he looked over to Marrin, "Is it okay to keep this link open? Are you in a safe place?"

"Yes," answered Marrin. "We are safe here."

"Good. I shall go and retrieve her highness then." The man turned and walked away, leaving the door open. It showed the other side of the roses inside of it.

"You must be important," said Marrin with a brow raised, "If it is a private conversation you require, I can leave you two here alone and still keep the connection stable."

"I'd prefer if you didn't," replied Victor with a sigh as he reached to lift his glasses and rub the top of his nose, between his eyes. He then realized that his glasses were back on his face, and they were unbroken. Plucking them off, he stared at them, "Wow, I've been wearing them so long that I even imagine myself wearing them."

"Here, we visualize ourselves as we wish to be, not as we are. And it seems you wish to have glasses."

"So, it would seem," said Victor as he placed the glasses back onto his face, just in time for Queen Clarissa to appear from inside the doorway. She was in a white and purple silk dress with a rose in her hair as she gracefully walked up to the table smiling.

"Hello Victor, I hope all is well," said Clarissa as she looked at the two of them sitting down at the table. "Excuse me, dear, if it's not too much trouble, may I request a seat for myself in this wonderful environment you have here?" She gazed over the field of roses and took a deep breath. "My, I can even smell the scent of roses here. You really have outdone yourself."

"Oh, yes, where are my manners, your highness," said the woman as she waved her hand at the Queen as an ornate white chair appeared before Clarissa.

"Lovely," said Clarissa before taking a seat at the table and turning to Victor. "Now, tell me, where have you been? Nevander pulled his troops back weeks ago. I'd expected your return by now. I mean, I knew you were alive, but I was still worried," said Clarissa in a sympathetic tone, while putting on a pouting face.

"Nevander sent me on a mission to chase down some bandits; in exchange for pulling back his troops."

"Oh, anything interesting?"

"Turns out some cult or whatever they were; had been implanting crystals inside the bodies of some nearby peasants."

"Implanting?" asked the queen with a raised brow.

"Yeah, it was weird to me also. But apparently, there were several dead bodies that had crystals embedded in their skin."

"Poor Nevander and his Kingdom of misfits," said Clarissa, feigning compassion. "I guess it's no surprise that his would be the environment that would engage in such debauchery." The queen looked over the horizon of flowers once again, "Okay then, where are you now? I hardly doubt such an exquisite visage truly exists in Burlus."

"Vontal, in Latrusa,"

"Vontal!" blurted out Clarissa in surprise. "Why are you in that bitch Yasmine's kingdom?" She coughed, regaining her composure, remembering that Marrin was listening to them.

"I followed the jewel bastards here, although I seem to have lost their trail. So now I'm here reporting in and about to seek passage back."

"About that, I'm going to need you to stop at the Royal Palace of Burlus on your way back."

"What? Why? What else could you have schemed up

with Nevander?"

Clarissa batted her eyes innocently, "Why Victor, whatever do you mean? How could you accuse me of scheming? I merely want you to attend the wedding of Prince Saffron as a way to show our support. And what better way than to have our ambassador attend the occasion himself?"

"You seem to be enjoying yourself in my suffering."

Clarissa reached out her hand and rubbed Victor on the cheek, "Well, I suppose if you're really so against going, I can have you return to me and we can finish where we left off last time."

"I'll make preparations," said Victor, twisting his lips and shaking his head.

"Good. I guess that settles the matter then." Clarissa sighed as she looked over the scenery once again and took a long breath, smelling the roses in the air. "Truly remarkable detail you have in this world of yours." She then turned back to Marrin. "Now, I trust that nothing you've heard here will ever leave from your lips, my lady."

"Ah... no, my queen. I promise to not tell a soul," said Marrin sheepishly. "It was an honor to meet you and finally get to see you. You really are as beautiful as the stories I've heard of you."

"Oh my, aren't you just the precious tongue flatterer," said Clarissa with a laugh. She then reached her hands out and placed her palms on the sides of Marrin's face. "Well, now, as a thank you for giving me this precious time with Victor, how about I reward you? Humm, Latrusa is a good bit away, but I guess it'll last a week or so from here."

"Your majesty, what are..."

"Shhh! It's okay," said Clarissa as she moved her hands up, placing her palms over Marrin's eyes and rubbing her thumbs across the woman's eyebrows. "And remember, no matter where you go, my power can always find you if you lie to me."

Suddenly the rose-covered world shattered like broken

glass as Victor was thrown back into the real world to the horrid sounds of a woman screaming in pain. He blinked several times, trying to will away the blackness from his mind. As his vision returned to him, he witnessed the sight of Marrin rolling around on the floor with her hands over her eyes. She writhed in pain, her legs flailing on the floor as she kicked over the bucket of water.

"What's going on here?" asked Ianwall as he entered the room to witness his wife's flailings.

He ran to her, wrapping his hands around her, then looked over to a disorientated Victor who was struggling to get his balance.

"What... what have you done?"

"Wasn't... me," said Victor as the world continued to spin.

"You bastard, I swear—"

"No... husband, it's... not his fault," muttered Marrin as she clung to the fabric of Ianwalls shirt, with her face pressed into his chest. "The queen, she... she has given me a gift."

"Gift? But you..." said Ianwall, staring into his wife's face. "By the goddess, what has happened?"

Victor's blurry vision slowly cleared to see Marrin's eyes as magical blueish smoke poured from them. The white of her eyes, replaced with a sterling, crystal blue.

"I... I... see you husband, for the first time. I see you."

"But... how? I mean... what happened?"

"Queen Clarissa, she... she gave me sight," said Marrin as the magical smoke slowly left from her eyes, replaced by the crystal blue of magical irises. She looked up into Ianwall's worried face and kissed him. "It is okay, husband. The pain has mostly subsided."

Ianwall looked over his wife's face, "I mean, are... are you cured? Can you really see me now?"

"You have a small nose and wide eyes, husband. But I can see you fine. But it is not a cure. The Queen said it may only last for a week, but a week seeing you is better than a lifetime of not."

"I... I... I don't know what to say."

Marrin rubbed her husband's face, staring at him, "You are bumbling your words, husband. But since I only have a week, I wish for you to show me this world we live in. May I ask that of you?"

"What? Of course. We'll close the shop and leave right away."

"I am still weak from the link; may I rest here for a while?"

"Oh, ahh, of course. Just, ahh... you rest here." Ianwall stood up, releasing his wife from his grasp, and headed toward the door as he saw Victor still staring at him. "Thank you, Sir. I don't know who you are. But I thank the goddess that you came here." And Ianwall headed out the door.

Victor watched the man leave before turning back to Marrin, who was gazing around the room at the plants and waving her hand through the beams of golden sunlight as they shined in through the window across her fingers.

"So this is what the world looks like. There really are so many different colors."

Victor struggled but stood to his feet and walked over to Marrin, extending his hand, "Am I allowed to at least help you up? Or is that also not needed?"

Marrin blinked, her eyes still watery from the spell as she focused on Victor and his hand. "I suppose this would be considered a special occasion to do so," she said, offering her hand to Victor, allowing him to pull her up on shaky legs.

"I didn't know such a thing was possible. I mean, healing is one thing, but what happened?"

"It's not healing; my eyes are still blind. It's just what she did. It seems to have just given me a different type of vision." She pointed ahead of her. "The window, please," allowing Victor to walk her over to a window.

Victor watched as she squinted magical eyes against the sun as she gazed outside. Turning back to Victor with blueish magical tears falling to her cheeks, she smiled. "What the Queen did would have cost a fortune and a group of the strongest mages in the land to even attempt. And to do such a thing from so far away. Victor, our Queen's power must truly be a monstrous thing."

Oscar sat at a table with Isha looking around at the crowds of people as they made their way through the city streets. He couldn't help but also notice how Isha's eyes nervously darted back and forth from people in the crowd.

"How ya holding up, Daughter?"

"Huh?" muttered Isha, turning back to Oscar, confused.

"You're not about to have another one of your screaming fits, I take it."

"No, I am not," insisted Isha sourly. "I'm fine."

"You sure? Those darting eyes and the way your leg keeps shaking are telling me something else. I thought Victor had you mostly fixed now."

"I'm fine... it's just... it's just there are so many people, is all."

"That so?" asked Oscar. "Place your hand on the table daughter."

Isha looked back at Oscar suspiciously; but did as he said, placing her hand on the table. Oscar reached out, laying his hand over Isha's small fingers, squeezing them softly.

"No one will hurt you, daughter. Not so long as I am around. Do you know that?"

"I'm not scared; I'm really not."

Oscar noted that she didn't try to pull her hand away and that her leg had stopped shaking. *So it seems the bastard spoke true.* "Of course not, daughter. Then just humor this old man will ya and keep a hold of his hand for a while."

Isha nodded.

"Oscar Highland, are you here?" asked a woman's voice through the crowd.

"And it seems my acquaintance has arrived," said Oscar. "Aye, I'm over here." Soon he noticed as an aged woman appeared from the crowd dressed in white and blue robes, accompanied by two women who were dressed the same. She spotted Oscar and walked over to him.

"Well, I can't say I'm happy to see you again. When I got the letter, I had hoped it to be a joke. But sadly, here you are. Why have you summoned me here?" asked the aged woman in an authoritative tone.

"Now, Soulden, I'd have figured you'd be happy to see me after all these years. Seeing as we're both old comrades, you and I."

"We were never comrades. And if I'd had the good luck to never have to see you again, then I would have counted it as a blessing from the goddess herself."

Even Isha could see the disgust in the woman's face as she looked at Oscar.

"Now, tell me why you've required my presence here so that I may be on my way and hopefully not see you again for another twenty-five years."

"Did you bring what I asked of you?"

"I did. Two healers from the academy; a recent graduate and one student. What do you want them for? Surely, you can't expect me to send them off with you. Even if the diplomatic relations nightmare didn't exist, I'd never allow it."

"Keep your mages; I have my own," said Oscar as he pulled Isha in front of him and placed his hands on her shoulders. "I'd like to introduce you to my daughter, Isha."

Soulden glanced down at Isha and frowned, unimpressed by the girl. "I see no reason to introduce myself to the child of one of your whores. Tell me why I'm here, or I'll leave this instant."

"You always were a high and mighty bitch," said Oscar, shaking his head. "Fine, have your little healers there use their sight to inspect the magical power of my daughter."

Soulden started laughing, "Surely you jest. You think I'd let anything of yours anywhere near Sceana. No, Oscar, I'm afraid you've wasted your time. Anything you touch turns to ruin, and I'll not allow it even if she were the goddess herself."

Oscar gave an evil smile as he saw the eyes of both the female healers behind Soulden light up and their mouths agape. "Seems as if you may not have a choice anymore, my old friend."

The older of the two female healers walked up beside Soulden and began whispering in her ear. Her face turned to shock as she looked to the smaller healer for confirmation of what was being said. She then glanced back to Oscar, looking between him and Isha. And after gritting her teeth for a moment, she let out a slow and disgusted sounding, "No."

"Yes," said Oscar with a grin on his face. "And those two healers you brought along are my ticket in. Unless you wish to tell that council of yours why you refused access to such a fine woman as my daughter here. A rarity in beauty just like her father."

"What monsters are you playing with, Oscar?"

"You mean, what monsters are *we* playing with Soulden? Because those healers there beside you, also report to that council of yours. Can you really expect those healers there to keep this a secret? Last I checked, healers only answer to their bitch of a high mother directly. Not to you."

"The high mother is not a bitch," declared the older healer.

"Clearly, you don't know her as well as I do," said Oscar with a chuckle before turning back to Soulden. "My point, my old friend, is either ya take my cute and precious little baby here, or ya risk answering as to why I was forced to take my daughter all the way to another kingdom to a lesser magic school. And I know Sceana prides itself on having the best and rarest mages in all the kingdoms. They won't be willing to let my little oddity go when word of her gets back to them."

Suddenly a ruckus was heard from the crowd as people gasped and stepped aside. They all turned in the direction of the noise as a group of Sakari pierced the crowd, making their way over to Oscar.

"Seems my trump cards have arrived," said Oscar with a smile.

Out of the crowd came Gregga, alongside Dessi, Prinja and Keltre, who were soon followed by Jomo and Momo and a set of Sakari warriors. The two Sakari children were gazing over the city and all the kingdom people with wonderment in their eyes until they spotted Isha and ran over to her.

"Sister Rana, we missed you," said Momo as the two girls hugged Isha with smiles on their faces.

Isha looked at Jomo and Momo, "What, what are you two doing here?"

"Old man asked mother to meet him here. We were waiting to show up," said Jomo.

Isha looked up at Oscar with a big curious smile on her face.

Oscar knelt, wrapping his hands around the girls. "What? You didn't think I'd let you go to such a big scary place by yourself, did you?" He then turned to Soulden, "Especially with that evil shrew of a woman." Oscar then stood and saw Victor slowly approaching them through the crowd. *Another card to play has arrived.* Oscar glanced over at Gregga as she gave her approval. After receiving it, he then turned back to Soulden. "Here you are, Soulden, as proof of my generosity to that magic school of yours. I offer you two magically talented Sakari to train, as well as my daughter. I don't think any magic school has ever landed Sakari before."

"Magical Sakari?" asked Soulden as she turned to the two healers for confirmation, which they both gave. She turned back to Oscar, still with disgust in her eyes. "How did you? Just... how?"

"Oh, I have more pieces on the board than you know, Soulden," said Oscar, gesturing to Victor, who had just made his way back. "Why, welcome back, Victor. That man there is none other than Victor Krill, the famous sixth general of the Kingdom of Mari and a good friend of mine. So, if by some miracle you can convince those two healers beside you to keep what you've seen here a secret. My good friend Victor here will ensure that word is sent to every magical school in all the kingdoms of the offer you've turned down this day."

Victor raised a brow at hearing the words of Oscar, looking between him and members of the school of <u>Scenea</u>. He then bowed to Soulden, "Greetings. I am Victor Krill, sixth General and current ambassador of Mari. You may contact Queen Clarissa directly if you doubt who I am. And I vouch for every word that Oscar Highland has just said."

Oscar noticed that Soulden's face went through a multitude of different emotions. Her lips twitching as if she was about to lose control of the muscles in her face.

Slowly Soulden peered around Oscar and his group before closing her eyes, taking in a very deep breath, and glancing down at the three girls. Her lips quivering as she spoke, "Well, it seems I've been outplayed. And as such, the school opens for new students in three weeks. I will send my personal airship to pick you up and bring your children to school. I look forward to seeing you girls there. Now, if you'll excuse me, I must go and make preparations and explain to the council why there will be three more students than expected this year." Soulden then gracefully turned on her heels and walked off into the crowd, followed by the two healers she brought with her.

"You could have warned me that you'd be using me

like that," said Victor, turning to Oscar after Soulden had vanished into the crowd.

"Spur of the moment thing. Didn't expect you to be back so soon. But it worked out well enough; it would seem."

"Yes, so it would seem," acknowledged Victor, still with a note of suspicion in his voice.

"Oscar, it seems we are done. I am leaving now," said Gregga.

"Aye, Gregga, I appreciate the help, as always."

"Mother, we wish to stay with Sister Rana, may we?" asked Momo.

Gregga looked down at her daughters, "Fine, they are your responsibility till you return them to me, Oscar."

"Agreed, I'll hold close your little ones."

Gregga then turned and walked off with her group of Sakari following behind her.

Oscar then turned to Victor, "Have you secured passage back to your queen then?"

"No, it seems I've been instructed to attend the wedding of Prince Saffron in the coming weeks. I'm sure you remember him; he's the young man you blackmailed into submission not too long ago."

"I'll have to ask you to be a bit more specific, as it seems I've been doing that so much recently."

Isha looked up at Victor, "Does that mean you're staying?"

"For another week or so perhaps, I had thought to just request a place in town to stay. But it seems so many years in the military have gotten me accustomed to camp life. So, I would be asking Oscar to grant me access to his camp for a little while longer until I make my way back to Burlus. And in that time, we can continue your training."

"I see no reason to deny that, especially seeing as you'll be doing me a boon by looking after the girl here," said Oscar as he placed his hands on the backs of Jomo and Momo. "Well then, what say we go get us something to eat?

All this scheming has given me quite the appetite."

"You all can go ahead," said Dessi. "It's been so long since I've been in a city with an actual creamer. I think it's time for little Isha and myself to go and get taken care of."

Oscar frowned, "And I'm paying for this, I assume."

"If you expect me to continue what I do, then what do you think? Creaming is very expensive."

"I'm very aware of that after the last time," said Oscar, and he reached to his side and pulled out a bag that jingled with the sound of coins.

Dessi reached out, taking the bag, "If there's anything left, I'll bring it back."

"Now there's a lie I'll never believe."

"Come on little Isha; it's time for us to go get pretty."

"We come with?" asked Jomo.

"We wish to stay with sister," said Momo.

"I see no reason why you girls can't. It'll be good for you to see the pain us women have to go through to look good for the men in our lives," replied Dessi as she and the girls headed back off into the crowded streets.

"Oscar, we need to talk," said Prinja after Dessi left.

"I figured as much. What have you two decided?"

"We're going to be leaving for a while to get things sorted out."

"Did you find Jasper's body?"

"We did. We buried him out in the woods near a river."

"Sorry I wasn't there. Will you two be heading back to Higgard?"

"We're not sure,"

"If you need anything, just stop by one of ours. Wherever you are, I'll send word that they accommodate you."

"Thank you," said Keltre.

"What about Gregga? Did she mourn him yet?"

"Not sure," said Prinja. "We don't know how Sakari mourn their loved ones. But she didn't cry if that's what you're asking. Even when we buried him, she just stood there and watched."

"Of course, she did." Oscar sighed, scratching his head.

"He really did like you, Oscar. Did you know that?" asked Keltre.

"Besides his stupid jokes, it was hard to tell what he liked. Well, the girl he brought me will be taken care of; I can assure you both of that."

"We have faith that you'll do right by her. And we will return when we feel it's right. Be well, Oscar."

"Be well, ladies," said Oscar as he watched Prinja and Keltre turn and disappear into the crowd.

Jomo and Momo held Isha's hand as they navigated the streets behind Dessi who would occasionally stop and ask for directions to a creamer. The more they traveled, the fancier the buildings around them appeared until they finally came to a colorfully painted building with a sign of a carved woman rubbing her legs outside of the door. The building had no windows, and the front was peppered in beautiful roses.

Dessi opened the door allowing the girls to step inside, and Isha saw a large man with red makeup over his eyes trimming some flowers. He wore a floral shirt that exposed his chest and trousers with red flowers stitched along the left leg. His long dark hair hung low to his chest, draping over his shoulders.

"Oh, customers. How can I help you? Oh, haven't seen you around before. And are those Sakari? Never seen those before either. If you're looking for me to perform some work on them, I might not be skilled enough for that job. Removing that much pigment is simply beyond my means."

"Ahh... no, I need the work done on her face," said Dessi, pointing down at Isha, "And well, I'm afraid you're going to have your hands full with me.

The man walked over and reached out for Isha's face. She jumped back as her leg started shaking again.

"Oh my, she's a jittery one."

"It's okay, Isha. He's just going to have a look at the scars on the side of your face."

"It's okay, honey. I've dealt with abused children before. Some noble father or mother went too far, many a time, and the result was brought to my doorstep to hide before someone found out," said the man as he dropped to his knees and looked at Isha. "Take your time, honey, and bring yourself over when you're ready."

Momo and Jomo tightened their grip around Isha's hands and slowly led her over to the man, till she was in front of him.

"Okay, now reach your hand out and touch my face," said the man.

Isha looked wary but released Jomo's hand and slowly reached up, placing her hand on the side of the man's face.

"There ya go," said the man with a smile as he reached into his pocket and pulled out a vial with some type of green liquid in it. Opening the vial with his thumb, he allowed the liquid to leak out and coat over his fingers. "Now I want you to reach down and grab this hand and place my fingers where those scars on your face are. Can you do that?"

"Yes, Sir," said Isha as she released Momo's hand and reached down and grabbed ahold of the man's fingers, slowly lifting them up to her face. Her breathing quickened a bit, but she was in control. She then placed the man's hands to the side of her head; the sticky liquid feeling cold against her skin. Her body trembled a little as she continued to feel anxious.

"There we go," said the man. "Now close your eyes, this is gonna hurt a small bit, but it'll be over soon."

Isha closed her eyes, and soon, she slowly felt a sensation at the side of her head. First, it was hot, then sharp, as if someone had a burning hot stick against her skin. Then the pain grew and kept growing until her face couldn't hide the pain anymore. She squinted her eyes and gnashed her teeth together, trying to endure it. And just as suddenly as the pain arose, it was gone, replaced by a cooling sensation.

"That's a brave girl. We're all done."

Isha opened her eyes to see that she was squeezing the side of the man's face so hard that it had turned red. She quickly let go, "I'm sorry, I didn't mean to—"

"It's all right, honey. I suppose it's only fair that I feel a bit of pain to match yours," said the man as he reached over to grab a mirror and handed it to Isha. "Have a look."

Isha held the mirror, turning her face, and noticed that the scars alongside her face were gone, replaced by unblemished skin.

"The scars are gone."

"Yes, they are," said the man standing back up to his feet, looking at Dessi. "Well, the baby has been taken care of. That'll be four gold pieces for the girl. But what about you? You said you needed some work done?"

"If you feel up to it later, Isha. We can come back and have that arrow wound also creamed over," said Dessi, reaching into the bag and giving the man four gold pieces, "You're good with children. You get a lot of abused girls here?"

"Girls and boys, the makeup and outfit help to get them to trust me. Since it's usually men who've done the damage, I have to try to look less like a man when working on 'em. Which, in my case, is particularly hard seeing how big I am and all. But we all suffer for our work."

"Well, your work's not done yet. I'm going to need a lot more than what you just did for her."

The man looked Dessi up and down. "What? You don't seem too bad, maybe that little gnash on your neck, a little work on your fingers, and you'll be good to go."

Dessi reached up to the string of her bodice and loosened it, allowing it to fall to the floor. She then grabbed the neck of her shirt and lifted it over her head, exposing her naked self to the girls and the man in front of her.

The man took a deep breath, looking over Dessi's scarred body, "I'm not going to pry about what you're into. But honey, I hope you brought a lot of gold."

Dessi handed the man the whole bag of gold. He opened it up, looking inside. "Your choice, honey. How 'bout I go and get you a piece of leather? I think you're gonna need something to bite down on."

CHAPTER 4

Saffron, Frenka, and Dekol were at a clothing shop in Burlus trying on different apparel for the wedding.

"Why we do this? Don't prince have people do things for him?" asked Frenka, lifting up the hem of a frilly pink dress with a frown on her face. "And why do kingdom women wear clothes like these? "It is big and puffy; it would get in way when fighting."

Saffron chuckled, "Not everyone thinks of fighting all the time, and you promised me you'd wear one of those puffy dresses on my wedding day. I won't have you trying to back out now."

"I only promise because you follow and pester me."

"Good, then I'm glad you remember. Father may get his way, but I'm determined to have at least one good thing come out of that day. And the sight of you all draped in makeup and fine linings is something I'm sure I'll only see once in this life. I'll not have you trying to weasel yourself out of it."

"Do they have dress in black?" asked Frenka, fumbling with the frilly laces along the side of the garment.

"As much of a wake as my nuptials might seem to me, this is an occasion that we both must suffer through. So, you put on the pink dress, and I'll put on the fake smile."

"Saffron, is it really wise to be out like this, given the reports on that cloaked figure attacking the nobles of the city."

"Oh please, I doubt anyone would be foolish enough to attack me with you two around. And I'm pretty good at defending myself. So, unless this one true king of all the kingdoms is on a suicide mission, I'd imagine I'm pretty safe."

"Excuse me, your highness," said the store clerk, "But is there anything else I can do for you. I was told to have these ready for your guests months ago. Any changes now would be nearly impossible to make."

The prince stared at the clerk and sighed. "No... no changes need to be made. Perhaps I'm just having the wedding day jitters, is all. I've heard that that happens to husbands who deflower a virgin, and the father drags them to the altar while holding a knife to their back. Seems quite appropriate given the circumstances." Saffron walked towards the door. "Come, you two. We might as well head back. I'm sure the ladies of the castle wish to reveal to me the joys of matrimony." Saffron exited the shop and began walking down the city streets with Dekol and Frenka.

"If not want to get married, why do it?" asked Frenka. "When partner came for me, I kill him. Surely Saffron can just say no. Or is it same for men here as it is for women in clans? Where men have no freedom unless woman dies?"

"Oh, goodness..." said Saffron, bursting into laughter as he clutched at his stomach. "You... you really are a gem of a woman, Frenka. The number of men who would agree with that statement. And you just blurt it out so casually." Saffron dropped to one knee and raised his hand to Frenka with tears of laughter in his eyes. "Marry me, my sweet mountain woman, and save me from my future wife."

"All men here are stupid," said Frenka, shaking her head. "If no want to get married, then do not. It is simple. Now get up, stupid prince, before I kick you."

Saffron's smile slowly faded from his face as he stood back up to his feet and shrugged, "For you maybe, but for a prince, things are never as simple. My marriage means a lot to the kingdom. The nobles would revolt if I didn't marry a mage, and those nobles own businesses that supply the people of the kingdom. Trade agreements, business partnerships, and the wealth of a large amount of the kingdom have been invested into this royal charade. And a prince must forever think of the will of the people before his own." *Otherwise, I'm no better than your local bandit guild to sit and watch the kingdom fall into chaos.*

"Speaking of your own personal chaos, it would seem your future lady wife is headed this way," said Dekol as he pointed behind Saffron.

Saffron turned to see his soon-to-be bride hurriedly walking towards him with her arms out holding up the sides of her large puffy dress. She was being followed by three of her handmaids.

"Hello, my lord," said Laura, trying to catch her breath.

"Where are you all headed in such a hurry?" asked Saffron.

"Oh, my lord hasn't heard? There has been a murder at the home of Hendrick Masterdane; the rumor is that it was the work of that Queen's Bane fellow who's been killing nobles in all the kingdoms."

Dekol and Saffron looked at each other.

"Seems I was right about one thing. He didn't come after me," said Saffron as he turned around, "Well, come along then. It seems we have an interesting mystery in our fair kingdom that needs to be solved."

They all quickly made their way across the city to the home of Frederick Masterdane. Upon arrival, the streets were filled with people as the city guard had blocked access to the house.

"If you ladies would excuse us," said Saffron as he, Dekol, and Frenka left the company of the ladies and made their way through the crowd up to the front gates of the manor.

"Stop who goes... oh Prince Saffron, what brings you here?"

"There's apparently been a murder of a noble in my own kingdom. Is that not enough reason to appear," said Saffron in an authoritative tone.

"Oh no, I mean, yes, it is your highness."

"Who's in charge of the investigation here?"

"Oh, that'd be captain Reynolds, Sir. He's inside with the family and—"

"Good, then I shall go and have a word with the captain myself then. Make way," declared Saffron as he intimidated his way past the guard and into the grounds of the manor.

"Haven't seen you do that in a while," said Dekol.

"What good is having power if you don't know when to use it?" asked Saffron with a smirk on his face.

They soon entered the manor and were greeted by the dead body of Frederick Masterdane lying next to a small table.

"Who let these two in here? Oh, it's you, Prince Saffron. Are you here to play detective again? I'd have guessed you'd be too busy planning your wedding to come down here and fool with this," spoke a gruff-looking man in armor along with a younger soldier beside him.

"Hey, Leonardo, nice to see you're staying busy. When did you get back to the capitol?" asked Saffron, smiling at the man.

"Around a week ago, Sir. Your father keeps me busy running around this kingdom of his. I'm scheduled to leave again for Grankall in the coming days."

"Perhaps one day you'll get to rest. I'd heard your daughter just had her first child. Do you not want to retire and become the doting grandfather?"

"Perhaps in another decade or so. But for now, your father still finds use of me."

"Well, murders and small politics seem to have no end, so your work will last forever."

"And I wouldn't have it any other way."

"Then perhaps you'll understand my involvement here. this mess is precisely the thing I need to keep my mind off that wedding of mine."

"Ha, I take it you're still trying to run from that wedding of yours. So Nevander hasn't been putting you in a vice yet?"

"I've accepted my fate," said the Prince with a shrug. "But that doesn't mean that I don't plan to keep up with my usual habits. But tell me something, Leonardo?"

"What's that, your highness?"

"You were there during the taking of Duke Richardson's manner, were you not?"

"Yes, your father asked me to lead in the capture of the man. But things didn't go as one would expect. Or perhaps it did, judging from your father's knowledge of the man."

"So, I saw. By the time I arrived in Passala, his manor was little more than rubble. Tell me, do you think there was anything odd about that mission? Anything that didn't feel right?"

Leonardo stared at the prince for a moment and then looked around the room. "There were many a thing not right about that night, but if your highness wishes for more details. I would prefer to tell them to you in more private arrangements."

"Yes, that will be fine. You can find me around the castle or in the city in the coming days. I guess we do have more pressing matters to attend to at the moment," said the Prince turning towards the younger soldier. "Tell me, Reynolds, what do we have here?"

Reynolds turned to the dead body, "Someone's finally off'd this bastard, Masterdane. At least we've got a solid lead as to who. Odd thing though, you can see the blood that's been scattered on the floor, but the victim doesn't have a mark on him."

"Huh, what do you mean?"

"Exactly as I said, there's a large amount of blood around the victim, but I'll be damned if I can tell where it came from."

"How do we even know it's his blood then? Maybe he died from a stroke or something during an attack, and the blood might be from the attacker. I mean, as much of a pain in the ass as he was, Masterdane was a mage of high renown to my knowledge, It's hard to imagine him being taken off guard."

"He wasn't. Take a look behind you," said Reynolds as he pointed to the side of the door frame where small chunks had been blown off. "Seems like he got off a blast or two for what little good it did him. But the man most certainly knew he was under attack."

"You think it was this Queen's Bane fellow like the rest of them?"

"Seems that way. He even left a note on the body."

"Oh, so the Prince finally made his way here," said Mova as she walked out of a room to the left with a young woman in a white robe beside her.

"There you were, Mova. I had wondered where you and Thaddius had gotten away to. Are you both investigating this as well?"

"Hardly. The king sent Thaddius down to Nyril to make

sure the troops are settled in properly down there. I just happened to be nearby when I heard about this."

"He sent Thaddius away? Aren't you both supposed to be my personal guards?"

"Hey, you're the one who left us behind and went on your fancy little trip throughout the countryside. Thaddius was just happy to get to do something."

"And what of you? Do you have issues about me not taking you on my adventures?"

"Goddess, no. Go travel the world for all I care. I'm perfectly content here in the capital than roughing it around in the woods with insects crawling on me. Just don't die in the process; I'd prefer not to explain to your father why I wasn't there."

"Oh, the wonderful delicate flower Mova, it's nice to know you have my best interests at heart." Saffron pointed to the body, "I take it you've already examined the body. What insights have you found?"

Mova patted the smaller girl on the back, "Go on, tell the prince what ya told me."

"Ah yes, well. He's had severe internal bleeding, and his lungs and heart were damaged heavily."

"So, poison then, maybe?"

"It would seem so, your grace."

Saffron smiled at the young girl, "Who's this pet you have with you anyway, Mova. You thinking of adopting?"

"Pfft, she's a healer on loan to replace old man Drylick. I was showing her around the city when all this apparently happened. But she's really timid, as you can see. Seems she's freshly completed her training, but here's the fun bit. Guess what her name is."

Saffron raised a brow, "Alright then I'll bite; what's your name, my meek, shy maiden of the Healing Order?"

"It's... it's Frenka, sir."

"Frenka?" asked Saffron, squinting his eyes. "Your name... is... Frenka?"

"Ah... yes, Sir," said the girl, dropping her head.

The prince immediately lost control, throwing himself at Dekol, placing his hands on his friend's shoulders, and burying his face into Dekol's chest, laughing and crying himself into a fit. "Ohh... Ohh goddess... help me. This..... Oh, this.... is just too good."

"I thought you might get a kick out of that," said Mova as she eyed the now visually annoyed guard Frenka. "Figured I wouldn't need to get you a wedding gift after revealing this little nugget."

The Prince struggled to hold in his laughter, "Oh... oh yes. This is indeed the best wedding gift. Goddess protect me. The difference... the difference is so night and day." The prince forced all his will to control himself, but after another glance at the innocent, fresh-faced young girl. He once again burst into laughter, using Dekol as his stability. "I can't... I can't look at her and not laugh."

"Oh, damn, both of you," said guard Frenka as she crossed her arms and turned around.

"I'm... I'm sorry, it's just. Oh Goddess," chuckled Saffron as he steeled his resolve once again to face the young healer, Frenka. "I apologize, my little healer, but we only allow one Frenka here. Do you perhaps have another name you go by?"

Healer Frenka looked around before turning back to the prince, "Well, in school, everyone called me Rayrah."

"Rayrah it is then. From now on, that is how you shall introduce yourself. Is that understood," said Saffron as he wiped the remainder of the tears from his eyes.

"Ahh... Yes, Sir."

"Okay, Miss Rayrah, please inform us as to your understanding of what happened to Mr. Masterdane."

"Well, seeing as I can't find any marks on his body, I would have to assume it would be poison, Sir. I didn't detect any magic traces left on him from any lingering spells either."

"Then where did all the blood come from? Surely, he didn't cough all of this up? And I fail to believe that any murderer would be able to escape after losing this much blood. This Queen's Bane fellow is a mysterious one. Leonardo, did you say he left a note?"

"Yeah, take a look for yourself," said Leonardo as he handed Saffron a piece of parchment.

Saffron raised the note to his face, noticing Rayrah staring at him, "What is it? Is something wrong?"

"Well, it's just... is death so common in this kingdom? I mean, a man is dead, and no one, not even the guards, seems to be distraught by it."

"Well, now, I guess you do have a voice then. But as to your question, that man there was hated by damn near everyone who knew him. Half the crowd outside will probably be drinking to his death tonight. If not for the way he died and this parchment here, I'd just have assumed it was his wife that had done him in."

"That sounds terrible."

"A word of advice, little healer. Save your tears for the people who matter to you," said Saffron, seeing the worried look on the girl's face. "You stay here long enough; you're going to be seeing far more dead bodies than this one." He then took a look at the parchment Leo handed him, *"Dark days are ahead for the fake kings and queens who hold pretend thrones. The kingdom of Burlus will now spend its nights trembling in fear as vengeance now walks its streets."* Saffron frowned at the parchment before handing it to Dekol, "Well, that doesn't sound too pleasant. Our killer sure does seem to have a flair for the dramatic. But I've never heard any stories about any true king."

"It's probably just some crazy person on a self-righteous mission," said Mova.

"Crazy or not, he was skilled enough to take down this asshole Masterdane. So, I'll be asking you all to be careful. Don't underestimate someone just because you don't understand them. Each of us here has had our asses handed to us once or twice because we underestimated our opponent. Let's see that we don't have another lesson that costs us our lives, shall we?"

Saffron, Frenka, and Dekol left the manor, headed back through the crowd to be greeted by the awaiting Lady Dunblane and her handmaids. Upon seeing the group, Lady Dunblane rushed over to see the prince.

"My lord, is everything well?"

"Yes, future wife, everything is under control. The guards have everything under control now."

"Was it that dreaded Queen's Bane as the rumors have said?"

"Yes, although with a name like that, one has to wonder why he's here in the only kingdom with an actual king. Honestly, that name is such bad marketing. If it were me, I'd..." said Saffron before he felt Lady Dunblane's hand on his cheek.

"My lord, your eyes are all red. Have you been crying? I hadn't realized you and Lord Masterdane were so close."

Now it was Frenka who started coughing, trying to contain her laughter, as she turned her back to them. Saffron narrowed his eyes at Frenka, who was visibly trembling in an attempt not to laugh, before turning back to Lady Dunblane with a smile looking at her in her beautiful green eyes. *She really is quite the beauty. A little on the dim side, but in terms of a wife, I guess she is rather affectionate.* "Masterdane was a good man."

Frenka let out a hard chuckle, and Saffron closed his eyes in annoyance and took a breath.

"But what's done is done. The palace guards will be on full alert to catch the vile beast who'd do such a thing." Saffron grabbed Lady Dunblane's wrist from his face and kissed the back of her hand. "But you lady wife, I shall ask that you be extra careful during this crisis. I most certainly can't have anything happening to my betrothed now, can I?

You and our ceremony are my top priority."

Lady Dunblane blushed and dropped her head as her handmaids giggled behind her, "Yes my lord, I shall be as careful as I can." Then she looked up at Saffron, her lovely emerald eyes focused on him. "Oh, I know, perhaps I can paint you a portrait of Lord Masterdane, you know, as a wedding gift. I'm quite skilled at painting and—"

"Oh goddess, no, I mean..."

Frenka threw herself into Dekol's back, clenching at his garb, biting her lip, her body twitching as she tried to contain the laughter.

"I mean, I'd much prefer to just remember him in my own mind, future wife, instead you should use your talents to paint more beautiful images. I quite like that image you've previously done of yourself and your handmaids there eating brunch together. Perhaps you could do another, this time with you all wearing your summer garbs in a field of roses."

"If that is what my lord desires."

"That is just one of my desires, Lady Dunblane; the rest of them you will find out after our wedding."

"Well... I mean, yes, my lord," muttered Lady Dunblane, her face blushing even more as her housemaids continued their giggling.

"But, until then, you'll have to excuse me. I, and my friends here, have kingdom matters to attend to," said Saffron as he turned back to Dekol and the now flush-faced Frenka who seemed to finally be regaining control of herself. "Come along, you two, we can discuss how we plan to deal with this threat as we head to the castle to inform father. Although I'm sure he knows by now."

Saffron and the group left Lady Dunblane's company and headed down the streets towards the castle.

"You will try to catch killer, won't you?" asked Frenka.

"Of course. You must admit it'll be a wonderful story to tell," said Saffron as he gestured his hand in the air. "The magical and magnificent Prince Saffron apprehended the dangerous and dreadful Queen's Bane, with the help of his merry friends, of course."

"I think you love yourself too much."

"Well, since you won't love me, I'd say it balances out well enough."

"What is next, idiot Saffron?" said Frenka with a frown.

"The standard affair, you two start asking around about any new faces, and I'll go and talk to my royal father about this.

CHAPTER 5

Early in the morning at the Black Jewels camp, Isha, Jomo, and Momo were sitting on the floor of a tent looking at books.

"Argh, book painful to read," said Jomo as she leaned back on the floor, looking up at the top of the tent.

"It's, 'this book is painful to read,' and Uncle Jasper wanted you to learn and you both promised him you would. Besides, it's not like it's easy for me to learn Sakari, but I'm trying."

"Uncle Funny man was better teacher; he would get us cookies from towns."

"It's, 'was a better teacher.' You must learn to use your in-between words. And I'll bake you cookies whenever I can get the stuff to do it," said Isha as she shook her head disapprovingly at Jomo, who began rolling around on the floor. "Look, Momo can do it."

"Momo always been study type. Sister Rana make us work too hard."

"Not Rana, no more. Old man and Mama say to call her Isha now."

Jomo stopped rolling around and sat back up, pointing at Isha, "And why you change name? You no like Rana no more?"

"No, it's so that I can hide from bad people. I changed my name so they won't find me."

Jomo narrowed her eyes at Isha, "Fine, if we now call you Isha, then you call us by our names too." Jomo dropped her head as a sad expression came over her face. "Uncle Funny man want us to do that, anyway."

Isha looked at the two Sakari girls and began to think, "Makeba and Jacinta, right?"

"Oh, sister Isha remember our names. I bet Momo that you forgot."

"Yes, now you owe me cakes," said Makeba, "Sister Isha smart, so I knew she remember."

"It's, 'she would remember.' Would is another in-between word. And why wouldn't I remember your names.? We are sisters now, right?"

Jacinta stretched out and began kicking her legs, "Sister Isha, what school like? Is it fun?"

"Probably, I've never been to one before. Father taught me how to read. But there should be more people our age there, I think."

"But none will be Sakari," said Makeba with certainty in her voice.

"Probably not; I never met Sakari before I met you two."

"Uncle Funny man used to tell us about lots of people

who used to live across water. He said he went there many times with people."

"Have you always known Uncle Jasper?"

"Oh yes, he was Momma slave till she gave him to old man."

"What?" blurted out Isha, dropping her book.

"Yes, he always been slave," said Makeba.

"But... how?"

"Oh, Momma made him her man before giving to Old man."

Isha's mind spun with thoughts of Jasper as a slave to Gregga, "In Sakari, what does a slave do?"

Makeba twisted her lips looking at Isha curiously as if the answer was obvious, "What you mean? He cook, clean, and took care of us. And at night he and Momma would have sex."

"Mama said she liked sex with Uncle Funny man because he made her laugh," said Jacinta. "That why we go to village that kill him and kill lots of people."

"When we got older, Uncle Funny man was supposed to teach us sex too, but he gone now. We must find other man who is worth teaching us. We should have strong mate to have strong babies. Sister Isha now has blood month, so she can have babies too."

They were going to have babies with Jasper? But... does that mean I was supposed to have babies with him? Isha's mind went in circles as she placed her hand over her stomach. *I know it's something girls do, but...* She looked between Makeba and Jacinta, who were saying these things as if they were just common knowledge, and leaned back on the rug and closed her eyes, "I think... I think I need to take a nap for a while."

Dessi walked inside Oscar's tent to see him sitting in his

chair, reading through Jasper's book.

"Are you sure it's a good idea to be sending your new daughter to that magical school in the next few days?" asked Dessi.

"No, but that's what I will be doing, nonetheless."

"You don't think it's too soon? You've barely had the girl two months."

"I appreciate your motherly instincts of wanting to protect the girl, but this is what's best for her."

"What if she's in danger up there?" asked Dessi as she paced back and forth. "No one will be there to protect her."

"I assure you I've made preparations for her to be taken care of," said Oscar as he flipped another page of his book. "She'll be with those Sakari girls, and we both know what those little demons can do."

"Well... she started her monthly cycle, she told me yesterday. She'll need to know how to properly see to herself."

Oscar placed the book in his lap and stared at Dessi, "I'm sure the Molan's of the world are rejoicing as we speak. But what's gotten into ya, I know ya fond of the girl, but I've never seen ya attach yourself to anyone like this before."

Dessi bit down on her thumb as she continued to pace on the rug, "I don't know, I just... I just don't feel right sending her away so soon. Especially after that mess with Molan and Jasper. I don't want her to feel like we're abandoning her."

Oscar just stared at Dessi as she continued to pace back and forth.

"What?" asked Dessi as she caught him staring at her.

"I'm just thinking, is all. Molan was a bastard for sure, but he must have known that even if he'd succeeded with his assaulting my daughter, that I would have had him killed. But yet he did it anyway. And then the boy Jasper coming to me for her, asking me to take her in. And now, here you are pacing in front of me like a love-struck kitten."

"What? You can't be serious. You think she's done

something to us? That girl can barely run without falling down, let alone cast any spells. And I doubt she made Molan do what he did."

"Perhaps not, but I'm thinking even more that I'd be wanting to distance myself from her for a while, just to see what happens."

"You're not planning to do anything to her, are you?"

"Nothing more than what I've already done, and that's secure her schooling. But ya can go on and continue playing mother to her for as long as she's here. No harm in that continuing I suppose."

Dessi then headed for the exit, stopping halfway out of the tent, before turning back to Oscar. "Why didn't you ever try to claim me as your daughter?"

Oscar looked at Dessi with a sad yet serious expression on his face, "Because I had already failed you as a father, just as I nearly failed with that little one you want to keep sheltered so badly."

Dessi took a breath, then headed out of the tent and down toward where the Sakari were camped. On her way, she spotted five captives that the Sakari had brought back with them. They had two women, and three men huddled together around a post. Gregga appeared from behind a tent and said some words in Sakari, and soon the captives were taken and led inside of another tent. After watching the prisoners being shuffled inside, Gregga spotted Dessi and walked over to her with a smirk on her face.

"Well, it is one of Oscar's favorite kingdom girls. What brings you over to the Sakari part of the camp? Always figured you all too scared to come visit. Only Amos and the Kingdom girl come down here unless the men be gambling."

"I came looking for Ra... I mean Isha. Is she still here?"

"Oh, that she is. She been training my babies on that proper kingdom tongue." Gregga gave Dessi a glance over. "They say you good warrior woman, and that killed you many men."

"When need be, yes. A woman needs to know how to defend herself in this world."

"Yes, woman needs to have many weapons. Often time, more than men, women are the hidden blade at the man's throat to keep him in line. When he is no longer a man, that is when we slash."

"That's an interesting way of putting it."

"That little kingdom girl showed my babies her knife throwing. I take it that you trained her in this."

"Yes, she's a quick learner for the most part. What of you? Do you train yours in magic?

"Oh no." Gregga laughed. "I do not have magic. You make mistake. My babies were given to me as honor." Gregga unbuttoned the bottom of her top and lifted the cloth, revealing a large scar across her stomach. She rubbed her hand across the scarred flesh. "I lost child and all coming children when this was done to me."

"I just had my scars removed. Perhaps next time, I'll come to you beforehand, and we can compare and tell stories."

"Agreed, a time I look forward to," said Gregga, allowing her top to fall back down, "For now, you follow, and I shall take us to our babies."

Dessi followed Gregga through the camp until they reached a large tent that was even bigger than Oscar's. Inside, she spotted Isha leaning over one of the squatting Sakari girls, pointing her finger inside the book she was holding.

"You teaching my babies that proper kingdom tongue?" asked Gregga as she walked over to the girl's.

"Yes, Miss Gregga, they... Hey Dessi," said Isha as she ran over to them. "Is it time for training?"

"Yeah, but if you're busy with the girls here, we can continue tomorrow morning. It's still a few days before you head off to that school."

"No, it's okay. They are getting better now."

"Yes, we learning our in-between words," said Jacinta.

"It's 'we are learning,' not we learning," corrected Isha, before turning back to Gregga. "We still have a ways to go, but Jacinta and Makeba are both learning. And they are teaching me Sakari."

Gregga raised a brow at Isha, "Oh, you call them their real names now?"

"Yes, Isha, change her name. Now, we tell her to call us by our name. So we all have new names," said Jacinta with a smug look on her face as she looked over at Isha.

Gregga looked down at Isha and reached out her hands and squeezed her face inspecting her, "So, it was Jasper who was the one who went and got you was it?"

"Wess Miss Wegga," said Isha through squeezed cheeks."

"Something wrong, Mama?" asked Makeba with worry on her face.

Gregga looked at her daughters and then looked at Isha, "Girl, do you consider Makeba and Jacinta to be your true sisters? Do you know what that means?"

Isha turned around looking between Jacinta and Makeba who were staring at her, then turned back to Gregga, "I don't know what everything means here, but I want to be their sister, if I can."

"Then it is decided," said Gregga, placing her hand on Isha's head. "Isha will have bonding tonight and in the morning, you will start calling me Mother."

"What?" asked Dessi, confused.

Gregga raised her hands up and then took a deep breath before closing her eyes, embracing the moment. "Oh, this world is full of wonder, but you did keep your word to me, Jasper Flannigan. Even claimed by death you have kept your word to me, for it seems that I shall have my little kingdom baby after all," said Gregga as she left out of the tent.

Dessi and Isha could hear her shouting orders to the people of the camp in Sakari.

"What... what is she saying, what just happened?" asked

Dessi.

"I don't know," said Isha, looking just as confused as Dessi.

"She is telling them to prepare for bonding ceremony tonight for sister Isha to be part of Sakari," said Jacinta with a smile on her face. "Isha is sister, but now she become daughter by rite. Me and Makeba did same when we fight for best daughter. It will be fun."

Dessi was listening to Gregga outside laughing and giving orders, but then turned back to Jacinta, "Wait, fight? Rana, I mean Isha is gonna have to fight someone?"

"Oh yes, since Isha is new sister, she will be part of fight with me and Makeba. We all fight for best daughter tonight. Last time I win, so tonight I win again."

"I don't want to fight anyone; I have to tell her to stop."

"It too late. You agreed to be daughter. To lie to mother now would be great insult to her. She really happy now. You take her joy away and you forsake all Sakari."

"But... but... Oh goddess, no, I can't fight. I can barely throw knives."

"It not fight to death; it just fight for best daughter. Will be fine. Last time was fun. Sister Isha worry too much."

Isha threw her face into her hands, "Oh goddess no."

Later that night, a small area of the camp was lit with fire as dozens of Sakari stood in a circle holding torches while two others banged on drums to a haunting rhythm. Even some of the camp's kingdom men had shown up after hearing about the spectacle that was about to take place.

Why... why is this happening? I don't want to do this. There has to be another way. thought Isha as she stood at either side of her sisters in the circle surrounded by Sakari. She was dressed in a white cloth that wrapped over her chest and lower body. Exposing her belly, legs, and shoulders.

Makeba and Jacinta, each dressed in the same manner, with smiles on their faces. Behind Isha stood Jacob, Victor, Oscar, and Dessi; with everyone except Oscar looking more than slightly worried..

"Now, I understand that I'm just a visitor to this camp," said Victor, scratching his head in confusion. "But can anyone properly explain how all this happened?"

"I think my daughter just has a knack for finding herself in situations like this," said Oscar, shaking his head.

Isha narrowed her eyes back up at Oscar, "It's not like I'm trying to do this."

"Perhaps not, but you're here now," said Oscar with a chuckle before he looked over to Dessi. "I suppose this brings some credibility to her having some effect on the people she's around, and apparently, it works on Sakari."

"Effect? Has there been a revelation on her magic?" asked Victor.

"Not so much a revelation, but a theory. I'll fill you in after this little show is over," said Oscar, looking down at Isha, "How's that leg of yours, daughter?"

"It's alright, I guess. It still feels funny. But it doesn't hurt."

"Good. We don't need you having another episode and burning us all down in the process."

"Why does this always happen to me?" asked Isha with a sigh.

The Sakari crowd split as Gregga walked between them and entered the small dirt arena, standing in the center between Isha, Makeba, and Jacinta. She raised her hands to the crowd and began speaking in Sakari. Isha caught a few words but didn't understand most of them. But after Gregga's final words, the Sakari men and women of the camp roared, and then Gregga pointed her finger down at Isha.

"And now, I will speak in the kingdom tongue so that my hopeful new daughter may understand my words. Fairline

Hayshair, Rana, and now Isha, you have had many names. But you seek for me to call you daughter and for you to call me mother. And this news brings me great joy, for you will fulfill a promise made to me so long ago."

"Anyone know what she's talking about?" asked Victor in a whisper.

"Yeah, Jasper and her were lovers when he was down in the Sakari wilds," said Oscar. "He became her husband shortly after they came back to the kingdom."

"Wait, what about those two ladies that said they were Jaspers lovers? How did that work?"

"You'd have to ask them. Far as I can tell, they all seemed okay with whatever arrangement they had. And I'm not one to pry as long as they do their jobs."

"I guess I should just be thankful it wasn't her in my tent that night. But seriously, this Jasper fellow must have been an extraordinary man."

"Step forward, my children," said Gregga, and Makeba and Jacinta stepped forward. Isha turned back, looking at Oscar.

"This is your mess, daughter; I expect you to follow it through. If it gets too bad, just scream Mula-ru."

"Mula-ru? What's that mean?" asked Isha.

"I think it means, 'I give up,' in Sakari. I've seen a couple of these trials before, and that's what they always say when they want to end the fight."

Isha sighed and faced forward, walking over to Gregga.

"My lovely children," said Gregga as she stood in front of the three girls. "Make your mother proud tonight. I wish to tell this story to the grandchildren that you will one day give me."

And with the sound of Gregga's words, the sound of small drums echoed, and Jacinta and Makeba squared off against each other. Both lowered their stances, spacing their legs far apart from one another as they dug their toes into the ground for stability. Isha placed her hands in front
70

of her, just watching the Sakari girls as they moved. Jacinta dashed towards Makeba, grabbing her arms, dropping to one knee in an attempt to flip her sister over.

Makeba placed her hands on the side of Jacinta's neck, using it as leverage to prevent herself from being thrown. She then placed her knee against Jacinta's shoulder, using her weight to ride her sister to the ground, forcing Jacinta to let go of her arm and brace for the impact.

Jacinta gasped as her sister landed on top of her, but with a heavy thrust upward managed to push her sister away before she could be pinned to the ground. She then quickly rolled over, grabbing her sister's leg to disrupt her balance. Makeba kicked at her sister only to have Jacinta leap on top of her as the two Sakari girls went rolling across the ground, tussling on the dirt, each one trying to subdue the other.

Isha just watched the girls roll on top of one another in the dirt. Each one trying to one-up the other in an attempt to gain control.

"Looks like Isha doesn't have a liking for battle, Father," said Jacob as he smiled down at the girls.

"Well, they can't all be blood-thirsty, I guess. Or maybe she just needs a push," spoke Oscar as he yelled out. "Hey, you little Sakari munchkins. Did you forget about my daughter? Or are you both too scared to fight a real warrior?"

Suddenly the cheering stopped, and even Jacinta and Makeba halted wrestling each other in mid-combat. Isha turned back to Oscar with a face of pure sadness. Her eyes squinted as her mouth frowned. Her face took on a mask of pure sorrow as her sister's released each other and stood up, slowly making their way over to Isha.

"Wait... I... I... don't know how to... ahhhh!"

Instantly the Sakari girls were each on top of Isha, as she tried to push them away. Makeba held her legs as Jacinta tackled her to the ground. Isha squirmed under them, trying to free herself. Isha pushed Jacinta away, then sat up and began hitting Makeba's hands on her ankles until she was forced to let go.

Then all three girls stood up, each one squaring off against each other again.

"Oh, she looks into it now," said Victor.

"That classic survival instinct. It's good to know she has it." Oscar cheered, "Go show those little darkies what my daughter can do?"

"I think you might be a little too into this," said Dessi, giving Oscar a disapproving look.

"I haven't had this much fun since Jacob was getting into scruffs with the kids in the Red Arrows. I won a lot of gold during that time."

"And I got my ass beat for a month straight because of you," said Jacob.

"A father is supposed to support his children."

"You call spreading rumors that I called all the other kids' mothers' whores, support?"

"Well, those fights supported my purse well enough. I doubt those bastards went home with any coin after that campaign. Oh, that looked like it hurt," said Oscar, turning his attention back to the fighting girls just in time to see Isha get slammed back down to the ground. "Fight harder, honey. Your father is here for emotional support."

"You're terrible," said Dessi as Oscar laughed.

Isha screamed as Makeba climbed on top of her as both girls grabbed at each other's hair and went rolling across the ground. Isha managed to get her legs under Makeba and pushed her off. But instantly, she regretted that move as she felt a sharp pain course through her leg. She rolled over, clutching at her ankle where the arrow wound was.

Jacinta saw this and seized the opportunity to beat her sister. As Makeba rolled over to balance herself, Jacinta pounced on her back, driving her to the dirt and twisting her arm behind her back.

"Mula-ru, Mula-ru," muttered Makeba quickly as Jacinta

let go of her sister's arm to the cheers of all the Sakari surrounding them. Isha forced herself to stand up and began favoring her leg.

"Looks like she injured her leg again," said Oscar. "Is that Sakari healer nearby? Probably going to her to fix Isha again after this."

"I think I see her in the crowd, but I'm not sure. It's too dark to tell," said Dessi as she looked on worriedly.

Isha watched as Makeba sat up, holding her arm. She heard her say the words and knew she was done.

Jacinta then turned her attention towards Isha and lowered her stance, slowly creeping towards her.

Oh Goddess, help me. Here she comes.

Jacinta stepped closer to Isha and, when close enough, reached for her wrists. Isha tried her best to keep her distance, slapping her sister's hands away every time she reached in. The Sakari men and women began clapping their hands as the two girls circled each other. Then in a blur Jacinta slid in under Isha's poor guard, dropping to one knee. She got her arm under Isha's wounded leg and flipped her up over her shoulders.

To Isha, the world was upside down before she knew it as she landed on her back, the dirt from the ground barely cushioning her descent. She winced from the impact, her eyes squinting from the pain as Jacinta stepped in front of her, raising her hand to the crowd in celebration as her Sakari tribe cheered her on.

"It's like an animal playing with its food at this point," said Victor, watching the spectacle of girls fighting.

"Well, my daughter gave it her best."

Isha narrowed her eyes at Jacinta as the frustration started to build up. *I'll show you, you big bully. Papa and I used to wrestle all the time. I'll show you I'm not helpless.* She reached out, grabbing Jacinta's ankles, and pulled back as hard as she could. The Sakari girl quickly fell to the dirt to the sounds of more cheers from the crowd. Isha forced herself through the pain in her leg and quickly jumped forward, latching on to Jacinta's back, wrapping her arms and legs around Jacinta's waist, and began to squeeze.

"Oh, well, looky there, seems my daughter hasn't given up yet?"

"If she wraps her arms around the neck for a choke-hold, she could win. I wonder if she knows that," said Jacob.

Isha continued to squeeze with all her might, and Jacinta wiggled and wormed, struggling to pry Isha's legs from around her waist as they both went rolling on the ground. Jacinta managed to get on her hands and knees with Isha still on her back. She then lurched herself upright, placing her hands on Isha's thighs, holding her in place.

"Oh, I know where this is going," said Victor.

Jacinta then jumped into the air with all her might and back down on her back, crushing Isha into the ground, knocking the wind out of her, and forcing her to release her Sakari sister. Isha rolled over, coughing and gasping for air, only to feel Jacinta quickly wrap her arm around her and plant her into her back. Instantly, she felt the pain of her arm being wrenched backward alongside the pain in her leg.

"Mula-ru, Mula-ru," screamed Isha as she felt her arm being released and the sounds of the Sakari around her cheer into the night. The torches around their small makeshift fighting arena flickering from the vibration of the cheers.

Jacinta then stepped in front of Isha, holding out her hand.

"Sister did good; you surprise us."

Isha sighed and took her sister's hand, allowing herself to be pulled up and hopping on her uninjured leg. She watched as all the Sakari clapped in celebration for the three girls as Makeba walked over to them and helped Isha steady herself on her shoulders. All three girls stood sweaty and covered in dirt beneath the moonlit sky, their breathing burdened under the weight of their exhaustion. But to her surprise, Isha felt an immense sense of pride standing there with her sisters.

Gregga stepped forward, clapping her hands with a wide smile across her face. She raised her hands, speaking in Sakari, but quickly switched to kingdom tongue, "Daughter Jacinta is glorious in her victory and has once again proven herself as the war daughter. She is who shall lead my children into battle. Well done, daughter."

Walking forward into the circle, she stood before her children. "All daughters have fought well, proving themselves all children of Gregga." The crowd around them burst into cheers as she looked at the three girls and smiled, "Whereas, at the start of this trial, I had two daughters, now at the end of it, I emerge with three. Truly these sisters will be fierce warriors one day, for tonight they have formed a bond that shall never be broken."

She knelt down, extending her arms out. First, it was Jacinta who walked forward and hugged Gregga. Then she extended her arms again, and Makeba walked forward, hugging her. Once more, Gregga stretched her arms to Isha, who looked at Makeba and Jacinta once again before hopping forward, keeping her foot off the ground and allowing Gregga to consume her in a warm embrace. "Well done, daughter. You are truly the child that Jasper promised me."

After a few seconds more of the embrace. Gregga stood and waved to the crowd, "These little warriors are covered in the world beneath us and must be off to get cleaned, but let us celebrate them now and eat and drink till ourselves become full."

Jacinta and Makeba escorted Isha over to Oscar as the rest of the crowd scattered.

"Well, that was quite the show. How's the leg?" asked Oscar.

"It hurts a lot."

"Sister Isha, a bad fighter," said Jacinta, "swings arms like child. But she try really hard. I think Mama was proud of that. Because tonight you fight for her."

Aukube stepped out of the dispersing crowd and walked over to the group with a smile on her face, "That was really entertaining. Everyone seems to have enjoyed themselves," she said as she knelt down and began to inspect Isha's leg. Closing her eyes, she allowed magical energy to leave her hands and flow out. "Oh, you really did a number on yourself this time."

"What's the damage this time?" asked Oscar.

"Yes, I would like to know the damage as well; it would be shame to have new daughter maimed," said Gregga, walking over to the group.

Aukube kept her eyes closed while moving her hand over Isha's leg, "She tore some of the muscle that was healing. It's not extremely serious, but she will need to go back on the crutches for another week or so."

"I guess that's to be expected. Why didn't ya just lay down in the dirt like I warned ya?"

Isha narrowed her eyes up at Oscar. "I didn't want to lose."

Gregga smiled, leaning down and kissing Isha on the forehead. "She not want to lose in front of her Mother. Yes, my daughter fought for Gregga, and I could not be more proud."

Oscar chuckled, "Well, that pride of both of ya has got the girl banged up pretty bad, but ya do have the spark to fight; I'll admit that. I'm guessing that more healing will be required though."

"I have healed and numbed the damage as much as I can for the moment. I expect she'd like to get cleaned up, but I will need to resume the healing after tonight's celebrations."

"Ya hear that daughter? You and them girls go get cleaned up. There's a watering tent over there. I'll have a few guards posted and—"

"Nonsense, they shall be cleaned in my tent. I will have hot water brought to them tonight. All my fierce daughters have earned that," said Gregga as she walked off, giving orders in Sakari to some nearby men who quickly began moving around.

"Come, sister Isha, we go to mother's tent," said Jacinta as they helped Isha along into the darkness, followed by Aukube.

Victor turned to the group after the girls left. "Now that that's over, I do believe I heard something about a revelation concerning that little girl's powers."

The girl's entered Gregga's tent, followed by Aukube.

"You girl's set her down over there, and I'll continue the treatment until the water is gathered."

Jacinta and Makeba helped Isha over to a stool where Aukube continued to apply magical healing to Isha's leg.

"It shame we cannot learn healing magic like Aukube," said Makeba as she watched the magic flow.

Aukube smiled back at her, "Don't worry, I'm still teaching you both your arts. And I'm sure they will teach you more in the kingdom school."

"You taught them magic?" asked Isha, looking surprised.

"Yes, for the most part. Not kingdom magic, but Sakari magic. I taught them to open their bodies to it by putting the marking on their backs."

Jacinta turned around showing Isha the marking on her shoulder again. "Yes, we have the markings to help us control magic. But we do not remember getting them."

"That's because you were young then."

"Is Sakari magic and kingdom magic that different? I

mean I don't have markings."

"Hmm. They are different and the same. The way you use magic and the way your sisters use magic, I think of it as eating different food. Kingdom and Sakari food taste different, but all come from the ground we stand on. We consume it, but in different ways. You do not eat an apple, the same way you eat a cow, but you still eat all the same."

"Sister cannot eat Sakari magic, she get fat," teased Jacinta with a smile on her face as she poked Isha on her stomach.

Isha slapped her sister's hand away. "Stop that." But the movement made her shift her weight and the pain in her leg flared up again causing her to moan in pain. "Owe,"

"Stay still, your will slow healing."

"Sorry."

What made you push yourself like that kingdom girl?" asked Aukube. "I'm sure Gregga had no intentions of you going so far. Tonight was more to reward the warriors for the last raid, but you sure did put on a show."

"Sister Isha surprise me when she grab leg," said Jacinta.

"I don't know; it seemed the right thing to do at the time."

Aukube smiled, "It is okay, you are young, and this will heal in the coming weeks, but you will look back on tonight with pride for a long time." She continued to apply healing arts until Sakari men brought in a huge wooden tub and began pacing in and out of the tent, coming back and forth with pales of steaming hot water and dumping it into the large tub until it was near filled. Soon after, Gregga appeared as the men left.

"Okay, daughters, we shall clean each other."

Jacinta and Makeba began unwrapping their balled-up hair and removing the cloth around their bodies until they both were naked. Aukube helped Isha strip out of her binding and escorted her into the water tub.

"Thank you, Aukube. You can go now; I wish to have a

conversation with my children," said Gregga.

"Of course, I shall leave you now," replied Aukube before walking out of the tent.

Gregga walked over, grabbing the stool that Isha was previously on, setting it into the large tub of water with the girls. She reached up to her neck and began undoing her clothes until naked. Stepping into the water, she took a seat on the submerged stool. She then reached over, grabbing a cloth, dunking it inside. "Come, Isha, and sit before me so that we may speak." Isha made her way through the water over to Gregga before turning around and sitting between her legs. "Now tell me, child, do you have any sisters or brothers?"

Isha thought about the question while looking forward to the two Sakari girls before her. "I don't have any brothers, but aren't Makeba and Jacinta my sisters now?"

Gregga laughed, "They are your sisters through blood and bonding now, but there are also born families. Children from the same belly of the same mother," said Gregga as she rubbed the scar on her stomach."

"Oh, I don't have any of those. It's always been just papa and me."

"Then look ahead of you and tell me what you see?"

Isha stared at Jacinta and Makeba while they stared back at her, "I see my sisters?"

"Yes, but what is a sister?"

Isha tilted her head in confusion, "I don't understand. Aren't sister's family?"

"You thinking like kingdom girl, you need to think like Sakari," said Gregga as she wrapped her arms around Isha, placing her chin on top of her head. "To Sakari, it is different; it is more. A part of you like an arm or leg. Together you share the same body, same spirit. Did you know that Jacinta and Makeba have different birth mothers?"

"No, I didn't know that."

"They were both girls born under the blood moon and

given to me after my birth child was taken from me. You should remember the father; it was Jasper."

"You and Uncle Jasper had a baby?" asked Isha in shock.

Gregga sighed, "No, sadly, our birth child was lost to us." She gazed forward as if looking into a memory, "Jasper was silly man. He would always say we gonna have half Sakari and half kingdom baby that would rule the world. And when my belly began to swell, he would jump around, tell stories, and rub the child inside me. But that was all taken away from me." Gregga kissed the top of Isha's head and took a deep breath, smelling her hair. "But before Jasper was taken from me, he brought me, you. A kingdom girl who would become sisters with Jacinta and Makeba and tonight would become my daughter."

Isha did not know what to say, so instead, she reached her hand up and squeezed the fingers of Gregga that were holding her close.

Gregga continued to hold Isha in her embrace as she began rocking back and forth, trying not to let the pain show in her voice as a single tear fell out of her blind eye. Makeba and Jacinta just sat in the water and allowed their mother to mourn.

"But... But as Jasper gave me the gift, I want... I want you to know and understand the gift you have. In front of you are your sisters; they will never betray you. As I will never betray you. And you are never to betray us. That truth is what will keep us strong. To know that through all of this life, you have someone who forever stands by you. Do you understand this, daughter? I look after them, but now I ask that you look after them. Share with them as they share with you, and that will bring me all the joy a mother could ask for. Can you promise me that, to become the Ala'mara of you three sisters; to look after them in this land that is not ours?"

"I do, I... I promise..."

"Thank you, daughter," sighed Gregga. "To hear you say

that now puts my mind at ease. But does my new daughter Isha wish to ask anything of Gregga?" She began to wash Isha's hair.

Isha thought for a second as she felt her hair being combed through, "Can... can you tell me more stories of Uncle Jasper?"

"Of course, daughter," said Gregga with a smile as she ran the comb through Isha's hair, "Did you know that he was my slave, and that I met him with five other kingdom men?"

"No. I mean yes, I knew the slave. Did you love him then?"

"Oh no, he tried to steal from the clan. I was going to kill him. But he was funny, so instead, I made him my slave. I did kill the other men, though. But they died too fast, so it was not a good hunt." She patted Isha's head, "Have you been on a hunt before, daughter?"

"No, I don't think I have."

"Then one day, I will take you on hunt with your sisters. Their magic eyes will help you in the hunt."

"What do you mean? They have magic eyes?" asked Isha as she stared at the faces of Jacinta and Makeba as they splashed about in the water with each other playing some type of interlocking game with their fingers.

"Oh, so you two have not shown your sister your eyes?"

"We never need to, we not hunt with her yet." said Jacinta.

"Never a need to use eyes, and it make us tired if use anyway," said Makeba.

"Now this won't do," said Gregga with a smile. "Things like this you should share with your sister." Gregga reached over, grabbing the nearby lantern off a stool. "Look closely, daughter, these are one of the gifts your sisters may be able to teach you." Reaching in, she turned a knob and the flames illuminating the tent went out, leaving them all in complete darkness.

Isha just blinked and tried to focus on her sisters in the

dark that she was sure were still in front of her. And slowly in the blankness, traces of four golden lights began to glow. And from them, hints of yellowish smoke.

CHAPTER 6

In one of the many taverns throughout the city of Burlus, Saffron sat with his eyes closed. In front of him sat a single candle that flickered on its wick. Its wax dripped down the side, not yet reaching the tray. In front of him sat a bottle of wine, the candle's flame reflecting off its glass surface, along with two cups that sat beside it. Through the floor beneath him came the sound of the many patrons of the establishment, chatting amongst themselves. The moon outside was high in the sky, giving cause for a few of the town's local four-legged animals to howl up in celebration of such an event.

A night like any other. But no night is like any other. There are always things that must be done. And soon, I'll have to do all of this as a married man. I can already feel the shackles around my neck. A noble highborn woman that anyone in the kingdom would be happy to have. And yet here I sit and pine for a mountain woman with speaking issues. The goddess is a cruel thing."

Interrupting his thoughts came a knock at the door, followed by three knocks in quick succession.

"And there is the first of the night's problems. Or perhaps it is an answer." Thought Saffron as he stood from the table and made his way over to the door. He opened it to see Leonardo Pendra standing before him..

"Your highness," spoke Leonardo before stepping inside with the prince closing the door behind him.

"Glad to see you could make it, Master Leonardo. Please, come in," said Saffron, gesturing back towards the table as he walked back over, taking a seat.

"How kind of you Saffron," replied Leonardo, accepting the seat. "Although I must admit, it's odd for you to ask to meet me at this hour and in such a location."

"Strange, yes. But there is a reason we are here. I will soon have business I must attend to and meeting here simply provided the most convenience."

"You're up to more mischief again, I take it."

"You could say that," said Saffron with a smile, as he grabbed the bottle and poured a cup for Leonardo, "I'm afraid the days of you covering for me from father are still long ahead of you."

"This isn't going to be like the time you asked me to teach you how to fish, is it? I still have the scars from the hook you landed in my leg," said Leonardo, taking the cup with a smile before having a sip. "I had a fun time explaining that one to the healer."

"Well, perhaps, but nowhere near as painful. Although I may have to depend on you for advice on how to handle a wife. You and Elora have been married since before I was born. Surely you have some marital advice for your old student."

"Plow her till she is with child and then pray for a war to keep you away from her wrath. That's how I survived it. Your father was gracious enough to send me to my death over and over shortly after our children were born."

"I'm afraid that may be harder to accomplish for me than it was for you," said Saffron with a shrug of his shoulders and a smile.

"The price of being a prince is a high one. It seems."

"So it is. But on to matters at hand. Before, when I asked you about your dealings in Passala. You said that the matter was... complicated. Care to enlighten me on that. I took a trip to the area where Dekol and Frenka were on a mission, just out of sheer curiosity. And needless to say, it turned into quite the little adventure. Perhaps you could shed some light on the subject."

"Yes, well. It seems that Duke Richardson had an item stolen from your father's personal collection. A silver star ornament. I wasn't tasked with retrieving it. Instead, the king seemed to care little for the item itself; ordering me to capture the members of the Richard's household. He seems especially adamant about the capture of the Duke's two daughters."

"His daughters? Did he say why?"

"No, only that he wanted them unharmed."

"The odd thing, though, was that he enlisted the assistance of an illusionist. She was to impersonate one of his daughters and convince him to surrender to us peacefully."

"Why's that odd? Seems to be a solid tactic if you wish to take them alive."

"Perhaps, but there was something odd about this illusionist. The first part of the plan went fine; we captured the oldest daughter or the Duke early on. But it's the way that this illusionist transformed. First, she was a man in my ranks, and then without any spells or chants, they transformed into a perfect copy of the Duke's daughter. I remember hearing that illusion magic is a tough skill and how even the best in the world take time to prepare the skill and to study the subject. But this one, it was just too natural. And that's not to mention her odd personality."

"Odd? How so?"

"It seemed a little too thrilled to be there. I've hunted down a few arsonists in my years. That person reminded me of them. The same excited eyes when the thought of causing chaos crossed their mind. The excitement of watching others suffer and panic because of their actions. Ever since that night, I wonder if she ever even mentioned the idea of surrender to the Duke. Because shortly after we arrived, the building began to burn. I hadn't even properly lined up my men before the place burst into flames."

"And you think that illusionist was behind it?"

"I have no proof, of course. But I wouldn't be surprised if that was the case. And that's not to mention its voice."

"Their voice?"

"Most illusionists choose not to speak much because while mastering the shape is hard enough, it takes an even more adept mage to mimic the voice. That requires the manipulation of air magic along with illusion magic. And after listening to Priscilla Richards speak for only a moment or two; she was able to perfectly copy her voice. It got to the point where even I began to question which one was the real or the fake. Was it the one in front of me or the one locked in the barracks. I'm not sure where your father found that person, but skills like that would not have been cheap to come by. That's the type of skill that could topple kingdoms."

"Father and his secrets; there's no telling who he has connections to," said Saffron, rubbing at his chin in contemplation before looking back at Leonardo. "And what of the other daughter? I take it you didn't find her."

"No, sadly. Some of the men assumed she was lost in the fire. Although one claimed he saw a girl running down the hill towards the wall. But after searching, nothing ever came of it."

"I see," said Saffron, rocking back and forth in his chair. He then sighed and stood up from his seat. "Thank you, Leonardo. You've been a great help. You can stay and finish up the wine or take it home to your wife if you like."

"I think I shall stay and drink for a while and ponder in my own thoughts. Tonight, this bottle will be my war to fight."

"Then I wish you victory, old friend," said Saffron with a smile as he tossed a hood over his head and walked out of the door and down the steps.

Through the crowd of celebrating townsfolk in the tavern, he made his way out into the city's cool night air. Being the opposite of the lively tavern, the streets were mostly quiet aside from the sounds of the familiar night environment. Creaks from the buildings, crackles from the torches, it was all commonplace in the city of Burlus.

Saffron made his way forward through the city but quickly turned, taking back alley after back alley into the shadows of the city. The blackness seemed to grow darker as he made his way between the buildings. Eerily the darkness persisted around him, even the few torches that he passed between alleyways seemed to do little to alleviate the presence of night that seemed to consume the area.

After another twist and another turn, he saw a body of a man sitting down on top of a crate. With a quick look behind him, he then made his way forward until he stood over the man.

"Enjoying your night?"

"I was wondering when you'd show up," said Dekol as he stretched out his arms, adjusting his neck so that it made a popping sound. "I was thinking you were going to make us do this alone."

"And miss another night alone with my friend. How could I?"

"Yeah, well, let's hope tonight is the last night."

"It's only our third night out here; do you really think he'd strike so soon after killing Masterdane? I mean, you'd think he'd have done it by now," asked Saffron while stretching his arms.

"Two of Masterdane's attendees said that they noticed someone tailing them days before the murder. But why did you ask Frenka to be the bait, what if something happens?"

"Frenka might not be as strong as Masterdane was, but she has far more combat experience. No one is going to surprise her. Plus, I have the opportunity to see her in another gown. You think I'd let this slip me by?"

"How did you convince her to—"

"Oh, there she is."

The door to a building opened, and Frenka appeared, followed by two men who had women in chains.

"I'm happy you seem to like the merchandise," said a large man of imposing size. "We will have the girls shipped up to the mountain clans in the coming days."

"Good, how fast can you get more? The Prince busy with wedding. This good time to move large supplies."

"Did she really need the dress for this? I mean if you're trying to convey her as a betrayer, wouldn't anything work?"

"Yeah, well, don't tell her that. I'd rather not have my ass roasted before my wedding day."

"I think I see something," said Dekol, pointing to a figure in the shadows.

"Did the bastard finally show up? Oh, they're moving. Dekol, keep up with them. I'll be behind."

Saffron watched as Dekol quickly began to move through the shadows of the building, being careful not to be seen. *Fast as always, I see.* He watched as Dekol vanished behind a shadowy corner after Frenka. Then standing up, he began rubbing his fingers against his thumb. "You know, if you wanted to get me alone, you just needed to pay a woman to seduce me. That would have saved you some time."

"Perhaps, but I thought this would be more fun," came a deep voice from behind Saffron.

Saffron turned around to see a visage of a man cloaked in shadowy tendrils that seemed to move and worm around his body as if they had a mind of their own, "Well, that certainly is a haunting appearance you have. But if you mean to do me harm, I do warn you; I'm quite strong."

"Yes, but you are in a narrow alley, and I am too close for you to properly wield your magic."

Saffron looked around his environment, "You seem to have put some thought into this. Wouldn't suppose you'd want to tell me who you are and why you're doing all this. That'd help us out so much."

The black tendrils seem to grow more prominent around the figure of Queen's Bane, "I am you; I am your shadow. You are my shadow, and the king and all the queens will pay. One by one."

"Well, that made absolutely no sense, and I think I'd remember having a shadow such as yourself. But did you just threaten my father just now? That means I really can't let you go. Especially with my wedding fast approaching. What say you, wanna give up here, and now, before I'm forced to kill you?" *Okay, how are you going to do this, Saffron? He's a legendary killer and he's only a few feet away from you. And he's a damned shadow mage. And a narrow alley, probably isn't the best situation to be in. But I guess it wouldn't be fun otherwise. Afterall, I wanted to capture the man, and here he is.*

"Lady Dunblane, your future wife, is another demon who hides their face."

"Ha, if that one's guilty, then even the goddess herself must be guilty in your eyes. Shame you won't live to see the wedding," said Saffron, quickly thrusting his hand forward, sending out a wave of force that rattled all the loose items in the alley, sending debris flying against the stone walls.

The shadowy figure dashed forward at the wave of energy. Upon contact, the black creature dispersed from the wave and came back together just as quickly and was in front of the Prince in an instant.

Okay, he's faster than I thought.

Saffron leaped back quickly, being propelled by the magical wind beneath him, but the creature was faster and appeared inches away from his face. *Shit, this speed,* thought Saffron as he brought up a magical shield around his body, just as he noticed a small glimmer appear from the shadow mages form and raised his arms to protect himself. *Fuck! It's a blade, is it magic or...* His question was answered immediately as the blade pierced through his shields and slid into his forearms so deep that it cut into the bone beneath.

Summoning a gust of wind, Saffron slammed the force not at the shadowy figure, but into his own stomach, sending him hurtling out of the alley, landing on his shoulder, and rolling out onto the cobblestones streets. He stopped in an open area of the dark city, with buildings around him in all directions.

"Fuck," said Saffron in pain from the blow. *I hate dealing with damn shadow mages.* He tried to raise himself up and saw the shadowy creature descending down towards him from up above. Saffron quickly summoned another gust of wind that hit him with such force that it sent him sliding across the ground again, but this time he rolled with the force, stumbling backward onto his feet. "Okay, so perhaps, I was..." A black tendril grabbed Saffron around the legs, snatching him up into the air. *Dammit. I don't know which part is magic and which part is mundane.* The creature spun Saffron around before releasing him, sending him towards the side of a building, into several planks of wood that immediately shattered on his impact and came crashing down on top of him.

The creature dashed over to Saffron, quickly grabbing a sharp piece of broken wood. It waved a tendril at the debris covering him, sending it exploding into the area around them. Then, standing above Saffron's body for only a second, it brought up the sharp piece of wood before driving it down towards Saffron's face.

"Die," said the creature as the wooded piece struck and shattered on the cobblestones beside the prince's head.

Looking up, the prince saw a sharp sword pointed inches away from his face. It was coming through the shadowy figure as Dekol had crashed into it, piercing it with his sword. The creature wormed as Dekol released the sword still inside him and wrapped his arms around what appeared to be its neck. Dekol wrenched back as hard as he could, forcing the creature to stumble back away from Saffron. A black tendril grabbed Dekol by the waist, ripping him from the creature and tossing him away. But Dekol flipped over in the air, landing on his feet, skipping twice to cushion his landing, and charged back at the creature once again.

Dekol dodged a black tendril from overhead and leaped for the creature again, dodging another tendril that came for his feet. He then rolled over behind the creature and reached out for the hilt of his sword, which was still inside of the shadowy figure. Squeezing the hilt of the embedded blade tightly, he ripped it free. Then spinning back around, he brought the blade down towards its head. The blade was deflected as the sound of metal clashing began to sound out through the street.

Dekol and the creature both rushed each other once again as more metal sounds clanged, but a tendril found its way around his waist again and lifted him off his feet, snatching him towards the creature. He shifted his weight just enough so that a sharp object grazed the side of his stomach, scratching the chainmail beneath his clothing.

Quickly, he dropped his sword and reached his hands into the shadows of the creature until he felt something solid and gripped tightly before slamming his head into it.

Once, twice, and then a third until the creature dropped Dekol to the ground by his sword. He grabbed the blade, spinning around to dodge the creature's thrusted tendril. He then placed his blade at his side, stepped backward with force, and drove the blade into the creature once again. Dekol then leaned forward then lurched back as hard as he could, slamming the back of his head into the creature's supposed face. Only then did the creature finally stumble back.

"I know you felt that," said Dekol as blood dripped down the side of his face, the mist from his breath hovering in front of him in the cool night air.

The shadowy creature paused in front of him once again before reaching out. Suddenly the night was engulfed in crimson as flames ravaged through the city's streets around the shadowy creature. Dekol turned to see Frenka walking towards them, her hands glowing as small flames nipped at the hem of her dress, slowly eating away at the fabric and sprinkling ash throughout the streets where she walked.

"I not know what you are, but I sure that everything burns."

Frenka squeezed her hands as the flames around the shadowy creature rose up around him. Dekol jumped back, feeling the heat from the blaze warm the skin of his arms. Dekol heard an odd sound from the creature before he saw it leap into the sky, attaching itself to the side of a building.

"Oh, it nimble. But I follow," said Frenka, pulling her arms down as the flames lowered, condensing the heat closer to the ground.

She then raised her arm at the creature as a trail of flame leaped from the pooled embers towards the creature. Queen's Bane leaped from one side of the building to another at an incredible speed as Frenka's flames chased it from leap to leap. Left, right, over, from wall to ground, the creature danced throughout the night with the flame as its partner, following behind its every step, sending a trail of fire circling them through the city streets as Frenka continuously rotated her arms in a dance of magic attempting to follow it.

The creature's black tendrils reached out, grabbing wooden crates and some lumber, tossing them at Frenka, who easily dodged out of the way and refocused her attention back on the shadowy figure.

"None are safe. I will return," said the creature as Dekol appeared behind it, over its head. He brought his sword down into the darkness as it split it in half, the black tendrils fading and disappearing into the shadows of the night.

Dekol landed back on the ground, staying alert with a sword in hand, and Frenka kept looking around ready to strike, but eventually, they both lowered their guard as they started to feel certain that the danger had passed them. Frenka reigned in her powers as the flame spread throughout the buildings and the streets below started to die down. She closed her eyes and began to concentrate till eventually, the last wary ember nipping at the roof of a nearby building died out. Dekol sheathed his sword, and they both rushed over to the mound of shattered lumber where the prince had been tossed.

"You two certainly are the best guards to have around," said Saffron, joyously when the two arrived.

"If you awake, why you no help?"

"Be that I could, but it seems I can't feel my arms at the moment." Saffron exposed his arms to them for them to see huge slashes so deep that they both could see the bone inside. *Focus... focus damn you. Dull the pain. Don't let her see you pass out. Don't.... Pass... out.*

Frenka grimaced, "Oh, it got you good."

"Yes, well, it was either my arms or my neck. I figure that healer could do with the arms. But not so much she could do with a headless prince. If whatever that was had not been magically enchanted, I fear I would have. But Frenka, I thought you didn't like using fire inside the city for fear of burning everything down."

"Well, I fear stupid dead prince more. So, I learn more control."

"I see. Well, would you two mind helping me through this mess? I'm doing quite a lot at the moment, trying to dull the pain and not pass out." *Focus on their voices. Control your breathing.*

Frenka and Dekol reached down, picking the prince up to his feet. They then escorted the prince through the streets until they heard the sounds of a large number of footsteps headed towards their direction.

"Quick, hide me," said the prince.

Soon from the shadows of a corner, Dekol, Saffron, and Frenka watched as a horde of soldiers went running past.

"Why we hiding from soldiers? They help stupid prince," whispered Frenka in the shadows.

"No, I can't afford for Father to catch wind of this, Frenka. Ah, your home is near here, right? Might I trouble you for a bit of hospitality?"

Frenka glanced over at both the battered and bloody men before sighing, "Fine, we go to my home. But you get healed, then you go."

"I am forever in your debt, dearest Frenka."

"Stupid prince always in my debt," said Frenka as the trio made their way down the streets of the city into the night. They took a series of twists and turns, ensuring that no one followed them. "Dekol, go get healer for stupid prince." whispered Frenka when she was sure that they were safe, and Dekol vanished into the shadows around a building.

Frenka and Saffron then continued and eventually made their way to the gates of a small home in the city where the lights were on. "Melana, I have returned." Soon a little girl answered the door, and the two of them escorted Saffron inside and sat him down on a chair by a table.

"Who's he?"

"Stupid prince is who he is. Go get cloth to wrap him. I not want him bleeding over house."

"Yes, ma'am," said Melana before taking off into the back of the house.

Saffron watched the little dark-haired girl run into the back. Then he glanced up at Frenka's dark hair and began to feel a small pang of pain in his heart that the magic couldn't numb. The girl quickly returned with bandages and a small basin of water, setting them on the table by the two. He continued to notice the similarities between Frenka and the girl.

Sharp eyes and nose, she really does look like a mini-Frenka.

"That all, go play for now," said Frenka.

Melana stared up at Saffron, looking at his bloody arms, then wandered back off into the house where he couldn't see her.

"Lift arms."

Saffron did as he was told and Frenka slid the water basin under his arms, allowing the blood to drip down into the bowl. She then soaked a piece of cloth into the water, lifting it out, squeezing the water over Saffron's wounds, cleaning it of the blood as much as she could. Once satisfied, she pulled one of Saffron's arms to the side and began wrapping the wound in dried cloth.

"Why you get hurt so bad? You supposed to be mighty prince."

"He was fast. Way faster than I expected. I didn't have a chance to use much magic. And before I knew it, he had already slashed me up. And no matter how strong I am, it becomes extremely hard to use magic if you can't feel your arms," said Saffron, looking at Frenka's face. He then turned his head away from her, looking down at the table, "Why... why didn't you tell me about the girl?"

Frenka raised a brow and stared at the prince before focusing back on his wounds, continuing to wrap them in the cloth. "Are you supposed to know all parts of Frenka's life?"

"What? No, I mean... I just mean if I had known, I wouldn't have brought you along tonight. I would have asked Mova or maybe Thaddius."

"Thaddius is out of kingdom, stupid prince. And Mova, maybe she help, or maybe Dekol would have killed it, or maybe you both be dead tonight."

"Be that as it may, you could have told me. Is her father here?"

"No, and Prince will not meet father. Now hand other arm," said Frenka as she grabbed the Prince's other arm, removing it from over the basin, and began the process of wrapping it.

Saffron shook his head, slumping his shoulders, "Do you really hate me that much?"

Frenka stopped wrapping Saffron's arms and stared at him until he finally looked up and returned her gaze. "Frenka does not hate prince, but Frenka does not belong to prince. Frenka hates that prince never says what he means; he makes jokes instead. Frenka hates that prince only thinks about self and not others. And now Frenka hates that prince almost died because really strong prince too stupid to take shadow thing seriously."

"Oh... well... I suppose I deserved that," said Saffron, dropping his head again while audibly blowing air from his nose and frowning his lips.

Frenka sighed and grabbed the water basin, lifting herself from the table, "Water needs to be emptied," and began making her way around the table. The prince closed his eyes for a second and took a deep breath before standing up from the table, blocking Frenka from passing with the water basin.

"What now? Move, I must empty—"

"I love you."

There was a moment of silence as Saffron stood with his bandaged arms dangling in front of him, looking down at the woman in her half-charred dress holding a basin of water and cloth covered in his blood.

"What?" said Frenka, narrowing her eyes up at Saffron.

"I love you. I've loved you ever since you knocked me in the dirt the day we met."

"Frenka will not be Prince's whore. Go find—"

"I want to kiss you so badly it hurts me; I dream about you when I sleep. I sneak looks at you whenever I'm around you. I love your long black hair; the way it rises every time you get angry with magic. I love the way you speak. The way you say your name instead of I when you are upset or nervous. I love that you don't listen to me. I love your big breasts, the way they bounce when you walk."

"What is it with you men and Frenka's breasts?"

"I love how you try to walk slow so that they don't jiggle as much. I love how you try really hard to pronounce your words. The way you blink too much when you're happy. The hint of sweet oil that you use in your hair as a perfume. That you sometimes sneak sweet cakes from the kitchen when you think no one is looking. I love all of it. I love all of you."

Another moment of silence passed as the two stared at each other before finally, Frenka sighed, "Is prince finished?"

"Yes, I… I do believe that was everything that I could think to say to you at this moment."

"Then move. Frenka has to throw out bloody water."

Is that it? I know I've told her how much I've cared before. But at the very least, I expected some type of reaction. Do you not care anything for me? Saffron sighed, then stepped back, allowing Frenka to pass. She walked over, setting the basin down on a counter before walking back over to Saffron.

"Your arms, they still numb?"

The prince tried to lift his arms but strained in the effort, "Yeah, I can't even feel my fingers. Between the magic and the blood loss. I think I'm going to be useless for a while."

Frenka reached down, grabbing the prince's arms by their wrists, lifting them up. "Good," she said as she stepped forward, smushing her breasts into Saffron's hands.

Saffron's face twisted into an appearance of pure agony, "But... but that's so mean and unfair."

Frenka looked up into Saffron's eyes with a gleeful smile and blinked, "Frenka knows." She then released Saffron's wrists, allowing his arms to drop to his side, walked back over to the counter, picked up the basin and towel, and left out of the back door. Soon the front door opened as Dekol and Rayrah entered. Dekol walked over to his friend.

"Saffron, are you okay? You look as if you've seen a ghost."

"The world is a strange and cruel place, my friend."

CHAPTER 7

In the mid-morning, Isha was back in the city of Vontal, sitting at a table with Jacinta and Makeba. Gregga had twisted all their hair the night before in lovely styles. Isha's hair flowed down, but the hair at the front of her face was braided down and hung low before connecting each side at the back of her head. Makeba's hair was fully braided at the top, but was released at the back, allowing for a large puff of hair at the end. Jacinta's hair had two small braids that cross each other in the back of her head, while the rest of her hair was pulled back to each side of her head and allowed to hang down, but on the way were several locking golden ornaments that exposed the hair in sections. She also wore a small ornate string atop her head that had a small jewel at the center.

They all were dressed the same, with Isha wearing Jacinta and Makeba's clothing with a leathery top and skirt that exposed her midriff. The city was still beginning to stir with only a handful of its occupants in the streets; mostly merchants finishing up the opening of their stores or stalls.

"Today is the day. Are you three ready to be going up to the big school in the sky?" asked Victor in a teasing manner.

"We not afraid, soon we get to fly like birds," said Jacinta.

"I wish to see flying school but will miss Mama while gone," said Makeba.

Gregga smiled, pinching Makeba on the cheek.

"And what about you, little Isha? Your journey seems to be taking you on another adventure. You've sure come a long way in a short time."

"Everything is happening so fast, I'm not sure. But I want to learn more. And Father said that I could come back if I didn't like it."

"That I did. There's more than one magic place to learn, after all. But seeing as I have connections to the best, seems to be a shame not to use it."

"Is there anyone you haven't blackmailed into submission?" asked Victor, shaking his head, chuckling.

"Oh sure, there are still plenty of people I haven't met yet."

"You are an absurd old man," said Victor, lifting his new glasses and rubbing between his eyes.

Dessi and Jacob walked through the crowd and over to their table. Jacob held in his hands a large wooden disk.

"The horses and carriage are at the stables," said Dessi as she pulled over a chair, sitting beside Isha. "Did you bring everything you needed? Your knives, more clothes, and stuff?"

"I did. I have them here," said Isha, holding a bag

beneath her legs.

"Good, Jacob and I brought you a present to take with you."

Jacob flipped around the circular piece of wood, exposing the paint on the other side that made a bullseye board.

"Now you can practice when you're in your room, you know, until your leg heals again," said Dessi as she turned to Jacinta and Makeba, "Will you girls help make sure she takes them with her when she's up there?"

"Yes, we will help sister Isha; we not carrying much."

"It's, *we are not carrying much. Are* is another in-between word," corrected Isha as Jacinta frowned back at her.

"Well, it seems our time is almost up. Your escort has arrived," said Oscar as he noticed Soulden accompanied by the same two healers and three more guards.

"I do hope you all have been doing well since we last met," spoke Soulden in a much friendlier tone than before.

"Aye, we're fine. Just a happy family out and about. Everything ready on your side?"

Soulden looked to the healers, and they nodded back at her, "Oh, everything is fine. The council is so excited to meet those three girls."

"Ya just had your healers check to see if my daughter still had her powers. Ya thinking I'm pulling a scam on ya?"

Soulden smirked, looking at Oscar, "Well, given it's you, Oscar, can you really blame me? You've never been known for honesty or any sense of strong justice for that matter."

"Depends on who's justice it is. Most certainly not yours."

Soulden frowned, "Well, come along then. I have a ship waiting for us outside the city, ready to depart."

The group stood from the table, and Isha grabbed her crutches as they began making their way out of the city.

"What happened to the girl? I don't remember her having crutches the last time I saw her," said Soulden as she noticed Isha's disability.

"Just a little scrap with the other children is all. Don't

worry, your merchandise is still in pristine condition for you to flaunt to that council of yours."

"As much of a heartless bitch as you think I am, Oscar, I do look after my students. All of my students. And I try to provide them the best that I can. And with that being said, I'm glad to be getting that girl away from your influence. You seem to have this knack for corrupting everything you come into contact with."

"Does that everything you speak of include you as well?"

Victor listened to the two bickering, "They really argue like an old married couple. What say you, Jacob? You ready to start calling her mother yet?"

"I'd sooner throw myself from a cliff," said Jacob, watching his father go back and forth with the aged woman.

They soon made their way out of the city gates, and there amongst the grassy plain, they spotted a ship hovering in the air with five guards on the ground beneath it. The vessel had the red glow of the scarlet liquid encased in glass as others of its type, but that's where the similarities ended. It had an ornate design etched into the wood that spiraled along the hull. The symbol's school was embroidered into banners that hung so long that they folded on the ground beneath it, and the bow was a wooden figurehead of a woman draped in cloth, holding a large bowl in her hand.

"Wow, that's the nicest ship I've ever seen," said Victor as he gazed up at the vessel. Its appearance looked almost majestic with the sun shining behind it.

"This is the Julamany, a vessel I had built specifically to my own design. I have personally worked on her for the last decade to ensure that she stands out as a beacon of what Sceana can produce. I am pleased to see that someone here appreciates fine art, although it's no surprise that it would be the general. Please give your queen my regards. I have had the pleasure of meeting her on several occasions; no doubt she remembers me."

"I shall keep that in mind upon the next occasion that I

meet her."

"I'd appreciate that," said Soulden, looking over the rest of the group, "Okay then, say your farewells. I'd rather not spend any more time than I need down here."

"Soulden, a final word if you will," said Oscar as he walked away from the group. Soulden frowned, but followed behind him.

Victor, Dessi, and Jacob watched as Oscar and Soulden spoke as they walked away.

"What do you think they are talking about now?" asked Dessi.

"Can never be certain with Father, but judging by the red in her face and how she keeps glancing back over here. I'd imagine a mix of threats, double-dealing, and blackmail," said Jacob, shaking his head.

Victor nodded. "Most certainly blackmail."

Gregga knelt and embraced her three children in her arms, "I shall miss my children. You all go on and come back to your mother, strong fierce warriors."

"We will, Mama," said Makeba.

"I will be strongest daughter, and make Mama proud," said Jacinta.

Isha began to speak but stopped and closed her eyes. Then, reopening them, she said, "El-dak maha, Mother."

Gregga gave a smile and rubbed the side of Isha's face. "That was good try, I will miss little Isha too."

"It is El-dak ala-ho maha. Ala-ho is in-between word," said Jacinta with a smug smile on her face.

Isha frowned at Jacinta, "I'm gonna get better."

"And so will we."

Isha hobbled over to Dessi. "Are people allowed to come visit?"

"Oh, she's so precious," said Dessi, kneeling and wrapping her arms around Isha. "Of course, I will. You just go and get strong, time will fly by faster than you know it."

"Plus, it'll be good to be around more kids your own

age," said Jacob with a grin. "Who knows, you might even find a boy up there you like. Then you can grow up and have magic babies."

"I don't want a boyfriend," said Isha, frowning at Jacob as he smirked back down at her.

"I'm gonna miss my little muddy princess. Try not to get into too much trouble up there, okay?"

Oscar and Soulden walked back over, rejoining the group.

"Well then, I hope you've said your goodbyes. She shall be departing now."

"Actually, with Isha's leg, how's she going to get on the ship?" asked Victor.

"What? We have a platform, of course," Soulden waved her hands up towards someone on the ship, and soon a small piece of the ship began to detach from itself, making a platform, and lowered down to the ground by ropes attached to the sides.

Makeba and Jacinta walked over, standing on the platform with Jacinta having the wooden throwing board strapped to her back. Isha hobbled over to Oscar with her sack in her hand.

"I guess this is goodbye for now, daughter; I take it you have everything you need?"

"Yes, Father," said Isha as she dropped her bag in front of her and pulled the string, revealing its contents. Inside were an assortment of items, but in the center was the head of the little wooden horse that Oscar had made her sticking out of the bunch.

"Right, well. Be off with ya then," said Oscar with a smile. "No need to prolong this goodbye. We will see you again soon enough."

Isha tightened the string on the bag once again, then huddled over to the ship's platform. It rose in the air; the girl's watching as their family down below began to shrink into the distance as they were taken away off into the sky.

"Okay, I guess this is where I am to say goodbye as well then," said Victor, turning to the others. "I must be heading back to Burlus if I wish to be in time for the prince's wedding and all the wonderful politicking and brown-nosing that that entails."

"Sounds like a pain in the ass, if ya ask me. I remember you saying something about retiring when we first met. What happened to that train of thought?"

Victor shook his head and shrugged, "Things in life rarely go the way we hope or plan for."

"Spoken like a man who's felt his fair share of misery," said Oscar as he extended his arm. "Well, no need to prolong this goodbye either. Farewell ambassador, if I ever see you again. I hope it won't be on the other side of the battlefield."

"And I wish the same. I'd rather not have to worry about your scheming," said Victor as he grabbed Oscar's wrist in a shaking embrace. He then turned to Jacob and Dessi, "You two be well also. It was a pleasure being in your company."

Jacob and Dessi both wished Victor well as he walked off, back towards the city of Vontal.

"Okay, what's next for us, Father?"

"Now, we get back to work, but first, we need to get ourselves another Molan. Except this time, preferably one that doesn't have an inkling for fucking children."

Isha, Jacinta, and Makeba stood by the railing, watching as the world below shrank.

"Everything so tiny now," said Jacinta.

"Not everything," said Makeba as she turned around and saw the grandeur of the school of Sceana.

The landmass of the sky was absolutely massive and

stretched on for over a mile. There were dozens of ships in the sky above the city as they hovered in the air. Explosions of colorful magic popped above the city as the sound of crowds and commands were heard. They could see the marble of the giant castle as it shone in the sunlight like a beacon does in the night.

"Pilot, take us for a trip around. I wish to give our students here a full view of the spectacle that is Sceana," said Soulden as she walked up behind the girls. "Take a good look, girls; this will be your home for the next few years. And once you've graduated, not only will you be one of the most talented mages in the world, but you'll be able to boast of being an alumni of the most prestigious school in all the five kingdoms."

The ship lifted higher as they flew directly over the city. Every building was made of marble, and the streets were all laced with large stones that seemed to shine different colors. Through the large city, there were trees far taller than the buildings. They appeared to be a part of the marble buildings as greenery littered the top of many of the houses below them. Down below, Isha could see a hundred or so children her own age all gathering in a line at the entrance of the city.

"It so pretty," said Jacinta, leaning on the railing of the ship, her eyes wide with amusement at the sight of the floating city. "Sister, sister, look. The trees, they Sakari trees."

"You have Sakari trees here in sky. Why?" asked Makeba.

"I've often wondered that myself. This school is far older than I. It has been this way since I inherited my role."

"You have Sakari trees in the sky," said Makeba. "But where water come from? I see no river, no lake. How you feed the trees?"

"That is a good question, and not one many ask the first time one sees Sceana. But the explanation is complicated. If you're really interested, come to me later and I shall give you a thorough explanation of the school's hydration system."

"Is that where we are going?" asked Isha, pointing to where all the other students were gathering.

"Normally, you would. That is where we accept new students and prepare them for orientation. But you girls are going directly to the council; they have taken a special interest in you three. Your orientation will be there." Soulden smiled down at the girls as they watched the people down below, "Do not worry, there will be plenty of time for you to make new friends once classes start." She turned back around to the deck, "Okay, pilot, that's enough sightseeing for now. Take us in."

The ship leaned in the air and made a sharp turn, heading for the back of the city where the large castle was. Around the castle were several other ships, all mounted on marble docks that looked to have giant pillows inside of them. And on each side of the docking area were a set of massive chains that were coiled up amongst themselves. Their ship floated in, slowly lowered itself onto the pillows, wedging itself perfectly into the V-shaped docking station.

"Finally, back home," said Soulden as she led the girls over to the edge of the ship.

The side-wall detached from the ship once again, lowering them to the ground. Stepping onto the docking area, the girls stared up at the castle in all its white marble glory.

"It's so big," said Isha, tilting her head upward, trying to make out the spire at the top of the school.

Ahead of them, before the castle, was a garden that appeared as if it were a maze. The brush was taller than the tallest guard around them, and the branches and leaves seemed to move oddly in the breeze. Soulden walked forward and waved her hand over a few of the leaves and twigs of the brush. Slowly, a path began to open between the leaves that allowed passage. Inside, it revealed a large pool of water that led up to the castle steps ahead of them.

"Come along then. No need to keep them waiting."

The girls walked ahead in wonder of the sight, with

Makeba cautiously reaching out a finger to touch a moving twig that seemed to respond to her touch by waving its soft dewy leaves across the skin of her fingers.

"Oh, it move."

The nearby trees did indeed look different than the ones below. The leaves were bigger and greener. Even from a distance Isha could see the spine of the leaves through the sunlight above.

Instead of walking around the pool, Soulden stepped a foot out onto the water and the girls watched as ripples formed beneath her feet as they hit the water, but she did not sink. Soulden took two more steps before turning around to look at the girls who were just staring at her.

"Oh come now, if you're surprised by this sort of thing, then you shall never make it past your training here. The water in the pool becomes more of a solid after the midday sun has arisen. This is Sceana; here is where you will learn the rules of the universe and the stronger you are, the more you will be able to bend those rules. Now step lively girls, I can assure you that it is completely safe."

Makeba was the first to step forward. Closing her eyes, she placed her right foot on the water's surface and then her left. She then opened her eyes after a second or two of not sinking and turned around smiling, "Me not sink. Look, sisters; the water has not taken me."

Jacinta was next as she stepped onto the water. After feeling somewhat safe, she began trying to bounce on the surface. "It really is walking water." She turned to Isha, "Come, sister, you try now."

"Okay, I'll try," said Isha, following behind her sisters, placing her crutch into the water, poking at it, feeling its firmness. *Please don't let me fall, magic water.* It felt solid enough, giving a little, but not very much. She placed her foot onto the water, feeling herself sink in just enough to give her caution, but not enough to frighten her. She hopped forward to her sisters, looking around at the hedges alongside the pool. The pool's outer area was covered entirely in roots that traveled over the marble, going deep into the water.

"I take it you girls are satisfied now?" asked Soulden, looking down at the children with a smirk.

"Why we not sink?" asked Jacinta.

"All questions will be answered soon enough. You wouldn't understand the principles behind it now. But over time here, you will. Now come along."

Soulden continued to escort the girls over the pool, through the hedges, and up the steps to the school's doors. Guards pushed open the doors to the school, revealing a completely marble interior. But throughout the castle there seemed to be root's and vegetation scattered throughout the floor, walls, and ceiling. Large roots exposed from the floors and went into the walls. But they didn't seem to break through the marble as much as the marble allowed the vegetation to pass through as it needed. Isha stared at the roots, noticing that every now and then she would see some type of orange light flow through them. A small shimmer that would vanish just as soon as it appeared but then appear near them again as they made their way down the hallway.

"Why you have trees in big house," asked Makeba.

"Big house? Hmm," said Soulden, smiling, "I guess that is one way of looking at it. The whole castle was once marble, but one thing the original designer didn't plan for was how odor would be trapped inside. So, one of our predecessors formulated a spell to have forestry congregate throughout the entire school. At first they found it to be a bit excessive, but the amount of magical power to keep everything smelling nice was also excessive. In the end, practicality won out, and thus we have a mixture of nature's greenery and man's marvels spread all over the floating city."

"It was like that in the city, too. There were a lot of trees and grass on the roofs of people's homes," said Isha.

"The city-part was actually unplanned for. At first, it was supposedly just meant for the school. But perhaps one day the spell got out of hand or it was decided to extend the vegetation. To all who visit here; it actually makes us look quite at one with nature; not knowing why it was really done. The same can be said for why we have openings in the walls so high up above so that bad air may leave and the sun may shine in for the plants. It reflects off the marble walls and feeds the entire system inside."

Jacinta marveled at the sight. "School built with trees. It's like garden."

Soulden stepped onto a circular platform with a red orb in the center. "Alright, you girls, come stand by me." They did as she bid, and Soulden placed her hand on the red orb, and the platform hovered in the air for a second before rising into the castle a few stories up.

Isha watched as the platform raised them higher and higher into the air until they reached the top of the castle, stopping at what seemed to be the highest level. Ahead of her were odd statues of people and golden double doors covered in roots.

"Alright, inside here is the high council. I am to introduce you to them. So do try to be on your best behavior."

"Yes, ma'am," said the girls as they stepped off the platform and walked over to the golden door. Soulden placed her hand on the door and pressed forward as the doors slowly lurched forward, opening the path inside. Isha looked ahead but only saw darkness inside of the room with a single lamp post with a dull light shining in the center. Inside, she could hear the sounds of flowing water.

"Watch your footing," said Soulden as she stepped down a few steps and walked forward into the center of the light. As the girls followed, Isha felt a small puddle under her feet as she hit the final step and made her way over to Soulden.

"Am I to assume you're all here?" asked Soulden.

"We are," came a voice that came from the darkness.

"I guess we are to assume that these are the three special girls that you wish to enroll in the school this year," spoke another voice that sounded throughout the room.

"Yes, they are enrolled, starting now. I merely wish to keep you all up to date on my plans and intentions," said Soulden as she placed her hand on the lamp post. Upon her touch the lamp's brightness expanded, illuminating the room even more to reveal eight statues that were placed on all sides of the room at varying heights.

They were mounted on a circular marble runway that connected them all as it spread throughout the room. Three to the left, three to the right, and two more up ahead. The symbols were an Ox, Bird, Salamander, Butterfly, a hand with its palm stretched out, a human heart with cloth wrapped around it, a large spider, and a piece of parchment and quill. A stream of water was running atop the marble runway and through the bases underneath the marble statues, emptying out at a drained reservoir beneath their feet.

"You seem fairly confident that we would approve of you taking such actions," spoke the Bird statue as it glowed red.

"No, I am just fairly certain that I am here, and you are not. The reason you all wished me to head this school is because you found me capable. That means you trust my judgement in these matters. Or am I mistaken?"

"We merely wish to impose the timing of you taking such action," spoke the large spider statue, also glowing red. "Are we not training the young champion candidate this year? Is it wise to add unknown and unverified samples to the pool? Where did you say you found these girls?"

"An old friend of mine, Oscar Highland, brought them to me. Seems he found them on one of his adventures. And he felt that I would be able to make the best use of them. Magical untainted Sakari are rare and a first for any school in the five kingdoms. And you all have received reports as to the one who is his own. It was simply an opportunity I wasn't willing to pass up."

"Oscar Highland, I've heard that name before," spoke the Hand. "Doesn't he lead a group of mercenaries? Strange bedfellows for Sceana to be in leagues with."

"I've met this Highland fellow before," spoke the Heart. "And it was my healers who verified one of the girl's powers. Step forward, children, and tell us your names."

"Go on," said Soulden as the girls turned to her looking nervous.

"I am Jacinta."

"I am Isha."

"I am Makeba."

"Well then, Jacinta, Isha, and Makeba, welcome to Sceana. Tell us, Soulden, is there any reason why one of them is on crutches?" said the Heart.

"They were with a band of mercenaries. I think we should count ourselves lucky that they made it here with all their limbs intact given the circumstances."

The sound of a sigh was heard as the Heart statue glowed, "I shall make a visit to Sceana in the coming months. It has been a while since my last visit. Then I will give the girl a proper inspection."

"I shall do the same," spoke the Butterfly statute. "I wish to see these oddities you have brought."

"Well then, I humbly await your arrival, but if there is nothing else. I must see that the students are properly enrolled in their classes. Seeing as they did not come from magical houses, I imagine the initial learning process will be quite the challenge."

"Until then, I look forward to meeting you all," spoke the Heart statue before the light in the room slowly faded as Soulden released the lamp post. And once again, they stood in a dark room with its dimming light.

"Well, that went better than expected," said Soulden. "Come along then. We need to have you tested and properly sorted." She led the girls back out of the room and down the floating platform, through the marbled castle halls until they reached a small wooden door. Soulden knocked twice.

"Come in," said the voice of a man.

"Hello, Tannor," said Soulden, opening the door to the room.

Inside, Isha saw a dark-haired man in a blue robe standing over a long table filled with odd instruments. He was young and had the stubble of a beard about to set in.

"Oh, headmistress, I didn't realize it was you. How can I help?" asked Tannor as he stepped from behind the table and came over to greet them.

What is all this? Thought Isha as she stared around the room, noticing all the odd items and instruments. Some even hung from the ceiling on ropes. They were all different colored things she'd never seen before. And spread across the table were an assortment of forestry: orange, brown, and green leaves along with branches of all sizes. *Is this where they make all their magic trees?*

"Just a little pre-test if you would be so kind," said Soulden, stepping behind the girls. "I just need to know if their magical cores have settled. They can do the affinity test with the rest of the current students, but I would like to get some baring now since you were on the way."

"With Sakari?" asked the man staring at Jacinta and Makeba.

"Yes, it seems we found two that are in their infancy. But I'd like to be sure that we caught them early enough."

"This is certainly an unexpected turn of events. Let me grab a rod then," said Tannor as he turned around and began searching through a shelf against the wall until he finally pulled out a black rod and walked over, holding it in front of the girls. His fingers had small paper patches all over them to stop the bleeding from where he had managed to cut himself numerous times.

So many bandages.

"Here," he said, holding the rod out for them. "Usually,

students are tested before they enter, but we can do it here. One of you just holds the rod and tries to channel your magic into it. If it turns white, your magical core hasn't settled yet. If it turns any other color, then it means it has. It'll be alright if it's white with a little bit of color. That just means it's beginning to settle. Which one of you girls will be going first?"

The girls looked at each other for a second.

"I will," said Jacinta as she reached out and grabbed the black rod in her hand. Soon the rod began to glow before turning white with traces of brown spots inside of it.

"Good, it hasn't settled yet, but I can tell you've been using earth magic. Your core seems to be headed in that direction. Okay, who's next?"

Makeba grabbed the rod and channeled her magic into it, and the rod appeared the same with a little less brown than her sister.

"Okay, and you're last up," said Tannor, looking at Isha.

"I... I... don't know how to channel magic."

"Oh!" said Soulden, "Don't worry, we sometimes get a few each year who haven't been trained properly. A week or two of remedial classes will get you up to speed. The Sakari girls can be placed a bit ahead, but you should catch up soon enough."

"We stay with sister Isha," demanded Makeba.

"Oh, don't worry now, it's just a—"

"We stay with sister Isha," asserted Jacinta. Both girls staring up at Soulden with defiance in their eyes.

"They both seem quite adamant about this, Soulden," chuckled Tannor.

"Indeed, they do," sighed Soulden.

I know father and mother asked them to look after me. But I'm fine now. I'm okay. They don't need to act so protective, thought Isha, looking at her sisters.

"Fine, you can stay together. Perhaps remedial classes would do all three of you some good," said Soulden, walking towards the door, "Let's finish getting you sorted then." They all headed out of the room and down some stairs, where dozens of new students flooded through the halls. "Seems they've finished with the first parts. Well, stay together then." After shuffling their way through the crowded hallway behind Soulden, they reached another door. She then turned around, looking at the two Sakari girls, "Now I'm letting you girls stay together, but the kids in here don't know how to use magic yet. So, do try not to one-up them too badly, will you?"

"Okay, that easy; we no use much magic," Jacinta assured.

"Good, then it's understood," said Soulden as she opened the door to the classroom.

"Learning the basics of magic is... oh, it would seem we have a couple of stragglers then," said an aged woman sitting down on top of a wooden table instead of in the chair behind her.

"Good day, Miss Huffles. I have three more for you."

"Ah, Soulden, well bring them in. They can take a seat and... Are those Sakari?"

"Yes, and we have them before their cores have settled. I figured you'd like this surprise," said Soulden as the girls peeped in behind her, gazing around the room and at the other eight students who sat down on marble stands in a semicircle shape around Miss Huffles.

"You're right, I do. What a blessing. Right, well... come in, then," said Miss Huffles, with a smile. Her head was full of gray hair except for one section that still held onto the brown that it all once been and she wore a black robe with white streaks that went down both sides of her shoulders.

Soulden stepped back between the girls and placed her hands on their backs, giving them a slight-push forward. "Go on then, take a seat with the rest of the class."

Isha couldn't help but notice the stares of the other classmates as she made her way forward on her crutches, taking her place on the marble blocks with Jacinta and Makeba sitting down in front of her.

"Enjoy the class; I will send a proper healer to have a look at that leg on yours at the end of the day," said Soulden as she closed the door, leaving the girls in the room.

"Okay then, I guess we start again. Hello, you three, I'm your teacher Miss Prenna Huffles. Now, I'd assume none of you know how to properly force your magic outside of your bodies." The class was silent. "Don't fret; in a week's time, we'll have caught you up to speed. So, let's not dawdle. I'm here to teach you how to draw out your magic, not teach you magical theory. All of you come and gather around me, forming a circle."

They all stood, making their way down to Miss Huffles as she placed ten stones in a circle around herself.

"Okay, now let's get started. First, for beginners, you are going to enable your magic like this," said Miss Huffles as she narrowed her eyes.

Isha felt the air surrounding her grow a bit thicker as it began to swirl the group, nipping at their hair as all ten of the stones she placed earlier began to glow red and float around her before slowing down and just as quickly lowering themselves back down to the floor.

The class stared at the magical stones.

"The stones react to magic and measure how much of your magic you're able to tap into. You won't need to do that every time you enable your magic, but for beginners, it's an easy way to remember the process. I can do all ten because I'm accustomed to it, so don't feel bad if you can only get one or two. The goal is to access your magic, not to become an archmage overnight. Now, who wants to try first? I'll give instructions of how the process goes." Isha watched as Miss Huffles tried to teach four of the other students. Two of the students managed to get a few stones to float, and two failed to get any at all. "Okay, next up is you, the girl with the crutches. Let's have you try your hand at it next."

Isha hopped forward.

Miss Huffles reached out and grabbed Isha's hands. "Okay, let's give this a go, shall we? Same as the others, I want you to focus on your fingers as I begin channeling magic. You should be able to feel my magic working with you. Now, close your eyes and focus."

Isha closed her eyes and tried to become aware of any changes around her that she could feel. There was nothing odd to her, just what she expected. She could hear the whispers of her new classmates and feel the heat from Ms. Huffles hands, but nothing else. *I don't get it. How am I supposed to use magic? Everything feels the same. Maybe it was a… oh, what's that? It's… it's warm.*

Isha's consciousness drifted in her mind as she felt something odd. In the blackness of thought, she felt something she could latch on to. *Is this magic? It feels weird. It keeps moving. I can't hold it. Where's it going? Can I follow it?* Inside her mind, Isha floated forward, trying to follow this new stream of light, but no matter how far she went, it just kept going. Little small waves of colorful light began flowing like a river in the blackness. It flowed through her mind, never stopping, just flowing in and out of the dark as if someone was breathing it in and exhaling it outward. Isha opened her eyes to see Miss Huffles smiling down at her.

"Not bad little one, it was a little rocky at the start, but you managed it."

Isha looked down to see the light fading from three of the stones as Makeba and Jacinta clapped their hands with gleeful smiles on their faces.

"Now, do you remember that feeling?" asked Miss Huffles.

"I… I think so."

"Good, now close your eyes again and try to locate it in your mind."

Isha closed her eyes once again and began to search the blackness of her mind and sure enough there it was. It was a lot weaker and farther off than before, but she could definitely feel it and now she knew where to look for it.

"I can see it now."

"Great, be sure not to forget, or we will have to do it all over again. When you get to your rooms tonight, those of you who accessed their magic are to explore it tonight for homework. Become acquainted with it so that it's no longer so hard to find."

Miss Huffles continued with the rest of the students; two more failed, with Makeba and Jacinta, both were able to lift eight stones. Which seemed to impress the class and teacher alike.

"Wow, we have second-year students who can barely lift five stones. You girl's sure catch on fast."

Miss Huffles stepped behind her desk, reached inside, pulling out a group of large pins. The pins were in the shape of bronze shields with wings extending beyond the plaque. "Just put these on your clothing. They'll signify that you're still in training. And if you get lost here," she tapped a larger identical pin on her own robe. "My pin allows me to keep track of yours, all you have to do is hold it in your hand and channel your magic into it, and I'll know you need my help. It's really easy for students to get lost here. We haven't had any incidents in the last twelve years, but it's best to be cautious, I think."

They all pinned the plaques to their clothing.

"Hey, that was good," said one girl to Jacinta, "How did you lift so many?"

"What you mean?" replied Jacinta. "We use magic."

"Oh, well, we can't use magic like that. Anyway, I'm Marlene, and this here's Serpene." She gestured to her friend.

"My name Jacinta, and these sisters Makeba and Isha."

"Hello," said Isha and Makeba.

"Cool, Sakari as sisters. What's that like?" asked Serpene.

"Hey," said a boy walking over. "Don't leave me out. I

wanna talk to the Sakari too."

"And this is Freedo," said Marlene as a dark haired boy walked up, joining the group.

"Wait! Marlene and Serpene…" Isha looked between the two girls. "Are you both sisters too?"

"No, our names just happen to rhyme. We've only known each other for a few days and made friends because our names rhymed."

"And I have a brother who's a second-year here," said Freedo with a smile as he turned to Makeba. "Hey, what's it like being Sakari? Is your skin like some type of magic? Is it hard or something?"

"What you mean?" asked Makeba, frowning at Freedo. "Makeba's skin isn't hard."

"Oh, well. Why's it dark like that."

"All Sakari have dark skin?"

"Oh, I'm sorry. I thought it was some type of magic."

"You weird kingdom boy."

"Don't worry about Freedo," said Marlene. "He's just slow."

"Hey, don't say that. I'm not slow. I just like asking questions, is all. And it's not like I was the only one curious," said Freedo, turning back to Makeba. "Hey, can I hold your hand?"

"Get away weird kingdom boy," said Makeba, standing behind Isha.

"Sister already find boy at school." Jacinta laughed. "But you must get permission from sister Isha."

"No approval. We not mate with weird kingdom boy," said Makeba, placing her hands on Isha's shoulders. "Come we go now."

The students then left the class, with Makeba keeping her distance from Freedo. Out into the hallway, Isha stopped at the door, looking up at Miss Huffles, "Where do we go now?"

"Oh, were you not informed at the front gate? Well,

Soulden did bring you in late, so I guess that makes sense," said Miss Huffles, looking out into the hall and pointing towards the direction the kids were walking, "Just head that way; all new students will be housed at the Fox House until they are assigned living quarters."

"Yes, ma'am," said Isha as she, Makeba, and Jacinta headed off down the corridor with the rest of their class, and they began rambling off questions to Makeba and Jacinta about all kinds of topics.

Down the hall, they were directed out into the courtyard of the castle where Fox House was said to be. The place was filled with what seemed to be over a hundred students all gathered together. Some were casting magic and lifting things off the ground, while some boys were using their talents to form colors above their heads to impress younger girls who giggled at their efforts.

"Look," said Makeba, "That one is making rocks float like us. And that one has fire in hands."

"Will we learn to make fire here too?" asked Jacinta, looking at Isha.

"I don't know. I mean, I guess so."

"Is that a Sakari?" said the voice of a girl from out of the crowd. "Oh my it is, I thought it was someone casting illusion magic. But someone actually found real Sakari and two of them nonetheless."

Isha turned to see a long-haired blonde girl with a group behind her.

"I simply must have one," spoke the girl. "Tell me, who do they belong to? I've heard the stories, how they share men and whatnot. Who is their trainer?" The blonde girl began looking around for someone of authority, while the group behind her laughed. "Look, they even have remedial badges. Oh, that means they have magic, even better. I simply must have one."

Isha shook her head, "Jacinta, Makeba, let's just go. We don't have to stay here."

Jacinta smiled, "Golden-haired girl funny, she wants to buy Jacinta and Makeba. You can't buy Sakari. Sakari must be given."

"Oh, is that the case? Is she your handler then, the girl with the crutches?"

"Not understand, 'handler,' but Isha is sister," said Jacinta.

The golden-haired girl laughed, "Sister? Oh my, you mean her father slept with a Sakari. Well, I guess that explains how you got your magic then." The girl walked up to Isha, looking down at her. "Tell me, sister handler, how much?"

Isha narrowed her eyes at the blonde girl, "They are not for sale. Now, if you'll excuse us. As you can see, my leg is injured. I need to go and rest."

"You should go now; sister Isha does not like you, and sister Jacinta is getting angry," said Makeba, looking up at the girl.

"What?" replied the golden hair girl, "Is that a threat? Are you seriously threatening an upperclassman? You three don't seem to understand how things work here. But since you're new, allow me to explain." She pointed her finger at Isha, "You, as an underclassman do what we say, and we, as upperclassmen, let you live. It's a fair exchange, the Sakari may not understand, but surely the cripple knows this." She extended her foot and pressed it against the base of Isha's crutch, threatening to kick it out from under her.

Isha started shaking as she began losing her balance on the crutch. The golden-haired girl slowly slid the base of Isha's crutch backward with her foot. Isha took a hop to stabilize herself only to then look up and see blonde hair flowing past her face and then downward as Jacinta grabbed her side, slamming her to the ground.

Makeba grabbed the golden-haired girl's arm while placing her knee on the back of her shoulder blade, wrenching the girl's arms upward. The blonde-haired girl screamed as Jacinta quickly crawled over her, wrapping her hands over the girl's face. Isha was shocked at her sisters' speed. She wasn't alone in her surprise as the crowd around them gasped. And as Jacinta began to wrench the girl's head back, twisting it, she realized what was about to happen.

"Jacinta, no, don't. You can't kill people here," yelled Isha as her voice carried over the crowd.

Jacinta stopped her twisting of the girl's neck before it snapped. But Makeba continued to hold the arm up, still wrenched upward behind her.

"Fine, we cannot kill. But you make fun of sister Isha for being cripple. So now, we make you cripple." And with a quick twist of the golden-haired girl's arm, a sickening crack sounded throughout the courtyard, followed immediately by the sounds of a young girl's screams.

"How could you?" asked one of the golden-haired girl's friends, and she charged at Jacinta, followed by two boys and two girls.

Isha struck one of the boys in the side of the face with her crutch that sent him reeling to the side and rolling over the marble streets into the feet of nearby onlookers, and instantly all three girls were in a brawl in the middle of Sceana's courtyard.

A little while later, Soulden Fegmont was in her office, and in front of her sat Isha, Jacinta, and Makeba. Their clothes were torn, and they had cuts and scratch marks all over their bodies. Isha had a black eye that was darkening more and more with each passing minute, and Jacinta seemed to have broken twigs in her hair. Makeba had a few cuts across her neck and upper chest. Soulden drummed her fingers across her desk and just stared at the girls for a long time.

"A little over four hours," said Soulden. "That's how long

it's been since I let you three out of my sight. A. Little. Over. Four. Hours. And in that time, you've managed to break the arm of one of our council member's daughters and smash in the face of one of our male students with your crutches. Not to mention the beating you gave those other poor girls." There was another moment of silence. "Have I left out anything?"

"They were mean to sister Isha," said Jacinta in confidence.

"Oh, I'm sure they were. I mean, breaking an arm or two is surely justified for hurt feelings."

"Sister Isha told us not to kill them. So, we followed rules," said Jacinta again.

"Oh, I heard about that bit. I do believe the exact words spoken were; you cannot kill people here. Is that right? And how many people have you girls killed, if you don't mind me asking?" asked Soulden with an eyebrow raised.

"I killed seven," said Makeba.

"I kill eight, so I ahead of sister."

"Oh, well, isn't that wonderful." Soulden began rubbing the side of her temples. "And what of you Isha? Do you have something to contribute to this body count?"

Isha lowered her head, "Just... just one ma'am."

Soulden twisted her neck looking at Isha, "Judging by the other two, I can only assume Oscar found you later than them. So, you haven't had the time to probably be trained in the art of butchering your fellow man." Soulden stood up from her desk and began pacing behind it. "I know I shouldn't be surprised. I mean, I received you from Oscar, of all people. But still, it hasn't even been half a day, and you three have already caused me more trouble than all of my students combined in the past year.

"I'm... I'm sorry... I really did try to walk away from them. But she wouldn't let me."

Soulden looked at the girls and sighed, "Well, no one died. I can still smooth this over with the council. But there was some good to come out of this, at least. You three caused such a stir that I'm fairly sure I won't have to worry about any students picking on you for some time. Especially those two," she said, pointing to Jacinta and Makeba. "They've gotten the students absolutely terrified. I do believe I heard whispers on my way back here of what they are calling Sakari Justice."

CHAPTER 8

Victor sat atop a horse, riding over the green hills of Burlus. The morning sun shone down upon him after leaving the forest area and heading into the plains surrounding the city. Accompanying him was a brownish gray-haired merchant, dressed in what looked to be old worn clothing on a horse-drawn wagon. His cart jingled with the wares of his trade; pots, pans, and other knick-knacks clattering as the horse leading the cart pulled it down the dirt road.

"Finally, we're here and there be the kingdom. Goodness, just look at all them ships," said the man pointing to what seemed to be over a dozen airships floating above the city of

Burlus. They all circled the city in the midday sun, each ship decorated in fancy colors and long large ribbons. "There's sure to be coin to be gotten with all them nobles running around."

"You mean you're not here to just offer your well wishes to the prince and his bride on their celebration day, Greenwill? I'm shocked the crown doesn't have your support," said Victor with a laugh.

"Oh, who cares about them? He's a fucking prince, and she's to be a princess," replied Greenwill as he bounced along the dirt road on his wagon. "They both surely have never had a hard day's work in their lives. I'm here for my own wellbeing; I got two little darlings to feed, and if swindling a few nobles keeps food in their bellies, then swindling is what I aim to be doing."

"I do believe truer words have never left a merchant's lips," said Victor with a chuckle as he looked at the old odd and ends that clattered in the back of the man's wagon. *Poor fellow, if he manages to sell any of this, it would be a miracle to behold.*

"What about you? Don't tell me you're here to dance with them nobles."

"Only a little. It's part of the job. Hopefully, after all this is over, I'll be allowed to run home, and the world will never see me again."

"Seems we're just two wandering men looking for a place to rest."

"That we are. And speaking of wandering men; seems we might have another kindred spirit to join us on our merry way," said Victor as he pointed to a cloaked figure walking the roads ahead of them.

It didn't take long for the clopping horses to catch up to the cloaked figure along the dirt road.

"Aye there, Sir, you a wanderer of the road also? Still a ways off to the castle. Want to rest your feet at the back of my wagon for the rest of the trip?"

The cloaked man turned up to them, "My gratitude Sir, I accept your... Well, the world is a small place. I hadn't expected to see you again so soon."

"Oh, well, here's a surprise," said Victor, recognizing Nahtalli. "It's Mr. Suspicious-Healer himself."

"It seems our paths have crossed once again," said Nahtalli as he looked over to the man driving the cart. "And yes, sir, thank you for the lift." Nahtalli lifted himself up and over the side of the cart, taking a seat amongst the goods and resting his legs on the wooden beams.

"What brings you to the capital of Burlus?" asked Victor. "Someone here needs the attention of a grand healer before the wedding?"

"No, I was merely requested to pay a visit by the High Mother. To let them know that the Healing Circle wishes their matrimony well."

"Seems like we're both in the same wagon then, so to speak. My quest has me here for brown-nosing as well. What have you been up to since our adventure on the ship? Off wandering the trees looking for adventures? Found any other shapeshifting assassins?"

"Ha, hardly," Nahtalli chuckled, "I'm a healer. I travel the land, stopping at random towns, providing my service to the common people in need. It is a job I find fulfilling."

"I'm actually curious about that, wandering the roads alone. I know it's outlawed to attack healers. But I don't think bandits and the like are known for following laws."

"Oh, I've been chased quite a few times, but with magic, I can increase my speed and strengthen my muscles. That has always been enough to ensure that I can escape unharmed. At this point, it's more of a game to see how far they will chase me than me actually having any fear that I shall get caught."

"That sounds like a dangerous game," said Victor, shaking his head.

"Given the times we live in, I imagine just trying to live

one's life would be considered a dangerous game."

"Considering the last few weeks, I've had, I imagine there are quite a few people who would agree with you."

They soon arrived at the gates to see the city covered in colors for Prince Saffron's royal wedding. There were artists painting murals in the streets along with traveling groups of entertainers practicing their tricks for the crowds that would gather around them. *Impressive. It's certainly more lively now than it was before.* The sounds of musical instruments bounced off the walls of the city as Victor dismounted his horse, leading it over to the stables where a young boy was there to greet him.

"Here ya go, lad. Tell me, how long has the city been like this?"

"Just a day or two, Sir, everyone's all excited for the Prince's wedding tomorrow," said the boy grabbing the reins from Victor. "A lot of fancy people have come here for it."

"That so?" asked Victor, looking up at the large amount of ornate and colorful airships floating in the sky above the city. "The noblest of the nobles have all come together to scheme and backstab in one grand procession." The boy looked up at Victor, confused. "Don't worry, just thinking out loud." He reached in his pocket and pulled out two silver, "Take care of her. She's had a hard ride."

"Yes, sir. I shall."

Victor smiled, watching the boy take the horse over to the stables before turning to Nahtalli and the man driving the wagon. *I didn't get the chance to enjoy the view last time I was here. I think this time a good walk will do me well.* The city was lively as children ran through the streets, and peddlers in the stalls hawked their goods to anyone who would give them the attention. "It seems your competition has already beaten you here, Greenwill," said Victor to the man.

Greenwill looked over the horde of street vendors ahead of him. "Aye, well, still I made the trip, so I'd best try to earn at least some profit."

"Here, have this as thanks." Victor handed the man five gold coins.

"What? Really?" asked Greenwill, the disbelief clear amongst the wrinkles of his face. "Are you sure? That's more than I'd make if I sold the whole lot of goods I have back there."

"Of course, you did say you had children to feed after all. Consider it thanks for providing me with your company on the trip here."

"Oh, Sir, thank you. I'll repay this one day, I promise."

"No need for thanks, go on and find yourself a place to set up shop before they have you set up outside the gates."

"Aye, that I will. Thanks again, Sir," said Greenwill as he pulled off with his carriage and headed down a street.

"You are quite generous with your coin," said Nahtalli.

"Not as much as you might think," said Victor as they walked through the streets together. "I just don't have much need for it as I don't travel with anything. Plus it's the kingdom's gold, and I'd wager they could stand to be a bit more generous with the people."

"Even people of a different kingdom?" asked Nahtalli with a side glance at Victor and a smirk on his face.

"Boil it all down; people are just people. The ground that they are standing on won't matter if they're all starving."

"Wise words."

The further into the city they ventured, the more Victor noticed the growth in the number of tributes plastered alongside people's houses. Symbols and paintings along-side statues or the gates to manors that represented the king and his son. Flowers magically enhanced and colored to represent the kingdom's colors. Banners hanging against the walls of buildings with the sigil of their houses below the Ox sigil of Burlus. *I wonder if they have these freshly made every time an event happens or do they perhaps keep them in storage until the proper moment to suck up arrives.*

"Is it much the same type of celebration for the High Mother when she comes back to the temple?" asked Victor, dodging a small group of children that went running through the streets. "I imagine her return to your happy temple is cause for quite the celebration."

"On occasion, but she very rarely tells us of her arrival. She just appears and guides those that need her instruction."

"Sounds like a hard person to keep track of."

"We all are. The life of a healer is one of service. This is no different, even for the High Mother herself. She leads by example, I guess you could say."

"Tell me, what is an immortal like? I imagine she can't be the same as us. I've never heard of there being a High Father. Has she never taken a mate?"

"Personality wise, she is very protective," said Nahtalli as he gazed up at the airships overhead as they continued their walk through the stone buildings of the city. "Much like a true mother would be. Especially if she finds that one of her children has been murdered. I once saw her hire three different armies to burn down the hideout of a bandit group that had cut off the hands of a healer."

"That sounds excessive."

"If you ever meet her, you will understand she can be quite the excessive person. But as to your question of a mate, I myself have never heard of her with or seen her with a partner. But I suppose anything is possible. She is a person, after all, and we all have the temptations of the flesh. I can't imagine immortality changing that. What of you, Victor? Have you found a mate as well?"

"As of yet, no, but after I get home, I do plan to find someone. Perhaps the daughter of some town baker. If I can have a simple life with a simple wife, then I'd count myself a lucky man."

"That sounds odd for an ambassador and general of an army. I would assume you, like many others in your position, would seek out a marriage of power and influence.

That seems to be the standard for the other men of power I meet."

"Perhaps, but I'm trying to avoid all that. My wife will be as plain as can be. No nobles, no mages, just a simple girl with pretty eyes and a nice smile to wake up to."

"That is admirable. I wish you luck in your search after you return," said Nahtalli as he stopped to gaze over a piece of art that was on display.

"What of you? Are there no healing girls you've got your eye on, or some grateful daughter whose father's leg you've healed?"

"No, unfortunately, there were a few that have tried. But I wish to continue to travel the lands for a while longer. There are still many whom I wish to help. Plus, you must understand. I am broke. A healer does not charge for their services, we merely accept what someone can afford to spare and we continue on our travels. I do not have exactly the highest marriage potential."

"I think you undervalue yourself. A grand healer surely can—"

"Aren't you that Emissary that was here a month or so ago?" said a feminine voice, cutting Victor off from behind them.

Victor turned around to see one of Prince Saffron's guards. She still had short blonde hair with the sides of her head shaved and wore a skirt that stopped at her knees. Beside her stood a small girl in a white robe carrying a bucket of colorful flowers in her arms.

"That would be correct. I'm sorry I seem to have forgotten your name."

She extended her arm, "It's Mova, this here is Rayrah, a little healer on loan from the circle."

"Well, it seems we've both shown up with healers then. This fella beside me is Grand Healer, Nahtalli."

"Hello, Master Nahtalli," said Rayrah. "It is good to see you again."

"Hello, Frenka, have you started going by your nickname now?"

"Frenka?" said Victor with a brow raised, looking down at the girl.

"Yes, Master. There is already someone here named Frenka, so I was advised to use my nickname."

"That's certainly a coincidence," said Mova, looking the two men up and down. "Tell me, is Mari such a prestigious kingdom that it's emissaries are able to get Grand Healers out on loan at a moment's notice?"

"Hardly, it was merely a chance encounter, I assure you. But since you are here, Nahtalli, I don't think the prince would be amiss to meet a grand healer. That's if you have the time."

"No, that would be wonderful. I am here to give the Circle's blessing after all. And it seems that being with you all shall expedite the process."

"Come along then," said Mova, as they all walked down the colorful street together to the sounds of musical instruments and the crowd cheering at random performances. "You can join me and baby Frenka here on our way back to the castle. They seem to have locked the prince in his room until the day of the wedding."

Inside the castle, Victor and company walked up the steps to the prince's room only to see a bevy of servants running in and out of the door with assorted goods and clothing in their hands.

"Well, things certainly seem busy," said Victor as they approached the flurry of people.

"You should have been here yesterday," said Mova as they entered Saffron's bedchambers. "The whole court was filled with clowns who all wanted to perform at the feast."

"Hey Mova, did you get the... Oh, we have guests,"

spoke Saffron as he stood on a wooden block while an older gentleman with pins in his mouth measured the inside of his leg. "And if it isn't the ambassador from Mari, who was lured away by that troublesome mercenary group?"

"That's an interesting way to put it. I much prefer putting it that I was captured, beaten, and held prisoner while on a mission for this kingdom. A mission that would have ended in success if one of the kingdom's own magistrates hadn't gone out of his way to sabotage it."

"All of this happened after our ship encounter?" asked Nahtalli, looking at Victor in disbelief.

"Unfortunately, yes," said Victor with a frown on his face.

Saffron extended his arms for the man below him to take more measurements, "That is another way of looking at it, I suppose. Tell me Victor, do you know what happened to the girl after your host so graciously released you?"

"No idea. She was with him last time I saw her. She seemed to have grown quite fond of them."

"I see. It's a shame we couldn't save her from that group, but father said he would handle it. So, I guess all I can do is leave the matter up to him. It was an adventure for a while, I guess. Oh, who is that gentleman beside you? A new friend of yours?"

"In a way, I guess. We met on the way. Allow me to introduce you to Nahtalli of the Circle. Apparently, he is a Grand Healer."

"A pleasure to finally meet you, your grace. The Holy Mother sends her best wishes on your nuptials."

"Does she now? I find that hard to believe. But I must admit, I've never met a grand cleric before. I've heard that's a hard status to attain. What are there like nine or ten of you in all the kingdoms?"

"Ahh, only five."

"Are your regenerative abilities as wondrous as the tales say?"

"With training, we are able to heal from most wounds, yes. But every mage has a limit. That is true even for us."

"And yet they allow you to roam the countryside like mere vagabonds. I once heard of a grand cleric taking up residence in a swamp for fifty years. I can't imagine there was much healing to be done there."

"Ah yes, that would have been brother Angles," said Nahtalli with a smirk. "He was more of an extreme case, even in our group. Each of us in the Healing Circle, from the highest position to the lowest, are allowed to choose our own path. It was made so after the Sunlight Accords, that no healer will be shackled to any kingdom unless they so choose."

"Shackled or not," said Saffron, adjusting his shoulder for the measurer. "A kingdom has to be a far sight better than a swamp. But still, having you might be a sign of blessing after all. The common folk look to that Circle of yours like your descendants from the goddess herself. Tell me, Sir, why is that?"

"The people just look for hope wherever they can find it, your highness. And they often think of our magic as a gift from their goddess. But the Circle itself praises no singular religion. We only try our best to serve the people when possible. There are many amongst us who praise no deity at all."

"All of the love and admiration, but none of the responsibility. How very convenient."

"It seems matters with the wedding are coming along nicely," said Victor as he walked over, rubbing his fingers against a flower. "Like the Grand Healer here, Queen Clarissa sent me here to offer her well wishes on your nuptials."

"How nice, so you both have been sent here as proxies," said Saffron, shaking his head and outstretching his arms as the seamster measured his back. "But don't feel bad about it; so did every other queen and noble. I always wondered why politics called for such formalities from people who

134

would more than likely wish me death than wish me health. What say you on the matter, ambassador?"

"Seems to be the way nobles have always been. I try not to think much of it nowadays, as there's not really much I can do to change it."

"Humm, perhaps I should take up that philosophy with my wedding at this point. Might relieve some of the mental burden at least."

"Still having the wedding jitters, I see," said Victor as he watched some ladies over in a corner talking and holding up fabrics with one another. "I seem to remember you not being too keen on the idea back at the magistrate's place."

"If by jitters, you mean me watching my life get traded away like a prized sow, then yes. I very much am having the jitters," said the Prince stepping down from the stool. "Well, if you gentlemen will forgive me. I still have wedding preparations to get sorted out. Feel free to enjoy the festivities of the kingdom as much as you can. I look forward to seeing you all tomorrow when my life is permanently linked to another. Except you, Rayrah, place those flowers over there; I require your services for a time."

"Does your highness require a form of healing of some sort?" asked Nahtalli, with excitement in his voice. "If so, perhaps I can—"

"No, no, she's merely assisting me in another personal matter. You gentlemen can leave."

"I wouldn't suppose the king has the time to speak with me," asked Victor to Mova as they left the room.

"I'm sure he would make time if you have anything to report," said Mova as she led the two men out of the room and back into the hallways of the castle.

"I wish to tell him of a few disturbing circumstances in his kingdom that may interest him."

"Follow me then, and we shall see what he says."

"I shall wait for you downstairs," said Nahtalli. "Perhaps even ask for a tour of the castle from a guard."

"Enjoy the tour, then. This shouldn't take too long," replied Victor with a smirk, as he and Mova set off up the stairs towards the king's tower.

"Tell me something, Ambassador," said Mova as she led Victor through more of the stone corridors.

"And what's that?"

"Have you fucked Frenka yet?"

Victor almost tripped over one of the steps as he placed his hand on the wall to stabilize himself, "Is there like a standard of boldness you need to have in order to become one of the prince's guards? I swear I don't know who's more brazen, you or Frenka."

"What? It's a fairly simple question. And Frenka does not hide her intentions. She's told me that she wishes to bed you."

Victor frowned, "I didn't realize you two were so close."

"Well, to be fair, I think she meant it as a warning. Perhaps her mountain clan thinking has overpowered her mind if she thinks you're my type. But if you want to speak of boldness, you yourself are the bold one. To put your dick in the object of Saffron's obsession. The prince can get quite jealous of any suitors of our little Frenka."

"I've noticed as much," said Victor as he lifted his glasses, rubbing between his eyes while continuing to climb the steps. "But no, I have not had the chance to intimately introduce myself to Miss Frenka. And if luck is with me, which granted it hasn't been, then I will escape this kingdom with my chastity intact and with the prince's ire abated."

"Well, good luck with that. I'm not sure you have a choice in the matter. Frenka can be quite forceful when it comes to getting what she wants."

"That too, I have also noticed," said Victor with a sigh.

"Years ago, I once saw her corner a man she liked in our shopping center. She pushed him down and demanded he fight her to prove he was a match for her in combat. The poor lad had his arms roasted and spent the next week getting himself treated for burns. After that, Saffron had the generosity to find the young man a nice line of work, halfway across the kingdom."

"How gracious of him." *I can't leave this Kingdom fast enough.*

They arrived at King Nevander's work chambers, and Mova knocked on the door.

"Come in," said the king's deep voice from inside.

Mova slowly pushed the door open, with it squeaking on its hinges, "Sir, the ambassador has returned and wishes to report."

King Nevander stood by a window overlooking the city, "So the emissary is choosing to visit after his arrival? Fine, let him in."

Victor entered the room with Mova closing the door behind him, staying outside.

"You excited to see your son falling in love and getting married?"

"Oh please, we both know love has nothing to do with it. She comes from a family that has been annoying to control. But with his daughter wed to my son, that should diminish any unrest and keep her father firmly in the fold."

"Now there's a love story that will stand the test of time."

"Love is for the common folk who have nothing," said the King with a chuckle as he peered out the window at the crowd of people below. "Love is easy; it costs nothing. Look at them all; they have nothing, so they are free to give nothing. But here, only power grants more power, and even then, it must be schemed away or taken by force." The king turned away from the window to face Victor, taking a seat at his desk. "So, why have you returned? You entered the city with that Grand Healer, Nahtalli. I was under the impression that you've completed your goal and wanted nothing more to do with politics."

"I was asked to come by the queen and offer my well wishes to the prince on his wedding day."

"Hmph, your queen just wants to keep us in her good graces," said the King as he pulled out a piece of parchment from his desk and laid it across the table.

"So it seems. And how did you know I entered with the Grand Healer?"

"Please. It's my kingdom, you two could have entered on donkeys, and I would have been informed. I am aware of more than you think, emissary. But since you are here, inform me of that mess down in Nyril. Your message said something about jewels."

"I was told that people were having red jewels harvested from their bodies."

"Told? By whom?"

"Oscar Highland, he told me that you're an acquaintance of his."

The king frowned, "Yes, I'm sure he did, but I doubt that any are thankful that they were ever acquainted with that one. Fine, tell me what was the purpose of these jewels you found?"

"No idea, but I did see one explode. It could be some sort of new military weapon. I didn't exactly have the opportunity to find out, seeing how I was captured at the time and all."

"Yes, I was informed that it was by Oscar Highland's group. Tell me, what did you think of the man?" asked King Nevander as he tapped his quill against his desk.

"Honestly, he's a manipulative bastard. I'm not sure if it's his age that has given him the knowledge he has, or if he's some mastermind controlling the five kingdoms like a puppet master behind the scenes."

King Nevander gave a hearty laugh, "Yes, you've met Oscar Highland alright. Then tell me, what of the girl I sent you after."

"As I reported, my last sighting of her, they were staring at each other in Latrusa."

"And tell me, while you were his captive, did you see her cast any magic?"

"So, she's a mage then?"

"If that's your answer, then I have mine."

Well, I didn't lie? Thought Victor as he walked over to the bookshelf, "I don't suppose you would like to inform me as to why this girl you sent me gallivanting after is so special?"

"Perhaps, if you would have returned her to me, you would get to see for yourself. But as it stands, I see no need to reward failure. But I guess in Mari, such things are commonplace."

"Really? From my view, it seems all royalty blame their own failures on their subordinates," said Victor, his tone growing harsher as his frustration grew. "Or were you not informed that not only did I find your secret girl, but I found her twice. The first time being so conveniently interrupted by your own magistrate. So, please tell me once more, where does that failure lie?"

"I see you haven't lost that sharp tongue of yours while you were a supposed hostage? A bold man, especially for a mundane like yourself," said the King as he leaned back into his chair, narrowing his eyes at Victor.

"It is because I am mundane that I can be brazen," replied Victor, turning to face the king and staring back into his eyes. "I have nothing, no land, no wife, no children. Just a title that I am desperate to be free of. And standing in this room, it's easy to see which one of us is carrying the heavier burden."

A moment of silence passed between the two men in the room before King Nevander laid down his quill, placing his elbows on his desk and brought his fingers together in front of his face.

"Just where did that queen find you? All the other Generals of Mari, have well-known histories. But not even my spies have been able to find anything about you. Tell me, how did you find your way into the position of general?"

"I'm a really good accountant," said Victor in a monotone voice.

The king smirked, "Fine, I've had enough of this conversation. You can see yourself out now, ambassador. I still have my own work to do. As you said, there is still a wedding to prepare for, and I'm sure you have plans to make."

"I appreciate your time, King Nevander," said Victor as he turned around and walked forward, opening the door to see Mova standing opposite him with her back against the wall.

"Everything done?" asked Mova.

"It would appear so." Victor took a breath. *Glad that's over. I hate dealing with nobles.* "Shall we head back down the stairs to see if my healer friend has finished with his castle tour?"

Downstairs, they saw Nahtalli sitting on the bottom steps waiting for them.

"How nice of you to wait. I take it you couldn't find your tour guide?"

"Sadly, no, none were available, but I did get to look around a bit."

"I guess since I'm here I should go out and take in more of the city's sights before I'm forced to attend tomorrow's celebration. What of you, Nahtalli?"

"It would seem that I am in dire need of formal wear for such an occasion. I'd assume I would be off to find an apparel shop."

Victor looked over his own dirty clothing, "Come to think of it, I guess we both don't exactly seem properly dressed for such an occasion. Well, if you have time, I know a shop nearby that may suit our needs. If I'm lucky, they might still have my old clothing."

"Oh, Mova, have you seen my lord husband? Is he still in his room?" asked an elegantly dressed woman, followed by three handmaids that were approaching them.

"Yes, Lady Dunblane," said Mova. "He's upstairs being tended to for his wedding attire."

"Good. I'll go..." Lady Dunblane paused as she looked

at Nahtalli and Victor. "I'm sorry, I don't know these two gentlemen. Are they also part of Lord Saffron's guards?"

"Ah, no, I am Victor Krill, Ambassador of the Kingdom of Mari."

"And I am Nahtalli of the Healing Circle."

"We're both here to give our blessings for the ceremony tomorrow, your highness."

Lady Dunblane grabbed Nahtalli's hand, shaking it, then grabbed Victor's, staring up into his face with her ruby eyes, "Oh please, I'm not a princess yet, just call me Laura. I've never been to another kingdom before. Is it much the same as this one?"

Victor was startled by the girl's quickness to get so close to him. "Well for the most part, yes, there's a castle and such. I imagine most kingdoms are the same." He couldn't help but glance back at the young woman. *She really is quite lovely. I guess royalty has different standards when it comes to finding a mate.* "Tell me your grace, should you not be preparing for the wedding yourself? I assumed weddings were days that the brides held in high regard."

"Mama and papa have long since handled all the logistics of such matters. Everything is perfect. Would you like to have coffee sometime? I'd love to speak more about this with you." She squeezed Victor's hand, rubbing her thumb against his palm.

"Ah, well, I don't think—"

"Don't you think it's time you let go of the Ambassador's hand Lady Dunblane? People might get ideas if you get any closer," said Mova with a smile on her face. "Especially since a certain ambassador already has the prince's attention. Let's not give him any more reason to be nervous, shall we?"

"Oh," said Lady Dunblane, "Sorry, I just got a little excited." She looked down as her cheeks reddened a little.

"Come, my Lady Dunblane," said Mova, grabbing her hand. "I'll take you to see the Prince, then you can look up into his eyes and blush as much as you like."

"I wasn't... I mean, it was just a greeting," replied Lady Dunblane, as she was escorted back up the stairs by Mova with her handmaids trailing behind them.

Nahtalli smiled at Victor, "I didn't realize you were such a ladies' man. Will you run off with the princess in the middle of the night?"

"I'm starting to wonder if the goddess punishes me with the women I meet," said Victor, shaking his head. "Come along then; I think I remember where that shop was. We can buy a new set of clothing for the ceremony there."

The two men exited the castle, making their way back down into the crowded city streets of Burlus. It didn't take them long before they reached the clothing shop.

"Welcome to... Oh, hello again, sir? What can I do for you?"

"I'm here to retrieve my clothes. You haven't tried to sell them off yet have you?" asked Victor.

"Of course not, sir, I would never. Our standard practice is to hold all loans for one month, and since you paid in full, I would have held your items for six, or at the very least, until I heard that you were deceased. That does sometimes happen, you know."

"Oh, I imagine it does. Well, I require them back since my mission is over, as well as a new set of clothing for myself and my friend here for the wedding tomorrow."

"Tomorrow? But sir, that is a bit too soon. I simply couldn't make the alterations in time."

"Don't worry, you'll be paid in gold again," said Victor as he walked over, feeling the leather of one of the belts on display. "Or are you willing to turn down the opportunity to service an Ambassador from Mari and a Grand Healer from the Circle? We will be in the highest company tomorrow, right next to the prince and his wife. Are you sure you don't want your clothing on display in front of every noble for a thousand miles?"

"Grand Healer, you say? And you're going to be paying in gold like before?"

"That's right."

The man stepped from behind the counter, walking past the two men. He then closed the door, dropping the curtains over it, and placed a closed sign on the hook above a window. "Follow me then; it seems I'm going to need to get started as soon as possible."

Victor and Nahtalli followed the man into the back of the store, and the store owner guided Nahtalli up on a box and began taking measurements.

"You both hear about that mess with Queen's Bane a few days ago?" asked the store owner.

"What is a Queen's Bane?" replied Nahtalli.

"Some lunatics that's been killing nobles in four of the five kingdoms, apparently."

So, he's finally made his way here, then?" asked Victor. *I guess it was only a matter of time before he made his way here or to Mari. But I wonder what his game is. Surely, he can't just be murdering nobles for his own personal pleasure.*

"Oh yes, he managed to kill Lord Masterdane some time back. The city was all in a fit over it if he would try anything at the royal wedding. The young maidens of the city are all doe-eyed over him, saying he'll take the future princess the day of her wedding and whisk her away."

"How romantic, being taken away by what seems to be one of the most proficient killers in the five kingdoms?"

"Ha! Well, maidens will be maidens after all. The allure of the mysterious has often been confused for romanticism," said the shop owner.

"Was anyone injured in his attacks, perhaps someone who still needs healing?" asked Nahtalli.

"Not unless you can heal the dead, Sir."

"You certainly have a one-track mind Nahtalli, does

public service compel so much?"

"It is my calling. You would not chastise a smith for banging his hammer or a sewer for threading his needle, would you? I wish to ease the suffering of those that are injured."

"Well spoken, I have no rebuttal. I'd ask you to join me for a walk around the city then. Surely you will find many a scraped knee amongst the children of this city."

Nahtalli smiled back, "Sounds like very pleasant work."

CHAPTER 9

The following day, the city streets were abuzz in celebration as Saffron began his ride on horseback. Beside him was Dekol as the city's guard trailed behind them both, dressed in black armor.

The streets were packed with people that had come out to wish him the best for his wedding day. Some shouted from their windows as he passed; others sat atop the roofs and clapped for him. Saffron waved back at the people as he passed and kept a smile stretched across his face.

"Oh, I can't wait for this day to be over."

"Looking forward to your future with your wife so

much?" asked Dekol, with a grin.

"You know, I really wish we could switch places and you could be the one getting married."

"I'd never rob you of that privilege, Saffron. Your father has put forth a lot of effort to see that you are wed as soon as possible."

"I'm well aware of that fact," said Saffron as their horses trotted through the streets, making their final turn and stopping at the castle steps. Saffron dismounted his horse, walking up the first flight of steps as a crowd gathered around to see them. Saffron continued to wave at the gathering people. "You know, this would be a perfect time for that Queen's Bane fellow to make another appearance. Surely that would be a good enough reason to postpone this mess until I can think of a way to make a proper escape."

"Wishful thinking; after that night we haven't been able to find any trace of him. I'm still curious as to what type of magic that was, though. Fighting him was difficult. Oh, it seems the bride has finally arrived," said Dekol.

Saffron looked over, watching as the crowd began to split. Soon, from around a corner, Frenka and Mova came sitting atop a carriage that housed Lady Dunblane. They made their way through the crowd, stopping a little away from the steps. Two men rushed forward and rolled out a red carpet in front of the prince down to the carriage and escorted the women down to the ground.

Frenka and Mova wore a royal garb with long skirts that had their swords at their side. Mova wore a wig of long golden hair that hung down past her shoulders with twin braids on each side of her face, while Frenka had her hair in a large braid that looped around a bun at the back of her head. On one side of her hair was the kingdom symbol on a golden pin. Both women dismounted and walked over to the carriage door. Frenka opened the door, and both women escorted Lady Dunblane out, holding her hands. Her silky white dress gleamed in the sunlight: it was backless, and she wore long white gloves that came up to her elbows. Atop her head sat a golden tiara with a large sapphire at its crown, followed by four emeralds, two on each side of the sapphire.

"She really is just so beautiful," said Saffron.

"I'm just going to pretend you're talking about Lady Dunblane," said Dekol.

The three women walked up to the steps together with Frenka and Mova escorting Lady Dunblane to her future husband. Once at the steps, they released Lady Dunblane to stand at Saffron's side. They both faced each other.

"Are you ready, my soon-to-be wife?"

"Ahh. Yes, my soon-to-be husband."

Together Saffron and Laura walked up the steps hand in hand, the door to the castle opening upon their approach. Inside the main hall, an older man in a white robe stood at the center of a crowd of nobles. To the left of him was Saffron's father and to the right of him was Lady Dunblane's parents, an older man with a beard and an older woman in a colorful garb. Saffron escorted Lady Dunblane to the center of the room in front of the old man in robes.

"Are you both ready to begin the ceremony?" said the robed man.

"Yes, Father, please, let us begin," said Saffron as he turned back to Lady Dunblane with a smile on his face.

"All gathered here today, we are here to form another great union of the kingdom of Burlus," shouted the white-robed man. "Prince Saffron Montavia and Lady Laura Dunblane, together may they be blessed with many children and ensure the prosperity of this kingdom."

You old fool, if only you knew. This farce of a wedding is such a pain. Oh, there's Frenka. Dammit, why didn't she tell me she had a child? I wouldn't have cared. Instead, I had to find out like that. He watched Frenka walk over to Victor and start chatting with him. Victor and Nahtalli were dressed in all white doublets and sir coats. *She looks so beautiful today. I wonder what they're talking about. Surely it's more interesting than this.*

He watched as Frenka rubbed the side of Victor's face with a smile on hers.

She's never smiled at me like that. I wonder if. No, Dekol would have told me. But still, she does seem quite comfortable around him. Wait! Could he be the child's father? Dammit, what am I thinking about? That child looked at least five, and they've only just met. How could she hide a child for five years? When did she have the time to have it? I would have noticed if she were ever with child.

He watched as Frenka grabbed Victor's arm in hers and embraced him.

Dammit, she's never shown me attention like she's showing him. Ah! I can't believe I'm actually jealous of that bastard.

"Your highness... Your Highness... are you okay?" said the robed man.

"Huh... what?"

"Do you agree to love and honor your wife?"

"Oh... ahh... yes... Sorry, it seems I got lost in my future bride's eyes. I sort of forgot where I was."

"Don't worry. There'll be plenty of time for that after the wedding, your highness," bellowed a male voice from the crowd, which got a round of laughs for the spectators and a blush from Lady Dunblane.

"And you, Lady Dunblane, do you promise to serve, obey, and honor your husband for the rest of your lives?"

"Yes, I so very much do."

"Then under the eyes of all the gods and goddesses, who have taken it upon themselves to visit this joining, I hereby acknowledge this union as complete and Lady Dunblane to be officially recognized as Lady Montavia. You may kiss your bride."

Saffron leaned down and kissed his wife as the crowd cheered. He then turned to the crowd, raising both their hands. "Now, everyone, let us start the celebration. I wish to enjoy my first day as husband and wife.”

Saffron escorted Laura over to the feast at a large table while music began to play, and the other attendees started dancing.

Victor allowed Frenka to lead him outside, over to a balcony where they could see over the kingdom together.

“Frenka is happy you come back for wedding. But you not come visit Frenka when you come back to city.”

“I only arrived yesterday. I had matters to attend to, and you seemed to have been pretty busy yourself. The hair is a nice touch, and somehow, I have trouble imagining you in a dress.”

“Dress is fine, just uncomfortable. Too big to move in and makes me slow.”

“Well despite that, you and your blonde friend over there look lovely.”

“Mova more the type for big puffy dresses. She enjoys the shoes that lift you up. But if Victor likes me in dress, maybe I wear more often for him.”

Victor shook his head, “You really need to explain this to me. Why are you trying to court me, anyway? We’re both in different kingdoms, and I highly doubt either of us plans to live with one another. Seems like a hard to manage relationship.”

“Does Victor not like Frenka?”

“Oh, I like you. Despite my better judgement, I like you. You seem like a fierce and capable woman, and you’re beautiful to look at. I’d need to be quite blind not to like you.”

“Then what else matters. We join and form Frenka’s own clan.”

“Just like that, huh, so simple. You want to do it, so you do it.”

"It not as if Frenka has not thought about it before. You will go back to your kingdom, and I shall stay here. But you will have a home here with Frenka when you desire it. In clan, men and women would spend months or maybe a year apart when men would hunt and war."

"I see. In kingdoms, that does happen, but not as often. Typically, the man and woman spend most of their days together."

"Frenka knows. That one reason Frenka chose Victor. He lives like clans live. Always moving. But Frenka will give you home to return to when war is done."

"I want to say that my war is done now. But I'm sure when I return back to the capital, Clarissa will have found some other war, rebellion, uprising, to send me off towards."

"This Clarissa, is Queen, right?"

"Yep."

"The one who sends you off on the stupid missions?"

"One and the same."

"Then, I thank her. Because of her, I meet future mate."

"Hey, I haven't accepted your proposition yet. How do you know I won't run away and never come back?"

"Yes, you have. You just not accept that you want Frenka yet. If Victor not want Frenka, Victor would not stand with Frenka now."

"Is that more clan wisdom?"

"No, that is what mother taught us," said Frenka as she waved her hand in the air. "When you meet mate, tell him so. And if he no runaway, then he is yours to keep."

"Is that so?" asked Victor with a chuckle. "Well, far be it from me to argue with your mother's wisdom. But still, I think I shall take some time to consider this, rather than just jumping into the mating rituals."

"That fine, Frenka will wait. Because she knows Victor will do what feels right."

"And how do you know that?"

"Frenka saw how far you went to save little girl. No good

man would go far; if he did not do what feels right. Victor stupid and tries to save everyone."

"Is that a bad thing?"

"No, but makes you easy target. Frenka will fix that."

"Do you really love me? I mean, don't you think it's kind of fast," said Victor, shaking his head. "It's not like we've spent that much time together."

"Not yet, but Frenka feels that she could love Victor."

"You feel like you could? That's a wonderful endorsement, if I've ever heard one. You do realize I'm not a mage. Probably won't be having any magic babies with me. I remember that being a thing you were looking for."

"Would be nice," said Frenka, raising a finger and placing it on Victor's head, "But there is magic here, as well. Maybe babies will get that magic instead. Or perhaps both. Only spirits will decide."

Victor closed his eyes and took a long breath, shaking his head. "Well, you got one part of being a wife down."

"Frenka does? What part that?"

"The part that says that I'm not allowed to win any type of argument."

Hours passed as Saffron sat at the table watching Frenka and Victor flirt with each other on the balcony. When his frustrations had built enough for the evening, he stood from the table. "As much as I would like to stay and enjoy the celebrations with you all. I think it's time for me and my lady wife to retire." He reached out his hand to Lady Dunblane and accepted his hand.

"Come, my wife, let us retire for the evening."

"Oh, yes, my husband," said Laura while keeping her head down as she blushed, not being able to look Saffron in the eyes.

He then led her up out of the back room, away from the

banquet, and up the stairs.

"I do hope you enjoyed your day, my lady wife."

"Yes, it was fun. Everyone seemed to enjoy themselves."

"Well, I hope you haven't tired yourself out too much. The real fun starts in our bedchamber."

Laura kept her head lowered, "I hope I please you, my husband."

Sweet goddess, she's timid. How did you ever survive being a noble? "Don't worry; I'm sure you will do just fine. It's more a matter of just me knowing what to do with it. I've had extensive practice learning how to please a woman. So, at the very least, I won't make the night difficult for you."

They entered the prince's room, and he locked the door.

"Will… will my first time hurt my lord?"

"No worries, I asked an herbalist for a vial of flowering oil. Tonight's our first night together. How about we just take things slowly?" asked Saffron as he walked over to Lady Dunblane and placed his finger under her chin. "Your eyes are back red again; did you practice that just for the wedding?"

"Yes, my lord, your father said that red was your favorite color, and I assumed it would please you. Was I wrong?"

"Whether emerald or ruby eyes, it makes no difference to me. All that matters is that I have you, lady wife." The prince leaned down, pressing his lips against hers. And Laura rose to her toes, pressing her lips against his. She then raised her arms to embrace the prince. And out of the side of the prince's eye, he caught a glimmer of light of a metal object.

Saffron quickly pushed the princess away as a blade grazed the side of his neck, with him falling to the floor. He rolled on the ground, coming back up to his knees to see his new wife charging at him with an impressively sized blade. *Where in the goddess's name was she hiding that?* Saffron leaped up, grabbing Laura's arm and trying to hold her in place. "Queen's Bane, I presume. I must admit, taking the place of my wife wasn't exactly something I'd think you would do."

"Oh, just shut up and die," said Laura as she jumped up in the air, holding onto the Prince's arms, and came down, planting her heeled feet into Saffron's chest. The impact forced him to let go of his grip while sending him flying back into the wall. Laura flipped over, landing on her hands and feet, and charged Saffron again, swinging her blade. Except now, her hair seemed to have been burned. The prince tried to dash away, but the blade sunk deep into his right forearm.

Dammit, again with the arms. Saffron swung both arms back at his new wife, hitting her in the elbow, making her drop the knife, sending it sliding across the floor. He then swung at her again, but she ducked under his arm, quickly sliding behind him and climbing on his back, wrapping her arm around his neck. Saffron then began backpedaling to the wall at full speed. His wife spun around Saffron's body, still holding on to his neck as Saffron's back hit the wall, and Laura planted her knees into his chest, knocking the wind out of Saffron, sending him falling to the floor with his wife landing on top of him and her hands around his throat.

"Goodbye, my husband," said Laura, pressing down on his throat. But soon, a look of confusion came over her face as she pressed down on his neck. "What—" she said before Saffron's fist connected with the side of her face, sending her flying to the floor. On hands and knees beside her, Saffron then pulled himself to his feet, gripping at his bloody neck and looking down at his wife,

"Why, why doesn't my magic work?" yelled Laura in confusion.

Saffron licked at the blood at the side mouth before spitting it on the floor. "My room's covered with alagon powder. No magic can be cast in here." He said, catching his breath and loosening his shirt collar.

Laura looked over the room with a scowl on her face.

"You know, I kind of wish you were my wife," said Saffron, looking at the blood covering his hand. "You've already proven way more exciting than she ever was. But still, I must ask what have you done with her."

Laura charged at Saffron, screaming. She slashed him across the face with her fingernails as he buried his fist into her stomach, coughing as the air left her lungs. Saffron grabbed her by the hair and spun her around, slamming her face-first into the wall. She screamed in pain as Saffron began to see smoke emerge from where her face was. She swung her arm around, dropping her elbow on his, forcing him to release her hair, and punched him in the throat sending Saffron stumbling back.

Saffron coughed as his eyes began to water and looked back at his wife, only to see that the side of her face had been burned, and the skin beneath seemed to shift and twist. He looked behind her and noticed the burn marks on the wall where her face had been. And slowly, in front of him, his wife began to change slightly. Her face transformed from a pale hue of pink to an ashen grayish color with greenish-red eyes. "What type of monster are you?"

It screamed and ran at Saffron again. He blocked it's attacks, but when it tried to kick him, he caught it's leg and grabbed it by the foot, then swung it around, ripping the shoe and stocking from its body. It rolled over and tried to stand back up to charge at him again. But the moment its foot touched the floor, it just created more smoke as the floor burned its foot, which made it start hopping on one leg. Saffron looked at it and smiled.

"Well… my darling wife. It is our wedding night, after all. And seeing as we've had our foreplay, what say we get you out of those clothes."

Saffron rushed at his fake hopping wife, clawing at its dress. It tried jumping out of the way, but the dress was too large, and Saffron quickly grabbed hold of it. He took a firm grip on the dress, yanking on it with all his might and sending it to the floor beneath him. He continued to claw at the dress, ripping off sections at a time, until it swung back at his head. Saffron caught its arm in mid-swing and pulled the long-sleeved glove from it's arm. Then planted his knee into its back and reached down, grabbing its other arm and ripping the other glove off.

"No, stop, get off me," screamed the ashened thing.

It writhed in pain beneath him as its hands and arms burned against the floor. Worming around, it finally managed to free itself as Saffron lost his balance, falling to the floor as it went crawling over to the bed and jumping up on the mattress. It looked around for anything and saw the blade it had earlier; it quickly reached down to the floor, picking it up and burning its knuckles in the process. It then sat up on the bed, holding the white bed-sheets in one hand, and pointed the blade at Saffron with the other.

Saffron stared at the sight of his supposed wife as he lay there on the floor, his back against the wall with his own blood leaking out of his head, arms, and neck. He suddenly began to chuckle and soon that chuckle turned into full laughter as he glanced around the room at the supposed princess's clothing now littered across the room: ripped gloves in his hand, a misplaced slipper to his side, and an unknown amount of the pieces of what had once been a beautiful wedding dress, now torn asunder.

And ahead of him sat his future wife. Half its face and arms covered in burn marks, its skin turned ashen, its hair turned white, and staring back at him with murder in its eyes as it sat atop their bed, the burned side of its face dripping blood down onto their wedding bedsheets. Saffron then keeled over on the floor with a smile across his face as he was unable to control his fits of laughter.

CHAPTER 10

Isha sat in class next to Jacinta and Makeba on the steps and watched as Miss Huffles finished teaching her final student how to control their magic. The whole class clapped when Marlene managed to lift two of the ten stones in the circle.

"Okay, and with that, everyone here finally understands how to channel their magic. It may have taken a few days, but we finished just in time."

"I knew I could do it," proclaimed Marlene, jumping up and clapping her hands as Serpene hugged her.

"Now we all know how to lift the stones," said Freedo.

"Does that mean we're mages now?"

"You still weak," said Makeba, pointing her finger at Freedo. "You only lift one stone."

"Hey, that's not nice. I'm gonna get better. Not everyone can be a magical Sakari like you two.

Makeba folded her hands in front of her. "Weak kingdom boy."

"You keep calling me that, but you'll see. I'm gonna get stronger than both of you."

"Now, now, children, you can finish your squabbles later. The school is still performing its housing assessment tests. Now, if we hurry, we can get you put in with the rest of the lot from this year. Come along all, let's go and get you sorted."

Isha grabbed her crutches as Miss Huffles led the class out of the room and down the corridor; eventually making their way to an auditorium that had students separated into five different isles, and at the end of each aisle sat an inspector next to a marble podium with a white crystal at the top. Students placed their hands on the white crystal, making it glow different colors and then were given a badge.

"Okay, children, line up in an aisle and wait for your turn. After the tests you will be given new badges, which will belong to your assigned houses for the next few years."

Isha and the other student entered into the lines, prepared to wait, as Jacinta and Makeba stayed behind with Miss Huffles.

"Aren't you girls going to be taking the test, too?" asked Miss Huffles, looking down at Jacinta and Makeba.

"No need. Soulden say we stay with sister Isha," said Makeba.

"Oh, be that as it may, there's still fun to be had in finding out where you would have been. Now come on, off with the both of you. Get in line with your sister there." Miss Huffles patted the Sakari girls on the back, shuffling them in line before they could mount any resistance.

Jacinta and Makeba were ushered into lines on either side of Isha. Despite any misgiving they may have had, Isha could see that they were excited to be taking the test with the rest of the students. Looking around, she noticed that the Sakari girls were still getting odd glances from the other students, but nowhere near as many as they were a week ago after their arrival at school.

"This is fun," said Jacinta.

Soulden walked up beside Miss Huffles, "I see you managed to get them ready in time for the last day of tests."

"It wasn't so hard; they just needed a little push, is all. But I don't remember you being the coddling type. Allowing those Sakari girls to just follow along with their little friend there."

"Coddling has nothing to do with it; she's the only one they listen to. Having her around ensures I have fewer students with broken arms."

"Yes, I caught wind of that. Wasn't that girl Evengale's daughter? How'd she take the news?"

"As well as to be expected, I'd guess. A lot of yelling, accusing, and threatening."

"Will you be cooking tonight?"

"What? No, it's your turn to cook. I did it last night."

There was a moment of silence between the two women, before Soulden sighed.

"Fine, I'll cook again. You know you really are a pain, Miss Huffles."

Miss Huffles linked her arm around Soulden's, "Of course I am. Oh, look, one of the Sakari girls is up."

Jacinta stepped up to the podium.

"Place your hand on the orb and begin channeling your magic inside of it, please," said the woman beside the podium.

Jacinta placed her hand on the orb, and slowly it began to glow white before changing to red, green, and finally settling on a grayish-brown color.

The woman reached into a cup beside her, pulled out a pin that had the shape of a Lizard on it and gave it to Jacinta.

"You are assigned to Salamander house."

Next, Isha stepped up to her podium and placed her hand on the crystal as instructed. Closing her eyes, Isha searched within herself for the magic as she had done many nights before and began trying to make it flow the way she wanted. It still wasn't easy, but she grasped some of it, and after some time, it began to follow her will. She opened her eyes and thrust the magic she had managed to grasp into the orb. The orb shifted color from blue to purple, and then just a clear white.

"Oh, congratulations. You'll be in the house of hearts," said the woman next to the podium. "Here's your badge."

"House of hearts? What's that?"

"You see those people in the white robes who are now headed over here? That's them. I bet they're excited to get another one. They've been waiting all week for another healer to show up."

"I'm a healer?" asked Isha.

"Yeah, probably. The Hilgard Orb is rarely ever wrong when it comes to tests."

Isha grabbed her crutches, stepping down from the podium and was joined by Jacinta,

"Sister Isha's orb was all white and pretty."

"Greetings child. We are very happy to welcome you to our ranks," said the older female healer.

"When I first saw you, I never expected that your magic would turn out to be healing magic, although it still looks a bit weird," said the younger healer. Isha remembered that they were the two healers that Soulden brought to the city to meet her and Oscar.

"Ah. Hello again, ah..."

"Oh, sorry, my name is Elena. And this is Darla; she is a graduate of this year. "

"I just wanted to see if any new healers would show up

this year, so I stuck around a little while longer," said Darla. "I can already tell that idiot Leo is going to be happy."

"Who's Leo?" asked Isha.

"Unfortunately, I'm sure he is," said Elena sighing, "Don't worry, you'll understand soon enough. If you want, I can take you to the heart house and show you around."

"I guess, but I have to wait for—"

Suddenly the sound of shattering filled the auditorium. Everyone turned to the sound to see Makeba standing on a podium, next to a blonde-haired man holding the side of his head as blood began to leak over his hands.

"You broke it," said Freedo, pointing at Makeba. "Now you're in trouble."

"You shut up," said Makeba, turning from Freedo to look over at her sisters. "I not mean to break it."

"Wow, I'm happy I was able to shield myself from most of it," spoke the blonde-haired man as he stood over the remains of a shattered Hilgard Orb.

"Well, that's never happened before," said Miss Huffles.

"Staff, go retrieve another orb, please," ordered Soulden. "Mr. Caudbell, are you okay?"

"Yes, I got my arm up when it started crackling and blocked most of it. Although it was certainly surprising," said the blonde-haired man.

"We'll have our healers look at your wound since—"

"No, don't worry about me. I have some patches on me for when the children scar themselves. It'll do well enough," said Caudbell as he reached into a pocket on his robe and grabbed a patch, sticking it on his head to stop the bleeding. "There we go, as right as rain. But I must admit, I'm curious as to the phenomenon that caused such a thing to happen."

But even after bringing another orb, just like the first, it shattered when Makeba tried to channel her magic into it.

"Amazing," said Caudbell. "Would you mind if I studied them? Perhaps this Sakari has a natural counterspell that reacts to the Hilgard Orb."

160

"If the girls don't mind. I don't see a reason why that can't be arranged," replied Soulden. "But it will have to wait for another day."

"Oh, yes, of course," agreed Caudbell with a smile. "For a day other than orientation."

"Go on with your sister, child," said Soulden as she knelt, inspecting the pieces of crystal that had piled up on the floor. "Apparently we're going to need a different way of testing your aptitude. No need for you to break any more of our equipment today. If nothing works, we'll just need to go by the cube that you used when you got here." She then looked to the two healers. "Go on and show them to their new quarters. We'll have their stuff moved over by this evening."

"Ma'am? Did you say, *their* quarters?"

"Yes, those Sakari will also be staying with that new healer you've acquired. You were there in Vontal; you should understand the arrangement."

"Ah, yes, ma'am."

The girls were then led out of the auditorium and out of the castle. Isha once again saw the small city that laid in front of the castle in the sky. As they walked through the city streets, she saw many older students standing around talking or sitting on park benches with books in their hands, while others were actively practicing magic. Eventually, they made their way over to a building with a heart statue in front of it. It seemed very similar to the heart statue that glowed when she was inside the council's chamber.

"This will be your home for the next three years when classes aren't being held," said Elena.

Isha looked over the wooden building with its two pillars at the doorstep, holding up its awning. It looked so out of place when she looked over at all the marble and stone buildings that had been scattered throughout the city.

"I'm Isha, and this is—"

"Oh, I know. I'd figure the whole school knows at this

point. We all heard about the fight with Blaire Evengale and her group. Everyone was talking about it. They brought her here, and Leo used her as an example of how to heal broken bones. I don't think she liked that very much".

"That was me. I broke her arm," said Makeba with a smile on her face.

Isha frowned at Makeba, "I remember."

"But still, it's good that they allowed you three to stay together. When I came in I overheard Headmistress Soulden saying how you are the only one who can keep them in line," said Elena, pointing at Jacinta and Makeba.

"But they really don't listen to me all the time; they just do what they want."

"Yes, we do what is best for sister Isha." said Jacinta. "Sometimes she not know what best for her. Once she tried to eat a bug, so I slapped it out of her mouth. Her face was really red."

"That was one time, and I didn't see it on the bread. I wouldn't have put it in my mouth had I seen it."

"Isha, the bug eat-ah. Oh, it rhymes."

"Shut up."

Elena laughed at the girls bickering with each other, "Well... either way. It's good that they are allowing you three to stay together. It's rare for siblings to be put into the same house."

"Hey, who's that down there?" asked a girl from an upstairs window.

A dark-haired boy with his hair in a bun popped his head out from around the building. "What do we have here, new recruits? And three of them this time, and the infamous two Sakari to boot. The Goddess sure is kind to me." The dark-haired boy glanced down at Isha's leg and crutches, which made her feel a bit nervous getting his attention. "What's this? We can't have a healer on crutches. It'd look bad for our branding. We're going to be taking care of that leg, don't you worry. You'll be feeling so good soon that you'll start thinking that you can fly."

Elena shook her head, "Sorry about him, that's Leo."

"He's the one I warned you about," said Darla. "The girl up top is Rima. She lives here too."

"What do you mean you warned her about me?" asked Leo, narrowing his eyes. "I'm a gentleman amongst gentlemen."

"An idiot lecher amongst women is more like it."

"Why are you still here, anyway? I graduated you. Shouldn't you be off on your journey now?"

"I wanted to stay and see if any new healers would come in this year. And perhaps warn them about your antics."

"Oh, hush you. You're just going to miss me. Admit it."

"Miss watching you make a fool of yourself? That's most certainly true."

"Stop it, both of you. You're setting a bad example for our new members," said Elena, turning back to the girls. "As you can see, it gets quite lively around here sometimes."

"Fine, I guess since I'm the oldest, that means it is my job to welcome you." Leo bowed to the girls. "My dearest ladies, it is my eternal pleasure to welcome you three here to Harem House."

"Harem House?" asked Isha as she saw Elena roll her eyes at Leo.

"This idiot couldn't last a minute, before making a fool of himself," said Darla.

"It is here at Harem House that you three ladies will be molded into the loveliest and most refined women for my pleasure. When you're older, of course, I can't have people thinking I like the kiddies. A prime example of my teaching skills are Elena here, Rima up there, and this bitch Darla here. Who, to my great joy, will be leaving us soon. Over the last three years I have personally molded these young ladies, except Darla, into the finest concubines a man could ever ask for."

Elena whacked Leo on the back of the head while he

bowed, "Stop that. You're going to give them the wrong idea."

Leo grabbed the back of his head while laughing, "Ah... you're always spoiling my fun."

"Don't mind Leo," said Elena. "He's a good guy and helps us a lot around here. He just has this bad habit of saying stupid things."

"I'll have my harem one day, just you—," said Leo, dodging to the side as Elena swiped at him again. "Ha! You missed that time."

Elena narrowed her eyes at Leo, then turned and opened the door to the house, "You can come on inside, and I'll show you around."

"He funny?" said Jacinta with a smile. "Is he slave of house?"

"Slave?" asked Leo, rubbing his chin. "Yes, I suppose I do feel that way sometimes. I'm the only guy here, and these ladies boss me around to no end."

"And you complain any time we ask you to do anything," said Darla.

"No, I complain any time when you specifically ask me to do anything because you demand too much. And you don't even dress sexy for me to look at."

"See, that's what we mean about you being an idiot. Think before you speak."

"Okay, you two," said Elena with a sigh. "Go on and finish up, Leo. We'll meet you inside later on."

"Alright," said Leo, looking over to Isha. "I'll come up and look at that leg of yours when I'm done down here. I still gotta finish cleaning the leaves off the roof," He then turned and walked off, disappearing around the corner.

"Ah... okay," said Isha, being caught up in the flow of the conversation as Leo disappeared around the house. *I'll be okay. I'm better now. I can be around them just fine. I'm... I'm okay.*

The three girls followed Elena through the door. The

house was wooden inside with nice furniture. Instead of carpet or a rug, the entire bottom floor was completely made of polished wooden planks. There were potted plants hanging from the ceilings through the bottom floor. Between the boards of the wall, she could see roots coming through as the greenery sprouted on the walls.

"It's not as nice as some of the major houses, but it's quite enough most of the time, and we all take turns doing the chores of the house," said Elena as the girls looked around. "Come on and follow me, and I'll show you to your room." Elena led the girls up the wooden stairs, to the last room on the right, where they heard Leo shifting around on the rooftop. They entered and found a small bed with a desk in front of a window. "Your stuff hasn't been delivered yet, but you can decorate it however you like." Elena looked to the Sakari girls, "Your rooms will be next door, so we can--"

"We stay in room with sister Isha," said Jacinta.

Elena raised a brow, looking over at Isha.

"You're not going to change their minds once they decide something."

Elena smiled, "Well, no worries. We got something for that too, although it's meant for group studying. I guess we can leave it open all the time." Elena walked over to the wall and raised her hand. "Shokram!" And as green light swirled around her hand, the wooden boards on the wall began sliding away, revealing another bed and desk from the next room. She then walked forward into the next room and repeated the process. "There we go, three beds, three desks, and one extra-large room."

Isha sat down on the bed to rest her leg. "Do all the walls work like that?"

"Only the ones on the second floor," said Elena, looking up to the sound of footsteps on the roof. "But Leo knows a bit more about the house than I do since he's been here longer."

"Oh, you're good at magic too. Are you going to be our

teacher?" asked Makeba.

"Me? No, I mean I'll help with your studies if you have trouble, but classes won't be starting for another week."

"Hey, I can teach you many things when you get a little older," said Leo, his face popping in from outside the window, startling Elena and Isha.

"Dammit, Leo, what are you doing outside the window?"

"Hey, I told you I was cleaning off the roof. I just so happened to hear you ladies talking and decided to make another appearance," said Leo as he climbed through the window, standing before the girls.

"Didn't anyone ever teach you not to climb in through a lady's window?"

"But I need practice for our romantic nights together. Our long passionate nights, and then I'll rescue you from the castle as the world tries to keep us apart. But that shall not stop our forbidden love."

"The only thing that should be forbidden is your stupidity," said Darla, walking into the room.

"Why are you still here? Shoo... shoo... Go on your journey already. I'm sure there are plenty of villagers with sore ankles for you to terrorize."

"I'm just getting my things, don't mind me."

Leo made a sour face, "Well, either way, I figured it'd be best to have a look at that leg. I may not look it, but I'm a really good healer. So, let's just have a look-see." Leo knelt and reached out for Isha.

"No, stop, please," said Isha quickly as she quickly backed up on the bed, bumping against the desk. Her eyes were wide as she started breathing heavily.

Leo pulled his hand back quickly and held his palms up in the air, "Whoa, sorry. It's not gonna hurt, I promise. I just wanna inspect the damage."

Makeba and Jacinta hurried over to the side of the bed beside Isha.

"Isha not trust men, ever since big man hurt her. You

cannot touch," said Jacinta with her hand stretched out over Isha protectively.

Leo stepped back, "Oh... ah... look, I'm sorry about that whole concubine thing. I didn't know..."

"Dammit, Leo, we are supposed to heal people, not open up scars," scolded Elena, whacking him on the shoulder.

"I'm sorry, okay... I didn't know she'd been... well, I didn't know, okay. It could have been a rape or a beating, who knows what..." said Leo turning back to Isha, "Ahh... shit... I didn't mean to say that." Leo began rubbing the back of his head, looking down at the floor. "I'm sorry, okay. I'll keep my distance from now on. You can even hit me if you like."

Isha looked over at Leo apologizing to her and began to focus more on Makeba and Jacinta, who had grabbed ahold of her arms. She noticed that her heartbeat had sped up and her finger had clenched the bed sheets.

"It... it's okay, I... I just wasn't ready. It's okay now. Please do check my leg."

"You sure?" said Leo, standing away from her.

"Yes, it's okay now. Just... please don't move so fast."

Leo looked at Elena cautiously.

"Don't look at me. You're the one who started this mess."

Leo grabbed a chair as Isha sat up on the bed. He then slowly walked over with the chair and placed it in front of Isha before taking a seat. "Okay, will you please give me your leg?"

Isha lifted her knee until her leg was in Leo's hands. His hands were cold at first, but she quickly felt their warmth as he closed his eyes, and green and blue magic began to appear around his hand tedd swirled around her leg.

"The bone's not broken. That's good. Just a large amount of scar tissue. It's slowing down the healing process quite a bit. But it's nothing too major." Leo rubbed his thumb over the wound, pressing into it softly. "Yes, I can fix this. The muscle around the wound is still strong." He opened his eyes and stepped back, away from Isha. "Okay, try it now. It should feel a bit better."

Isha lifted her knees and noticed that the ping of pain was lesser than before.

"Yes, it… it doesn't sting as much now."

"See, Leo's probably the best healer in the school. It'd be perfect if he didn't blab off at the mouth so much," said Elena.

"I did apologize, you know," replied Leo, looking sourly at Elena before turning back to Isha. "If you'll let me, I think if I perform treatment twice a day until classes start, you shouldn't need the crutches anymore by then. But that is if you don't mind me touching your leg a few more times."

Isha looked down at her leg. "I… I don't mind."

"And I'll be here during every session if that makes you feel comfortable," said Elena.

"Jacinta and Makeba will be here too," added Makeba as she tapped Jacinta on the arm and pointed to the bed at the edge of the room.

"Good, I look forward to starting the treatment. I know it's a little late, but I usually cook for the new members of the house. But we didn't have anyone show up all week, so I just assumed we didn't get anyone new this year. If you don't mind waiting, I can head down to the market and get something started."

"I don't mind. We haven't eaten all day," said Isha as she looked over to her sisters who had started moving around the furniture.

They pushed their desks to the side away from the wall, and then they both raised their hands as magic began to swirl around their fingers. One of the beds began to shake before rising off the floor and hovering over beside the other bed, setting itself down.

"Wow, I never seen Sakari use magic before. They didn't even use words," said Elena.

"I don't see them use it that much either. I guess, woah…"

said Isha as she went tumbling across the bed as it was lifted into the air and began bouncing its way towards the girls. Isha gripped the side of the bouncing bed and peeked over the edge to see Jacinta and Makeba smiling back at her, making the bed sway in the air.

"Stop that, you two. What if I would have fall... ahhh!" screamed Isha as the bed jiggled in the air even more.

CHAPTER 11

Victor stood atop an airship looking out at the city of Burlus as more passengers walked across the tower's bridge over to the deck. He took a deep breath, turned around, and placed his back against the railing. *Finally headed back. The adventure has ended.*

"Hello sir, I believe I saw you at the royal ceremony," said a well-dressed man with a sword at his side.

And, of course, someone bothers me. "Yes, like many, I was there to offer my well wishes to the prince and his wife. And you are?"

"Oh, where are my manners? I'm Fernando Figarella.

And if I'm not mistaken, you are Victor Krill, are you not?"

"That would be me, yes. But I'm afraid I don't know you. Have we perchance met somewhere before?"

The man laughed, "Yes, you can say that. The last time we met, I was a refugee, and you sheltered my children and me in your tent at Provain the night of that bandit raid."

Victor stared at the man for a moment, remembering the raiders that had attacked the small town years ago. Along with the group of four that he allowed to stay in his tent those nights. "Seriously? Well, you certainly clean up nice. You look different without all the blood and mud on your face. Are your kids okay? Hopefully, that night didn't scare them too bad."

"They are fine now, thanks to you. I have them living with their aunt in the north of Mari while I was here doing business."

"Humm, I think you owned a vineyard the last time I checked. Is that still your profession these days, or have you taken on other hobbies?"

"I actually ended up selling my vineyard to the Goose in Passala some years ago. He and his wife became friends of mine. He was supposed to supply the wedding with wine himself, but it seems he had other matters to attend to. He asked If I could oversee the shipment here, so here I am."

"Ah. I know the man. I met him a while ago on assignment here in Burlus. Quite the round fellow."

"I can't argue that," said Fernando with a chuckle. "But he's good-natured enough. Bought my vineyard for a tidy sum more than it was worth and often pays me decently to overview any areas he may be having troubles in."

"You travel the five kingdoms looking after barrels of wine?"

"Four kingdoms, actually. He has no vineyards in Ursjun. Says that the land isn't fertile enough to grow good grapes properly."

"I'll leave that bit of expertise to his judgment as it's out of my range," said Victor as he yawned and stretched out his arms. "Still, though, it's nice to have a friendly face on the trip home; what mysteries do you think awaits us back in the land of roses?"

"For me, it's my children running me crazy. For you, saving more refugees like myself, perhaps. Oh, speaking of which, it seems we're about to take off."

Victor watched as the men on the tower pulled back the large wooden bridge.

"Hey, what's that down there?" said Fernando pointing down to the ground below them, next to the platform.

Victor peered down over the edge and saw Dekol and Mova talking to the guard down below. "Oh no. This has to be a joke."

"What's wrong?" said Fernando, looking at Victor worriedly.

"I'm not sure, but I'm thinking that someone is trying to involve me in something bothersome again."

Victor watched as Dekol and Mova walked up the steps of the loading tower and saw the men once again lower the bridge onto the ship. Dekol and Mova walked across onto the deck and began looking around.

"Victor... Victor Krill, are you on this ship?" shouted Dekol.

"Oh, for the goddesses sake, Dekol, why? I was about to go home."

Dekol walked over to Victor, "Sorry sir, but the prince would like to have a word with you."

"He's doing this on purpose, isn't he? He knows this is the last ship out to Mari. Does he intend to have me walk home?"

"Oh, I promise, it'll be worth your time," said Mova.

"Sorry sir, but it's more serious than that."

Victor noticed how serious Dekol was acting and sighed, "All right, lead me to his royal highness. It's not like I actually wanted to go home or anything. Enjoy your trip,

Fernando. One of us should at least get that opportunity."

"Ahhh, you do the same," said Fernando with a puzzled look on his face.

Dekol and Mova escorted Victor down the tower, and they mounted onto horses heading back off to the castle.

"Don't suppose you two would like to tell me what all this is about?"

"Queen's Bane tried to kill prince Saffron on his wedding night, but she failed," said Mova. "We've been interrogating her since."

"What? Seriously? How did he... wait, you said she... Queen's Bane is a she?"

"Seems so."

"Okay, that was unexpected information. But why tell me this; what do you even need me for?"

"Don't know. Saffron asked for us to find you, if you were still in the city, and bring you to him."

"Goddess help me. I'm not hunting down whoever sent her. I'd rather just live in your castle than go on another one of your kingdom's annoying missions."

They soon arrived at the castle, with Dekol and Mova escorting Victor down multiple stairs into a dungeon far beneath the castle. The air was thick and stale as they led Victor through the brick catacombs. He could hear drips of water hitting the floor from somewhere unseen from what must have been a waterway nearby. Gone were the bright lights of the castle that illuminated every corner of the main building above. Here, there was only dim torchlight and a large amount of shadows in between.

"Well, this seems like a fun place; I can practically hear the screams bouncing off the walls."

"Every kingdom has a darker side to it," said Mova as she held the torch ahead of them, turning a corner into another dark corridor. "Or is your queen's dungeon filled with flowers and draped in linens."

"No, it's pretty much the same, a dark, depressing hole for people to die in. You ever wonder why all dungeons look the same? Surely they would have managed some type of innovation over these last generations." Victor rubbed his fingers along the wall, feeling the cold moisture of the bricks as he passed, "But no, just brick walls and dim lights. Is there a waterway near here? The coolness here seems chilly even for a dungeon."

"You've noticed it, huh. Yes, but not just the castle. The city itself has several waterways beneath it. I suspect that was one of the main reasons the castle was built here. When all the rest of the Queens have castles near the sea."

"Perhaps I should have been a builder. It seems like a much more rewarding profession to have people appreciating your work hundreds of years after you've passed."

"We're here," said Dekol as he opened a cell door for Victor to step inside.

Victor frowned but glanced inside to see the prince sitting in the darkness with a small torch behind him.

"Ahh, they managed to reach you before you left. Good, I so hoped we'd get another chance to conversate."

"Yes, well, I would never have imagined that this would be the place of our next conversation," said Victor walking into the room cautiously looking around into the darkness.

"Neither would have I. But there has been a development."

"I heard. It seems you've caught Queen's Bane, and it appears that she's a woman to boot. I'm sure the daughters and housewives of all the nobles will outlive the shock."

"It seems my guards have spoiled the surprise," said the prince, tossing up his hands and shaking his head. "Oh well, it's not like I forbade them from giving you the information." Saffron stood up from his seat and walked over to Victor, placing his hand on his shoulders. "But there is still one surprise that I hope they haven't spoiled."

Victor noticed that one of the Prince's arms was wrapped and there was a small trace of blood on it. His face had scars from what appeared to be someone's fingernails that had dug into his skin, and his hair was hanging somewhat loosely over his face.

"I was told you caught her right after the wedding. That was a few days ago. That should have been enough time for you to request a healer and repair the damage that's been done to you."

"Oh, you're right, but I've been a little busy with the interrogation. Such superficial matters aren't important when trying to uncover a plot of assassination."

"And I am to assume you want my help navigating this investigation?" asked Victor, narrowing his eyes at the prince.

"In a way, yes. But first, it's time for the big reveal," said Saffron as he let go of Victor's shoulders and turned toward the darkness ahead of them inside the dungeon cell.

Saffron's hands began to glow red as two balls of flames appeared over both his palms. He flicked his fingers and the balls of flame floated off to the back of the room, illuminating the dungeon's walls as they went, before finally landing on two large torches at the end of the room.

Is that just a special party trick all nobles use to show off to the mundanes?

It was in that light that Victor saw an ashen faced woman wearing a torn, bloody, and very muddy wedding dress. Her skin seemed burnt as it was chained and stretched across the dungeon's wall. Two chains across her ankles, two across her wrists, and one large chain around her neck. Her eyes were closed as she hung silently against the wall.

"Well... this is a surprise."

"Oh, and in what way is that, Victor," asked Saffron in an accusing tone.

Victor walked over to the woman, staring at her. "I think

this is the woman that attacked me on the ship on my way across the Avadose Sea. And you say that this is Queen's Bane?"

"Well, I find it hard to believe that there are two psychotic murder mages in this kingdom who have been trying to kill me."

"A fair point," said Victor as he continued to examine the woman and the damage done to her. "I assume you've already attempted to torture her from the burn marks and the bruises along the face and shoulders."

"Yes, and in our interrogation, your name came up quite a few times."

Victor paused, glancing at the woman. He then closed his eyes, taking a deep breath of the stale dungeon air, "And that would explain why you've asked me to come here."

"Indeed, it would. Do you have anything you'd wish to reveal?"

"Other than my distinct hatred of politics and how I keep finding myself in these situations? No, sadly, I do not. But you seem to have some ideas rolling around in that head of yours. So, go ahead and give me your understanding of all this," said Victor, the tone of his voice shifting to one of aggravation.

The prince walked back over and sat back down in his chair facing Victor.

"At first, I thought either you or that queen of yours had attempted to have me killed. But soon that idea fell apart. I mean, yes, killing the son of a king makes for a good story, but you had an opportunity or two to kill me yourself. Or try and have those mercenaries do it for you." Saffron reached over and grabbed a long white rectangular cube, flipping it over in his hand. "No, try as I might, no conclusion I came to made any sense." He then walked back over to Victor waving around the white cube. "Hold this for a moment will you?"

Victor took the cube, rubbing his hand over the surface

and placing it to his nose. "Humm, it's an alagon stone. Did you think I was a mage?" He handed the cube back out to Saffron.

"No, but one can't be too cautious, especially after the last few nights I've had," said Saffron as he walked over to the creature in chains. "You assumed that we burned this thing in our interrogation, and while you're not wrong on that." Saffron pointed to the ashen-skinned woman's arms. "You see the burn marks alongside the shackles on this creature? Well, these shackles are laced with alagon stone to keep mages from escaping. And it seems this particular magical creature has quite the adverse reaction to the stone." Saffron raised the stone to the creature's face and pressed it softly against its skin.

Victor watched as the woman's skin began to smoke and burn against the brick. It moaned and writhed in an attempt to distance itself from the cube, but was shackled too tightly.

"Wakey wakey my wonderful assassin, someone's come to visit you,"

The woman coughed and slowly opened her eyes, looking up to see Victor. She snarled and grit her teeth before spitting blood at him, landing on his chest.

"Oh, it doesn't seem to like you very much," said Saffron as he walked over getting close to the creature. "Now, now, behave yourself," Saffron lowered the cube and began rubbing it up her leg through the ripped part of the dress. "Be good, or I'll stick this cube where my cock should have gone on our wedding. I can't even fathom what the burning sensation would feel like in there."

The woman turned her hateful face at Saffron but was quiet.

"That's a good monster; showing that you can follow directions is the first step to proving that you can be trained. Perhaps I'll make a pet of you after all."

"If the stone burns her skin, why aren't the shackles

doing the same."

"Oh, you certainly are a masochist, Victor," said Saffron with a smile on his face. "You want to watch it burn?" He wagged the alagon cube at him. "But if we used pure alagon stones, I'm not even sure it'd survive the night. No, the shackles are a lesser grade of the stone. It seems to burn it a little, but not so much as to kill or keep it unconscious for too long. We've been able to extract a few details from it over the past few days, but it refuses to give up it's handler, which has been a bit of a pain. But in between the fun we've been having, your name slipped out of its mouth."

Victor sighed, "Of course it did."

"You said you encountered this creature over the Avadose Sea. Care to elaborate more on that or introduce us to some witnesses that may be still around? It's not that I don't trust you, but we must be thorough."

"The healer I introduced you to was also a passenger on the ship, he's the one that uncovered the mystery of her identity. Looking at her dress, I take it she was disguised as your wife? Well, while aboard the ship, she was impersonating a crewman that she most likely killed and threw overboard."

"Dekol, see if you can't find out if that healer is still in town anywhere. Is there anyone else?"

"The captain of the ship and his crew, but I doubt you'll reach them anytime soon."

"Okay, for now you're free of suspicion. But not allowed to leave the capital until we confirm your story."

"Oh, I don't plan on leaving this room. Not now, when the answer to a few of my questions is locked up against that wall in front of me."

"Really now," said Saffron with a laugh. "I didn't expect you to be a torturer. But still, I'm afraid I can't let you do too much harm. It has become quite the precious commodity to me over these past few days."

Victor stepped forward, inspecting the creature even

closer. She stayed silent, but Victor could see the rage dancing behind those emerald and ruby eyes. "No, while torture has its place, I simply wish to use this opportunity to perform a negotiation."

"With that creature? With what leverage will you use since acts of violence are not an option?"

"She's not brainless. She snuck into the ship I was on and more impressively imitated your wife so well that even up until the wedding, no one realized it was her. That shows she's capable of critical thinking; I just need to make it so that answering my question is in her best interest." Victor looked the creature in the eyes, "What is your name?"

She was silent.

"What day is it?" asked Victor in a soft voice.

She stared at him but didn't speak.

"I don't see why you insist on calling that thing a 'she,'" said Saffron. "It has a vagina, but so does a dog and at this point, I don't very much see the difference."

The ashen woman stared daggers at the prince. Victor could see the intent to murder written so blindly on her face that he half assumed Saffron would die just from the will of it.

"Judging by the claw marks on the side of your face and the blood on her nails, I imagine I can see your perspective. But let's try to be civil as long as the moment will allow us."

Victor turned around, walking back and grabbing the chair Saffron was sitting in, before coming back to the creature, placing it before her, and taking a seat. "I'm willing to stay here with you as long as it takes for you to answer. Days. Months. Even a year if need be. Granted, I might have to ask to have a bed brought down. I don't think that the dungeon floor is good for my back."

"Surely you can't be serious," said Saffron.

"Take a seat, your highness. This could take a while."

"You're in my seat," spoke Saffron with disgust in his voice.

Victor looked down. "So it seems I am." He then looked back up to the creature with a smile on his face. "Now tell me, what's your name?" He waited a moment. "What day is it?"

For another few hours, the questioning went on with Victor asking the creature for her name and what day it was every few minutes.

"Wha... what's... your name? Oh, it seems my voice is getting dry. Can I ask for a bucket of water and a sipping spoon?"

Mova looked at Saffron, who was sitting in another chair that was brought to him. Giving his consent, Mova went off to get the water.

"You've been at this for hours. I had thought to humor you at first, but this has become quite tedious."

"Such is the way of things. You yourself said you had been at this for days. Surely you can afford me a few more hours today."

"What do you mean to accomplish by doing this? She's most likely compelled not to speak of these things?"

"Spells have rules. I merely wish to understand the rules of the one she's under. And to do that, I need her to speak. And for her to speak, I need her to understand I am not the type of man to hold hot irons against her skin."

Victor heard the sounds of footsteps before the door to the cell opened as Mova entered back into the room, splashing water on the floor from a bucket with a sipping pale. Wet footsteps splashed in the bucket's fallen water as Mova set the pale beside Victor.

"Thank you, Mova, just leave them beside me," said Victor as he dipped the spoon into the water and took a sip of the cold water, allowing some to drip from the side of his mouth and drop to his chest.

While holding the spoon to his lips, he watched as the creature stared at the bucket of water. Her mouth opened as she swallowed unconsciously. *There we go, just focus on the water.* Victor dumped the spoon back in the water. "That's better, now what is your name?" Her eyes narrowed at him. But they would slowly keep gazing back at the water from time to time every few minutes.

"Would you like some? You keep looking at the water. Would you like a drink?"

The creature turned its head away from the water, looking down at the floor.

"Well, I didn't hear a no, so I guess that's a yes."

Victor stood from his seat, dumping the spoon back into the water. Then walking with it over to the creature, he lifted the water up and away from her mouth. He held it just far enough where she would have to struggle against her chains to reach it. Despite her misgivings, the chains around her neck began to jingle as she slowly pulled her neck forward.

"There we go," said Victor, placing his hands under her chin and lifting her head. "Take your time; we can't have you choking."

He waited until her need overpowered her reason, her mouth opening just enough for her trembling outstretched tongue to slide between her cracked lips. Only then did he begin to slowly pour the water onto her lips and into her mouth, taking his time, allowing trickles of the cold liquid to flow over her skin. She swallowed twice before the water was gone.

"There we go," said Victor before he went back to his seat and watched the woman in silence. For another hour, he didn't speak a word. "Now, what is your name?"

Another two hours passed, and Victor continued to sit in silence. Saffron had fallen asleep in his chair, and Mova was nodding off against the wall. Only Victor and the creature were there to stare into each other's eyes.

"Once again, what day is it?"

More silence followed, but the creature's eyes glanced down at the bucket of water and then back to Victor.

"If you want water, you're going to have to ask for it. I'd at least think I've earned that much courtesy at this point. If you won't give me your name, I understand. But to not ask for water, now that's just being stubborn for stubborn sakes, isn't it?"

Another hour passed before Victor saw the creature's cracked lips begin to move.

"Wa... wa... ter... please."

Victor dumped the spoon into the water without saying a word and once again brought it upwards, making the creature struggle against her binding, sticking out her tongue again before he would release the small amount of water onto her lips.

And once again, he went back, sitting down and quietly refocusing his attention on her. After a few minutes as the torches flickered, he heard from her lips.

"Silk."

Victor never let his gaze leave her eyes. "Hello, Miss Silk. I'm glad to make your acquaintance."

Hours later, Saffron awoke to the sounds of roosters somewhere outside of the castle. He almost fell out of his chair, but Dekol placed his hands on his shoulder to stabilize him.

"Thank you, Dekol. Wait, when did you get here?"

"Sometime last night, I figured I'd let you rest. You seemed to need it."

"Good morning, Saffron," said Victor, who was still sitting in his chair, staring up at the ashen-skinned woman.

"Victor? What are you? Oh yes, right... The creature. Did you sit here all night and just stare at that beast you call a woman?"

"On the contrary, we had a wonderful night, discussing our hopes and dreams. She made me realize that I had this

182

inner desire to be a farmer out in the countryside. Me and my two children and a dog named Nunally."

Saffron shook his head, narrowing his eyes, "You got the creature to speak? How?"

"Don't worry; I'm sure your father will reveal it to you soon enough. But now we can move on to the fun part."

"And what part would that be?" asked Saffron, shaking his head, trying to shake off the sleepiness. "Wait, has Father been here?"

"Yes and no, but I'm referring to the part where you release this woman into my custody and care."

Saffron shook his head again and began whipping his eyes, "I'm sorry, I must still be dreaming. Have you lost your mind?"

"Unfortunately, no. But a rattled mind would make me feel better about what I'm about to do," said Victor as he turned around to face Saffron. "Your highness, it seems that I owe this woman behind me my life. Supposedly, she saved me aboard that ship. So in order for you to grant her parole, I am willing to pay a price for her."

Saffron looked back and forth in confusion, "This is ridiculous; how do I know this isn't some elaborate plan to get her back and try to kill me again?"

"It's not," said Mova. "The healer verified the story and said he would be arriving sometime today to converse with you personally."

"And you didn't drag him here?" asked Saffron, who was growing visibly annoyed. "He could be long gone from the kingdom by now."

"He is a healer, Saffron; we do not have authority to compel them to do anything. The same goes for Victor as well."

Saffron looked around the room and started laughing, "This is all ridiculous, but fine I'll play along. Okay, Ambassador, you say she speaks; let's hear her speak."

Victor turned her head around, looking at Silk, "If you

would be so kind."

The ashen woman stared at the men, "My name... is Silk."

Saffron twisted his lips as the creature spoke, "And what assurances do I have that she will not try to assassinate me again?"

"I assume you have a mind mage in this kingdom somewhere. Use a word bonding spell."

"That only works if the creature willingly accepts the bonding as truth."

"And I assure you that she will. So, if that's all you're worried about, why don't we start the real negotiations?"

"And what of my lady wife? I can't just let that creature walk out--"

"Lady alive... hidden," said Silk in a meek voice.

Saffron stared at the creature and then at Victor for a few moments, "You really are quite serious about this, aren't you?"

"Unfortunately, it would appear so. Trust me, your highness; I am as flabbergasted in my decision as you are."

"Fine, if you wish to play the noble role of this thing's savior. Then so be it. First, you will submit yourself to the Sakari bonding ritual. But not to me, you will submit yourself under the control of the creature you're trying to save."

"And?"

"You will commit yourself to five years of service in our kingdom's military. Where in which you will publicly and officially resign from your post with the kingdom of Mari."

"Is there anything else?"

Saffron stood from his chair and pointed his finger at Victor, looking down at him "And most importantly, you will stay away from Frenka. I've seen how she looks at you. I will have you stationed in the northeastern most part of the kingdom to ensure she never sees you again."

Victor closed his eyes and took a deep breath. "Okay,

and here's my counter-offer."

"Counter offer? There is no counter offer. If you want that thing, then you will accept the terms given to you."

Victor raised his hand, waiting for Saffron to quiet himself, "I did say that this was a negotiation, did I not?" He folded his arms in front of him. "I will participate in the bonding ritual because I feel I should take some risk in asking you for this. But I will not join your military; I will not disown my kingdom, and I will not forbid myself from being around Miss Frenka.

Victor placed his hands on his knees. "Instead, if you do not give me what I want, I will instead claim Miss Frenka as my own and take her back to Mari with me. For, as you have so generously pointed out, she does seem ever so fond of me. And I do believe that the agreement was for her to train here until she was sent back to her husband. So, if I, in fact, were to become said husband, then she would have every right to leave with me."

"Dekol, draw your blade. It seems our guest won't be leaving this room."

Victor stood from his seat, staring daggers back at Saffron, "Do it, I dare you. Your little kingdom would be wiped out in less than a year. Your father claimed I was the Queen's little miracle boy. And you just allowed a boatload of people to leave Burlus; all headed back to Mari. All of whom whose last visage was of the little golden boy being taken off by your men. I can promise you that if I were to disappear here, you'd be under siege in less than a month."

Victor stepped forward and stood face to face with Saffron. "Tell me, your highness, which of the other four queens won't jump at the chance to wipe out the last remaining king in the five kingdoms, especially considering the history of how your ancestors attained these lands. Unless you think one of them will join you? And despite their misgivings, what Queen wants to see King Nevander wipe out another Queen?"

Saffron's eyes twitched as he gritted his teeth, and suddenly the sound of clapping echoed throughout the dungeon cell. To the left of them, the corner of the wall began to shift, transforming the image of the shadowy brick wall into a running river of black and brown colors sinking to the floor to be replaced by King Nevander.

"Well done, well done. I haven't seen my son so thoroughly destroyed since the day Frenka pounded him into the dirt. And it was at the hands of a mundane no less. Ah, now this is a lesson I'm sure the boy will remember well," said King Nevander, looking over at Victor. "Tell me, did Oscar teach you that?"

Victor turned to King Nevander, "I was wondering when you would show yourself. And you may be right, I've seen him blackmail at least two people into submission in just the last month."

"I'm sure you have, and when did you realize I was here?"

"When Mova came back in with the water, there was the sound of another set of footsteps right after she dropped the bucket before me."

"Perceptive bastard, aren't you? But I accept the terms of your negotiation with two extra caveats."

"Which are?"

"If you find any plots that involve my kingdom, you will inform me as soon as you can."

"And the other?"

"You and this creature are to investigate the matter of those jewels you informed me of. And ascertain what purpose they are made for."

Victor narrowed his eyes at the king.

"You want this, emissary? Well, there is the price. I'm handing you a legendary assassin. I'd imagine that what I ask for in return is a fair trade."

Victor turned back to look at the ashen woman, before turning back to the king, "I accept the terms of the negotiation."

"But Father, you can't just—"

"Quiet boy, you've lost. You probably lost the moment you invited him down here. Let this be a lesson to you that magic isn't the only weapon worth using. I'd have figured you'd have learned that after having your ass handed to you in the streets that night."

"You knew?" asked Saffron, with a look of confusion on his face.

"Of course, I did," said the king waving his hand dismissively at his son. "What father doesn't keep watch over his idiot son?"

"He did stand by all night and watch you sleep after all," said Victor. "I imagine if I had tried anything against you, I would have found myself severely damaged."

"Speaking of which, your interrogation was quite masterful. Answer me honestly. How many have you performed? A man like you doesn't not keep count."

"Counting tonight, four-hundred and seventy-eight."

The room was quiet for a moment as they all just stared at Victor.

"And here I lose a torturer every few years because their stomach isn't enough for it. But yet and still, so many of the common people call us monsters when people like you are walking around," said the king as he began to leave the room. "Well, either way, a deal has been struck. Get the creature to tell you where my son's bride is. After that, then we'll continue with the rest. Dekol, you and Saffron will be in charge of retrieving Lady Dunblane. Gather as many men as you think necessary. A husband's job is to protect and save his wife. Perhaps you can still manage the second act."

Saffron's lip twitched with a snarl at the comment.

"Yes, Sir," said Dekol.

"Mova, go and retrieve Eunwalt, tell him we require the use of his magic."

"Yes, Sir,"

King Nevander turned back to Victor, "It's nice to have you under my employ again, emissary."

They all gathered in the tower, in the king's study. The furniture had been placed against the wall, leaving a large open area in the center of the room. Victor stood against a wall with his hands folded over his chest.

I must be the dumbest man in all the kingdoms. I was so close to freedom and now look at me, about to chain myself to another complicated mission. And for what? Because I just couldn't let it go.

The door opened and, escorted into the room by Dekol and Mova was the ashen skinned woman, still in her magical chains. They brought her forward, forcing her to her knees before the King.

"Well, creature, it seems your caretaker and I have arrived at a solution for your freedom. But the trick to mental magic binding is you have to accept it willingly. So, what say you?"

Silk scowled at the king, "I… accept."

"Well then, we will start when you're ready, Emissary."

Victor took a deep breath and walked over, dropping to his knees alongside Silk. "Let's get this over with."

Eunwalt walked over and stood in front of the two, "This will only take a moment. It's a fairly simple process, you see. I will ask you a question, and you will agree with it inside your mind. After which, you will be compelled to do it. It's strong, just enough to always haunt your dreams unless you are on the path to completing your compulsion." Eunwalt looked over at another mage in the room that Victor had never seen before. "The bonding ritual on the other hand, that will be more taxing, I'm afraid."

Eunwalt looked over at the creature, "If you would remove the shackles please, they would interfere with the linking process."

Dekol walked over and began unshackling the metal binding around the creature's ashen skin. Then, with an audible clicking noise, the fixtures fell to the ground one after the other with a heavy thud. Her skin was charred black where the bindings had been and provided a stark contrast against its milky white skin.

"Let's get started, shall we?" asked Eunwalt, as he began waving his hand over the creature as the space around her began to glow in blue light. Eunwalt's fingers also glowed blue as he placed them on the temple of Silk's head. "*Fenom extromite.*" And with those words spoken, Silk's eyes matched the blue coloring of the magic. "Now, do you agree never to assault any member of the royal house again?"

"I... I... will not harm... members of royal family of Burlus."

"And do you agree to help Victor on the mission that the king has given him?"

"I.... agree.... to help Victor."

Victor watched as she barely formed the words. Her mouth gaped open as her head spasmed against the magic.

Eunwalt pulled his hand away from Silk's head, and her eyes slowly began to lose their light, turning back to the greenish-red they were before. Silk then dropped her head and began coughing.

"I guess it would be hard on those that were already weak, to begin with," said Eunwalt, turning to Victor. "No worries though, you're in a much better state than that thing. I imagine you'll fare better."

"Thank you for the vote of confidence," said Victor.

Once again Eunwalt's fingers began to glow, and a blue light began to surround Victor. Eunwalt placed his hands on Victor's temple. "Do you agree—"

"Stop," said King Nevander, and the light on Eunwalt's fingers and surrounding Victor vanished as everyone in the room turned to look at the king.

"Your highness? Do you not wish to continue?"

"No, it was enough to see him willing to go through with it. Instead, start the bonding ritual."

"But Father, what guarantee do we have that he will actually investigate the crystals? He could just as well take the creature back with him to Mari."

The king shook his head at his son, "This is why you aren't ready to be king. Being king means using every piece you have to the best of its ability. This untalented man became a general of Mari. How do you suppose he accomplished such a feat?"

"I don't know; what does that have to do with anything?"

King Nevander placed a finger to his temple, "It's his mind, boy. Putting a shackle on his mind and sending him off is like hunting with a prized hound and cutting off one of its legs. No warrior will intentionally dull his own weapon."

"Then what assurances do we have that he will start his orders given to him?"

"Idiot boy, we never had any to begin with. While the bonding process is permanent to our knowledge, tell me, Emissary. How many mages does Mari have nearby that are strong enough to break mental links?"

Victor smirked, "There are three I can rely on in neighboring cities if need be."

"Of course, there are," said the king with a chuckle. "So, tell me then, what will you do since you won't be compelled?"

"I'll follow the rules of the agreement and investigate the jewels. But I'm not going to sacrifice my life trying to find out this information."

"I never assumed you would, but your word is good enough."

"Okay then," said Saffron, "I know I suggested bonding him to her originally, but since we don't have a mental link, then why not bond him to one of us instead of that... she-creature?"

The king twisted his face in disgust at Saffron, "Did

you not listen to a word he said when you were down in the dungeon? We link him to us, and his Queen is at our doorstep trying to kill one of us to free him from the spell. But if he's linked to that creature, then the story changes. He wants to protect it, so he can't let it be killed. But the only way to break the bonding is through death. Are you able to comprehend any of this? That bitch Clarissa might spend the rest of her life trying to undo what we've done. And nothing she can do to us will matter in the slightest in resolving it. Either he lets his new little pet die, or Clarissa watches as her little miracle boy slaves under this thing for the rest of his life."

The prince was silent as he clenched his fist in disgust, looking down at Victor.

"Pensola, start the ritual," said the King.

"Yes, your highness," said the blonde-haired mage in black robes as he began walking around Victor and Silk. "The Sakari do have their uses. Their version of the bonding technique is actually quite impressive. The control it maintains over the conscripted has less damaging effects than other methods of this magic." He took black sand from out of a pouch as he walked around them, spilling it on the floor. "*Un-kal Gresha,*" said Pensola after completing a rotation around them and snapping his fingers, and the black sand burst into flames around the two as black tendrils of magic crept towards them.

The moment the tendrils touched Victor's body, he shook in convulsion as his eyes bulged and his teeth gnawed against each other. Soon grey veins appeared on his hands and neck, slowly crawling up his jaw, then to his cheek and entered his eyes, turning his pupils back as night, right before he let out a horrendous scream.

Suddenly everything went black, and a second later, Victor found himself standing in complete darkness. He tried to gaze around, but there was nothing but blackness. He couldn't even see his own fingers when he tried to raise them in front of his face.

Well, never figured I'd have to live through that again. I wonder how long it'll be before I wake up. Goddess, how do I always find myself in these situations? Is it really so much to just ask to retire to a quiet life?"

Slowly a white light began to appear above him. It was dim at first, but it grew till it reached around half the size of Victor. It then swooped down and began circling him.

And it seems we meet again, whatever you are. Are you planning to drag me out of this again? If so, then I'd...

Suddenly the space Victor was in began to glow completely white as the darkness was pushed away. Victor turned around to witness a ball of light so massive that it dwarfed him and the other smaller ball of light.

"Okay, well, this part is new," said Victor as he squinted, trying to shield his eyes from the massive ball of light as it came closer. But it was too bright, and within a moment, he and the other smaller ball of light were wholly consumed within the massive sphere of radiance.

Victor awoke on the floor, unable to move as his blurry eyes began to focus on the white mass in front of him. Soon, while lying there, he would see the ashen woman also crumpled up on the floor, looking back at him with her emerald and ruby eyes.

"It is complete, your highness, although this one seems to have gone a bit rougher than expected. Perhaps because of the creature's origins, I'm not too sure."

"But you are sure that it succeeded?"

"Yes, your grace, the bonding is secure. I was able to feel it."

"Then that's all that matters. How long before they are not sprawled out on my floor?"

"I'm not sure. As I said, it was rougher than usual. That one is a none mage and the creature's health was severely diminished. Perhaps in an hour or so they will be able to move. A few hours after, they should be able to walk."

"When he is able, I want him and that thing out of my kingdom as soon as possible. They no longer serve a purpose and having them here now is just a nuisance."

Mova opened the door to the room breathing heavily, "Sir, I'm sorry I have bad news."

'What is it now?"

"Queen's Bane has killed Sir. Hornsteen."

Everyone in the room just stared at her as a sound of coughing was heard amongst them. The prince looked down to Victor, who seemed to be convulsing on the floor. Then rage filled his eyes as he realized that Victor was laughing.

"So, it seems this was not Queen's Bane," said the king. "I think it's time we take this threat a little more seriously." The king stepped forward. "Grab those two and drag them downstairs. I want them gone as soon as they are able. Prepare a carriage to dump the creature in; I don't want anyone spotting that thing leaving the castle. We already have enough problems without rumors of abominations being created here."

Three hours later Victor found himself upright in a carriage with the reins in his hands. Dekol sat beside him with a small item wrapped in cloth in his lap.

"Are you my only escort out of the city?" asked Victor.

"I don't think anyone else has the stomach to look at you two anymore, it seems."

"What about you? Have I burned that bridge too?"

"There was no bridge to burn. We both are soldiers doing our job."

"A question for you then. If Saffron would have given the order to cut me down back in that dungeon, would you have done it?"

"Yes."

"A quick answer, but then, I guess I should just be

thankful the king intervened when he did. I really don't think I could have beaten you in a fight."

"Probably not. Your movements are too slow, and your footwork is sloppy. You're resourceful, but you came down to the dungeon unprepared; you didn't have your belt equipped."

"You paid attention to all of that, did you?"

Dekol shrugged. "Where are you headed now?"

"Back around Nyril, I guess. That's where the trail starts off, and I wasn't there long enough for anyone to remember my face."

"You're probably right. We received reports that a gang of Sakari raided the town and killed every guard in the city, making off with some women and men."

Victor nodded.

"You knew?"

"I had a guess, but wasn't sure until you just confirmed it."

They both looked ahead and saw Frenka standing by the gate to the city.

"Ahh shit. You won't be telling the prince of this, will you?"

"Why? Do you think it's possible for him to hate you more?"

Victor laughed despite himself, "You know, I do believe that's the first time you've told a joke around me. Maybe you are more than just a murder machine."

"Maybe, just a little more," said Dekol as he jumped off the carriage as it stopped at the gate. "I'll leave you two alone. See you back in town, Frenka." Leaving the wrapped item on the seat, he walked back through the city's gates.

"I not see you after wedding night?"

"Yeah, well, a lot has happened. I was actually in your castle for a few days. Did you know that?"

"Stupid prince had guards refuse me from castle."

Victor sighed, "Of course he did. That explains that part,

then." Victor looked at the dark-haired woman as she gazed back up at him with a genuine smile. "Why do you look at me like that?"

"Like what?"

"Like... that, like you feel sorry for me, but care about me."

"Because I do."

"But why?"

"Because I choose to."

Victor threw his face into his hands, "Goddess, you make no sense. People trying to kill me and manipulate me, I understand. But you are just—"

"I'm Frenka."

"Yes..." Victor sighed again. "Yes, you are. Frenka, do me a favor."

"What is favor?"

"Slap me."

Frenka frowned for a second, then slapped Victor across the face.

"Ow. You didn't even ask why," said Victor as his jaw reddened.

"No, I do first, but now I ask why."

Victor stretched his jaw, shaking his head, "I kinda used your affection towards me as leverage to threaten that prince of yours."

Frenka stared at Victor for a few seconds, "And why you do that?"

"To save her life," said Victor gesturing into the back of the wagon where Silk laid on top of the hay with a blanket covering her body.

"She has pretty white hair; you save old lady?"

"Not so much. It's a long story."

"This person you save, she good or bad person?"

"I don't know yet. Good, I hope, or at least good enough."

"Then if she good person, you did good thing and if she bad person, you make her good person."

Victor laughed, "I don't think it works that way."

"It will, because Victor do right by Frenka."

"And how does Frenka know that?"

"Because Victor told Frenka what he did, bad man would not have told."

"I... I... have no response to that."

"Men are stupid," said Frenka as she stepped up into the wagon, sitting on Victor's lap and began kissing him. After a moment, she pulled her mouth away from his. "You should do what feels good."

After a long pause, Victor responded, "I really am stupid, aren't I?" He gazed back into the eyes of the mountain woman.

"Yes, very stupid. But Frenka accepts you."

"When I return, we will continue our discussion on that forming of a clan thing. Perhaps the best thing for me is to be the man of a fiery mountain woman."

"There, you see. Now you do what feels right. When you come back, we make Frenka a clan."

"Goddess, help me."

"Victor's goddess sits on his lap."

"Ha! Okay, off with you."

Frenka hopped down back to the ground and turned away, walking back into the city, "Come back to Frenka when done saving old lady. And no king first. Now, Frenka comes first."

"Yes, Dear," said Victor, shaking his head with a smirk on his face. *Do what feels right, huh? Why not? A murderous assassin with me, a jealous, vengeful prince behind me, and a mountain woman who wants me to join her clan beside me. This certainly is a far cry from that simple village life I dreamed of.*

Victor leaned over the side of the wagon, watching Frenka walk away.

"You... didn't... say, I love you," came the cracked and hoarse voice of Silk behind him.

"Oh, you shut up, back there," said Victor as he snapped

the reins, making the two horses pull the wagon away from the city gates. "Might as well see how far we can make it with the little light we have left."

Leaving the city of Burlus behind him, the carriage squeaked down the dirt road.

They made it quite a few miles before the sun set and the chill of the night came over their wagon. Victor pulled over to the side of the road to let the horses rest for the remainder of the night. He took off his coat and placed it over his chest, trying to shelter himself from the chilled night air while he gazed off into the darkness. *I don't think anyone would have any real reason to follow me this time. Well, except for that prince. I seem to have made a powerful enemy in exchange for the assassin. This will surely continue to bite me in the ass till I die. Go on Victor, why not royally piss off a future king? That can't possibly be a bad idea.*

Victor heard the sound of Silk shuffling around on the hay in the wagon. Then soon was followed by the sound of her coughing.

"Hey, you alright back there? You can't die on me. Not after the price I just paid for you."

"Co... cold," she managed to speak before another round of coughing fits.

"Of course, you are," said Victor, peering into the darkness around them one last time, before turning around and climbing into the wagon with Silk. He laid down beside her, wrapping his arms around Silk before covering the thin cloth over them.

"It'll get warm soon enough. Just try to rest for the night." *The things I get myself into.*

CHAPTER 12

Isha woke from her bed to sounds of tumbling coming from downstairs. Blinking, she tried to adjust her eyes to the shining sun that came through the window. Rolling out the bed, she placed her feet on the cool floor and began looking around for her sisters, but they were nowhere to be found.

I guess there downstairs. She thought as she made her way towards the door. *It's been a week now. I wonder what Dessi, and Jacob are doing. How long will it be before I see them again.* She stepped out into the hallway and made her way towards the steps, the wooden floor creaking beneath her weight.

After taking the first set of steps down, she was surprised to see Jacinta and Makeba in their new school attire, pinning Leo to the ground with his hands behind his back.

"Damn, you Sakari warriors," said Leo, wiggling under the girls as they sat atop him. "One day, I'll beat you and claim you both as my warrior wives."

"You never beat us," You too weak," said Jacinta.

"Hey, I'll have you know that healing magic is the most powerful magic in the world. You just break people, but I save them," Leo replied with a proud grin.

"Oh, sister Isha awake," said Makeba as the girls bounced off Leo, causing him to make an audible "Oof" sound.

"You two look ready for class already," said Isha, looking the girls over.

The school's outfits were a darkish blue half top with a hood that cut off at the waist. Beneath was a light blue fitted dress with a white front that split at the sides. Beneath the dress was a dark blue skirt to match the top that came down to their knees. Both girls had a heart pendant on one side and the winged pendant that Miss Huffles had given them earlier, pinned to the other side.

Elena walked from around the corner with a tray of sweetmeats. "They've been wrestling down here for an hour, while you were knocked out. They really don't seem to tire," she said, lowering the tray for the Sakari girls who hurriedly began munching on the treats. "I really don't see how you keep up with them, Leo."

"That's the power of healing; you will be learning muscle retention this year. As long as we can draw in magic, then we should be able to run for hours and never get tired."

Isha pulled at her nightclothes. "Do I have an outfit?"

"Oh, yes, they brought them over this morning. I have yours here," said Elena, plucking a set of robes from the couch. "Come on; I'll help you change." She walked into the back with Isha following behind her.

"So, are you excited about being a healer?" asked Elena as they entered the backroom.

"I don't know," said Isha, slipping off her night attire and bringing the light blue robe up over her head. "I don't know what I'm supposed to do." Her head popped out of the top as she tried to straighten it around her waist.

"Whatever you decide, for the most part, I'd guess. A lot of healers take up residence in small towns or a few who become wanderers that travel the land healing others."

"What will you do?"

"Me?" asked Elena, fiddling with the attire. "I'll probably stay here as a teacher with Leo. Someone's gotta keep him out of trouble."

"What about the girl from before?"

"Who, Darla? Your guess is as good as mine. She actually left this morning, but never told us what she had planned. Leo and her bickered a bit, and then she took off, saying that she'd see us down below one day."

"Oh, they didn't seem to like each other very much," said Isha as she slipped on her skirt.

"Don't let them fool you; they get along well enough. They just bicker a lot is all. Darla knows Leo's a good guy. She just has a hard time showing it. He's the one who trained us, after all. They used to stay up all night bickering with each other over healing techniques." Elena grabbed Isha's night clothes. "There ya go, all done. Now you look like a proper student."

The two came back into the living area to see Leo lying down on the floor, with Jacinta sitting ahead of him, trying to braid his hair.

"Now, what are you doing?" asked Elena with a smile.

"Shush, we're bonding. I'm having them teach me their Sakari ways."

"Goddess, you're an idiot."

A knock came at the door as Leo stood up from the floor. "Alright, hold on." Walking over, he opened the door to see a blonde-haired man with a patch above one of his eyes. Under one of his arms, he held a crystal-looking block.

"Ah, hello, Mr. Leo. Are those Sakari girls here? I was told that they were placed in this dorm."

"Hey Caudbell, what brings you and Tannor here so early?" asked Leo as he stepped aside, allowing them in.

"Hello, Miss Elena. Ah well, after past events, I decided to put more effort into our testing spheres. They were outdated, after all. And I made this," said Caudbell as he extended out the marble-looking block for them to see. It glowed different colors as a liquid swooshed about inside. "It's a new testing device for recruiting,"

"And I'm here to watch it break," said Tannor. "Apparently, I missed the fun of orientation, so I tagged along as well. Now which of the two Sakari girls broke the old one? I'm wondering if she would humor us with another try."

"Oh, that me. I break big glass ball," said Makeba excitedly with a smile as she strolled over, looking at the swirling colors inside the block.

"Okay would you two mind?" asked Caudbell, looking between Elena and Leo.

"Oh, no. Go ahead, Caudbell," assured Elena as she walked over, clearing the table for him.

"Thank you so much," said Caudbell as he walked over, placing the unit down. "Okay, so in order not to be pelted by shards like yesterday. I infused the container with a spell so that if its structure fails, that it will crack in on itself, rather than having a repeat of yesterday."

"I can heal that for you Caudbell," said Elena pointing to the patch above his eye.

"Oh, no, I'm still doing testing on the cut to test the days it takes for a full heal after getting nicked by a Hilgard Orb."

"Ah, okay. I guess."

"Don't mind him," said Tannor, shaking his head. "Caudbell's always been a stickler for his experiments. Even the ones he does on himself."

"Why our first test thingy no break when we come to school?" asked Jacinta. "They not the same?"

"Well, they are, but the rod then was a much lower grade and test variant. It has a limit as to how much magic can be put inside, the rest just is negated. The Hilgard orb and this here is to test the limits of someone's compatibility with magic. So there's no limiter placed on it."

"I don't understand."

"You will one day," said Caudbell, turning to Makeba. "Go ahead, child, we're all waiting on you. Just put your magic inside of it, the same as yesterday."

"Okay, I try now."

They all walked up and watched as Makeba placed her hand on the flat, colorful block. Her hand started to glow and instantly, the colors inside shifted, then swirled around. The block changed from red to brown to green and to a bright yellow.

"Well, I didn't expect this," said Caudbell. "I wonder—"

Suddenly the block cracked and shattered in on itself, the colorful liquid spilling across the table, down to the floor as they all jumped back.

"Oh, it broke again," said Makeba.

"So, it seems," said Mr. Caudbell with pursed lips as he rubbed his chin.

"Seems like you're going to have to start over again, Mr. Caudbell," chuckled Tannor, shaking his head.

"But that was the strongest one that I could make. I'm not sure what my next action will be." Mr. Caudbell crossed his arms. "Well, I guess I should help clean this mess up."

"Oh, don't worry about that," said Elena, "You have to teach soon, so Leo and I will clean up here."

"Oh, I couldn't ask you to clean up my mistakes."

"When do classes start?" asked Isha, still fidgeting with her clothes.

Leo picked up a shard from the broken device and held it up to his face, examining it, "For Elena, in a little over an hour. But for you new students? In about twenty minutes."

Isha's eyes shot open, "What? Why didn't you wake me up?"

"Ahh, but you looked so cute sleeping," said Leo.

Isha ran towards the door with Jacinta and Makeba following behind her.

"Hold up there, you young ladies," said Leo in an authoritative tone, causing the girls to stop at the door. He then walked over to the wall, grabbing three golden sashes with heart imprints at the bottom. "Wrap these around your waist; it has our house sigil on it." Leo tossed the sashes to the girls only to watch them put them on in completely offsetting positions. He sighed then looked over to Elena, handing her one of the sashes. "Come on, momma bear; you handle Isha, I'd rather not cause another panic attack. I'll handle the two Sakari."

After the girls had the sashes properly tied around their waist to hang in front, they ran out of the door, joining into the morning crowd of students that were on their way to class.

"I love you, Isha honey. Enjoy your first day of school," yelled Leo, waving at her from the door.

Isha turned back, frowning at him before throwing her hood up over her head and walking forward with the crowd.

"Why do you embarrass her like that?" asked Elena.

"You saw how she first freaked out when I tried to touch her leg. I'm just trying to get her accustomed to me."

"Are you sure embarrassing her is the way to do that?"

"It worked on you, didn't it, momma bear? You still got any of those sweet meats left?" asked Leo, walking back inside their home.

Isha, Makeba, and Jacinta followed the crowd and were eventually given directions to their first class. They walked inside and took their seats amongst the other students and faced a beautiful woman standing in front of the class. She had long brown hair with a blue flower pendant attached as she stood watching the students walk in. Unlike Miss. Prenna or Soulden, she wasn't wearing a robe. Instead, she wore slacks and a dress shirt with a few bottoms at the top left open, exposing a decent amount of cleavage.

"Okay, calm down, calm down," said the woman, "I know you're all excited to be learning magic, so let's get class started. Now, for those of you who don't know, you all will have three classes throughout your first year here. The first is myself. My name is Miss Gallows, and I am here to teach you the basic principles and understanding of magic. That would be your spells, chants, hymns, and such. Second, will be Mr. Higgins' down the hall. He will teach you basic strengthening, shields, and fortitude spells. I'm sure the few boys we have here will love that, hmm? And finally, you will be taught by Miss. Webblebottom at the end of the hall, where you will learn magical theory. Altogether, that means we will teach you basic magic structure, proper use of magic, and the principles of creating your own magic."

Mrs. Gallows clapped her hands, "Okay, so in this class we have six, people who favor water magic, four that favor fire magic, three that favor nature magic, one healer, and whatever that Sakari girl who broke the crystal is." She said, looking upward with a brow raised at the girls. "Okay, which one of the two of you is the one that shattered the orb?" The class all turned to stare at Jacinta and Makeba.

"I did. Orb fell into many pieces," said Makeba.

"It wasn't her fault, though," said Freedo. "She... she didn't mean to do it."

The girls glanced over at Freedo, and he glanced back at them, but then shyly turned away.

"I'm sure she didn't," said Miss Gallows. "But understand that just because your magical core favors a specific type of magic, that does not mean you must specialize in it. Here, we will teach you to control and expand your powers further than you could have ever imagined." She then walked around behind her desk and pulled out a large bowl filled with little pointing sticks. "So, who here's ready to get started?"

The children all came down, and each picked out a pointed stick.

"Now, throughout your whole first year, you're going to be using your wands as conduits to channel your magic point."

"But most of us here can already do magic," said Serpene, tapping the wand against her finger. "Why do we need wands?"

"Oh, so you're already accustomed to handling magic?" Miss Gallows asked, "Then, you see one of those chairs up there? Who here knows the spell to pull it to them?"

"I do," announced Marlene. "My mother already taught me that one."

"Okay then, pull that chair down here as hard as you can. I'll stop it from endangering anyone."

Marlene walked in front of the rest of the class and reached out her hand in the chair's direction. "Pull," she shouted as the chair shook and slid forward across the floor, coming towards them. It reached the edge of the steps and tumbled down, stopping at the bottom in front of the class.

"Good, that was a solid try," said Miss Gallows as she grabbed the chair, dragging it back up the flights of steps, placing it back in its original spot before making her way back down.

"Okay, now once again, except this time, focus your magic through the wand."

Marlene raised the wand, once again pointing it at the chair, and took a breath, "Pull." The chair and the chair beside it launched at the class at incredible speed, causing them all to scream as they raised their arms, trying to protect themselves. After a few seconds when the screams had quieted down. Isha drooped her arms and opened her eyes to see the two chairs floating in the air, harmlessly just spinning around in a slow rotation.

"And that is what having a wand can do for you," said Miss Gallows as she poked the floating chair with her finger, sending it harmlessly floating backward. "There are many mages that stick with wands their entire lives as their magical weapon of choice. Purely because they are easy to carry and as you have seen, are quite effective."

Will you teach all of us that magic?"

"Of course, let's start now. It's a simple spell really. Since mundane objects do not have magic, what we are doing is extending our own magic into the mundane objects like an anchor for us to grab on to." She reached out her hand and one of the large tables ahead of them began to shake. "After you've secured your magical anchor, that's when you pull like this." She gripped the space between her fingers, then raised her arm, lifting the table into the air."

The crowd clapped at the display of magic by their teacher.

Hours later, Isha found herself along with the rest of the class standing in a large marbled room. Unlike before, this room was just a large flat open area with blue padding placed against the walls and certain sections of the floor. Above her were large windows surrounded by forestry that allowed the sun to shine in. The roots went all through the roof, making their way down the walls, stopping at the blue padding.

"Alright," said a large man with short dark hair standing in between all the children as they looked around the room. He also didn't wear a robe uniform like she had seen from the rest of the staff. Instead he wore a blue uniform of some sort. "My name is Mr. Higgins. I'm here to teach you magical strengthening and shielding. Which means I'm here to watch and make you beat the life out of each other until I am satisfied with your progress. Now, has anyone here used these techniques before?"

The class was silent.

"That's fine," said Mr. Higgins as two students rolled over carts filled with rubber balls. "You are here to learn after all. Now, what I teach is very simple to understand. First, magic blocks magic. So, if someone shoots a magically imbued ball of fire at you, you can activate a magical shielding to protect yourself. But magic shields don't block the mundane objects. So, if someone throws a rock at you or your average soldier swings a sword at your head, then you will use magic to deflect that attack. I'm sure Miss Gallows showed you that push and pull magic earlier. Well, keep that in mind because that's going to be your main defense against mundane attacks."

Higgins had all the children pair up, standing opposite each other. Jacinta and Makeba paired up with each other, and Isha ended up being paired with the blonde boy from the first class. Standing in front of him, she could see that he seemed quite slender and had a slim face. She looked over at the other two boys in the room. Who both had stockier-built frames with broader shoulders.

"Hello there, I'm Pavel, what's your name?"

"Ah... I'm Isha."

"Glad to meet you, Miss Isha. You're the girl with the Sakari. I bet there is a story there."

Mr. Higgins went around the room, tossing the leather balls to each set of students. Pavel caught the ball, holding it to his chest in front of Isha.

"Okay, here's how this works. You are to toss the ball at your partner. Not hard! I don't need you brats bleeding on my floor until we've assigned cleaning duties. When you see the ball coming at you, you are to use that push-pull magic that you should have learned earlier to deflect the ball away from you. This will teach you to anticipate the speed of an incoming attack and learn to judge when and where to focus your magic."

"Shouldn't we have wands?" asked Freedo as he plucked a ball out of the cart.

"Those are soft and slow leather balls, not swords or arrows. Use your hands to guide your magic."

And soon the sound of the leather orbs being passed around and hitting the floor echoed across the large room. Isha passed the ball back and forth between her and Pavel, trying to use the push magic that she half-learned during the previous class, but every time she tried the ball would just harmlessly bounce off her fingers, landing on the ground. Pavel on the other hand seemed to be a natural. She passed the ball to him and watched as he caught it with magic and made it hover above his hands.

"How do you do that so easy?"

"Are you sure you should be asking me that?" asked Pavel with a smile, shifting his attention over to his right, where Makeba and Jacinta were both making the ball hover in the air and spin around them. "Your friends over there seem to be having a grand time as well."

"They're a lot better at magic than I am," said Isha as she watched Mr. Higgins walking over to the Sakari girls, with Freedo following behind him.

"Well, what do we have here? Two little Sakari naturals, I see. Tell me, do they actually train you little brown babies over down in them jungles where you're from?"

"We learn by playing krump," said Makeba.

"Krump harder than this. Much harder to catch," said Jacinta.

"Can you show me how to play?" asked Freedo.

Mr. Higgins rubbed at his chin. "Krump, huh? I guess that's some game they play down there in the trees. I heard about that mess you girls caused one of our other students. Said you broke her arm."

Jacinta smiled. "Yes, we break good; she scream a lot."

"The report said there were three of you, where's the other one."

"Oh, that sister Isha. She over there, playing with boy who pretty like girl."

Half the class that heard the comment started snickering, dropping their balls on the floor.

"Jacinta!" Shouted Isha.

Pavel started laughing, "Oh my. Am I really that pretty?"

"That so?" said Mr. Higgins as he walked over to Isha, looking down at her. "And what's your story? Those girls called you sister. Your daddy went down in them jungles trying to fuck them dark ladies and came back with those two?"

Isha stared up at the big burly man and felt her body freeze up. He looked so much like Molan to her. Her hands began to shake as she swallowed.

"I... I..."

"What? You don't wanna share with the rest of the class?" asked Mr. Higgins, leaning down and staring Isha in the face until he was inches away from her.

Tears began to form up in Isha's eyes as her lips shook and her mouth began to open.

Makeba started to run over, "Wait, Sister not good with—"

"Watch out, Isha," said Serpene's voice from somewhere nearby.

Isha's eyes turned to the sound of her voice only to catch the last glimpse of a leather ball speeding in her direction, and then suddenly everything went black.

Isha sat in the school's healer office with a large black eye as Jacinta poked at her cheek with her finger.

"Sister Isha's skin dark like ours now. If we hit her with small balls every day, then she become real Sakari," said Jacinta with a smile across her face.

Isha narrowed her one good eye at her sister. "Oh, quiet

you." In front of her sat Leo across the room, just staring at her, shaking his head.

"How do you wind up injured so much? You're supposed to be a healer. You know it really makes us look bad if one of our healers is the one that comes in for the most healing."

"It's not like I hit myself in the face," snapped Isha.

"You sure? You seem awfully good at it. I mean, look at the size of that bruise," said Leo with a chuckle.

Isha frowned back at Leo, "Why are—" Jacinta poked her at the black spot on her face again, causing Isha to slap her finger away. "Stop that."

"Oh, sister angry," said Jacinta, smirking mischievously, while waving her fingers.

Isha sighed, "Why are you here, shouldn't you be in class?"

"We watch over, sister," said Makeba.

"Not you two. I mean him," said Isha, pointing to Leo.

"Who, me? I finished my training in my first year. I'm one of the teachers now."

Isha narrowed her eyes at him, "What?"

"Yeah, don't you remember Elena saying how I was teaching her? Well, that goes for everyone else in the house. You can call me Professor Leo if you like. Speaking of which, let's have a look at that face of yours." Leo slowly made his way over to Isha, placing his chair in front of her. "Now lift your head and turn your face to the left, so I can have a good look."

Isha turned her face to the side, looking out the window.

"Now, is it okay that I touch your face?"

"Yes, I... I'm ready," said Isha as she closed her eyes and reached over to grab hold of Makeba's hand.

"Okay, now just like with the leg, tell me if it hurts okay?"

"Okay," sighed Isha.

"Good," said Leo as he placed his thumb on the side of her face, "Does it hurt yet?"

"No, not yet."

Green magic left Leo's hand and began rolling over the bruises on Isha's face. "Okay, now how's that feel?"

"Cold, but it doesn't sting as much."

"You were supposed to tell me when it hurt."

"It didn't hurt that much."

Leo continued to massage the side of Isha's face for a bit as the magic worked its way into her skin. "Okay, that should do it, for now. I'll finish you up when you get back home. But you should be able to make it to your next class before it gets started." Leo slid his chair back, standing up. "Off you go then."

Isha left the room still with a black eye, Jacinta and Makeba beside her.

"Bye Isha, Jacinta, and Makeba. See you girls at home. I love you," shouted Leo into the crowded hallway as hard as he could.

Jacinta and Makeba smiled back, waving at Leo, while Isha's cheeks reddened below her blackened eye as she blushed. She lowered her head trying not to be seen by the few students that glanced back at Leo being foolish.

Eventually, they made their way back to the side of the school where their classes were. The girls entered Ms. Webblebottom's class only to be stopped at the door.

"Stop right there, and who is it that is coming late to my... Oh my, what happened to your eye?" said a young woman in the similar black robe to what Soulden and Miss Huffles had worn. Except that going down her shoulder on the garb were green stripes. She wore glasses and her reddish hair was tied into a bun.

"Sister was hit in face with leather ball," said Makeba.

"Oh, that sounds horrible. Are you okay?"

"Yes, mam, I'm okay," said Isha, noticing that some of her classmates were now staring at her.

"Well, go on then," said Miss Webblebottom, pointing up to the class. "You can take a seat there and we can—"

The door opened, and another girl entered the room,

standing beside the girls.

"What, why is everyone coming to my class late today?"

"I'm sorry, I'm late. They needed to get me sorted," said the voice of a girl.

"Oh, goodness. What happened to your hand?" asked Miss Webblebottom.

"It's fine; it got caught in a fire, but I'm told the healers here can help me."

"Well, I most certainly do hope so. Just looking at you two, it has me wondering what's happening to our girls these days?"

Isha looked over and saw the burned hand on the girl. The skin was disfigured and patched in different shades of burned darkness. She raised her head to look at the new student, only to see the brown-haired girl staring back at her as if she'd seen a ghost.

"Is... is something wrong?" asked Isha.

The two stared at each other for a few seconds more before the girl lunged at Isha with her hands around Isha's neck, forcing her back as they both went tumbling over chairs to the floor.

"It's your fault, dam you, dam you, dam you," shouted the girl, as she struck and clawed at Isha as they continued to tumble over each other.

"Oh, my word," said Miss Webblebottom.

Isha began clawing and striking back at the girl as they tussled with one another, with the rest of the class watching on in amazement.

"Oh, sister is getting better at fighting," said Makeba.

"Yes, but she still no good," said Jacinta to the sounds of the girl's screams echoing across the classroom.

Isha was once again back in Leo's office. To the left of her sat the girl who had attacked her. Red scratch marks littered both their faces and neckline from the earlier tussle with each other. Ahead of them sat Leo, who just stared at them both as if they were something he'd never seen before.

"Has it been an hour yet? Actually, I don't think it's been twenty minutes since you left," said Leo, shaking his head.

Isha turned her face away from Leo, frowning down at the floor.

"You two mind informing me how this happened?" asked Leo, turning to Makeba and Jacinta, who were both sitting in chairs next to the wall with candy straws in their mouths, kicking their feet out.

"The new girl jumped at Isha trying to hit her, then they fell over chairs," said Makeba.

"But sister punch and kick her back. It was fun. She still not good fighter yet. She was hit too much," said Jacinta.

"And you two look pretty unscathed. Did you not participate in the fun?"

"No need. Sister in no danger. New girl bad fighter also," said Jacinta.

The other girl frowned at the comment and turned her head away.

"Is that so?" asked Leo, placing his hand under his chin, looking at the disheveled girls. "Alright then, no need to waste time. You're both pretty banged up now, and classes are done for today. So, you both can follow me home and think about what you've done on the way."

"I'm not going anywhere with her," snapped the girl.

Leo stood up from his seat and walked closer to the girl, "Really? Because it seems to me that I'm the only one in this whole school that can heal that mess of an arm you got. So, if you don't follow me home, I'll make sure that they send your little butt back to where you came from, messed up arm and all." Leo walked to the door, "Now, come along you three. I think Elena is cooking vegetable soup tonight."

Jacinta and Makeba hopped out of their seats, leaving the room with Isha behind them. As they left the room, Isha saw the new girl start trailing behind them.

After leaving the castle and taking a short walk down the street, the group arrived at Heart House, where Leo opened the door to see Elena cooking behind the counter.

"Oh, you're back," said Elena, "Leo, can you come and… Oh, what happened to Isha? Her eye's all black." Elena snapped her fingers, extinguishing the fire, and went over, rubbing her fingers across Isha's face.

"The same as every year," said Leo. "A girl gets hit in the face with one of the practice balls so hard that she passes out, then the girl gets into a fight with another girl minutes later." Leo walked into the kitchen and popped a sweet meat into his mouth. "Happens every year. You females are just naturally violent creatures."

Elena spotted another girl peeping into the door of the house. "Oh, hello. Can I help you?"

"He… he made me follow him."

Elena frowned back at Leo, "And what's this one then?"

"Her hands all messed up. I didn't want to stay at school anymore. Or risk Isha blowing up the whole castle if I sent her off again. So, I had her just follow us home for the day."

Isha narrowed her eyes at Leo, "It's not funny. I'm trying to be good."

"Of course, you are, you little walking catastrophe, you," said Leo as if talking to a baby. He then walked over, grabbing two chairs and setting them in front of each other. "Okay, you with the bad hand, you come here and sit in this chair."

The girl with the scarred hand fully entered the house, walking over and sat down in the chair. And Isha sat down on the couch with her sisters and began going over a text book. Both girls were careful to keep an eye on one another as they passed.

"Okay, little miss scarred hand; what's your name?" asked Leo.

"Chloe."

"Chloe is a cute name. Well then, Miss Chloe, you mind telling me what you and Isha were fighting about."

Chloe looked over at Isha scowling, "No, I... I made a mistake. I'm sorry."

"That look on your face sure doesn't say you've made a mistake," said Leo with a smirk as the girl remained silent. "But if you promise not to randomly attack our little Isha there again, then I'll let it go."

Chloe dropped her head, "I promise."

"Don't worry, you'll both get plenty of time to beat up on each other in battle practice under Mr. Higgins. You're a first-year, right? Then you've got three years to sort out whatever you two have going on." Leo raised up the girl's sleeve, following the damaged skin with his thumb. "Your hand and arm have been through the wringer; that's for sure. But after we've healed the skin and smoothed it out, then we can worry about creaming over the arm to get the skin back to normal."

"So, you can fix it?" asked Chloe, looking back up at Leo with wide eyes.

"Of course, I can. It's going to take a good amount of time, maybe even a full year of treatment. I'll have you start showing up twice a week from now on. But this won't be free. What I'm doing is going to cost a lot of gold."

"I don't... have much money anymore."

"Humm... tell you what; if I'm going to provide a year-long treatment. I'll have you helping us out around here to pay off your debt. We don't have that many of us here. So, you'll help out with the chores like everybody else."

Chloe raised her head, "Yes sir, I can do that."

Good, then it's settled. There's not much else I can do today. So, you can head on back. Just show up for either tomorrow or the day after for your first treatment. We gotta get you on a schedule"

"Yes, Sir," said Chloe hopping down from her seat. "I'll be back tomorrow." She then walked out of the door, scowling at Isha on her way out.

Elena walked over to Leo, whispering in his ear, "Can't you fix that in a few weeks?"

"Yeah, but they don't know that. Now shush, momma bear," said Leo as he looked over at Isha. "Your turn again little woman. Bring your butt over here so I can give you one final check-up before I send you off."

"Yes, sir," sighed Isha as she walked over with her shoulders slouched and sat down in the chair opposite Leo.

"Okay, now turn your head to the right and look towards the wall." Isha did as instructed. And Leo reached up, rubbing the side of her face with his hand and pressing his thumb against the side of her temple.

Jacinta and Makeba's eyes went wide as they began to speak, but Leo placed a finger over his lips at them and smiled.

"Now, do you feel any pain when I place my hand near your ear, neck, or shoulder?" he asked as he moved his hand over the body parts he mentioned.

"No, I'm fine now."

"Humm. Okay then, I guess I can let you go for a while, but I'm going to continue doing check-ups on you to make sure you're okay. Especially if you keep getting into trouble."

"Yes, sir," said Isha with a solemn look on her face as there was a knock at the door.

"Who's that?" asked Elena as she walked over to the door, opening it. "Oh, hello there, can I help you."

"Hello," said Freedo's voice. "Ah, we were supposed to come over and study. Is Makeba here?"

"Oh, really? Well, come in, I guess," said Elena as Marlene, Freedo, and Serpene walked inside the home, each of them gazing around.

"Cool, everything is made of wood," said Freedo, walking inside looking over the house. This is much better than Ox House, with its stone floors."

"Yeah, and it's so much smaller than Butterfly House,"

added Marlene. "There's only one upstairs."

"Well, what do we have here?" asked Leo, "Even more little people have come to visit."

"They friends from school," said Jacinta, standing up. "They help us study. The kingdom boy follows Makeba around. He likes her."

"Hey," said Freedo. "You don't have to say it like that. I'm... I'm just curious, is all. I wanna know why the Sakari got so strong."

"I Sakari like Makeba, but you not follow me around like you do her."

"That... that's not true. I... I don't follow her around like you say."

"Freedo, you come sit," said Makeba as she patted the rug beside her. "We practice magic now."

"Okay," said Freedo, a smile across his face as he hurried over and sat beside Makeba.

"Wow," whispered Leo to Isha, "Would you looky there? She's already got him under her control. I wonder if he knows the rumors of what Sakari do to their men."

Isha watched as her sisters and their new friends huddled around each other on the floor and began chatting amongst themselves.

"Well, go on," said Leo, patting Isha on her leg. "Don't allow yourself to be left out of the fun. Go on and play with your friends."

Isha stared at Leo for a moment before getting down and walking back over to the group as they began to talk more about magic. They all sprawled out on the floor as they guessed on how to use magic until night had finally taken over the room. And even after their guests had gone home, the girls stayed on the floor talking about their classes, trying to understand their courses.

"Sister, we tired now," said Jacinta as she rolled across the floor, stretching her arms out. "It hard learning all the kingdom words. We go to bed. You come too."

"I'll be up soon. I want to read a little more. You two go on."

The girls stared at Isha for a moment, but shook their heads and left for up stairs. Isha lit a candle and continued reading.

So healing magic is the art of sending your magic into another person's body. It says that there are two types of healing. Healing of mundane and healing of people with magic requires two different techniques. But for each one to work, the healer has to inject their own magic in the patient's body. "Inject? How am I supposed to put my magic in someone else's body?" Isha thought about all the healing she had received from Leo and from Aukube back at the camp."

I wonder how everyone is doing. Is Dessi off on another mission? Or maybe with Jacob somewhere? She shook her head. *No stop, think about magic. You're supposed to be learning magic. I missed class, I'm going to be behind and I need to be ready for class. I can't freeze up again when the teacher comes near me. I need to be okay. I need to be strong.*

Isha's eyes went back to the book in front of her. And as the candle's flame in front of her began to dim, so did her eyelids as they began to close.

Suddenly, Isha was back in class, but everything seemed out of place. There were more shadows in the room. Chairs were arranged randomly. Off, away from her, between the shadow and the light, she could see her sisters. They were just standing there, holding hands, not saying a word.

"Sisters? What's going on?" said Isha as she tried walking towards them.

But the more she stepped forward, it didn't matter. She couldn't reach them; it was as if her body was slow. As if she was moving through water. Soon her sisters were out of her sight, gone into the shadows that seemed to surround her.

Alone in the darkness, she could feel the hair on the back of her neck stand up.

"Hello... hello," she called out into the void.

But as she shouted out, only silence was given back to her in return. That is until the sound of something hitting the floor creeped into her ears. Soft at first, but as it slowly began to develop a rhythm, the thumping started to grow louder.

"Who is that? Who's there?"

The thumping sound grew louder once again. But this time, out of the shadows came a small leather ball, bouncing towards her, creating a thumping sound before finally losing momentum and resting at her feet. Looking at the ball, her hands began shaking. But after looking around again, she knelt to pick the ball up.

"Well, ain't you just something?" said a familiar voice.

Isha quickly looked up to see Mr. Higgins standing directly in front of her: his tall stature, a towering and intimidating sight.

"You think you can just walk out of my class?"

"Wha.... I... I..."

"Don't wanna speak, huh? Well, I got something for people like you," said Mr. Higgins as he reached down, grabbing Isha's arm.

"Wha... no, please I'm sorry... I..." Isha's words froze in her mouth as she realized the man holding her was no longer Mr. Higgins, but someone more horrible. The clansman Molan now held her hand and began dragging her forward. "No... please. I'm sorry, please let me go."

"I told you I was gonna break you in," said the gruff man's voice as he dragged her forward through the shadows ahead. Her feet slid along the floor as she struggled.

"Please let me go. Please, I..." her words froze again as she saw up ahead a bed, the same bed where Molan had climbed on top of her. Where he had inserted his fingers inside of her. There was blood all over the sheets and on the floor. The wood was still burned, and there were knives on the floor to the side of it.

"No... don't take me back. I... I don't want to go back."

Molan was silent, only continuing to drag her forward towards the bloody cot.

"No.... no."

He lifted her into his arms as she banged on his chest trying to free herself and dropped her face down onto the cot.

Quickly she turned around, "No, don't touch..."

She was alone again. Molan had disappeared. No one was there anymore as she sat up on the bed, frantically looking around. Instead, only the silence had returned. Something then caught her eye. Something shiny that pierced the darkness. She peered at it as it began to glow in the shadows. Illuminating the area around it, she saw that it was the jewelled dagger that Oscar had given to her. Except now it was back where it shouldn't be, in the neck of the dead man's body that lay in front of her. He lay on the floor surrounded by dirt as blood pooled out of his neck and mouth, but his eyes were open, and they seemed to be staring at her.

"No, that's not right. This... This isn't real. It's..." she muttered as she felt something moist and cold on her fingers.

Looking down, she could see more blood on the sheets of the cot. It was as if blood was seeping out of the bed and as it covered her fingers. Raising her hand, she could see the blood sliding down her palm onto her wrist. But in front of her, beyond the vision of her hand, at the edge of the bed, she saw another hand. It was burned. No, it was burning. Its fingers searing the cot as a moaning noise came from in front of her.

"You..." the voice moaned as its fingers pulled at the sheets of the cot, gripping the fabric in its hand as Isha watched it begin to ignite in its grip. And soon the burned figure lifted itself slowly from under the cot, and Isha's face filled with horror as she saw the scorched body of Molan climbing up. His body lucent in red heat; his eyes replaced with dark holes that oozed blood down his face. Slowly, his corpse climbed onto the bed.

"You… did… this…"

Isha froze as the burned body crawled forward over the cot until the bloodied and burning face of Molan knelt atop her.

"You… are… mine…" said Molan, the empty dark sockets of his eyes staring down at Isha as her own eyes were wide with terror. She felt Molan's hand crawl up her waist, then to her arm, and up her shoulder until his hands rested on her neck. Isha could feel the burning sensation in her throat, as Molan's finger began to tighten and her ability to breathe began to leave her. Molan forced her head up to look at him once more.

"Mine."

Elena walked down the hall of the heart house with a candle tray in her hand. Turning the corner towards the washroom, she stopped. *What was that?* Turning around with a candle tray in hand, she narrowed her eyes, trying to see in the dim light.

"Hello? Leo?"

She stepped forward, hearing more sounds as if someone was trying to catch their breath.

"What game are you playing now, Le…" Her words froze as their front on her huddled in the corner of the house sat Isha with her hands around her knees.

"Isha, what's wrong? Are you okay?" said Elena as she slowly stepped towards Isha. But Isha didn't respond; she just stayed in the corner trying to catch her breath. Elena took a few more steps, then kneeling in front of Isha, she placed the candle tray on the floor. "Isha, it's okay. You're going to be okay." She reached her hand out. "You're safe here," she said as she touched Isha's arm."

"I'm sorry... Please.... I'm sorry.... Please..." said Isha, mumbling over and over.

"Isha, Isha. Look at me. Look at me," pleaded Elena repeatedly under Isha finally quieted down and began to look around as if in a daze.

"E... Elena?"

"That's right, It's me. You're safe. I'm here with you... It's going to be okay."

Isha began frantically looking around into the darkness of the house. "He was... I mean... He... He..." As the words fumbled in her mouth, tears began to flow down her eyes.

"Oh Isha, it's okay. I promise you're safe now," said Elena as she slid in beside Isha and wrapped her arms around the small girl, feeling her trembling.

"I'm sorry... I... I didn't.... I thought..."

"No, it's not your fault. It's not your fault."

"Please... please don't tell my sisters. I... I... I need to be okay."

CHAPTER 13

"Okay, let me see your leg," said Victor to Silk as they both sat in the bag of their wagon on the road outside the village of Nyril. The early morning sun shining through the wagon's fabric as small pieces of hay flew through the air from them, shuffling about.

"I'm fine, you don't... ouch," yelped Silk, still wearing the torn wedding dress.

"You're not fine. How long before you're able to shape-shift again?" asked Victor, rubbing healing oil over her leg.

"I've been trying, but it just doesn't work," said Silk as a white stream of magic flowed around her finger. "I can kinda use some magic, but it's a lot harder than it should be."

"I wish Nahtalli was here now; he might be able to figure out how to fix you. Okay, give me your other leg."

Silk extended her other leg to Victor, "Why... why did you save me?"

"Was I not supposed to?"

"I mean... you could have just left me... anyone else would have."

"Well, if we were to go by the word of that charming dark-haired woman. It's because I'm stupid, and at this point, I'm inclined to believe her." Victor held out the oil vail. "Give me your hands. And seeing how you can't really walk right now," He rubbed the oil over her wrists. "I'm guessing I'm going to be your caretaker till we get this mess sorted out."

"It's not like I like this either. I'm not a child. I don't want anyone treating me like one. And why aren't you scared of me?"

"Why? You planning on trying to kill me again anytime soon?"

"I didn't, ow... try to kill you."

"Then why would I be afraid of you?"

"I told you don't treat me like a child. I'm not," said Silk, pulling herself away from Victor. "You know what I mean. Most people would run away or try to kill me if they saw me. Or... start calling me.... monster."

Victor released her leg and leaned his back against the wagon, "Alright, you look odd. That ghostly hair and milky white skin you got make for a haunting image. So, what type of magic are you using to do it? I've seen illusion magic before, but something tells me that's not what you're using."

Silk shook her head, "I don't know, we've always been like this."

"We?"

Silk sighed, closing her eyes. "I have a sister; she also

looks like this."

"That's good then."

"How is that good?" asked Silk, a bit of frustration in her voice as she rubbed at the black mark on her neck.

"Means you're not alone, you don't like people calling you a monster? Well then, imagine being the only one of your kind. At least that sister of yours gives you someone to relate to. There aren't many things in the world worse than being alone, with no one who understands you."

Silk just stared at Victor.

"What?"

"Nothing... it's just... you're weird."

Victor raised a brow at the remark, "And you're going to tell me you're not?"

Silk smirked back.

"So, tell me, how does that spell work? Is there only certain things you can say or do, or you just can't answer specific inquiries?"

"I can't directly answer any questions that I think will reveal any missions I've been on or put the people I work for at risk," said Silk stretching out her leg and looking up at the top of the wagon. "But I'm allowed to talk about things if I don't think it has anything to do with my missions."

"That just means I need to ask in the right way," said Victor as he stretched his shoulders creating an audible popping sound.

"Pretty much, yeah, as long as I don't realize that the question reveals the answer to a mission, then the spell won't stop me from speaking."

"Well, this sounds like a fun game to play. Unfortunately, we don't have the time for that right now. Turn around and give me your neck, I'll use the last of the oil and we'll take off. The first thing we gotta do is get you some clothes. You currently have a quite startling image with that skin and that bloody white dress. So, I'll start looking for something else for you along with myself. You prefer trousers or tunics?

"Doesn't matter, I can play both when my magic starts working again."

Victor finished rubbing the oil on Silk's neck, "Okay then, let's head off, you get some rest, and I'll start the trip back into Nyril."

"Victor."

"Yes?"

"I... no, it's nothing."

Victor hopped out of the back of the wagon and smiled back at her, "You know, you're a lot nicer than I'd assumed for a murderous assassin." He closed the wagon flaps, walked around the cart, jumping up into the seat. And with one snap of the reins, the horses began pulling the wagon down towards Nyril.

After arriving at the city gates, Victor could see a lot of guards walking around on patrol along with the worshippers of the goddess in their white robes scattered through the streets. Throwing his hood over his head, he rode through the city until he reached a large barn with a man sitting outside.

"Excuse me, sir, mind if I kept my wagon in your barn here?"

"Huh, why's that? You can just leave it in the stable with the rest at the head of town."

"I'm a salesman. I'd prefer to leave it with a trustworthy fella, such as yourself."

The man chuckled, "Five silver a night, and you can just pop her in the back. I won't be using it fully for a few days still."

Victor gave the man fifteen silver, "Just in case, a little bit extra to ask you not to peek inside. I got something dangerous in the back. It might kill you to ever look at it."

"Don't worry. I don't care much for your little trinkets. Just don't disappear and expect me not to sell the damn thing after a few days."

"A reasonable request, but I shall return soon enough,"

said Victor as the horses pulled the wagon into the barn. "You gonna be okay back there?"

"I'm fine. I know I'm no good like this," replied Silk's muffled voice from underneath the blanket.

"Okay then," said Victor as he hopped down to the ground, "I'll try to be back around nightfall with some clothes." Victor left the barn and headed back out into the city, and began moving through the streets, seeing the cathedral off into the distance. *So, it didn't burn down then.* He continued walking through the city and made his way down to the waterfront where people were worshipping.

"Hello, sir," said a young man in a white robe.

"Hello there, your group is enjoying a fine day of worship, I see. Is the Kemlor here as well?"

"Very rarely is there a bad day to worship the goddess, but no, if you're looking for the Kemlor. I'm afraid he's moved on from here." said the old man with a chuckle.

"I heard that there was an incident here a while ago." *An incident that kinda involved me, but let's not bring that part up.*

"Yes, it seems robbers broke inside the cathedral and tried to burn it down. It's hard to imagine someone who hates the goddess so much."

"There are truly some terrible people in this world."

"Sadly, yes, there are."

Victor gazed down over the water, down at the rest of the worshippers, "Why aren't you down there with the rest? Have you finished the water prayer today?"

"Oh, I rarely go down these days. These old bones don't shrug off the water's cold as well as they used to. I mostly spend my time watching over them from up above while looking for a partner for four queens."

Victor took a look up the hill, seeing the playing tables, "I need to waste a few hours. If you're looking for a partner, I could go for a game or two."

"Young man, I'd enjoy nothing better."

The two walked back up the hill and set up the game

and began to play as the sun traveled over their heads.

"I won again, but you're surprisingly capable at this game," said Victor.

"I can't tell if old age has taken my wits or are young people just getting smarter. Both you and The Kemlor are quite formidable in this game. I'm usually able to beat everyone else."

"The Kemlor sounds like a good guy to play with. Perhaps we shall meet up one day, and I will get my chance. Where'd he head off to?"

"He, and that commander of his left to go to Molask the day before someone tried to burn down the cathedral. We've had dark days since he left. Having been raided by Sakari and Goddesses only knows where they even came from. They killed every guard in the city and made off with some of our people."

"Sakari? What were they doing way out here?" *I guess that explains where Gregga went off to.*

"No one knows. They came out of nowhere and left just as fast. We were afraid of them coming back, but that's when the king sent more guards down here to protect us. I pray to the goddess that it works this time."

Victor looked up into the sky and saw the sun high above him. "It seems I've been here a little longer than anticipated; I must make my way to buy some supplies for my trip. It was a pleasure playing with you, Mr?"

"Belvac Dunlow."

"Well, good day to you Mr. Dunlow; my name is Victor. I hope you find another partner for your next set of games."

Victor bid farewell to the old man before heading back into the city, asking questions as to where an apparel store might be. After a few directions, he purchased another set of clothing for himself along with a tunic and undergarment which appeared as if it would fit Silk. He stuffed the clothing into a sack and tossed it over his shoulder, heading back out into town.

He continued to walk around, asking the residents questions until he noticed the sun getting lower in the sky. Somewhere along the way, he noticed that more than one person was following him. *Guess I can't head back just yet.* His stomach began to growl as he caught wind of food from a nearby tavern. *If I'm going to get robbed, I'd rather not do it on an empty stomach.* Entering the tavern, he took a seat at a table.

"What can I do for you, honey?" asked a waitress wandering over.

"Any type of meat, please, and water. Oh, do you have anything hot that I can take with me? I have a kid waiting for me."

"Sure do, we can put some meat in a potato, and it'll stay warm for over an hour."

"Thank you, that will work fine."

Two of the men stood by the door as Victor was delivered his food. He quickly munched down a few pieces of meat before someone stepped up behind him.

"Ya know at first; I thought I had mistaken ya. But it seems I wasn't wrong."

Victor took off his glasses and placed them on the far side of the table, then turned around with the knife he was eating with lowered at his side. In front of him stood a dark-haired man with a scar on his cheek looking at him, "I'm sorry sir, seems I don't remember you. Have we met before?"

"Yeah, I mean, why would ya remember me? All ya did was put a knife to my throat and take my damn wagon before ya hightailed it outta town with them girls of yours."

Victor closed his eyes, biting his bottom lip while shaking his head, "Yeah, you have me there. I do think I remember doing that."

"They found them guards that chased ya dead in the trees bout a mile away from here. Ya wouldn't happen to know anything about that, would ya?"

Victor sucked on the side of his lip while continuing to shake his head, "Nope, sorry. Now that you mention it, I don't seem to remember much about that day. Perhaps I was drunk."

"Oh well, poor fella. Drink's always been a weakness of mine too," said the man as he leaned in close to Victor, "But ya don't seem all that drunk now. So, why don't ya tell me where that pretty wagon ya rode in on is at? I figured since ya done wrecked mine, I think you giving me yours would make us even. Either that or everyone finds out ya was with the group that dam near burned the town down."

Victor sucked in air through his teeth, "You seem like a nice guy. Would you believe me if I said that the contents of that wagon are dangerous, and it's best if you would stay away from it?"

"Between you and me, I think I'll take my chances."

"Of course, you will," said Victor with a sigh as he dropped the knife from his hand, letting it sound off the floor. The man glanced down at the sound of the knife hitting the floor, only to catch Victor's fist to the side of his head.

Suddenly three more men jumped up into action as the man went flying backward.

Well, that's two more than I anticipated.

Victor ducked under one of the man's arms as he swung at him and punched the man in the ribs before bringing the palm of his hand up under the man's chin, sending him falling backward. The two other men grabbed at Victor's arms, forcing him back on the table sliding it across the floor with force. He kneed one man in the back of the head, only to be struck in the face by the other.

The impact rattled Victor's jaw as he headbutted the man who struck him and stood up on the stool he was sitting on earlier, kneeing the same man in the face sending him stumbling back crashing against the bar.

"Oh, that one's a fighter. Looks like ya got your hands

full with that one, Sirius," said someone in the crowd of spectators.

"Oh, shut it, Mackave!" yelled the man with the scar on his cheek as he ran at Victor, swinging wildly. Victor jumped back, trying to dodge the man's blows, but found himself grabbed by the man he kneed in the back of the head earlier as he wrapped his arms around Victor's neck.

"I got him, Sirius," said the man.

"Good, now hold 'em still. Bastards got a beating coming."

Victor struggled as the man's grip tightened around his neck.

Sirius punched Victor square in the gut, making him gasp and lose his breath. Then struck him in the face as Victor grit his teeth.

"Not so proud now, are you?"

Victor leaned forward and threw the back of his head into the face of the man holding him. Forcing him to reel back in pain, lifting Victor up with him. Victor then used the momentum to kick the scarred man in the face with both feet as they all went tumbling to the floor. Quickly Victor began elbowing the man holding him in the side until he was forced to let go, doubled over in pain trying to protect himself. Victor stood back up just in time for the two men from before to grab a hold of his arms.

"Throw the bastard outside," said the man with a scar on his face walking up, shaking his head, trying to fight off the effects of the kick Victor gave him.

Both men lifted Victor up, dragging him out the door and throwing him down the stairs when he went rolling across the ground. He tried to stand only to feel the scar-faced man boot crunch into his ribs, sending him rolling on the ground, grabbing at his side.

"You like that, huh? You bastard."

"Not... so much... no," said Victor with his face covered in dirt.

Victor rolled over again, and the scarred went for another kick at his ribs, only for Victor to catch his foot in his hands and yank him to the ground. Victor then pounced on the man, grabbing the back of his head and slamming him face down into the dirt. Quickly the other two men pulled Victor off, punching him in the face.

"Hold... that bastard there," said the scar-faced man, wiping the blood and dirt from his face. "We'll throw him off the bridge into the water." They kicked the back of Victor's legs, making him kneel on the ground.

"What's going on here?" asked a man with two other soldiers walking one of the men who ran away from the brawl.

The man with the scar on his cheek stopped and turned to the guards, breathing heavily. "This bastard... is the one who tried to burn down the cathedral, and he stole my cart and horses."

"That so?" said the man walking up to Victor, whose face was still planted into the dirt, "Well, never thought we'd be meeting like this again."

Victor looked up to see Thaddius's brawny face smiling back down at him, "Oh, I had wondered why you weren't at the wedding."

Thaddius looked to the two men holding Victor, "Alright, let him go."

"But what about all he's done?"

"I assume everything you did was for that little mission the king had you on?" asked Thaddius.

"Yeah, I needed his cart to make my getaway. Didn't do much good, though; it broke about a mile or two from here."

"Alright, the crown will pay for your cart and horses, just visit my office in the morning, now all of you, go on home. You're done here for the night."

The scar-faced man spat on the ground. "Bastard, don't think this is over," before slinking off down the street with the other men. "Alright, boys, let 'em go."

The men released Victor as he rubbed at the side of his face and stretched out his jaw.

Thaddius reached his hand down to Victor, "You look like you've seen better days."

"Story of my life," said Victor, grabbing Thaddius's hand and pulling himself up to his feet. "Why the hell are you out here? You got tired of living in the castle?"

"In a way, yes. I'm here to stabilize the town after the mess you caused down here. But it's most certainly more fulfilling than watching after Saffron. What about you? Why are you back here?"

"Your king's managed to recruit me into another one of his damned assignments. I'm out here getting my ass kicked again for the glory of his highness."

"Well, come along then. You can explain it on the way. Unless you have somewhere else, you must be?"

"You got wine where we're going? I didn't exactly get to finish my meal."

"Both wine and food can be had at the cathedral where I've set up."

"My stuff's inside, let me just grab it, and you can lead the way."

After retrieving his items, Thaddius escorted Victor down the streets to the cathedral.

"This place was a mess when I got here. Seems someone set fire to the records room down below," said Thaddius, opening the door to his office and walking in, taking a seat behind his desk. "It's a wonder the whole thing didn't go up in flames. Found some poor bastard dead down there. Half his body burned. Gruesome thing. Not sure if the fire or the smoke got him first."

"Yeah, I was here for that part. Smoke was pouring out of the top when I got here. Do you know what happened to the previous captain and Kemlor of this town?" asked Victor as he looked around the room, noticing the stone walls still had traces of black smoke at the edges of the roof, along with singe marks along the wooden support beams.

"The previous captain died some years ago; the town was mostly self-managed before all this happened. But I heard that Kemlor was assigned to another town. Why? He part of this mission you on?"

"Not sure yet," said Victor as he took a seat in front of Thaddius. "But he left town right before all this happened, so it at least gives me somewhere to start asking questions."

"Tell me, how goes things in the capital? Information has been slow receiving out here."

"Well, your prince is married now, sorta."

Thaddius raised a brow, "How does one get 'sorta' married?"

"That prince of yours is a special man. Oh, and Queen's Bane has appeared at the capitol. When I left, he had already killed two nobles."

"What?" asked Thaddius, standing up from his desk. "And I haven't been called back?"

"The king said he would handle it,"

"But you said he's killed two already. Ah, dammit!" Thaddius slammed his overly large fist on the table. "I'd love to be there to have taken him down; that would be a tale to tell."

"I'm not sure they will. I mean, how many kingdoms has he killed nobles in so far? Two? Three? He seems quite elusive."

"That just makes the hunt more thrilling, Ah, to be there now," said Thaddius, calming down the passion in his voice and re-taking his seat. "But I must finish my work here. A soldier has his duty and all. I imagine you know that as well as I do."

"Unfortunately."

"Well, far be it from me to keep you from your mission. I doubt those fellas will bother you again tonight. You're free to go."

"I appreciate that. I'll take some wine and bread with

me if ya don't mind. A pouch for water if ya have one lying around."

"Sure, go ahead. There's enough here to spare a bit for your travels."

"How long will you be here enjoying the countryside air before you're called back to babysitting duty?" asked Victor as he stood back up and stretched his shoulders.

"Sadly, I have another week or so before I'm expected back in the capitol. By then I imagine that bastard would have been caught or moved on."

"Well, when you get there, don't be surprised if that prince of yours isn't so fond of me anymore."

"Why; did something happen?"

"I may have gotten too much attention from Frenka while I was there."

"Ha! Yeah, that would do it. The prince's been hung up on her ever since I've known him."

"Well, I'd prefer if he turned his interest elsewhere," said Victor as he headed for the door. "I think I have more than enough problems, so I'd prefer not to add dealing with a jealous prince to that ever-growing list."

"I'm afraid you might not have much say in the matter if Frenka has her sights on you. Your best option is to run away or submit. Either that or have the prince send you away to the northern border like he did that poor bastard before.

"I think someone mentioned that. Well, I'll be off then. Be well, Thaddius. Perhaps the next time we meet; we'll have a round of drinks together."

"Would you like an escort on your way back?"

"Nah, I'll be fine. You seem to have scared them off well enough," said Victor as he left the room and walked out of the cathedral after grabbing some supplies.

Darkness had taken over the city as nightfall had come while he chatted with Thaddius. *Right, well, let's hope the assassin princess hasn't gotten lonely and went on a rampage while I was gone.* Victor made his way across town to the barn where he stored the wagon. The moment he saw the barn, he knew something was wrong. There was a light inside. *I doubt murder princess decided to turn on a light show.*

He crept forward into the night until it reached the walls of the barn. Through the old wooden boards, he was slightly able to see inside, but couldn't see much. There was hay, the side of the wagon, and to the right, the sight of Silk leaning against a wooden beam. She was breathing heavily. Her torn wedding dress was smeared with more blood than it was before. *Shit, of course, something had to happen.*

Victor slowly approached the back of the barn. It was quiet inside except for the sound of the horses neighing and stomping restlessly. Victor dropped his sack of supplies and slowly opened the barn door, trying to peer into the pale lit area. To the left of the entrance was a bloody lantern leaning on a wooden beam to the left. Sticking his head inside, he froze. His breath catching in his throat from the sight of Silk. Blood covered half her white head, dyeing it crimson as it slid down the side of her face. The barn looked like a butcher's shop before someone had to clean up the mess. Body parts and blood covered random patches of hay and grass all throughout the building. An arm here, a leg there, a headless torso ahead.

And over to the right was Silk, half her body bloodied. In her hand she held a broken piece of wood.

Victor stepped cautiously inside and felt a soft mushy feeling beneath his feet. Before he could look down, he felt something wet hit him at the top of his forehead. Reaching his hand up and rubbing at his temple, he already knew the outcome before he saw his bloodstained fingers. Twisting his neck up upward, she saw a man's body. Well, it was half a man. His lower parts were surely scattered somewhere around the barn, but his upper torso was impaled on one of the support beams as his entrails dripped what was left of his life down onto the hay. Victor looked down only to see the man's guts beneath his feet. He quickly closed his eyes in an attempt to steel his stomach for fear of throwing up.

"You... didn't come back," said Silk, dropping the bloody piece of wood to the floor.

Victor opened his eyes, gaining back resolve, and pointed to his blacked eye and scars. "Yeah, well, take a good look at my face, and you'll see why."

Cautiously, he stepped closer to Silk, trying not to step on any of the random assortment of men's body parts scattered through the barn. "What happened?" To him, Silk looked far worse than before; her eyes had dark spots under them, as if she hadn't slept in weeks.

"They came... wanted to steal the wagon. The lantern... they saw me... tried to run. I couldn't let them tell."

Victor looked ahead and saw the scar-faced dark-haired man's severed head and sighed. "Yeah, well... let's get you back into the wagon. We're done here, anyway."

Victor lifted Silk into his arms and carried her back over to the wagon, letting her crawl back inside. He then walked ahead, opening the barn doors, and headed back around to grab his supplies. On his way back inside he could help but shake his head at the slaughtered body parts all around them. *It's a wonder the horses are still here. Kingdom horses are just used to blood I suppose.* Hopping back into the seat of the wagon, and tossing the bag down, he snapped the reins on the horses, and pulled off into the night, headed out of the city of Nyril.

CHAPTER 14

Victor stood naked over a stream of water. His bruised face stared back at him as a reflection in the cold liquid as he reached his hand in before bringing it out, splashing his skin. The previous night's smell of dirt and blood being replaced by the fresh air of the surrounding forestry.

Well, all things considered, I guess it could be worse. I mean, a few more people are dead. I'm pretty sure that's my fault, or the king's, or just the luck of the draw. Fuck, this really has become a mess. Dumb bastards really should have listened. Victor grimaced, thinking about the past day's actions while rubbing at the skin on his knuckles until they turned red.

Kneeling down above the water, he closed his eyes and focused on his breathing. *Okay, Victor, think. That's what you're supposed to be good at. I'm out in the middle of nowhere. I don't have any tools because they rushed me out of the castle. And no place around here will be able to resupply me.*

Victor splashed water on his face. *The next step is to find The Kemlor and or that commander. That's who knows about the jewels. Well, maybe The Kemlor. Definitely, the captain, since Oscar said Dessi got the jewels from him. And apparently, they're off in Molask.* So that's my next move. He opened his eyes and glanced over to the wagon to see Silk's head poking out the back flap, staring at him. *And it seems my next problem has awoken. Great!*

Victor walked out from the water and slid on his small clothes before walking over to the wagon. "Hey there, sleeping ghosty. How're you feeling after your late-night murder spree?"

"I'm fine, and you don't look much better," said Silk looking Victor up and down, "You're skinny."

"Well, I'm sorry I don't meet the legendary assassin's standards as to what a man should look like," he said, frowning. "I would say you don't meet mine, but I'm still not exactly sure what standards I should have for you." He noticed the dark spots under Silk's weary-looking eyes. "Why do you still look tired? Didn't you get any sleep last night or were too busy dreaming of a male ashen skinned shapeshifter for you to have babies with?"

"Oh, just shut up. It's not like this is easy for me either," she said while turning her head away from him.

"Now's not the time to be stubborn. Come on out of there." Victor made his way back towards the wagon, taking a seat on the grass. "I washed the blood off my clothes. Now you can wash the blood off your everything. I got some new clothes in that bag there and you can clean yourself in the river. Shouldn't be anyone around to see you way out here."

Silk slowly stepped out of the wagon onto the ground,

walking towards Victor, and looked down at him.

"What?" he said, looking back up at her. She still seemed surreal as half her face still had smears of blood on it. Along with the bags under her eyes, she gave off a chilling appearance to him.

"I need help getting out of it."

"You're a mage. Can't you just magic your way out of it?"

"It doesn't work like that. I can't focus on tiny things yet, and if I use too much, I might hurt myself."

"Oh, for the Goddess's sake," said Victor standing up and grabbing his blade from atop his drying clothes. He noticed Silk's eyes focus on him as he came back up with it. "I'm just going to cut you free. I don't need you getting any funny ideas."

"I know, I... I'm just not used to people helping me, is all."

"Well, I'm not used to any of this, so let's try to get along. Now, turn around and give me your back."

Silk turned around lifting her long hair and exposing her back to Victor along with an assortment of strings and laces that held the wedding dress together. Victor once again looked ahead to the water.

"Actually, when you fell from the boat into the water. I'm curious, how did you survive? I mean, we were in the middle of nowhere. Are you going to tell me you can turn into a fish or something?"

"No, I caught hold of a rope at the bottom of the ship and pulled myself back up and just stayed hidden until you made it back to port. But if needed, I can transform parts of myself, so that I breathe underwater.

"Sounds like quite the useful magical talent to have," said Victor as he cut two strings and the top of the dress loosened. Silk placed her hands around her waist to keep the dress from falling down. "Well, you do have some modesty. That's a surprise. Would have figured an assassin to have no shame."

Silk turned around, with growing anger filling her eyes. She removed her hands from the dress and let it fall to the ground. "Do you want to have a look so that you can make fun of me too?"

"That's not what I..." said Victor, squinting and lifting his glasses to scratch between his eyes as he tilted his head back. "I apologize. It's just... I'm a very analytical person. So, I observe things and speak without thinking. I'm not... I'm not making fun of you or how you look."

"Then how do I look?"

"We're both near naked. Okay, well, you are naked, and half covered in blood. I don't think now is the time to ask how you look."

"Do I look like a woman to you like this?" said Silk, lifting her arms.

"What's happening right now? How did we get here?"

"Answer me."

"Yes, you look like a woman. A very ghostly, murderous woman. Are we done here?" asked Victor, looking away.

"Then what ab—"

"Nope, not going to continue this conversation." Victor placed his hand on Silk's shoulders, spinning her around towards the river. "As your reluctantly appointed caretaker, I say it's time for a bath." He then gave Silk a light push, sending her off towards the water. "Now, off with you."

"Fine," said Silk in frustration, before heading off into the stream.

Victor went back and sat down beside his clothing, watching as the naked assassin splashed around in the water.

The great sixth general, Victor Krill, now reduced to the caretaker of a temperamental ashen-skinned assassin with acceptance issues. One really can't predict how one's life will turn out. I can predict battles, enemy movements days ahead of time, but it's the dangerous women who seem to be the weakness I can't overcome. Maybe I should have become a Precebal Monk.

I don't think they accept women yet.

Well, at the very least, Frenka protects me from becoming seduced by the murder princess over there. Maybe she was right. Having someone who wants you to come back to them doesn't feel that bad. Although if she heard me say that she'd call me stupid for arguing in the first place.

Oh, and here she comes. Her naked and scary splendor only matched by the ridiculousness of this situation I'm in.

Silk walked back up to Victor, grabbing the wedding dress and placing it down beside him, and sitting down on top of it.

"You're not going to put your clothes on, are you?" asked Victor, taking a deep breath and closing his eyes, trying to accept the ever-growing complications of his situation.

"I want to wear myself for a while."

"Of course, you do. But wearing yourself? That's an odd way of putting it. Do you stay transformed a lot?"

"All the time, mostly. We aren't allowed to be out in front of people wearing ourselves. I probably haven't worn myself this long since I was a child. It's just easier to wear other people. No one likes it when I'm wearing myself."

"Well, I'll admit, you took some time getting used to. Even for me," said Victor scratching his head looking over the water. "Where are you from? Surely not here."

"Sister and I are from Ursjun, or that's where Grennok says he found us."

Grennok huh? I guess that's who I need to look out for, or maybe look for, depending on what I can find out, thought Victor as he picked up a rock off the ground, rubbing it between his fingers. "That's far away. Have you ever left Ellendor before?"

"No, we've only been in the five kingdoms. He probably wouldn't let us go anyway."

"You said you had a sister. Is she back home?"

"Don't know, haven't seen her in a year. We were close though, I felt her when I was in Mari."

"Felt her? Another odd term, how does that work?"

"We can feel each other, and share memories. I'll know she's there if we get close enough to one another."

"I guess I will just chalk that one up to the long list of magic powers I will never truly understand. Why were you in Mari, trying to find a vacation spot?"

Silk laughed, "You seem to think we have an easy life. We had to—" Silk's words vanished in her mouth as she reached for her throat in confusion. Then, with eyes wide, she looked at Victor.

"I guess I was pushing my luck with that question."

Silk narrowed her eyes at him and frowned.

"Maybe we'll get farther next time," said Victor, standing up and wiping off his small clothes, then reaching down his hand to Silk. "Well, come along, my naked friend; we've got a long way till we reach Molask."

CHAPTER 15

In an open field in the middle of the day, the wind blew across the green grass as Oscar and Jacob sat atop their horses with their army in full armour. Their black armor shining over the green grass appearing as if a black cloud hovered just above the land. Ahead of them were dozens of mountain people who stood brandishing their weapons. They were dressed in fur clothing, some even shirtless. The sound of the screams carried across the battlefield as they yelled and whistled, ready for their war.

"I don't really see anyone worth keeping," said Jacob.

"Well, we were informed that this was the largest clan in

the area. Someone here must be the reason for it," replied Oscar.

"You think he's holding up somewhere?"

"If so, that's a new development. The mountain folk aren't exactly known for their tactics."

"I think that's him now," said Jacob, squinting as a large man wearing the fur of a bear across his back appeared from out of the trees on horseback, accompanied by four other riders.

The mountain men rode through their clan, halting ahead of them but still within arrow range. The big man began pounding his chest before sticking his fist out towards Oscar and Jacob.

"Seems he wants to talk," said Jacob.

"Good, it'll make the slaughter less costly to us. Let's go," Oscar turned back to his men. "Three of you follow me; the rest stay here."

After three more riders joined alongside them, Oscar and Jacob rode forward to meet the mountain man, stopping within speaking distance of them.

"I am Whastet, Leader of Red Shield clan. Why have you come here?"

"I am Oscar, leader of Black Jewels clan. I've come to have you all join my clan."

Whastet laughed, looking around and waving his arms, "Why we join you? You have small clan. We are strong and mighty, and there are many of us. We even have magic in our clan."

"We have many more of us, but we only bring what we need to defeat you. If you join us, we will give you many women for your bed and strong men for your women."

"We kill you and take your women."

"You may try... ah, a question before we start. We have small children in camp. Small girls, what will you do with them when you kill us?"

Whastet gave Oscar an odd look, "We turn boys into

warriors, and when girls are women, we give them to warriors to make strong offspring for clan."

"You're not the type to fuck children then? Good."

"What a thing to ask before a battle." Jacob chuckled, looking at his father. "I think our little baby has made you soft, Father. Never thought I'd see the day when you planned a battle around someone who's not even here."

"Well, we can't have the home looking like a mess when she returns. Otherwise, we risk giving her a second chance to burn the camp down. It'd be a shame to have to go through that mess again." He turned his horse around, before turning back to Whastet and his men. "Feel free to attack us whenever you like; we'll try to leave as many of you alive as possible before you surrender." He and his men then galloped back off to their army.

Whastet shook his head, "Old man crazy, prepare to attack. We take their women and keep only their men who kill one of ours. We not need the weak ones."

The sun had barely moved before the battle started, with Jacob rushing ahead in the vanguard. Ten mounted men ahead of him in formation with spears at the ready. Arrows flew through the air towards Jacob and his men as they galloped into battle, only to be carried off by gusts of magical wind before they ever came close to the charging men. The Black Jewels spearmen plowed into the mountain men, quickly breaking what little formation they had. The following explosion of sound was the screams of men as the horses trampled through the brigade.

Once routed, then came the Sakari rushing in on foot, with their short swords and shields. The first wave crashed into the mountain men like a battering ram, sending the frantic mountain folk falling on their backs only to then be stabbed by the spears of foot soldiers that trailed behind the Sakari as they hacked their way through the crowd.

The mountain mages began casting spells of fire that were quickly blocked by shields, whisked away, or negated completely as they themselves met another mage of the Black Jewels in combat. The sounds of screams and clashing metal sounded throughout the air as the battle waged on.

Jacob saw Whastet on the ground fighting off two men. He cut down one with his axe, blocking an attack with his shield, and slicing the throat of another man. He noticed Jacob ahead of him, grinned and began making his way through the crowd. Jacob dismounted, sending his horse off in order to meet Whastet in combat. The large man rushed at Jacob swinging down with his axe. Jacob blocked it with his shield. The impact rattled through his arm as he shifted his weight back and thrust his sword forward at Whastet's chest.

The large man dodged, bringing his axe down hard once again on Jacob's shield, forcing him back as Whastet followed up with slashes. Jacob nimbly jumped backward every time Whastet lunged at him, keeping his shield forward to take any blow he had to prepare for.

"Does all the Black Jewels clan know how to do is run?" taunted Whastet, the annoyance in his voice as clear as the blade in his hand.

"Just... getting a bit... of exercise is all? Feel free to keep attacking me."

Whastet walked up and kicked Jacob's shield with such force that it sent him stumbling backward trying to balance himself. The large man was strong, as Jacob had expected. Molan had also been strong. Jacob quickly stood back to his feet, balancing himself, and began looking around. He then backed up again, with Whastet following behind him.

"Right, well, I guess that'll do for now," said Jacob as he tightened his grip on his shield and sword, planting his feet into the ground in an attacking stance.

"Oh, will you fight now? Or is plan to kill me by running away?"

"So sorry about that. I was told to take you alive, which would have been harder to do with so many people around.

But we're far enough away that that shouldn't be a problem now. So... whenever you're ready."

Whastet turned to see his clan downhill from him. They were fighting and losing to the Black Jewels clan, "After I kill, I will return to them."

"Simple-minded, but honest. I respect that."

The large mountain man charged at Jacob as their shields clashed against each other. The wood of the bucklers crackled under their force as each one tried to push each other back. Whastet's strength won out, forcing Jacob to relinquish ground, allowing Whastet to send him floating back. He landed only to see the large man closing in on him, Jacob swung his blade at the Whastet's head, which he easily blocked with his shield.

Whastet tried to bring down his axe on Jacob's head. Jacob stepped forward into the attack dropping his shield and gripping Whastet's shield arm by the wrist while jumping forward and using his shoulder to hit the man's elbow, forcing him to release his grip on the weapon. Jacob dropped his blade and punched the large man in the face which didn't seem to have much effect at all.

"Good, but I am stronger," said Whastet with a smile on his face as he dropped his own shield, gripping Jacob by the arm with one hand and around the neck with the other. "You will die now."

Jacob felt Whastet tightening his hand around his throat, but smiled back at the large man, "Sorry... seems... I win." Jacob raised his arms, gripping the man's head in his hands as his palms began to glow.

Stop, release me. The mountain man froze and slowly began to loosen his grip around Jacob's neck before standing in front of him with his arms at his side. He then began focusing his magic into Whastet, trying to send a command into his mind.

Okay, big man, you're feeling tired. It's time for you to take a nap. And the large man dropped to his knees before passing out on the ground next to him. Jacob sat down beside the mountain man, shaking his head. "It's always a pain in the ass, taking them alive." He rubbed at his throat, "I guess I should be happy I didn't get choked again. I wonder what that bastard is up to."

Later, Whastet awoke to find himself on his knees, his arms bound as all his surviving men knelt on the ground behind him, their weapons taken from them. Around them all stood the Black Jewels soldiers, holding their weapons.

"Oh, he finally moved. Must mean he's awake then," said Oscar behind Whastet.

Whastet turned around to see Oscar sitting down in his chair, looking down at him with Jacob standing beside him. "What happened? Why am I alive? Why you not kill me?"

"Because I will have you and all your men join Black Jewels clan. I will give them homes and wives in exchange for loyalty."

"Kingdom lives, rather die than become kingdom man. Kill me, keep men if you want, but I not become your man."

"Sadly, that's not how this works. I didn't come here for them. I came here for you, Whastet of the former Red Shield clan. I require strong men, and to get strong men; I will slaughter hundreds." Oscar looked to Jacob, who then walked over, grabbing one of Whastet's men by the hair and placing a dagger under his throat.

"What, stop, why you do this?" asked Whastet, looking up at Oscar,

"Because that is what I am, Whastet of the former Red Shield clan. I am the World Burner, and if you do not join me, I will make you watch as I have each of your men murdered before you. Then I will drag you back to your village to make you watch as I murder all the women. And if you do not join then, I will have you watch as I murder all the children." Oscar leaned forward in his chair, a sadistic smile taking over his face. "You will watch it all burn until Whastet of former Red Shield Clan is the last of the Red Shield Clan."

Whastet looked up at Oscar and back to his men, "You demon-man."

"Aye, that I am. But only you can save your clan from this demon. You either serve this demon clan, or you watch as everything burns. It is your decision." Oscar smiled, leaning down looking Whastet in the eyes. "I want to see how many of your people we must put down before we break you."

Whastet looked back at his men, before turning back to Oscar once again with gritted teeth. "If Whastet joins, then you not kill clan?"

"They will become part of Black Jewels clan. I will allow them to stay here to live. But you will come with me, along with twenty-seven of your men, Three for every one of mine that died here today. Your women and children will be safe, and you will be given new wives and husbands to live in that camp of yours."

"Kingdom wives and husbands?"

"Black Jewels' wives and husbands."

Whastet looked back at his men before turning back to Oscar and lowering his head. "Whastet will join Black Jewels' clan."

"Good," said Oscar, who then nodded to Jacob and watched as his son released the man's hair, removing the blade from his neck. "Unbind him and give him and a few of his men horses." Oscar looked down to Whastet, "You will arrive back here in three days' time with your men to serve me. The rest will be left with the women to protect your Village. Let it be known that you are now part of the Black Jewels clan, and if any other clan dares to attack you, then I, Oscar the World Burner will personally come and wipe them out."

Oscar turned to Amos, "You go with them and answer

any questions their Jalahe has for you.”

“Yes, Sir. But why do you always have me do it?”

“Because you’re a scrawny lad, that’s not intimidating and there’s no need to send an army to a land I’ve already conquered. You will do fine enough. Sending troops with them, means we’re scared of them; sending you with them proves we are not.”

“Doesn’t that just mean no one’s afraid of me?”

“Aye, that it does. But don’t worry, we all have a role to play. And the role of a weak nonthreatening man is one you play perfectly.”

Amos sighed, “I’ll go get my horse,” and walked off.

“Cheer up, Amos,” said Jacob as he followed behind Amos, placing a hand on his shoulder, “You’re the ambassador of The Black Jewels clan. Father just has a bad way of putting it. I promise if anything were to happen to you, he’d be quite upset.”

“You really think so?”

“Have you ever wondered why he never lets you go off into battle?”

“I thought that was because he thinks I’m weak.”

“Then why does he always wait for you to show up before he starts planning a battle?”

“He does that?”

“You never noticed? Father said it himself. We all have a role to play; yours is not in combat. So, try to think about what Father is using you for?”

Amos dropped his head. “I shall try to think about it, Sir.”

Remember, that lad Victor was also an ambassador, and he bested me in combat. Just because you look weak; doesn’t mean you have to be weak.”

“Hey, I didn’t think of that. Thank you, Sir Jacob.”

“No problem, lad. Now mount up. You’ve got some ambassadoring to do.”

Amos chuckled, “Yes, Sir.”

Oscar watched Amos, and his new crop of mountain men leave off back up into the mountains. "You fought him; what do you think?"

"He's probably not as strong as Molan was. Molan was just a monster in human skin. But he's strong, and his men seem to respect him. He might even be a better leader than Molan. Why did you ask for him to return with three times the men? They only killed a few of us and I think just a single Sakari."

"They killed half a dozen well-trained soldiers, and I have to replace them with untrained men. Three to one should do to properly balance it out until they are trained correctly."

"And I'm guessing; I'll be doing this training."

"Volunteering yourself for the job, eh? I didn't realize I raised such a dutiful son."

"One day, this way you have of going about things is going to get us all killed."

"Happy to hear you approve."

A soldier rode up and handed Oscar a piece of parchment. He opened it and began smiling before giving the paper to Jacob.

Jacob raised a brow at his father as he took the paper from his hand and began to read. "A noble wants you to kill both sons of a duke. And here I thought that nobility were above such forms of treason."

"As they say, loyalty only lasts a lifetime because you can't stay loyal to the dead."

"Apparently, no one is trustworthy these days."

"And weren't ya just saying that my way of doing things would get us killed." Oscar stood from his seat. "Seems to me that there are a lot of others out there with far worse ways about them. Just call everyone into the tent. We can decide how to get this done inside rather than out in this damned sun."

Inside the tent, Oscar sat around a small coffee table with Gregga, Jacob, and Dessi, along with a few other soldiers.

"Okay, it's the city of Orlana. The Duke there has two sons that apparently have been arguing over succession rights and not a few nobles have died trying to pick sides. So, an invested party has taken it upon themselves to ask us to do their dirty work. Any ideas?"

"How big this city? Why not just rush in and kill them?" asked Gregga.

"Two main problems with that. First, I don't want to be known for this murder. It's all well and good if we'd meet on a battlefield, mercenaries would be expected to take out a noble or two. Second, they want it done in the city and to make it look like an accident."

"Are the two guarded?" asked Jacob, folding his arms. "There should be plenty of ways to go about this. Carriage falls into a lake, gentlemen's duel with another noble, any of the classics should work, really."

"I would assume they both have guards who are fairly competent at fighting, but one of those might be the best option. Maybe have it look like one of the guards killed one of them. Doesn't have to be at the same time. Just within a day or two of each, so that neither son can claim the title of future duke."

Dessi placed her finger down on the parchment, "Didn't you say this came from a noble? Aren't these types always throwing some fancy balls? Why not just kill 'em there? That way they'd all be too busy suspecting each other to come chasing after us."

"And who's going to be one to pull off this stunt of yours?" asked Oscar.

"Well, you did just fork over all that gold to cream over this body of mine. I figure I might as well get some use out of it. They're both men after all."

"A point I would concede if this didn't seem as if it would cost me even more gold."

"You're the one who said you wanted it to look like an accident, and we both know I'm the one here who does that. And besides, your son hasn't taken me out on a date in forever. This'll be good for you to play the supportive father."

Jacob smiled at Dessi, "You're really having fun this time, aren't you?"

"So come on, father-in-law, let the children go out and have their fun."

Oscar shook his head and sighed, "We'll head to the city after we're done here, where I'll have some men ask questions. And as suggested, Dessi will take lead on this job."

CHAPTER 16

A few days later, Isha sat in class as Miss Webblebottom pointed to several shapes on the board.

"The way magic works is through the mind. Your body is able to absorb magic from around you as your mind filters it for use. If some of you have ever tried continuous use of your magic, then you've experienced the trauma that too much magic at one time will do to you. The overabundance of magical energy on the brain will have several adverse effects. That is because magic itself is toxic and the brain acts as a filter. If you overload the brain, then you will pass out because the brain literally shuts itself down to protect itself."

"But my father uses magic all the time," said Freedo with his hand raised. "And I've never seen it affect him like that."

"That's because your father most likely has had proper training. With training you can increase your brain's tolerance in terms of filtering magical energy. But make no mistake, we all have our limits, and it is here where you will find them."

"Excuse me, teacher," said Pavel. "But magic is the same for everyone, so why are some mages stronger than others?

"A good question, Pavel. The answer for that is simple. Not all of us are made the same. Some people are better at running than others, some are better at swimming. For those physical traits, we say they have a natural talent. Well, the same can be said for magic. Some children are said to have started using magic at ages as early as three. And while I feel terribly sorry for the parents having to deal with such an occurrence, it does prove not all mages are made equal since most of us didn't find our magical talents until our early teens. I myself found mine at fourteen."

Miss Webblebottom waved her wand, and an image of the human body appeared in bright colors in the air.

"We've found that many things can affect the adaptability of a mage; from their breathing habits, to the type of food that they consume over their lifetime. Our Sakari students up there should be proof of that. Despite their lack of proper training in magic, they have shown a remarkable potency for magic over this last month. It makes me wonder what other gems the Sakari wilds are hiding."

Jacinta and Makeba smiled down at Miss Webblebottom before a magical bell appeared above the class and began shaking and ringing in the air.

"Well, it seems our time is up," said Miss Webblebottom as the students stood up from their seats. "See you all tomorrow and be sure to practice with your wands. You will be needing them for tomorrow's class."

Isha stood from her seat and saw Pavel smiling at her. Waving at him, she walked over.

"Are you ready for the big test?"

"I hope so, but I don't think I understand how to use shields yet."

"Don't worry, we still have some time to practice. They did put us together as a team, so I think it's best if we get some practice in. I can come by Heart House later if you have time."

"Okay, I'd like that," said Isha with a small-blush.

"Hey, don't leave us out just because you're flirting," said Marlene as her and Serpene walked over.

"We are not flirting," replied Isha, feeling embarrassed.

"Girly boy coming to visit again?" spoke Jacinta, walking up with Makeba.

"How many times do I have to tell you to stop calling him that?" asked Isha, blushing even more.

"Oh... it's quite alright," said Pavel, laughing. "I'm quite aware of what I look like. If anything, it's sort of refreshing to have such honesty. Usually, people either stay away or treat me like some type of king when they are around me."

"Why? Are you the son of a noble person?"

Pavel twisted his head, squinting his eyes, "Do you seriously not know?"

"Know what?" asked Isha.

"No, it's nothing. If anything, it's something that you'll find out on your own sooner or later, anyway. Until then, let's just continue our training as usual."

"Ah... okay."

"Does pretty boy have special magic?" asked Jacinta as the other children began to leave the room. But they were soon parted as Soulden entered and began gazing around until she spotted them.

"Pavel, a moment of your time, child," said Soulden.

Pavel looked down at Soulden and sighed before turning back to Isha, "Seems I must be going. I will stop back by

Heart house before it gets dark. See you then." He made his way down the steps as Isha watched Soulden lead him out of the room.

"Does sister intend to make pretty girly boy her mate?" asked Makeba.

"What? No," said Isha in a fluster as she turned to her sister. "He's just my training partner."

"Good, he's too skinny for sister. Sister needs big strong man like Jacob. We approve of Jacob."

"Wha... I'm not gonna marry Jacob. And besides he has Dessi."

"We know, both Dessi and sister marry Jacob. Then you will be happy."

"Wha... how... how can you know what will make me happy."

"Because we know sister and sister likes Jacob, and Leo, and maybe Pavel. But Pavel is girl boy and sister needs strong man."

Isha placed her hand over her eyes shaking, her head, "How do you two just say these things so easily?" She then pointed a finger at Makeba and then Jacinta. "Fine, what about you two? You must like someone. What about Freedo, Makeba? You two always pick on me, but I bet you're too afraid to admit who you like," she said with a smug look on her face in satisfaction, knowing she finally got her sisters in their own teasing game.

Jacinta and Makeba looked at each other, and Makeba scratched her head in confusion.

"What sister mean? We marry who sister marries."

Isha's face twisted as her eyes squeezed together, her lips sinking in as she sucked in her cheeks. "Wha... what?"

"Sister Isha silly, mother was to give us to Uncle Funnyman. But he gone now, so now mother make you care-sister. And we marry who you marry. Sister Isha say she would do this when in bath with mother."

Isha's mind began racing back to her time with Gregga.

Indeed she did agree to share and become one with her sisters. But she didn't know what that meant then. "Oh... no."

"We think Jacob good for you. Strong man, make many babies when we ready."

"Hey, Makeba," said Freedo, walking up with a smile on his face, holding a textbook. "You wanna practice with me. We can learn... what's wrong?" he asked as he noticed the stunned look on Isha's face.

Isha stood there for a moment and just stared into the innocent faces of her sisters after Makeba told her their marriage plans. She then slowly raised a finger and opened her mouth, but no words would come out. Instead, all she managed was an, "Oh...no... no no no no," and she just headed down the steps and began to leave the room with her sisters following behind her.

They left the school and eventually made their way to the Heart House, where they found Elena and Rima working outside, picking up leaves.

"Welcome home, you three. I hope you enjoyed class-es today," said Elena as she ran the rake over a pile over the grass. "Isha, are you okay? You look as if you've seen a ghost."

"It's fine. I'm... I'm fine." *I don't wanna think about it.*

"We will practice using shields tomorrow," said Makeba.

"Oh, you're that far along, now are you? I guess classes are going well for you then," replied Elena as she rotated her hand around, causing the leaves in the yard to swirl in around themselves in a pile on the ground. Then she slashed her hands, splitting the stack in two, and spaced them apart next to her.

"Oh, wow, Elena good with magic," said Jacinta as she picked up a leaf from the pile.

"I've had a lot of practice over the years. Hey, Rima, mind giving me a hand?"

"Sure," said Rima as she looked at the Sakari girls.

"Wanna help?"

"Yes, we help," said Jacinta.

"Okay, show me that push magic and let's lift these leaves into the air."

Rima and the two Sakari girls began channeling magical energy as the wind started to blow around the stack of leaves and lifted the pile into the air forming a giant ball of hovering leaves spinning in rotation with a few stragglers orbiting the mass of brown and green shrubbery.

"Okay, just hold her there for a little while longer," said Elena as she focused on the mass of lawn debris. "Spark." Slowly from the inside, the large mass of leaves began to burn until the swirling air turned the once swirling mass into a small inferno that quickly consumed the leaves. "Okay, girls toss it away and try not to burn the roof, or Leo's gonna be very upset with us."

They all raised their arms, sending the fiery ball of magic into the sky and released their magic when satisfied with the height, watching as the fire streamed out and vanished in the air.

"Wow, you girls have gotten good at this fast," said Rima. "It usually takes years for people to start using their magic together. Timing is usually a pain in the butt."

"Jacinta and I always play together to see who can make magic longer. I always win"

"Hey, that only cause it boring. Me rather do something else."

"What do you girls have planned for today? Just gonna go inside and sleep?" asked Elena.

"Today we teach Isha more Sakari words. She still very bad at it," said Makeba.

"Hey, I'm trying. Sakari is hard, and there are too many *ah* words."

Makeba smiled at her sister, "Then Isha will have girly boy and friends come to visit. I think that she likes him."

"Makeba stop that, we are just practicing. And Freedo is

always chasing behind you."

"Yes, but Freedo weak, not strong. Will be bad mate. We think sister should pick Jacob for man. Will make strong babies and he has strong magic."

"I'm not talking about this," said Isha as she placed hands over her ears and quickly stepped toward the door. She reached for the handle only to have the door open before she could grab it; losing her balance, she fell forward, burying her face into Leo's stomach.

"What's everyone doing out he... Oof," said Leo as Isha crashed into him. "What's going on here? Am I under attack by little girls again?" Leo pushed Isha back, holding her up, "You, okay?"

"Sorry, I'm fine."

"Oh, you should hug Leo now. Make sure sister no longer scared of men," said Makeba.

Isha turned back to her sister, "I'm fine; I don't need that anymore."

"Hey, just because you don't need it doesn't mean I don't," said Leo, mockingly pouting, sticking out his lip, and shaking his head. "I've grown accustomed to our daily hugs. Are you telling me that I am now forced to go hugless? That's so heartless. Makeba, Jacinta, why is your sister so mean to me? And after everything I've done for her."

"Ah, fine," blurted out Isha before closing her eyes and wrapping her arms around Leo.

"See, there we go. Now count to ten," said Leo while patting her on the head.

Isha held onto him tight with her face red and counted to ten. They had done this dozens of times now. And with Leo, Isha no longer felt frozen around him. Although the sheer embarrassment of everyone watching her attach herself to him was its own form of torture for her. She finished counting to ten in her head, then released her hold on him before running upstairs away from everyone.

Elena shook her head, smiling, "You're going to

embarrass that poor girl to death. You know that, right?"

Leo turned towards Elena with his hands out, "Sounds like someone over there needs a hug."

"Hey, you keep your hands to yourself, I don't—"

"Get her, girls."

Jacinta and Makeba latched onto the sides of Elena.

"Ahhh, let go! You little traitors," said Elena before she was consumed by Leo's arms as they went rolling across the other bundle of leaves together.

Chloe stuck her head out of the door, watching everyone playing with leaves falling down around them. "Ah, I think the sweet meats are ready, Mr. Leo, Sir."

Leo raised his head up with leaves in his hair, "Oh good," He then turned to Jacinta and Makeba. "You two hungry?" The girls nodded, and they all went inside the house, half-covered in leaves and dirt.

"Ahh, no you don't. We just cleaned up in there," said Elena, who was just as covered in dirt and leaves as she chased after them.

Later that night, they all relaxed around the house. Elena sat teaching the girls about magic. While Leo sat in front of Chloe, healing her arm.

"Well, it seems to be coming along nicely," said Leo, moving his hand down Chloe's arm. "How has it been since I started healing you?"

"It… it doesn't hurt to move my fingers anymore."

"Yeah, I wanted to heal the nerve endings first. You should be able to move your fingers a lot more these coming days in terms of range of motion. But I won't start healing the skin until I am sure that you have full mobility back into your hands."

"Yes, Sir."

"And stop calling me that. Call me Leo, like everyone

else does."

"But you're a teacher and—"

"And this teacher is telling you to call him Leo, or are you the type to disobey a teacher?"

"No, Sir... I mean Leo."

Leo reached to his side, pulled out a vial and began rubbing oil over Chloe's hand and arm. "Okay, that should do it for today. It's getting dark. Come on, I'll walk you home."

"No, you don't have to."

"It's fine. I need to go see Soulden, anyway. Apparently she has something for me."

"Oh, okay... Ah, thank you," said Chloe as her cheeks began to redden.

"Oh, does the scar-handed girl like Leo too?" asked Jacinta, walking up to the table and grabbing a piece of candy.

"What? No, I just—"

"Your face turn red like sister Isha when she look at Leo."

"My face does not turn red," said Chloe as her face reddened to a deeper shade.

Leo smiled, "I knew you girls would come around to my charms eventually," Leo threw out his arms. "All of the girls here should just marry me, and we could all be a happy family."

"Leo, stop being an idiot."

"Don't worry, Elena, you can marry me first. I think it's only fair since we've known each other the longest."

"Oh well, how nice of you. I can't wait for the day you make me a real woman. But until then, stop being an idiot, and walk Chloe home."

"Yes, Dear, I'm sorry dear," said Leo in a monotone voice.

Rima and Isha laughed at Leo and Elena, bickering like a married couple.

Leo stood up from the chair. "Come on, Chloe, let's get

you back."

Chloe followed behind Leo, frowning at Isha, who was sitting on the floor next to Jacinta and Makeba as they tried teaching her more Sakari words.

"I swear, what are we going to do with that idiot," said Elena, walking up to the three girls on the floor. "What are you three up to? Practicing your magic? I didn't think you will learn how to link words until your second year."

"We teach sister Isha Sakari. She still bad at it," replied Jacinta.

"I'm getting better, and you're still bad at using your in-between words. Don't act like you're all perfect."

"Why are you learning Sakari? Do you plan to go live there?"

"No, I just..." said Isha, trying to think of the right words to use.

"Our Mama is Sakari, so sister Isha is trying to impress her and make her happy," spoke Makeba.

Elena squinted her eyes, looking at the girls, "I've actually been wondering about that. You call each other sisters, and you're so white, and your hair is blonde. Is your father from the kingdoms, then?"

"I've been wondering about that too," said Rima walking over, looking curiously at Isha, "What do you mean her hair is blonde. It's black like her sisters, isn't it?"

"No, it's blonde," replied Elena, "How are you confusing that with black? It's almost perfectly golden."

"Oh," said Makeba, shaking her head. "That because sister Isha has magic hair and eyes, it look different to everyone?"

"What?" asked Elena in surprise.

They all made a round of telling each other what color Isha's hair, and eyes were.

"What? How is that even possible?" asked Elena, leaning down and rubbing a lock of Isha's hair between her fingers. "I mean, I've heard of illusion magic, but magic that affects everyone who sees you differently? That's not something I've seen before. Who taught you that spell?"

"I don't know. Everyone just says that's what it is. I never knew it was there or how to even turn it off."

"Why don't you ask Miss Fowler?" asked Rima.

"Who's that?"

"Oh yeah, since you're a first-year, you wouldn't know her. She teaches advanced magical research. If you ask her, she might know what's happening with you and how to fix it."

"Where do I meet her? I don't know the school all that well yet."

"That's fine. I'll take you to see her tomorrow. I'm sure she'll be interested once she hears about it."

"Okay."

Makeba looked outside of the window at the stars in the sky. "Sister Isha, where is the pretty girly boy? Wasn't he supposed to come visit today?"

Isha glanced outside the window, "I don't know, I guess he couldn't make it." She then turned to her sister, frowning. "And stop calling him that. Use his name. It's mean when you call him that."

Elena sat down in a chair, "Come sit between my legs Isha and I'll pin up your hair before bed." She then began twirling Isha's hair after she crawled over. "Now, what's all this about a pretty boy? You falling for a boy already?"

"What? No. He's my training partner in Mr. Higgins' class. He said he would come by today to help me train for tomorrow's shield test."

"Well, it's too late for that now. I wish you would have said something. I would have been happy to help teach you shields."

"It's fine. I've done it a few times. I'll be okay, tomorrow, I think."

"Okay then, what's the boy's name?"

"Pavel."

"Pavel, as in Pavel Hemmington?"

"Yes, why? Do you know him?"

"The whole school knows him; he's the prodigy of the Hemmington family. He's one of those special types who's been using magic since he was a toddler. All the second and third years talk about him. He's even stronger than some of the teachers here." Elena playfully shook Isha's head. "Well, you sure did pick up a popular friend."

"So, pretty girly..."

Isha narrowed her eyes at Jacinta.

"I mean, is Pavel boy really strong?" asked Jacinta, looking up at Elena.

"Yeah, if anything, he's one of the strongest in the school."

Jacinta turned to Makeba, "Then maybe sister did pick good man for us."

Elena finished with Isha's hair, "What do you mean, pick man for... us?"

"Yes, sister Isha picks mate for us. Mother gave her the right and sister accepted. She now care-sister."

"Well, that's a big responsibility; I didn't know..."

Isha quickly stood up, "No, I'm not doing that. That's just weird, I'm not doing it. I don't care what I promised. Don't you both see how wrong that is?"

"But you promised moth—"

"I don't care. I refuse. I won't do it, and I'm tired of both of you acting like it's okay," said Isha as she quickly ran up the stairs to their room, leaving her sisters looking bewildered down on the floor with Elena.

After entering the room she saw their three beds all pushed together that they slept in every night. Isha frowned but crawled into bed, throwing the blankets over her head. *I'm not wrong. They're the ones who are wrong. They can pick their own boyfriend. Why is everything always my responsibility? They're both thirteen, too. But maybe I didn't say it right; If I just explain to them, then they'll understand. I just need to get them to understand.*

She waited for her sisters to come join her in bed, but she never heard them. Never heard their footsteps in the night making their way to the room. Until she would fall asleep, all she would hear was silence and the inner voice of her own thoughts.

The next morning Isha awoke to the sun shining down upon her in an empty bed. She quickly got dressed and made her way downstairs, where Elena was busy casting spells on one of the pillars of the house.

"Oh, good morning. Did you sleep well?"

Isha looked around the house, "Where's Makeba and Jacinta?"

"They've already left. I think they're quite upset with you about last night."

Isha shrugged her shoulders, "They are just being unfair; they do and say whatever they want and don't think about how I feel."

Elena sighed, "Are you really sure about that, Isha?"

"Of course, I am; you've seen how they play around all the time. They only think about what they want."

"Isha, I have a question. Why do you think those girls are here at this school?"

"What? I don't know."

"Because I was talking to them last night, and they said the only reason they came to this school was so their sister wouldn't get lonely,"

"I didn't ask them to do that."

"Maybe not, but I bet you didn't try to stop them from coming either."

"No, But... it's still... I mean."

"And who were the ones calming you down when you were too scared to let Leo touch you."

Isha sighed, "They were."

"And who was fighting with you when you got into trouble on your first day here."

"Okay," said Isha, shaking her head in frustration, "Do you think I should apologize?"

"That's up to you, honey. All I know is that me and you fit in nice and easy around this school. We look like everybody else, but them girls don't have anybody else but you, and last night, the only person they had, who they followed here, practically told them she didn't want them anymore."

"I didn't say that."

"Maybe not, but that's what they heard."

Isha screamed, "Why does it always end up like this," and headed for the door.

"Wait, what about Miss Fowler today? Oh dear, and away she goes."

Isha went to class alone for the first time since she arrived at the magical school. On the way, she found herself being more aware of other students talking to one another and suddenly started to feel a lot more alone than she did before. Making her way into the castle and through the corridors towards class, she entered the room. Immediately she noticed Jacinta and Makeba sitting next to each other near the front of the class next to Freedo, who had the happiest grin on his face.

"All right, everyone take your seats," said Miss Gallows.

The class all sat down as Isha walked up the steps, sitting down by herself in her usual spot.

"Now today, we will talk about the ratio between women and men when it comes to mages. Surely you all have noticed the abundance of females in the class compared to the four male students. Now, why do you suppose that is?"

"Because girls are better at magic," said Marlene as the class laughed.

"That's not entirely wrong. As females, our bodies are simply more receptive to magic than our male counterparts.

Which simply leads to more female mages being born than males. Now, who here knows why?"

The class murmured amongst themselves, but no one spoke up.

"Ah, well, the answer is quite simple, really. And that is babies. Magic itself is a form of life. It blows in the wind all around us and is a part of the trees that give us the air we breathe. And as females, since we are able to grow life within us, we naturally are more receptive to the thing that grants life. In short, magic is much like motherhood."

"So, we're all magic babies then," chuckled one of the boys.

"In a way, yes. You laugh, but some children whose parents were predisposed to a certain type of magic have been sold or held hostage for a substantial sum. Why, just a few months ago, it was found out that the Starlight Queen's child was stolen. Now, how that even happened is beyond me. You'd think a castle filled with guards would be the safest place imaginable for a child. But If any of you boys or girls were born with a natural talent for mind or shadow magic, you would be looking at quite the bachelor's life in high society, with your pick of any suitors of your choosing."

"My father married a shadow mage after my mother fell from a tower," said another girl in class. "She's the one who helped me get into this school. Why are they so important?"

The class was silent for a moment after the girl's words.

"I'm not sure help is the right term for your situation, darling. But after graduation you may want to look at having an extended stay here, rather than going back home. Perhaps you have a future as a teacher of sorts," said Miss Gallows with a pitying look on her face. "But as to your question as to why shadow and mind mages are so valuable; it's because they are oddities, mutations in the normal magical spectrum. Typically, you'd have your fire, soil, and the occasional mage who can call up water. But every now and then, the mixture of mage genes transforms and creates a child that is able to bend the laws of what we know as traditional magic."

I wonder what a shadow mage looks like. Does that mean there's also a light or sun mage?

She walked over to her desk and picked up a paperweight of an apple. Magic began to circle her hand and the apple changed into a small wooden wagon. "You see, I used illusion magic, which is a mixture of essential water and fire magic to reflect the light in the room to appear as whatever I desire. If you're good enough, you can transform anything."

Wow, will I be able to do that?

Placing the wooden horse back on her desk, it glowed and slowly turned back into an apple. "But shadow magic breaks this rule, whereas it reflects darkness and is able to make solid constructs that are able to interact with the world. Imagine being able to fly on a giant shadow bird, or control an army of shadow soldiers. This is exactly what Propel the Shadow King did over eight hundred years ago. He was a mage so powerful and talented that he was able to fight off the attacks of entire armies with his shadow soldiers. It took the combined might of the three golden kingdoms to bring him down. If not, we might all be living in a shadow kingdom now."

"Why is mind magic so important, then? Surely they can't fly with their mind" spoke one of the boys in class.

Thats Jacob. He has that magic. Thought Isha as she remembered the night when she first met Jacob.

"No, but if truth be told, mind magic is probably even more dangerous if applied correctly. Simply because you can't really see it and how it can affect you. Remember, I said that magic is poisonous and that the mind is a filter. Well, what if someone managed to remove that filter and you tried to use magic, granted that would take someone so adept in mental magic that I've never even heard of them? But if they were to turn off your mind's filter, then you might be dead the first time you tried to use magic, or at the very least, knocked senseless. Remember, we take in magic unconsciously all the time. There's no telling what kind of tragic effects it would have."

"That sounds freaky," said Freedo.

"Yes Mr. Tolliver, I imagine it feels quite freaky. Especially if you think about someone controlling your mind. The ability to make someone do whatever you desired, certainly sounds like something a tyrant would do. It's even possible to make someone fall in love with you, or walk around the school naked. There was once the story of a princess in a faraway land who had over one-hundred husbands and all of them were controlled through mind magic. Now some of us adults shiver at the thought of having to deal with a hundred of you boys, but she seemed to handle it fairly well. A durable woman if there ever existed one."

The magical bell appeared in the room above the students once again, making a ringing sound.

"Okay, students, time for you to be off. And you, Miss Lolaine, stay behind. I think we need to have a talk about your family situation."

Isha began to make her way down the steps of the classroom, wanting to talk with Jacinta and Makeba, but her sisters were already out the door by the time she reached the bottom step.

Dammit, what's wrong with them? They could at least speak with me.

Isha left out of the classroom and headed over to combat training with the rest of the class.

"Okay, each of you square off with your partners and we're gonna see what you've learned so far," said Mr. Higgins, grabbing one of the leather balls from a nearby basket and holding it in his hand. "Now remember, your shields can only block objects that are magic or are infused with magical energy. If I throw this ball at you and increase its speed with magic, then it should bounce off your shields

271

as long as you have properly prepared your defenses. But if I just toss the ball with no magical energy on it, it will hit you. You can cushion the ball's impact by using magical padding, but technically, it still hits you. And that'll be another lesson for another day."

Mr. Higgins slapped the ball against his hand, "Alright, all of you come up and get your balls and let's see what you got."

Isha watched as the students each came up grabbing different colored leather balls. Jacinta walked up, grabbing a ball, but refused to look in her direction before heading back over to Makeba.

Fine, be like that, I don't care. Both of you are just being stubborn and selfish.

"But Sir," said another boy in the class. "If that's true, doesn't that mean that we just have to infuse whatever is trying to hit us with magic before it hits us, and then we can shield ourselves from it?"

"How very astute of you, lad. That's exactly what it means. And thank you for volunteering to prove this theory in combat."

"Huh, what do you mean?" asked the boy looking around the room.

Mr. Higgins grabbed a ball, "Okay, everyone, Mr. Brusells has volunteered to be target practice for us. So, on the count of three, I want you all to launch your balls at him as hard as you can. Don't worry about the injury; Sceana has one of the best healers in all the five kingdoms. So really lay into him."

Isha watched as evilish grins overtook the faces of her fellow students.

"Hey, I didn't mean—"

"Get your shields up, boy. I want to see you deflect all these incoming attacks with them skills of yours."

"But that's not—"

"One."

"Wait, wait," said the boy, looking around the room with his hands out in a panic.

"Two."

"This isn't fair, if you do this, I'll report you to the—"

"Three."

"Noooo!" Screamed the boy before he was assaulted by dozens of small leather balls from every direction. Isha watched as the boy's shields didn't deflect a single ball as he raised his leg and arms to cover his face as he was bombarded with attacks from the rest of the class. After it all ended, the boy laid on the floor huddled over in pain as a final ball, that was suspiciously late, came flying in and whacked him in the head.

"The best thing about children is how horribly cruel they can be," said Mr. Higgins with a smirk of pride across his face as he looked down at the boy, "Now, in theory. It is possible to block every attack from every direction. If you are able to make your shields strong enough to repel each attack the moment it hits and focus on the split-second timing that it would take to do such a thing. Then yes, it most likely is doable."

He pointed to the boy on the ground. "But as you can see, it is extremely difficult to manage, and even if you could, the sheer amount of magical energy required to do something of that nature would be ridiculous. So, instead of trying to achieve the impossible, I would suggest you learn to dodge and parry the damn attacks. Anyone else have any questions?"

The class was silent on the matter as a few other students took the boy off the floor and over to a bench, laying him down.

"Good," said Mr. Higgins. "Now, pick up your balls again so that we can start practice."

The students each walked around picking up their leather balls and resuming their position with their partners.

"You there, where's your partner?" asked Mr. Higgins,

calling out to Isha.

"Ah, I don't know." yelled Isha, feeling her body beginning to grow stiff as Mr. Higgin to a step closer to her. "It was supposed to be Pavel, but I haven't seen him since yesterday."

Mr. Higgins rubbed at his chin, stopping in the center of the room, "So the little golden boy's too good to show up for tests, aye." He turned to Chloe who was sitting down in a chair watching everyone. "Alright, fine. Chloe, get your butt over here."

Chloe got up from her seat and walked over to Mr. Higgins and Isha.

"You've been getting that arm of yours worked on, haven't you? You think you're okay enough to throw this ball around."

Chloe turned her attention to Isha and narrowed her eyes, "Yes, sir, I can do it."

"Okay then, let's get started, and I'll..."

A leather ball zoomed past Mr. Higgins smacking Isha on the side of the head, sending her to the ground with the ball bouncing into the air and landing beside her.

"What the..."

Isha's world turned blurry for a second as she hit the floor. Shaking her head and blinking her eyes as she came back to her senses only to see Jacinta and Makeba looking at her for only a second and then turn their eyes away from her. Isha clutched the leather ball that struck her. *I'm... sick.... of this, it's not fair. Everyone only cares about themselves. Nobody cares about me.*

"Dammit Chloe, you were supposed to wait until I—" said Mr. Higgins as the leather ball zoomed by him, striking Chloe in the face sending her flying to the floor as Mr. Higgins stumbled back in surprise, tripping over the cart full of balls and sending them rolling over the floor by the girls.

"Oh, I'm sorry, did that hurt?" said Isha, looking down at

Chloe on the floor. "Now you see what it feels like."

Chloe gritted her teeth at Isha and stood up, grabbing a nearby ball from the floor. Isha saw her and reached down, grabbing another ball of her own. The two girls squared off against each other with their balls drawn back, glowering at one another as if daring the other to make the first move.

"Screw it," said Mr. Higgins, standing up and scratching his head. "I don't know what's gotten into you girls, but if you're gonna fight, then dammit, put up your shields and do it the right way."

And suddenly, leather balls were sent flying across the room as the girls' personal shields went up. Both girls went down several times as their shields broke, and they stood up, activating them again. They hit each other everyplace they could get a good aim in. Arms, legs, especially the face. Nothing was safe from the magically accelerated, fast-moving leather balls. It didn't take long before each girl was breathing heavily, both their faces drenched in sweat as their brown hair hung over their faces.

"It's... all your fault that I'm here like this."

"I... don't even... know who you are."

Chloe ran at Isha, tackling her to the ground with tears in her eyes. Both girls went rolling on the floor, clutching at each other's hair, scratching and clawing at each other.

"Aren't you going to stop them?" asked a girl to Mr. Higgins, who was watching Isha and Chloe fight, while shaking his head.

"Nah, they're too tired now to do any real damage to each other. Best to let them just get it out of their systems,"

"What kind of teacher are you? They might hurt each other?"

Mr. Higgins nodded. "Yeah, there's always a chance of injury in a scuffle, even with those two babies. But, if you're so concerned, how about you get in there and break them up."

The girl turned back to Isha and Chloe, who were now

involved in a fierce slapping contest with each other as their arms flailed through the air. "I… I think I'll wait here."

"Smart girl."

A little while later, Isha and Chloe were back in the healer's office, sitting on a bed next to each other with their heads down while Leo and Elena just stared at them.

"I distinctly remember saying that you couldn't attack Isha anymore if you wanted me to continue healing your arm."

"That's not true," replied Chloe, raising her head. "You said I could if it was in combat class,"

"You did say that," agreed Elena with a smirk on her face, looking down at Leo in his chair.

"Thanks; who's side are you on, anyway?" asked Leo, frowning back up at Elena.

"Just keeping track of the facts. You can't go back on your word now."

Leo sighed, "Fine, And I'm guessing you still won't tell us why you're so mad at Isha?"

Chloe looked away, "I can't. They'd send me away if I did."

Leo rubbed his face in frustration, "Fine, so let's make a new deal. You two can beat the hell out of each other. But no killing, and no broken bones. I figure I can just heal the less severe things."

"I promise," said Chloe.

"It's not like I started it," said Isha.

"I know, I know," said Leo, shaking his head. "Come on, Momma Bear, you grab one, and I'll get the other. We got some healing to do."

Both Leo and Elena began healing the girls' injuries: a few small cuts among them both, a little swelling around Chloe's eye, a few scratches across Isha's cheek. Elena wrapped both girls' hair in buns while Leo wrote down in his notes for the day the medical care he'd given.

"Can I go now?" asked Chloe.

"Yeah, go ahead and try not to get into more trouble," said Leo.

Chloe hopped down from the bed and left the room.

"So, who's your next opponent, champ? I heard about your fight with your sisters. Should I be preparing to heal them next?"

"Why is everything my fault? Everyone is blaming me. Jacinta and Makeba do what they want, and nobody blames them. They are always having fun, messing with people, and no one says anything."

"Are you sure about that, Isha?" asked Elena, standing next to a window. "Cause it sure doesn't seem like they're having fun."

"What do you mean?" Isha hopped down from the bed, walking over to the window by Elena.

She peered down to see the school courtyard filled with people, and over in a corner holding hands were Jacinta and Makeba. They were sitting down at a table just watching as people walked by, when three girls approached them. Isha couldn't hear what they were saying, but soon Makeba and Jacinta stood up and tried to leave, but the three girls blocked their path.

"Looks like we might be healing someone else after all," said Elena with a sigh.

Isha looked up at Elena after her words before turning and taking off, running out the door.

"Hey, don't run yet. Your leg… and she's gone."

Leo looked at Elena with a brow raised, "What did you do?"

"What any Momma Bear would do?" asked Elena with a smirk. "Although I didn't expect her to dash out of here like that."

"It just shows how much she cares, I guess. But don't

worry, we can heal whatever damage she does."

Isha ran down the corridor and down the steps to the lower floor and out into the courtyard. Breathing heavily again, she frantically searched the area for her sisters but couldn't find the Sakari girls anywhere. She ran through the crowd but still couldn't find them.

"Well, if it isn't the owner of those Sakari. You out here by yourself?"

Isha turned around to see the same blonde-haired girl whose arm Makeba had broken when they came to the school.

Isha frowned at the girl, feeling the heat of anger rise at the back of her neck, "Where are they? Where are my sisters?"

"I honestly don't know and don't care, but since they're not here to pay for what they did to me. How about I show you what happens when you attack an Evengale, and think you can get away with it?" asked the girl as brown magic began to circle around her fingers and up her arms. The crowd around the courtyard started to step away. "I'll have you pay for what you did to me." Suddenly the marble stones beneath their feet began to shake as pebbles broke free from the ground and rose up around the golden-haired girl.

Isha raised her hand in the attempt to use the pulling spell they learned in class, but she dropped her arms quickly when she saw a hand land on the shoulder of the golden-haired girl.

"Who dares touch—"

"I dare, Miss Evengale, or would you like to try that spell on me?" asked Soulden Fegmont, glowering down at the golden-haired girl.

Instantly the marble pebbles dropped to the ground as the magic around Miss Evengale's arms vanished.

"Oh, hello, headmaster. We were just having a discussion and—"

"Correct me if I'm wrong, Miss Evengale, but I distinctly

remember asking you not to involve yourself with that girl or her little Sakari friends. Or am I mistaken?"

"We just happen to run into each other is all,"

"Really? Then you won't mind if I have a conversation with her, since of course, you weren't trying to disobey me."

"No, ma'am, of course not," said Miss Evengale, lowering her head. "I... I was just about to leave."

"Good, see that you do." Soulden looked toward Isha. "And you child, come with me. I would like to have a discussion with you."

Isha followed behind Soulden, glancing back to see Miss Evengale staring daggers back at her. They both entered back into the school and walked down the corridor.

"It's been almost two months since you've entered this school. Tell me, are you enjoying yourself here?"

"Ah... yes, ma'am."

"Then perhaps you can explain to me why in these last two months you have been in three fights and were about to start on your fourth before I intervened. Even for a child of Oscar's, I find that quite excessive."

"Oh, you know about those."

Soulden laughed, "Child, there is far little that goes on in this school that I do not know about.

"No one believes me, but I swear I'm not trying to do any of this."

"No, my dear, I very much believe you."

"You do?"

"I learned quite some time ago that there are some people in the world that trouble always tends to find, no matter what they do? I myself, am one such person."

"You are?"

"Of course, how else could I explain that bastard Oscar dropping you on my door steps after twenty-five years of being free of him? No dear, for people like us, we must be extra careful, for the world seems to have malicious plans for us both."

After talking with Soulden for some time, Isha left her office and headed off to search for her sisters. But noticed that the sun had already set. *Was I really in there that long? Maybe they're back at home.* She made her way back downstairs to the first floor, realizing that the halls were empty as all the regular students and teachers had gone home.

The school's darkened halls gave off a surreal feeling as small amounts of dust sparkled in the empty corridor. Moonlight shined through the windows, illuminating the hallway through the classroom doors. To her left, a pale orange light began to glow. She turned, seeing the orange light hovering inside one of the roots that went through the walls. Stopping, Isha knelt and tried to touch the orange light, only to watch as it moved ahead, stopping down the hall. It bounced from side to side inside of another large root as if waiting for her to catch up.

Isha looked around the moonlit corridor for signs of anyone else, but after not seeing or hearing anyone, she stood and began following the orange light. Back upstairs, she went through more hallways, through parts of the school she had never seen before. Isha continued to follow the orange light as it danced in and out of walls. It moved from the tips of leaves to the trunks of roots until finally, it reached the wall, hovering in place. After catching up to it, she noticed it was above the disk platform where Soulden had taken her when she had first came to the school to meet the council. She was hesitant to step on the platform, but the orange light danced among the plants beside the large stone disk as if compelling her. Taking a deep breath, she placed her feet on the platform and walked over to the orb at the center.

I don't know what to do next.

She remembered Soulden placing her hand on the orb, so she reached out to do the same. But before she could, the platform lifted off, taking her into the upper levels of the castle. She stared up as she passed several orange rings of light before finally stopping on a level of the castle she'd never seen before. Gazing back upward, she could see that she was still a far cry from the top of the castle where Soulden had taken her. Instead, she was in a middle area of some sort. Ahead of her were leaves and small roots blocking a corridor. Between the roots, she could see the orange light ahead.

The words of Soulden only hours ago ran through her mind. *No dear. For people like us, we must be extra careful, for the world seems to have malicious plans for us both.*

Isha shook her head. *I'm sorry, I don't think I'm going to be careful.*

She walked over and took a deep breath before placing her hand between the roots and leaves in front of the corridor before slipping through. The hallway was illuminated by different colored lights coming from the doors that stretched downward. She walked forward and lifted herself on her toes in an attempt to peak in through one of the windows. Inside, she could see people wearing the school's robes next to stone pillars. They were chanting words and casting spells, and every now and then, the huge stone pillars next to them would glow a different color.

I'm probably in so much trouble now.

She continued to make her way down the hallway, poking her head into doors. One room seemed to have water floating in the air as fish swam through it, and in another, she saw a man consume what looked to be lightning. He held a small ball of blue and white light in his hands that sparked violently, before he then opened his mouth and placed the arching ball inside, seeming to swallow it.

Is... is this magic?

But while she could see inside, she couldn't hear anything. Outside was as quiet as a mouse. That was until she heard a familiar voice coming from down the hall. She left the window and slowly crept down the hall until she reached an open door. Leaning slowly into the frame, she peered inside. And to her surprise, she saw Pavel talking to someone that she couldn't see.

"Well, besides the headmasters' follies, how is that body of yours holding out?" asked the unseen female voice.

"I get regular checkups from the doctor; it still hasn't been a problem so far," replied Pavel as he raised his hands to his face and began opening and closing his fingers into a fist. "But it still feels weird. I'm not sure what I'm supposed to do."

"Don't worry, you will learn in time."

"Have you heard anything about when they are supposed to attack?"

Attack? Attack what? A dorm? The school?

"Soon, we've already got people inside waiting on the order; it's only a matter of time now."

"Well, we've got to do it before they suspect something. They're not idiots. If they catch on to it, then everything will be wasted."

Isha tried to stand up and leave, but her leg buckled as she fell back down, smashing her knee against the floor. She made a short moaning noise as she bit her lip from the pain.

"What was that? Who's out there?" asked the female voice.

And suddenly, Isha heard the sounds of footsteps coming closer. Quickly she turned, trying to run, but her leg had frozen on her as she fell forward to the floor.

No... dammit, it was supposed to be better. Why now?

Pulling herself forward, her elbows scraping against the floor, she saw the orange light again inside of a large root sticking out of the wall in front of her. The light seemed to dance, and she instinctively reached her hand out for it.

A moment later, Pavel and the woman ran into the hallway, but there was nothing there. All that could be seen was darkness and the glint of light from the opening in the doors up ahead.

CHAPTER 17

Isha's eyes were closed, or at least she thought they were closed. Everything was just so dark, wherever she was. Blackness filled every corner around her.

"Un licht... Treum bleulm," came a deep voice that echoed from the darkness around her.

"Tre... tre... I don't understand," said Isha into the darkness. "What's happening? Where am I?"

In front of her, out of the void, a small pale orange light slowly appeared. "Treum bleulm, Treum bleulm, Treum bleulm," it repeated, seemingly directly into her mind.

"I don't... I don't understand," said Isha to the pale

orange light. She tried to grasp the orb in front of her, but her hands just went through the barely shining orb.

The light began to emit heat and slowly began moving forward. It bumped against her chest, before forcing its way inside her. Isha felt her chest warm as the light entered her before a shock hit her body, forcing her to gasp for air.

Instantly she was thrown out of the darkness and found herself in a fit of coughing, hunched over the large trunk of a tree. She placed her hand again on the bark, trying to catch her breath. Isha could feel the heat inside. It felt as if it was flowing through the wood, passing over her hand. She blinked over and over as her eyes slowly focused on the world in front of her. Peering around, she found that she was in a massive open room somewhere in the castle.

Where am I? How did I get here?

The room was filled with tiny orange trees that emerged from the marble floor and stretched all the way to the walls. She looked above her, and the orange glow instantly made sense. The tree that she was under was enormous, and while the bark was brown, every leaf upon every branch was glowing in a deep orange light that cast its radiance through the room onto all the trees that were around.

What in the goddess's name...

Isha watched as a single leaf fell from the tree, slowly gliding its way down before finally landing on the marble floor. But instead of resting upon the cold marble surface, Isha's eyes opened wide as she witnessed the leaf sink into the marble stone as if it was being swallowed. In a state of awe and curiosity, she crawled over and slowly ran her fingers over the stone where the leaf had sunk in. The blueish-white stone felt as hard as one would have expected.

How?

Treum bleulm spoke tree into Isha's mind.

Isha looked back up towards the tree, "I don't... What does Treum bleulm mean?"

Suddenly the sound of stone rubbing against stone

began to echo throughout the structure. Isha's face darted from left to right as she searched between the trees, looking for the cause of the sound. She quickly found it on the other side of the large tree as she witnessed a hole in the wall open as a large stone slab raised from the floor. And from inside a dark room appeared five people. It seemed to be three women and two men wearing the school's robes. They quickly spread out and seemed to start searching the room.

Are they looking for me? Of course, they are. I have to leave here. But I don't even know where I am. Or how to get out.

She peeked over the large tree trunk once again and watched as robed figures continued to get closer. She realized that one of the men was Caudbell, the man who came to test Jacinta. The blonde-haired man still had the patch above his eye as he walked around pointing to the trees.

"Okay, we won't be able to take all of them, obviously," said Caudbell as he placed his hand on the bark of a small tree. "But instead, look for the ones that are the healthiest. Those we will get for transport since they will have the highest chance of success. Make sure you have a good look. This will be a learning experience for all of you."

Okay, I don't belong here. I have to get out. I need to get out before they see me.

Isha tried to slowly crawl again when she heard the large tree in her mind also.

Estot Valrium.

Isha turned her head back, looking up at the tree. *Estot Valrium? What does that even mean?* She quickly felt something cold come over her hands and knees, and when she looked down, she saw that her fingers were covered entirely in marble. Not only that, but she was sinking into the floor. She tried to struggle to free herself, but it wouldn't allow her to budge. The marble had a hold on her and was swallowing her like quicksand. She wanted to scream but didn't know what the robed people would do to her. Soon only her head was above the marble, and with one final gasp for air, she was swallowed by the stone, once again finding herself in a world of darkness.

She held her breath as long as she could, but gave out. Her mouth opened in a gasp. To her surprise, she found that she could breathe. Her heart was beating fast. Focusing on her body, she could feel herself falling through something. But falling wasn't the right word. Maybe sliding, or she was being guided was the right way to describe it. The experience was disorientating, because for Isha, there was no up or down anymore. There was only a sudden shift on her chest or on her back and then a movement of some sort.

The little orange light didn't appear this time. She merely just stayed in darkness for a time she never could get a grasp on before she felt something cold on the side of her face. She could smell the wood of the large tree and the roughness of the bark against her face, along with the coldness of the marble. And once again, she opened her eyes as if from out of a dream to a dark and blurry world in front of her. As her eyes slowly focused once again, she realized that she was back at the bottom floor of the school, in the hallway of the first years.

She forced herself to her feet and once again felt the pang of pain in her leg and fell against the wall to balance herself. *What's happening? What was Pavel doing? What type of attack is someone planning? Did that person really swallow lightning? I don't understand what's going on anymore. And what was that giant tree?* Isha shook her head and headed down the corridor and out of the school. *I have to get home. Please be safe, Jacinta, Makeba. I'm so sorry. I'm not a good sister, I should have told you.*

Isha left the castle school grounds and hobbled her way home, noticing that it was still nighttime. *Maybe if I tell Soulden what happened, she might be able to do something.*

It took her a while to hobble her way home through the streets. The roads were empty as the street lamps that littered the road guided her through the night. After a while, Isha finally managed to make her way home and opened the door. She saw Elena and Leo talking to Pavel. She froze as Pavel turned to her.

"Oh, thank the goddess," said Leo as he and Elena rushed over to Isha.

"We're so glad you're safe? Where have you been?" asked Elena.

"Huh?" asked Isha as she felt the embrace of Elena and Leo's arms around her. "What do you mean, what's wrong?"

"What's wrong?" asked Elena. "You've been gone for two days and you come back hopping in the door covered in sweat, and you ask us what's wrong."

"Two days? I've been gone two days?"

"Are you okay, Isha? Is everything alright?" asked Leo, rubbing the side of her face.

"Yes, it's been two days," said Elena, "Pavel here even came to check on you when you didn't show up for class."

"The teachers asked me to check on you since we're assigned partners. And I think Soulden has been worried too."

Rima came downstairs, seeing everyone embracing Isha, "Oh, she's made it back. Has she said where she's been?

Isha dropped her head, trying not to look at Pavel, "Oh, I... I'm sorry. I guess I got lost."

"Got lost?" asked Leo, "For two whole days? You even have twigs in your hair. Where have you been? And you've hurt your leg again; let me have a look."

"I'm fine. It doesn't hurt that bad anymore. Can I... can I just go and lay down? I'm really tired."

"Oh," said Leo, letting go of Isha, "Of course, we can treat your leg in the morning if you want."

Elena brushed the few leaves from Isha's hair, "Come on, Isha, let's get you cleaned up, and then you can go to bed." Elena leaned down and placed her shoulder under Isha, and led her into the back of the house.

"Well. I guess I should be going," said Pavel, "She's home safe now, and I'll report this to Soulden first thing in the morning."

"Thanks for coming to check on her Pavel, you should stop by for your physical check-up tomorrow, if you have time."

"Thank you, Mr. Leo. I will do just that," said Pavel as he left the house and walked down the street into the darkness of the night as small street posts with hanging lanterns with glowing stones illuminated the path back..

Leo turned around and began to clean up the leaves and twigs from the floor that fell out of Isha's hair. He picked up one leaf, noticing that it felt oddly warm. For a second, the leaf glowed bright orange in his hand. "What the," he said before it turned a dull brown. He then looked down the hall where Elena had taken Isha, narrowing his eyes.

Elena led Isha into the bathroom and stripped her down, tossing a water bucket over her head before helping her into the steps of the bath water.

"Okay, now just sit on the steps and I'll give you a good wash."

"I'm okay, I can..."

"You've been gone two days and come back looking like that. You are most certainly not okay," said Elena, plucking more twigs out of Isha's hair.

"Have I really been gone two days?"

"You most certainly have. Just what kind of—"

Isha's eyes jolted open as she turned around, grabbing Elena by the collar, "Jacinta, Makeba, my sisters, are they okay?" Are they—"

"Yes, yes, they're okay. They're in the room sleeping."

Isha's breathing slowed down after hearing Elena's words, "Okay... okay... that's good. I... I was worried."

"You were worried?" asked Elena with a brow raised, "Those poor girls were worried sick about you. They, along with Freedo, searched for you all night last night, refusing to come back, inside and insisted on staying up waiting on you."

"Freedo?"

"Apparently, he saw them walking without you and noticed them acting odd. So, he wanted to help as much as he could. Those poor things, when they had exhausted themselves, Leo and I had to drag them back in."

"I'm sorry, everything... everything is just so... so much. I'm... I'm just so tired."

Elena wrapped her arms around Isha, "Everything is gonna be okay now, you're home and safe."

After feeling Elena's arms embrace around her and hearing her words, all the tension in Isha's shoulders faded away. Her arms dropped, and she took a deep breath, smelling the rose-scented perfume of Elena's hair as it hung down over her head, sliding over her cheek. Isha reached up, gripping Elena's arm, and rubbed her cheek against it, feeling its comforting warmth.

"Thank you, Elena."

"You're welcome, honey. Now come on, let's get you ready for bed. You seem as if the world has beaten you up pretty bad." Elena wrapped Isha's hair, tossed one of Leo's oversized shirts over her head, and walked out of the bathing room and over to the stairs.

"Alright, you go on and head upstairs and get some sleep. Leo and I will finish up here."

Isha slowly made her way upstairs, favoring her leg. The door to her room was in front of her, but she was scared to enter. She turned around to see Elena, peeping her head above the steps.

"Don't run away from it. It's best to get it over with. Those girls love you. I promise if you're honest about what you feel, it'll all work out."

Isha took a deep breath and made her way over. Placing her hand on the door, she felt the ridges of the wood between her fingers as her hesitation set in for a few moments. She closed her eyes, took a breath, and with one final look at the supportive Elena by the steps, she opened the door of her room.

Inside, it was dark, the silence of the room adding to her tension as she glanced over and instantly noticed that their three beds that were pushed together previously were now separated again. With her bed over in a corner on one side of the room and Jacinta and Makeba's bed still pressed together on the other side.

Feelings of shame washed over Isha as she hobbled her way over to her bed and crawled on top of it. She looked over at her sister's beds. The Sakari girls had themselves covered with the sheets.

As Isha looked over at the girls, her father's words popped into her head. *Friends fight and then they make up, even if they beat the hell out of each other. Sometimes that's the only way they will ever get past whatever the problem is. So, if you've decided you're gonna make up, then you best go and get it out of the way. If you want something to happen, then you usually are gonna have to make it happen.*

Isha closed her eyes and rolled out of bed, landing on one leg to balance herself before slowly making her way through the moonlit room through the room and standing in front Jacinta and Makeba's beds.

"Makeba, Jacinta, are you awake?"

There was a moment of silence in the room before Isha got her answer.

"Bad sister, go away. We no want to talk to you," came Jacinta's muffled voice from under the sheets.

"I know… I was bad… I shouldn't have said what I said… I'm really sorry."

"Lie, sister lie and run away."

"I didn't. I got lost… I mean, I couldn't come back. I didn't know how to."

Suddenly, the sheets flew up and Jacinta rose up from the bed on her knees, staring Isha in her eyes. Isha could see the sparkle of moonlight run down the sides of her sister's faces like tiny crystals in the night, and she realized that Jacinta and Makeba had both been crying.

"Why sister throw us away? Why she break promise to mama? Why... why sister no come home?"

Isha watched as more tears began to flow down Jacinta's face, and she stood there in shock. She'd never seen them cry before. She'd never even seen them sad before. And this sight of both the girls crying, it was just too much. And without warning, Isha's world turned blurry as tears whirled up in her own eyes.

"It's not... I... I... I didn't throw you away," said Isha, and as more words blurted out of her lips, so did the tears fall from her eyes. "I didn't mean... Nothing ever... No one understands..."

"But sister no understand us," said Makeba. "We want to stay with sister, but sister not want us."

"But that's not... I wanna stay with sisters too..."

Makeba wrapped her arms around Isha, then reached over, pulling Jacinta over to her as both girls continued to cry and fumble their words.

"Then sister not allowed to run away again," said Makeba. "We worry, we worry lots."

"I'm sorry... I promise I won't run away anymore."

And soon, all three girls would find themselves asleep atop one another in bed, with Leo and Elena peeking their heads in through the door.

"You think everything's okay now?" asked Leo, looking into the room.

"Aww, that's cute. You're actually worried," said Elena, pulling away from the door with a smile on her face.

Leo frowned, turning around to her, "What? Am I not allowed to be?"

Elena stepped closer to Leo, placing her hand on his chest and looking him in his eyes, "You're cute when you worry, Papa Bear." She then leaned in on her toes, lifted her chin and pressed her lips against his.

CHAPTER 18

Moonlight sparkled off the leaves of the trees. The night's dew providing a glimmer into the shadows below the forest's brush. Crouched in the darkness, surrounded by the forestry were Saffron and Mova as they peered out at a disheveled looking Villa, alone in the center of a forest. Its misuse was apparent by the chipped lumber, the broken windows, and the vegetation that had long since started to reclaim the building.

"Why am I here?" asked Mova, picking a twig out of her hair. "Didn't I say how much I hated these country outings of yours?"

"Because you're one of my trusted guards. Who else would I hand over the duty of rescuing my wife?"

"Anyone, literally anyone else. And why not just send in a bunch of guards? Why must we be out here alone?"

"The risk of them panicking and hurting my bride to be is too high. Don't worry; Dekol is already off somewhere providing us assistance. And besides, you're more suited for these types of missions?"

"Yes, well, I much prefer to be sneaking in a castle, rather than whatever the hell this creepy place is."

"Come on, let's get this over with."

They moved between the trees, keeping their eyes on the house as they went. But try as they might, they couldn't notice anyone inside.

"I don't like this," said Mova, her eyes dart from one side to the other, suspiciously peering into the shadows. "Aren't there supposed to be guards? If this is where they're holding a princess hostage. There should be lights, spells, something."

"This is what the location that thing gave, or at least it's the most we could get out of her before it started choking on its own words. There was a spell that forbade it to speak on certain matters. This is all we could get before it would pass out."

"So for as much as we know, the actual location could be miles away in a completely different creepy house and a different creepy forest."

"I never took you for the type to be scared of ghosts, Mova. You're a mage, just cast magic."

"I'm not afraid of ghosts. I'm afraid of what I don't understand, and what I don't understand is ghosts. There's a difference."

"I'm sure there is," said Saffron, shaking his head. "Come on, let's go have a look."

"Oh, did you hear nothing I just said?"

"Best time to get over your fear is the present," replied

Saffron as he patted Mova on the back. With his touch, the world around them morphed and twisted before their bodies had completely faded into the darkness and become transparent.

"Argh, I hate when you do that. It feels so weird to have your magic sliding over my body."

"That sounded sexual. You do know that, right?"

"Just shut up."

"Let's go! The ghost house awaits us," said Saffron as he dashed forward under the cover of darkness, towards the side of the house.

"Damn you," said Mova as she followed behind.

Everything seemed quiet as they reached the side of the villa. Peeking inside one of the broken windows, they could see a few guards' silhouettes in the shadows. They stood, not moving as if they were waiting on something.

"You think they know we're here?" whispered Saffron.

"Well, they most likely know you're not dead. And their assassin hasn't returned. So, they know something is not right."

"Good point," said Saffron as he made his way towards a side door of the house.

Placing his hand against the wood, he slowly edged the door open. Creaking on its hinges, it opened a path inside the villa's kitchen.

Stepping inside, his fingers began to tingle and the smell of lavender came into his nose. He rubbed his hands together. "Be careful. There's some type of magic here." No response came. "Mova?" Saffron turned around, but there was no one there. *Okay, then. Perhaps a few more guards would have been a good idea after all.* He took a deep breath, smelling the scents of old weathered wood and furniture. *I guess I can't turn back now. And I doubt that Queen's Bane's made his way all the way out here.*

Saffron crept into the house. His feet sliding silently over the floor as he made his way through the kitchen.

That's odd. One would think there would be guards at the door. He made his way out through the kitchen towards the door leading into the main hall. Clutching the hilt of his blade around his fingers, he peered inside. Scattered over the floor were assortments of clothing being shined down upon by the moonlight piercing in through the broken windows.

What the... just what is going on here? Thought Saffron as he looked ahead to see the two guards he had seen through the window. But they weren't guards. *Mannequins? What is this about?* He stepped out into the main hall, coming under the steps into the center of the room. The scattered clothing dragged along his feet as he stepped. There, underneath the moonlight, he stood before one of the two mannequins. On display for the moon above, it held a wooden sword and shield in its hands. And there, at the crown of its head, sat an embedded red jewel.

That... is that what father... Before he could finish the thought, the sound of children giggling passed over his ears. He turned around in a rush, but was only greeted by more piles of clothes lying on the floor. A slight breeze came in, cutting through the holes in the walls, creating a whistling sound that made the hair on the back of Saffron's neck stand up,

Okay, so there's something to be said for ghost sto... Turning back around, he quickly realized the mannequin that was before him was now gone. Replaced by nothing but air. He waved his hand ahead, testing the space in front of him. But there was nothing there. Again, came the sounds of the children. They're giggling sounds bouncing around the room. Saffron couldn't help but look around once again, but he could only watch as the surrounding space began to spin. The darkness inside replacing itself with light. The broken pieces of the windows seemed to reverse in time as the glass picked itself up off the floor, resealing back into the window panes.

"What is this?" asked Saffron as his own spell became

dispersed as the world melted around him, slipping between his fingers like water falling off his body. "What in the goddess is strong enough to break my spell?" And in one final blinding spot of light, Saffron opened his eyes to find himself in a room filled with people.

Men and women all wore the finest clothing. Above him hung crystal chandeliers with magic light reflecting off the crystal. As he looked over himself, he realized that even his own clothing had changed. Gone were his black cloak and attire beneath that would blend into the darkness, replaced by a formal black and red uniform that he had worn to dozens of social events in the past.

Another illusion. Thought Saffron as he narrowed his eyes. "One strong enough to disperse mine. This isn't—"

"Why, if it isn't Prince Saffron," said a familiar voice as a man made his way through the crowd.

Saffron turned his head to see Highman Masterdane, as the older man walked up to greet him.

"How are you, lad? Your father still giving you trouble about your adventures in the land?"

"Ah, you know Father, he's always been that way," Saffron found himself saying in response without even trying. *What the.... Am I a puppet now? Do you wish for me to converse with a dead man? Is that it?*

"I've told him before. The boys got to get out there and spread his wings; test the waters."

"I'm sure father has my best interest at heart." *Am I? Because I'm fairly sure he had something to do with that assassin thing that tried to kill me.*

"Of course, I do," said his father as he came up behind. "I worry my boy is going to get himself in some type of situation that he can't get himself out of."

"Ah, your highness, I'm glad to see you arrived."

"Are you now? You seem to be enjoying yourself with my son."

"I was just about to give a bit of sage advice. You and I

both have lived quite a long time. Passing on our wisdom is part of our duty."

"That may be true," said the king as he made his way in front of his son, then gave him a look over with a smile. Reaching out, he adjusted the collars of his son's uniform. "But leave the fatherly advice for his actual father."

"Will you be training me in swordplay this afternoon again, then father?"

"Of course, who else is going to whip you into shape."

Leonardo and Humfrey taught me the sword, because you never had the time. "I look forward to your lessons, Father. But I'm fairly sure I will beat you today."

"Ah, will you look at that," said the king with a broad smile across his face, turning to Masterdane. "The boy thinks he can best his father already."

Okay, now this is actually offensive. Who here is behind the charade?

Suddenly a knock at one of the side doors came. It pounded through the room, such that the ornaments above began to shake, and the waiters with their glasses of wine found it hard to balance their trays. The entire room turned towards the door.

"Just what in the world is the meaning of that commotion," said the king.

And with one final knock, the door burst open, and out came a shadowy figure. His ominous size barely fitting through the door. The crowd in the room cheered at the sight of Queen's Bane.

"Ah, so the guest of honor has arrived!" said the king.

What?

An ominous black cloud began to fill the room, pooling at Saffron's feet. He tried to move, but his body refused his every command. Instead, he just stood there frozen as from the black cloud beneath his feet came the same black tendrils from before. They wormed their way up his body, wrapping themselves around his waist and over his shoulders. He remembered the cold feel of it as it crept over his neck.

"You are no king," spoke the shadow figure as he stepped forward. "Only I am worthy." Queen's Bane reached out his hand, placing it over Saffron's face so that all he could see was darkness. "And soon, the world will know."

Saffron struggled in the darkness only to then open his eyes and find himself at his own wedding night. Beside him sat who was supposed to be his new wife.

"Husband, are you alright?" asked Laura.

"Why yes, of course, my wife. I'm just enjoying the night's activities," said Saffron's voice with no will of his own. His lips continued to spout words as he lay trapped inside of his own body. *What is this? What kind of illusion spell plays with one's own mind?*

"I'm glad. I was worried I'd not have made you happy."

"Nothing could be farther from the truth," said Saffron, smiling back to his wife. But out of the corner of his eye. He saw Frenka out on the terrace with Victor. They both were smiling at each other. "Excuse me, dear wife. I wish to go and congratulate another happy couple." *What? The lies of the Goddess, I do.*

Saffron stood up from the table, placing his hand on his wife's shoulder before taking a step away, heading over to the main hall of the ballroom. The floor was filled with people offering their congratulations and well wishes to Saffron as he made his way across the floor and out on the terrace overlooking the kingdom.

"Well, if it isn't the happy couple," said Saffron as he approached Victor and Frenka.

"Oh, prince is here?" said Frenka as she turned around, grasping Victor's arms, wrapping them around her waist. "You come to wish us best."

"Of course, you two make quite the lovely couple." *When I find out who's behind this perverse heresy of an illusion. I swear on the Goddess herself that I'm going to have them bleeding from the eyes as I am right now.*

"Yes, although we haven't known each other long," said Victor as he squeezed his arms around Frenka's waist, kissing her on her neck. "This mountain woman has taken it upon herself to claim me as her mate."

"I have chosen him, and we will have babies soon."

Hot molten lead directly into their eyes. Just death alone would be too generous for making me witness this assault on my senses.

"Prince's new wife and Frenka babies will play together. Oh, but I will go live with Victor soon, so maybe not. Saffron will come to our wedding."

"I will have the Queen marry us, and the assassin will serve as our maid," said Victor as he pointed behind Saffron. "On and here she comes now."

Saffron turned around to see the ashen-skinned thing making its way towards him. It still had the same dress as his bride. It's white hair was pulled back in a ponytail with a black ribbon holding it together.

"Hello husband," said the assassin as it laid its hand against Saffron's chest. "I missed my new husband."

"What already? It's barely been a few minutes. Or are you just excited for our wedding night?" asked Saffron with a smirk on his face as he wrapped his arm around the assassin while turning back around to Victor and Frenka.

"Aren't we the happy couple," said Victor, I and Frenka, you and the assassin. "I think the future is going to be very wonderful for us both, your highness."

And with that, sparks began to explode in the sky. Making both couples gaze upward as the airships above them launched magic that exploded across the kingdom in celebration.

"This is such a beautiful night," said the creature.

"But not as beautiful as you, my ashen skinned princess," said Saffron as he leaned down and closed his eyes, kissing the assassin on it's reddish lips. *Disgusting.*

After another moment, the touch of the creature faded from his lips, but then another one of his senses became filled with the smell of the soil beneath him.

Saffron opened his eyes once again and the night sky upon the terrace was gone, along with the sight and feel of his fake wife. Now he stood as a ghost. The image of a set of stables outside of his family's summer manor was in front of him.

Green forestry and level plains surrounded the area. The sound of children giggling filled his ears once again, but now it wasn't a mystery as to where the sound came from. Because out of the stables, covered in hay, came a boy with mud smeared on the side of his face. But not an unknown child. Instead, Saffron was greeted with an image of his younger self. A fresh-faced boy, no more than ten years of age.

"Ahh, got you," came a man's voice from out of the stables as a younger version of his father appeared from a stall, grabbing his son from around the waist and lifting him into the air. Both father and son, wearing smiles across their faces as they enjoyed each other's company.

Okay, enough. I have had enough of these lies.

"I got you now, boy. No more running away," said his father as he held his son high into the air. "Now admit, who's the better man."

"No, no, I won't give up," said his younger self as he squirmed in his father's hand. "I want to win."

"Oh really," said his father as he placed little Saffron down on the ground and began tickling him. "And how about now?"

"Ah, no fair... no fair," said the younger Saffron as he continued squirming until it became too much. "I give up, I give up."

The king let go of his son, sat down on the ground, and let out a huge burst of laughter. Only to then get tackled by his son as they went rolling around on the floor. There they both laid, their clothing covered in dirt, out of breath. His younger self laid atop his father's chest as the king stroked his son's head.

Whoever you are, you wish to torment me with false images of a life I'd never known. Is that it?

"It is good to have a day like this," said his father looking up towards the sky. "To be a father, rather than a king."

"Will I be king one day?"

"Of course. Eventually, one day I will no longer be here. Or I'll be foolish enough to stick around too long and end up being a burden more than a king. Then it will be your turn to lead."

"Are you going to go away?"

"We all must go away, son. As I will to you and as you will to your sons. Our goal is not to linger, but to instill what knowledge and principles we have before we go."

"I don't want you to go away?"

"Ha," came a chuckle from his father. "I'm sure that's the way of it. But sadly we don't get a choice in the matter. Just know that I loved you and your mother well. If I can leave that much, then I'm sure the goddess will welcome me."

"I... I love you too father."

This farce has gone on long enough. Thought Saffron, as he could feel the anger building up inside of himself.

"Do you, now? And what else do you love?"

Enough! He thought as the taste of blood and disgust seeped into his mouth.

I love mother, and you, and Mr. Leo, and sweetcakes.

"Sweetcakes? Well, I'm happy that I'm second, I guess. But remember that no matter what happens."

Don't...

"You're my son and I will always love you."

Lies shouted Saffron in his mind. So much so that the image of the happy father and son began to distort in the false world. *You wish to torment with false memories. Is that it? Well, I refuse to play witness to this corrupt world you've brought before me.* Although he didn't see it, he could feel his fist tighten as he gathered power into himself. *I am Saffron Montavia, and I refuse to stand as a spectator to this atrocity anymore. Release me.* Suddenly the world around him shattered into small pieces, like a glass wall being broken.

Saffron gasped in the darkness as his mind was thrown back and as he opened his eyes once again. The taste of blood fresh in his mouth as he realized he had bitten into the flesh of his bottom lip. Surrounding him once again was the inside of the moonlite villa. The furniture and clothing that was spread through the floor before were now against the wall and the statue that stood in front of him no longer held the mock sword and shield, because both its arms were now gone. Blown away somewhere. But another thing caught Saffron's attention. The red jewel that was inside of the mannequin's head now had a crack along the center and was now turned completely black.

"Saffron, are you okay?" asked Dekol from upstairs on the balcony.

"Ah yes... yes. Where have you been?"

"I was caught up in some type of illusion spell," said Dekol, making his way downstairs and towards Saffron. "Damn thing plagued me with false memories."

"You aren't the only one," said Saffron pointing to the now black jewel against the mannequin's head. "I'm not sure, but I think our troubles may have been caused by this."

"There you two are," said Mova, poking her head out of the kitchen. "I lost track of both of you."

"Saffron," said Dekol, stepping in front of his friend. "Wipe your face."

"What?" asked Saffron, reaching up to his face and feeling the wetness below his eyes and realized that he had been crying. He quickly took his sleeve and began wiping at his eyes as Dekol walked over to Mova.

"There's a room downstairs. I think she might be in

there. Come on."

"Okay, hold on," said Saffron as he turned around and walked over to the wall, grabbing a loose piece of cloth from the floor and wrapping it over his hand. He then walked back to the mannequin and plucked the black crystal from its head. Then wrapping it in the cloth, he placed it in his pocket before following behind Mova.

Together, the three made their way to the back of the house, where a bookshelf had been moved to the side, exposing some stairs.

"How did you even find this?" asked Saffron.

"While looking around, I felt a cool draft coming from behind the shelf. I moved it and found this passageway," replied Mova.

"What's down there?"

"That's what you two are going to find out."

"Ever the selfless heroine you are," said Saffron shaking his head and peering down the dark steps. "Fine, lets go, Dekol." Saffron squeezed his hand into a fist, making it glow white. Then opening his palm again, he allowed a white light of magic to float above it, lighting the way down the stairs.

"Do you really think she's down here?" asked Mova as the three traveled down the steps.

"That's what that assassin said, although I still have trouble believing that thing's words."

"Does the king still have her then?"

"Why are you asking that now? You were there when that bastard from Mari took her?"

"I just mean wouldn't it have been better to keep her till we found what we're looking for?"

"Yeah, you weren't there for that part. Father wanted them both out of the kingdom as fast as he could. For all we know that bastard is halfway back to Mari now with his little trophy monster."

Making it to the bottom of the steps, they found

themselves standing before a short corridor that led to a wooden door at the end of it. From beyond it, he could see a light shining through the boards of the door.

"I guess that's our destination. You think there are any traps?" asked Dekol, his hand on the hilt of his blade.

"If so, I hope it's someone we can actually kill, rather than more mind games."

Saffron crept forward into the shadows of the small corridor, making his way towards the door. The cold air from being below ground running its way over his skin, bringing a shiver down his spine. He looked to his side to see Mova on the other side of the wall beside him, with Dekol bringing up the rear.

"I thought you were afraid of ghosts?"

"Am I? I guess that shows I'm more afraid of being down here and longer than I need to. Let's just get this over with and kill who we need to kill."

"Well spoken. You're finally sounding as if you're enjoying yourself now," said Saffron as he extinguished the light above his hand and reached for the door.

Placing his hand on the door, he leaned in closer, trying to look between the cracks in the wood where the light was shining through. Inside, he saw a bundle of clothing that raised up to a height half his size.

He nodded back to Dekol and Mova before turning around and slowly pushing against the door. It swung open easily, squeaking on its hinges as they all stepped into the room with their blades drawn. But there was no one inside, just a table and two candles on each side of the room. Saffron then noticed a chain mounted into the wall that led into the mountain of clothing ahead of him.

"You, underneath the cloth; come out of there," announced Saffron.

There was a moment of silence in the room before a meek voice was heard.

"Is... is that you, my lord?" came the voice of Lady

Dunblane as her head popped out of the large bundle of clothing. Her hair was disheveled, and she had bags under her eyes. But underneath her chin, Saffron saw a metal collar, much like the same he had used on the assassin down in the dungeon. "Oh, my lord, it is you!" she said as she struggled to free herself from the mass of clothing.

"What have they done to you?" Mumbled Saffron as he witnessed his supposed wife in her current state. She had lost so much weight since he had last seen her. Her cheeks had sunken in around her face.

"I had hoped you would come for me. I... I dreamed you would," said Lady Dunblane as she stepped forward towards Saffron, small arms reaching out towards him as the chain around her neck caught against the wall, making her lose her balance and fall back down to the floor.

Saffron rushed forward, dropping his sword and wrapping his arm around her as his mage light vanished. "Dekol, it's an alagon collar. I won't be able to release it. Can you?"

Dekol walked over and examined the collar. "No, the sealing latch has been broken. I can cut the chain, but we won't be able to remove it without a blacksmith."

"Cut the chain then. I would do it myself, but I don't want to risk injuring her."

"Okay, lay her down on the floor; I'll cut as much of it off as I can."

"You... you called me your wife," mumbled Laura as Saffron held her hand, laying her gently down on the floor.

"That's because you are. Nothing will change that. Now close your eyes, my wife. We are going to free you now."

Dekol placed his boot as close to Laura's head as he could, stepping on the chain, making it taut, before raising his blade. And with one swing of his blade, the chain and the stone beneath it were cut in two as if it was nothing but parchment.

"Come on," said Saffron, lifting his wife back up from

the icy floor. "We're getting you out of here."

"I don't see or hear anyone. Come on, let's go," said Mova, standing in the door. "I don't wanna get caught down here if there's a fight."

"Agreed," Dekol pried one of the candle fixtures from the wall and moved to the doors opening beside Mova.

Saffron escorted his wife to the door. "Let's get out of here."

Dekol led the two back down the corridor, candle in one hand and sword in the other. The three reached the steps and made their way back up the stairs. Leaving the room, they made their way back through the villa into the main hall. Where Dekol stopped in his tracks, gripping his blade.

"Dekol, what's wro..." said Saffron as he stood staring at the doorway of the manor. Or more precisely, the person standing in the doorway.

"Where have you two been? I've been searching everywhere for you," said Mova.

Saffron quickly turned around, but noticed that the Mova that had been with them was now gone.

"What? Why are you two looking at me like that?" asked Mova.

"Mova, have you been downstairs?" asked Saffron.

"What. No. What's downstairs?"

"Mova, tell me. How did we meet?"

"What? Why?"

"Just do it."

"We met at my father's horse stables. Your dumbass tried to ride our horse Drexler and fell on your ass. That's how we met," said Mova, placing her hands on her hips. "Satisfied now?"

Saffron took a breath and shook his head. "That'll have to do. For now, let's just get out of here. I want to be as far away from this place as I can." He then headed towards Mova, walking past her out of the door.

"What... did something happen?"

"I'll tell you after we get clear of here," said Dekol.

The three walked out of the villa and down the stairs, headed back towards the woods.

"Let's just hope the horses are still where we left them," said Saffron as they entered the forest. As they entered the brush, he turned his head, taking one final look back at the villa only to see what looked like himself standing back in the doorway, watching as they made their way into the shadows.

I don't know what's going on. But when I find out. Be it ghost or not. I plan to kill everyone involved. And that place... that place will soon be burned to the damn ground.

CHAPTER 19

Victor rode into the town of Molask. It was an old wooden city downhill from a lake that had seen better days. Where shady bridges ran over half-dried and muddy waterways. A city where brown and dirty seemed to be the theme of its depression. Smoke could be seen from multiple city angles as fires blazed from blacksmith ovens of what smelled like the burning of bodies.

"It stinks here," said Silk's voice from inside the wagon as they rolled through the muddy streets.

"Yeah, this city isn't exactly the highlight of the five kingdoms," replied Victor as he passed what seemed to be the city's market area, watching its people and the depression that seemed to be written across their faces as he passed by. "How's your body? You still stuck in your own skin?"

"Seems like it. I've been trying to change, but it starts hurting too much and I can't concentrate."

"That's fine. No need to rely on tools you don't have. Now that we're here, I'll start asking around about the clergy, but judging from the look of this place it won't be too difficult to find them. The atmosphere here doesn't exactly scream 'town of the goddess."

"So how are we going to find him?"

"*We* aren't going to do anything yet. I'm going to get us a room, and you're going to stay put. I'll go around the city and find out if The Kemlor has been through."

"I'm not helpless, you know."

"Helpless? No. Extremely dangerous and with a visage that could scare children. Yes. Just wait a little longer till we find a place to stay for the night," said Victor as they continued to ride through the city.

After traveling through the streets for a while longer, Victor picked a small tavern at the farthest end where few people seemed to venture. He tied the reins of the horses to a post and walked inside. The place was empty except for an old man who was asleep at the counter.

"Excuse me," said Victor, walking in and examining the building. The place was old and not well kept. Dust was on the tables, and half the chairs were keeled over and missing legs.

"Huh, what's... oh someone's here, what can I do ya for?" said an old man at a table. His gray hair looking as disheveled as the dusty clothing he seemed to be wearing.

"I'd like a room for a night or two here."

"Aye, and I take it that one over there be with ya then?" asked the man while nodding behind Victor and scratching his head.

Victor turned around to see Silk in the doorway, covering herself in the blanket from the wagon. The sun shining through the door, forcing the sheet to cast a shadow over her face. Victor exhaled and turned back to the old man, "Yeah, that one's with me."

"That'll be two silver a night and four silver for me not to ask any questions about the girl ya got with ya," said the old man as he walked behind the counter, grabbing a set of keys from under it.

"Seems like a fair deal. Don't suppose this place comes with breakfast."

The old man nodded to a rat over in a corner. "If you can catch it, breakfast is yours."

With a smirk Victor placed five silver on the table before fumbling around in his pockets and pulling out the last silver and placing it among the rest. "I'm sure I'll manage."

"Thought as much," said the man, sliding his hand across the table and scooping up the coins. "Just head upstairs, pick any room you want."

"Thanks," said Victor turning around to Silk, "Alright, come along, honey, and we'll let you lay down for a while."

Silk walked up to Victor, and he stood behind her, leading her upstairs into one of the rooms. The room they chose was dusty, but it was the only one that didn't have a hole in either the wall or the floor. Silk walked in, looking around before dropping the blanket and revealing herself in the blue and white tunic that Victor bought her with oversized brown boots.

"Well, at least you put on your clothes."

"You asked me to."

Victor walked over, looking out the window down at the streets below. For the most part, the roads were empty, except for the occasional passerby.

"You said wearing yourself felt better. What's it like in that body of yours?"

"What do you mean?"

"I mean, the rest of us can't reshape our bodies at will, and if anything gets twisted out of place, then it's extremely painful. Doesn't it hurt when you change?"

"No, it's... it's hard to describe." Silk walked over to Victor, "Give me your hand."

Victor extended his arm and Silk took Victor's hand in hers, taking a finger, and slowly ran it down his arm. Not too hard, but just enough where her ashen finger sunk into his skin and pushed it aside as if she were kneading dough.

"Think about what this feels like. Now imagine this feeling all over and throughout your body. As if someone was able to shape you. It doesn't hurt, but you can feel it. That's probably the best way I can describe it."

"And you and your sister have always been like this?"

"We have, but we didn't learn we could change until one day my sister turned into one of the boys that they had in chains. He was the only one who wasn't scared of us. We soon found out why; it turns out he was blind and couldn't see what we looked like." Silk's lips quivered while she rubbed at her shoulders, her mind thinking back to days that had long since passed. "They... they kept us down there with them, and my sister became friends with the boy. Then one day they came down for him and saw that they had two of him. Sister had transformed and didn't know it."

"And what about you? Did you do the same trick with the boy?"

"No, but after that, it didn't take us long to figure out what we could do. At first, it was hard, but being locked down there, we had plenty of time to learn. As we grew older, they'd bring us up and strip us, making us transform for them."

"That doesn't sound pleasant."

Silk rubbed at her eyes, trying to prevent her tears, "It's fine; we are who we are. But now it's your turn. You have to answer my question."

"Okay, fair's fair. What do you want to know?"

"Why did you save me?"

"Seemed like a good idea at the time. I figured, why not? It's not like—"

"Stop that!"

"Stop wha—"

"I'm not a child, and you always run away from answering my questions. I want you to be honest with me. Tell me why you did it. Grigguk treats me and my sister like his pets. Is that what you want? Are you gonna lock me away and only use me when it's suit's you? Is that all you people care—"

"Woah, woah... hold on...," said Victor, watching the frustration grow in Silk as she clenched her fist. "You're the one who owns the bonding thing, remember. You're giving the orders. I'm not your boss."

"Then why did you save me? Tell me."

Victor looked down into her ruby and emerald eyes as they still had traces of water left at the edges of her eyelids and slumped his shoulders.

"Because you asked for it."

"I didn't ask—"

"Not verbally, but remember that night in the dungeon. After you had given me your name. You just looked so tired, like you had given up and just wanted to die. And I just thought, that's not the face of a person who enjoys killing." Victor raised his hand, wiping another tear from the face of Silk that had escaped from her eyes. "I've seen the faces of people who enjoy maiming, murdering, rape, and none of those faces looked like yours."

Victor took a breath, pulling his hand away from Silk's face. "At the time, I had a decent amount of leverage to use on the Prince. So, I made a simple wager with myself that if I could get you out of there and away from whatever was controlling you. Then you might go on and try a life that didn't involve what you had been doing. I had planned to drop you off in a nice quiet village somewhere." Victor tapped his knees and looked around the room. "Gotta admit, though, I didn't expect all of this to happen. But as they say, every choice you make comes with a price you must pay." *Plus, you might end up giving me some information on who was trying to assassinate me. That bit of information needs to be explored more.*

Silk stared up into Victor's eyes, just focusing on his face.

"What? Why are you looking at me like that?"

She raised her hands, placing them on each side of his face. "I think... I think I see it now."

"See what?" asked Victor, looking at Silk in confusion.

"What that dark-haired woman sees."

"Dark hair? Wait... you mean Frenka?"

"Yes, and you really are stupid."

Victor sighed, "That seems to have become the anthem of my life at this point. He looked out the window once again and saw a man in a white robe walking through the streets. "And there's our first lead."

"Are we going to follow him?" asked Silk as she peered out the window.

"*We* aren't going to do anything. You still can't transform yet, remember. So, until then, you will wait here. I won't be too long."

"That's what you said last time," responded Silk with her hands on her hips.

"Last time, I didn't expect to meet up with an old friend. There's no one in this city that should have a grudge against me."

"And that old man downstairs, do you think he won't try something the moment he sees you leave without me? Men like to pray on small women, and in this form I appear a lot smaller than you. He knows I'm female."

"You know the nature of men very well. But I'm confused. What are you afraid of? Being left alone or having to kill more people?"

"Can't it be both?"

Victor looked out the window again before shaking his head and lowering himself to the floor with his back against the wall. "We'll wait until nightfall, but you must keep yourself covered."

"Are you serious? You really are stupid nice."

"What?" asked Victor in annoyance, "So you don't want me to stay."

"Of course not. I just wanted to see if you would. Goodness, Victor. I can wait here for a few hours," said Silk as she walked over, sitting up on the bed with her legs crossed.

"Goddess help me, you're a pain in the ass," said Victor as he walked over to the door and opened it."

"Wait, Victor."

"What, you feel like teasing me again?"

"No, it's just… I've never had anyone care about me before. It… it feels nice. Thank you."

Victor turned around to see Silk with a big smile on her face, "Yeah, well, try not to kill any more people before I get back."

"Then try to get back before they die."

Victor left the room shaking his head, but with a smirk on his face. "Smart ass." He walked down the stairs to see the old man having a drink at the bar. "Is there a temple of the goddess in this town?"

"Yeah, those damn things are here; there's two on the other side of town. Just go out and head toward the big ass bell. You can't miss it."

"I take it you're not a believer then."

"Ha, look around you, lad. Does this look like the type of place that's gotten the goddess's blessings lately? This town's been a shit hole for the last thirty years that I've been here. And those new robed fellas ain't gonna be changing that."

"Spoken like a man who's lived a happy life here."

"Ha, I'm a man who's lived long enough to know bullshit when I see it."

Smiling at the man's humor, Victor made his way out the door and into the muddy streets of the town. Easily, he spotted the bell tower off in the distance that was mentioned and set off down in its direction. The people of the town walked the streets in dirty clothes with expressionless faces, as if the life had been sucked out of them. The children of the city walked about like malnourished half corpses, their bare feet sinking in the mudd. Up ahead he could see a man followed by two young girls carrying buckets of water in their hands. Their ragged, torn cloth clothing exposing the skin beneath. Their sad faces reminded him of the girl named Rana he was sent to find.

If there was ever a city that just existed for the sake of existing, it would be this place. I've seen war cities where the people had more life to them.

He continued his walk through the city, inspecting its people. Men gambling on decks of taverns, and women washing cloth by the wells. There were three wells only a few feet apart from one another. It seemed to be the town hub for the women here, judging by the many poles with strings on them and large amounts of linens and undergarments hung to catch the sun for drying.

Victor continued on his way and turned a corner towards the bell tower. There, out in front of the tower, a man in a white robe stood on a wooden box, preaching to a crowd of five or six while others walked by.

"The goddess will bring to you her blessing if you only believe. The nobility have forgotten about their people. They serve only themselves. Their castles of magic only hold up their false wealth. But if we want to be held up, we must do it not with their magic, but through each other," said the brown-haired man on the wooden box. "The goddess does not ask for your money. She only asks for your time. And with it you will be rewarded with the fortune of her blessings."

"And what has the goddess done for us down here, huh?

We slave our asses off down here," said a man in ragged clothing. A hole in his boot, a slouch to one side indicated that this man had clearly seen better days. *Or perhaps it hasn't, this environment might just foster such types.*

"That is why she sent me here. I will guide you if you would only give me a chance. I only ask for an hour of your time each day. Just one hour so that I may properly teach you to receive her blessing."

"Ah, this is a bunch of nonsense," said the man as he walked off.

"I want to believe in the goddess, but... but nothing good ever happens to us down here. My first son died because he was ill. Where was the goddess then?" asked a woman in muddy clothing, holding a child in front of her. Her hair was tangled, dirt showed under her nails, and arms seemed skinnier than they should be for a woman her size.

The man stepped down from his box and approached the woman, "I grieve for your lost child and the pain you must have suffered through at his passing. Please, just come and give me an hour of your time, and I promise you will come to understand the love of the goddess." He then turned to the rest of the people around him. "All of you, come visit me again tomorrow, won't you?" Soon after a few more words, the crowd dispersed, leaving the robed man in front of the bell tower.

A little dramatic, but the man knows how to take advantage of the people who need to be taken advantage of, thought Victor before stepping forward. "That was a nice speech."

"Thank you, although I am afraid that it will be quite the daunting task to bring the goddess's glory to this city. Its people have been living in such a state as this for quite some time."

"And how did you guess I wasn't one of these people?"

"Look around you, do you think anyone else here could afford a pair of glasses," said the man pointing towards Victor's face. "It's a small item, but such a small item would

318

be a luxury here. But your clothing, while not especially noteworthy doesn't seem worn down, compared to the crowd that just dispersed."

Observative fellow.

"The robed man walked over to a horse watering trough to wash his hands. "Tell me, what brings you here to this part of the kingdom?"

"Just passing by with a friend on the way to Burlus. It was on the way, so we decided to stop in. What brings the Will of the Goddess here? There doesn't seem to be many people who wish to be saved in this city."

"That is a true thing upon first appearance," said the brown-haired man wiping his hands on his robes, "But these people, like all people, are just looking for hope. If you can supply that to them, then what better purpose is there?"

Victor watched as a few other white-robed figures came out of the bell tower carrying buckets. "I was told this city already had an old place of worship. Why use the bell tower?"

"Oh, there's a simple explanation as to that. It has a bell, whereas the previous place did not. If we want to renew the faith in the people here, we will need a symbol that they can look to, and what better symbol than a loud annoying one that rings throughout the whole town itself," said the man with a smile on his face.

"Who am I to argue with that logic?" asked Victor, extending his hand. "Amadeus Jacobs."

"Retallia Kolgin," said the man as he shook Victor's hand. "But people just call me Kemlor."

"How long will the Will of the Goddess hold station here?"

"We will stay here as long as needed to earn the people's trust. Afterward, I must leave, but I will leave the city in the hands of my brothers after it's been settled. I must go where the Will of the Goddess takes me."

"The church or the actual will of the goddess? Your naming schemes have often confused me."

"I wonder that sometimes as well," said The Kemlor with a chuckle. "But you are welcome to join us for services in the morning or evening if you so desire. We would welcome your company."

"I'm not much of a believer myself, but I do understand the need for people to have a symbol to believe in. Whether that takes the form of an army, a king, or even a goddess."

"Even so, all are welcome here; the offer still stands."

"I appreciate the offer; maybe I will take you on it then," said Victor as he gestured goodbye to The Kemlor and walked off down the street.

He continued through the city, taking stock of the situation he was in, noticing more guards patrolling the streets and white-robed figures conversing with the people as he wandered. *They certainly are a proactive bunch. They even have their own guards. But when someone has guards, it immediately makes one ask, just what are they guarding?*

He passed by a shop. *Well, now's as good a time as any to try and resupply.* He walked inside and saw wooden shelves half barren and a man sitting behind a desk carving at a piece of lumber with a knife.

"What can I do for ya?" asked the man.

"What, indeed?" asked Victor, taking stock of the place. "Do you have any fire powder and molding clay?"

"We got none of that. Maybe blacksmiths might have clay, but you ain't gonna find any fire powder here. That stuff's expensive."

"Okay, perhaps some sleep root or mangle weed."

"Nah, I think ya might be in the wrong place for the type of stuff you looking for."

"It would seem so," said Victor with a sigh. "Okay then, do you at least have a hammer and a rolling wheel?"

"I got a hammer."

"I suppose that'll have to do."

He made a few stops at the local stores, finding nothing but the grinding wheel, and headed back to the old tavern where he was staying. As he entered, he noticed the old man at the counter was gone.

Let's hope you kept your word, old man. It'd be a shame to have to hide the pieces of your body. Victor walked back up to their room, opening the door to find Silk looking out the window.

"Oh, you've returned."

"Here, I brought you food and wine."

"Good, I'm starving," said Silk as she walked over, taking the wine and piece of meat, and began chewing.

He watched her munch down the food, focusing on the black burn marks that were still on her arms, ankles, and wrists.

"Do we go out tonight?"

"Huh... ah no, for once I am tired. Between traveling and the fighting, I think I would very much like to just sleep for a few solid hours without having to worry about bandits on the road." Watching her, he noticed that the exhaustion had still not left her eyes. "What's going on with you? You've seemed more and more tired as we've continued our travels. Why is that?"

She wiped the wine from her mouth and rubbed at her tired eyes, "It's nothing. I just haven't been able to sleep well, is all."

"You're lying. You were like this before when I came back to the barn. You looked exhausted. What's going on with you?"

Silk sighed and walked over, sitting down on the bed. "I thought it would get easier after I healed up, but I guess that's not the case."

"I can't fix you if you won't tell me what's wrong."

"The spell the king placed on me; you remember it?"

"The bonding spell?"

"No, the mental spell."

"Okay, what of it?"

"Well, turns out the king knew what he was talking about when he refused to put the spell on you. It really does wear down on you over time. You remember what the side effects of the spell were?"

"Yeah, you were compelled to help me solve the case, so what's the issue? You've been with me this whole time."

"I've been with you, but I haven't done anything. You go out and leave me behind. Does that sound like helping to you?"

"But that spell causes mental pain if you don't..." Victor stomped over to the bed and grabbed Silk's face, looking into her tired eyes, "That was more than a moon ago. You mean to tell me you've been dealing with that this whole time?"

"It wasn't so bad at first; only recently has it started affecting me this much," she said with her face looking even more exhausted.

"Fuck," Victor let go of her face and began to pace the room. "And the reason you probably haven't been able to transform is because of that damned spell. And you couldn't help because you couldn't transform, which only made the spell even worse. Well, this is some screwed up circular logic."

"Sorry, I thought things would get better once I healed, so I didn't want to bring it up."

"It's fine... just... just give me a moment to think."

Victor paced around the room dozens of times. *When did the spell start taking effect? When we first left the capitol? No? There was nothing for her to do. I wonder if she knows that. If so, then maybe since Nyril. Shit, stop thinking about the cause. How do we fix it? Not helping makes it get worse. But she can't help until she can transform, right?* Victor turned around to see Silk staring at him as she watched him pace. *Ok, fine. If helping fixes it, it's a risk that needs to be taken.* He finally stopped. "Fine, we're going out tonight."

"But you said you were tired."

"I am tired, and you're even worse than me. The goddess's followers are setting up base in some bell tower down the way, but I saw a few of them exit the previous chapel in town when I was making my rounds. So, we're going to pay that old chapel a visit tonight and see what they have in there."

"But I can't change yet."

"And you probably never will again if I don't start taking you along with me. So, before this gets any worse, we're leaving tonight. Try to get some rest until nightfall; I'll take the floor for a few hours."

Victor sat down on the floor by the window and tried to close his eyes.

"Sleep in the bed with me," said Silk.

"The floor's fine; I'm used to it. Military life has got me accustomed to hard surfaces."

"You cuddle up with me in the back of a wagon for over a month and now is when you choose to act prudish?"

"That was different. It was cold, you were weak, and hadn't eaten in days."

"And now I'm still weak and have gotten accustomed to you being beside me. You want me to rest, well I want you to lay beside me."

"Goddess help me. You're a pain in the ass," said Victor as he stood, walking over to the bed and laying down beside Silk. "Happy now?"

"Surprisingly, yes. Yes, I am," said Silk as she laid down beside Victor and snuggled her head under his chin. "I really have grown accustomed to this; I didn't lie when I said that."

"Well, don't I feel flattered? Just try and get some rest. We'll leave after the sun is fully down."

And soon, they both found themselves asleep in each other's arms.

CHAPTER 20

A handful of the Black Jewels arrived at the city of Orlana, with Oscar, Gregga, Jacob, and Dessi sitting inside a carriage. Magic lamps littered the walkways of the stone topped streets as horses clopped along carrying men and women in elegant clothing. The tapping of men's canes was the backdrop to conversations of magical theory and high society living. All the buildings seemed as if they were made of hand-crafted stone, with each house having ornate doors that showed off a name or a symbol of a family.

"Once again, back in the midst of the rich. I never did like being around so much hypocrisy," said Oscar, "And why am I here? I doubt this mission required an old man."

"For no other reason than I wanted you to be," replied Dessi. "And besides, you need to get out of that musty old tent."

"I do my best thinking in that musty old tent."

"Then why ask me to join?" asked Gregga. "I doubt you need a Sakari to kill these men. Jasper say you were good killer."

"Because you will distract them, the beautiful exotic queen from the Sakari wilds."

"And what is this plan you've made up?" asked Oscar.

"I'm still working on the details, but I just have to seduce one of the men, and Jacob can mind control the other. Then we kill them at the same time and make it look like a brother's quarrel."

"Sounds simple enough," said Oscar. "However, I don't know if you've noticed lately, but things haven't exactly been going according to plan."

"That's why I said; I'm still working on the details. Jacob and I will go around and gather information on the targets, and you can meet with the clients to make sure everything is set up properly. The plan will change based on the information we both receive."

"Fine, let's get this over with." Oscar banged his fist against the carriage, causing it to come to a halt. "We'll be at the Humphrey's, I've used it before when coming here."

"All right, me and Jacob will meet you there when we're done," said Dessi, extending out her hand.

Oscar sighed and reached to his side, pulling out a small coin purse and placed it in Dessi's hand, "Ya gonna send us home poor."

"Good service costs good coin, and besides, we have to blend in. And we'll need new clothing to do that."

"Yes, yes, off with you then."

Dessi stepped out of the carriage and onto the stone streets, gazing around at the well-sculptured city.

"What's the plan?" asked Jacob, approaching her on horseback.

"The plan is for you to accompany me on some information gathering. So, get down from there; we'll do the rest on foot."

Jacob dismounted his horse, handing the reins to another soldier as the carriage and men continued off down the streets of Orlana. "Alright, you have me at your command, so what's first?"

"First is that we find ourselves some clothes and a bath. We both stink of sweat and horses."

"Seems to be the smell of the trade."

"Well, we're performing a different trade in a different city, so come on."

"I shall follow your lead on dress attire, I guess."

"Just something quick, this is just to fit in, not to stand out. Simple attire will do just fine for now."

It didn't take them long to find several clothing stores to choose from. Splitting up, they headed off to separate stores, meeting back up half an hour later with their supplies.

"You took a little longer than expected," said Jacob as Dessi approached him on a bench.

"Female clothes are much more complicated than men's and your basic attire. What did you get?"

"Just a shirt and trousers? And you?"

"You'll just have to wait and see, but nothing too fancy. Nonetheless, that was annoying."

"What? And here I was told women like shopping," said Jacob and they began walking down the street."

"We do when it's stuff we actually want. What I have is something for the mission. That's a totally different set of clothing."

Dessi and Jacob ventured into the city until they reached a large hotel. Walking inside, they noticed the ornate furniture spread through the first floor and a large red carpet that flowed from the lower level up the steps up to the second floor. Ahead of them was a woman in a flowery dress with her hair tied in a bun. Her face was heavily pressed in makeup and eyeliner as she smiled at they approached.

"Greetings and welcome to the Shay-Lon. Will you be staying with us for a while?"

"Only for a few nights. We just got off the road and would like to not smell as if we were born in a shed."

"Oh, I do so understand. The travels of the road can make even the most civilized smell like a commoner. Shall we have someone follow up with a tub of water for a bath and perhaps some scented oils for your pleasure?"

"Thank you, that would be lovely. I can't wait to get out of these clothes and into a bath."

"Well then, that will be one gold for the night, and we'll have someone escort you to your room."

"Thank you," said Dessi as she reached into the purse Oscar had given her, handing the coin to Jacob. "Honey, pay the woman, please."

"Thank you, madam," said Jacob as he stepped forward and placed the coin in the woman's hand, smiling at her.

They both were escorted up the stairs by a boy in uniform and led into their room, with Jacob dropping their new clothing on the bed.

Soon a well-dressed woman with a wand in her hand came into the room along with two servants. The two servants carried with them a large ivory tub, placing it on the floor in front of the bed. They were quickly followed by several other servants carrying buckets of water and soaps, pouring the water in the bucket and filling it.

"Thank you, you may leave now," said the woman with the wand to the servants after the tub had been filled. She then turned to Dessi. "Do you prefer your water hot or mildly warm?"

"Whatever you think is best suited to wash off days of dirt and sweat from the road."

"Hot it is then," said the woman with a smile. She placed

her wand over the water, "Beauty in all things," and streams of red magic began to flow from her fingers, across the wand, and over into the water until soon they all saw steam begin to form. "There, that should do it. The water should stay hot for around two hours. That should be more than enough time to wash away your travels and perhaps a little time with your gentleman there."

The lady bowed to Dessi, then smiled up at Jacob and winked. Jacob extended his hand, and the lady placed her fingers in his palm. He then bowed, kissing the lady's hand and sending out a message with his magic. *Thank you, my lady, you have been most kind.* The woman glanced around the room in confusion before looking back down at Jacob, who smirked back up at her.

"Mind magic, oh my." She then turned to Dessi with pursed lips and a sly smile on her face, "Well, aren't you in for a good time. Wherever did you find this one?"

"Old childhood friend, he's traveling with me till we reach my father's home."

"Yes, well," She turned to Jacob. "It's always good to have friends. Perhaps one day I'll find one of my own." And she walked out of the room.

Jacob followed behind her, locking the door. "Well, she was a charming woman."

"They always are when you pay them enough."

"You seem so comfortable in places like…" said Jacob, turning around to see Dessi's boots already across the floor and her leaning over, pulling off her trousers.

"Oh, come now," said Dessi, smiling back at him, catching him staring at her, "You've seen me naked plenty of times. Surely you're still not surprised by it." She kicked off her trousers and lifted her shirt over her head, exposing her breasts to him.

"I don't think a man ever really gets used to the sight of a nude woman," said Jacob, staring at her body. "But your scars, they've gone again. When did you have the time?"

"When we took Rana, I mean Isha into Vontal. I got her face cleaned up and got myself taken care of as well. Do you approve?" asked Dessi, placing her hands on her hips and standing stark naked before Jacob.

"I hardly think my approval matters on the subject."

"You think so? Well… oh, that is hot," said Dessi as she stepped into the tub, slowly lowering herself into the water. "You're the only man I prefer to lay with, even if you seldomly touch me."

"You know I can't control it when we—"

"I know, I know," said Dessi with a sigh. "Now come over here and bathe me, surely that's not too much to ask of you."

Jacob shook his head, "Yes, my princess." He grabbed a cloth from the water and submerged it before running the soap across it. Placing the towel across Dessi's neck, he began rubbing it across her shoulders, watching the heat and steam rise from her body.

"Oh, that feels so much better," said Dessi, embracing the hot towel as the water dripped down her shoulders.

"I'm glad you approve."

"Did you influence them? Or was that woman just naturally turned on by your charms?"

"Probably the influence. Both of them won't remember your face. They will only remember mine."

"Good, I haven't decided what role I'm to play yet. No need to pretend to be something unless it serves the purpose. And now that that woman knows you're a mind mage, you're likely to become the most popular man in town when the rumors start spreading."

"Words cannot express my joy," said Jacob in a depressing tone.

Dessi laughed, "You must be the only man in the world who doesn't like to be pursued by women."

"Well, since father has sold me out to the nobility since the moment my cock could get hard, it hasn't exactly made my experiences with women anything more than formal.

All looking for children who might have my talent. How many bastards do you think I've fostered by now? Sons and daughters that I'll never meet?"

"Who knows, but outside of your bastards, is there much difference between us? How many men have I seduced into bed only to kill them when they're in their supposed passions? There are certain things that can't properly be explained, like the feeling of watching a man die while his cock is still inside you."

Jacob squeezed the rags against Dessi's skin as he listened to her words.

"Don't worry, all things must come to an end. We've survived this long. We can survive a bit longer," said Dessi, placing her hand upon Jacob's.

"You think this is what normal couples talk about?"

"Is that what we are? A couple?" asked Dessi, turning her head upward to gaze at Jacob.

Jacob looked down at her face and saw tears appearing in her eyes. Whether it was from the steam of the hot water or from the emotion of the conversation, he couldn't tell. Lowering his head, he placed his forehead against hers, allowing his hair to brush over her face.

"Couple or not, we are together, and that's enough for me," said Jacob as he pressed his lips against hers and allowed the rag to slide from his hands into the water.

They both took their time and bathed each other. A bit longer than needed as they allowed their fingers to wander over each other's bodies in an attempt to satisfy a growing lust, and if not satisfy it, then perhaps abate it.

But soon they headed out of the hotel, Dessi dressed in a long blue dress that exposed a decent amount of her cleavage with a large bonnet over her head partly covering her face. Jacob adorned a dark blue dress shirt and trousers.

"Well, don't we look like a distinguished couple. How do people spend all day in these getups?"

"You're not the one wearing a petticoat and garter belt.

330

I might as well just give up on breathing all together in this thing."

"What's with the big hat?"

"It's a bonnet, and I'd prefer to keep my face hidden a little while longer."

"Well, it's your show, my lady. Where are we off to first?"

"They are the Duke's sons, so they can't be hard to find. Come my pretend husband. Show your wife around town," said Dessi as she linked arms with Jacob and let him escort her down the stone road of the city.

The streets were filled with similarly dressed people, all in fine clothing. As they made their way through the city, they stopped by several merchants to shop and asked questions about the city and its residents. In those conversations, Dessi was sure to bring up the Duke's two sons. Before stopping at a jewelry maker and striking up a conversation.

"Are the Duke's sons in town? I'd like to meet them while I'm here," said Jacob.

"Aye, Henry was here just a few days ago looking for a trinket for one of his lovers, I'd guess. And Franklin usually spends most of his time down near the barracks; he helps the men train down there now. Brothers, they may be, but the similarities stop at the bloodline. I watched both of them boys grow up and oil and water is what they are."

"And would you know where I might find Henry?" asked Dessi, picking up a small ornate hair pin, holding it up in the light.

"Around this time of day, he'd probably be at the park with his men or in the town library."

"Thank you, Sir. I'll take this pin if I can."

"Of course, that'll be eighty silver, but for your pretty face, I'll let it go for fifty."

"I appreciate that. Honey, please pay the man."

Jacob placed the coins into the man's palms and left the shop owner there in a daze for a few seconds.

"So where to first?"

"Barracks. Best to get what will probably be the more difficult one out of the way."

Eventually, they made their way down to the city's barracks, where the town guards were housed in a large building. Jacob looked down at all the soldiers going back and forth with their morning training.

"You won't be able to hide your face in there. And that's way too many for me to influence."

"That's fine, as long as no one knows where I'm staying or that we've been asking around about the two sons. You stay out here. I'll do this part alone," said Dessi as she took off her bonnet and allowed her hair to flow downward. She then ran her hands through her hair, making a mess of it.

"Now, what are you doing?"

"Making myself look just a bit disheveled," she said as she slapped her hands against her face a few times for her cheeks to turn red.

"And why's that?"

Dessi placed her hand on Jacob's chest and leaned into him, looking into his face innocently while batting her eyelashes. "Because I'm a weak and harmless innocent woman, who those types eat up." She tapped him on the chest, "And you, my lumbering husband are tall, muscular, and give off the scent that you're ready to kill at any moment." She lightly pushed him back. "So, if you'll excuse me, it's time for a lady to do her job." Dessi walked her way down the hill, swinging her hips in an exaggerated motion for Jacob to watch.

She reached the barrack's door and took a seat alongside a few others who were sitting on a bench and waited for an opportunity. She didn't need to wait long as soon a man who seemed to be in charge came walking by with four other men following behind him. *Well, either that's him or the general. And outside of Victor, I ain't met a general that young before.* She watched as the four men followed him around, praising him and following his orders. *That much ass-kissing; he must be the Duke's son, and those lackeys would spend the next decade trying to improve their station. Well, you're in luck, lackeys; that man's going to be dead soon. So, you'll have to find someone else to suck up to. But first, let's figure out what type of women you like.*

Dessi walked up to one of desks near the supposed Duke's son to speak with the guard sitting behind it, "Excuse me, Sir, a pickpocket stole my purse with all my coins inside, and I don't know what to do."

"I'm sorry, ma'am. Ahh… do you know what he looked like?" said the man at his desk as he performed a double-take at Dessi.

Dessi glanced over at the Duke's son, but he didn't move. He just continued to talk to the men around him. *So, damsel isn't your thing.* "It was a small boy. I chased him into an alley, thinking it was just a prank, but two men grabbed me. One of them had the nerve to reach down my top and fondled my breasts." She leaned over, allowing the man to look down her cleavage. "See, they're all red from where he grabbed them."

"Well… I… ahh… I see… they certainly are ah… red," said the man fumbling his words.

Dessi glanced back at the Duke's son to see that he was undoubtedly glancing in her direction now. *Oh, so you like the dumb ones. Well, come and get me, Mr. Wolf; this little bunny needs you.* "I know, and this was a new dress too." Dessi crossed her arms and started pouting, "What am I supposed to do? They took all my money. Papa's gonna be furious with me."

"Excuse me, Miss, perhaps I can be of assistance. My name is Franklin Delik. I'm the future Duke of this city."

"Oh, hello, can you help me find the people who took my purse?"

"Yes, ma'am, come with me, and we can discuss how to best solve this matter."

"Thank you so much, Sir. I was so scared. Papa really is going to be mad at me if I don't get the purse back."

"Don't worry, just come with me, and we'll get an investigation started. Now tell me exactly what happened. You said two men grabbed your breasts?" said Franklin as he placed his hands on Dessi's hips and led her over to a room.

A little while later, Dessi left the barracks and found Jacob sitting on a bench down the street.

"How'd things go?"

"About as well as could be expected. We're meeting up tomorrow for supper. After he investigates my make-believe purse snatcher."

"Your ways of seduction are as impressive as always. It makes me wonder if you ever use them on me."

"Of course, I do. But the difference there is that I love you."

Jacob's eyes opened wide, "That's... that's actually the first time you've said that."

"Well, a certain little girl asked me that question some months ago, so I figured I might as well answer it for myself."

"And when did you answer it?"

"When we were bathing each other and I wished that we could stay like that forever. That's when I knew."

"Well, I know I've said it to you before. But it's nice to hear it back from your lips. Sorry I couldn't have given you a better time to say it."

Dessi linked arms with Jacob again, "There is no right time, other than the time I choose to say it. Now come on, you're going to help me seduce another man."

"Oh, how romantic you are, my lady wife."

They headed off through the city once again towards it's park. Eventually, they reached its gates but stood there in surprise at the visage before them. There was a lake in the center of the park where people were dining on a wooden platform above the water. Children ran around the area, hiding up in the trees, casting magic that sparked colors of all shades at their limbs. But the leaves absorbed the magical sparks changing colors throughout the park. Many of them weren't just one color, but instead a cornucopia of beautiful colors that slowly changed from one shade to the next.

"I've never seen anything like this before," said Jacob.

"Oh, this is a fairly new development to the city," said a nearby man overhearing Jacob's words. "This exquisite display of foliage was a gift from the school of Sceana this year. The spell the children are using was taught to them by Master Tannor, specifically for the trees here; between you and me, it has worked wonders as a pseudo-babysitter for an hour or two a day."

"Thank you, sir," said Jacob as they both walked into the park gazing over the foliage in all its colorful glory. "Little Isha spends her days in a place filled with magic like this? I wonder if she will be the same girl by the time she returns. Perhaps she'll come back to us and be able to change the weather or move mountains." Jacob reached up, plucking an orange and green leaf from the tree, holding it out for Dessi.

"We all have to grow up one day, I guess," said Dessi, taking the leaf in her hand, rubbing it between her fingers.

"You want her growing up as fast as we did?"

"No, but given Oscar's nature, she may not have much of a choice."

"Your first time was an accident. Father had no intentions... I saw the anger in his eyes. He regrets it still to this day."

"And your first. Was that an accident as well?"

"That's different; I'm a man."

"A fourteen-year-old man who came to lay in my bed the moment he returned home."

"I did ask you."

"How could I refuse? The look on your face was heartbreaking."

Jacob sighed while patting Dessi's arm, "Well, there are those Sakari girls she is always with. Would it be so strange for her to find comfort and safety in their arms?"

"Perhaps not, but I'm pretty sure she likes boys."

"How do you know that?"

"Call it a guess."

"Then perhaps that school holds her future husband within its walls. And together they shall become the greatest mages in the land."

"For Oscar to manipulate to no end." Dessi sighed. "That sounds like a bigger threat than the shadow king."

"Ha! Despite his manipulations, Father has never once lied to me about what he was asking me to do or for what purpose. He does at the very least place his trust in his children to make our own decisions."

"You ever wonder why he never called me his daughter? Was it because I never had magic like you two?"

"That's a question you'll have to ask him yourself one day. I'm sure if you ask sincerely, he will tell you the answer."

"Perhaps one day, I'm not sure I could handle that truth right now."

The two continued walking around the park together, taking in the colors of the trees and the shows of magic that were on display throughout the area. But soon they found themselves in awe of their next target, even more so than the spectacle of magic. Henry was sitting near the water gazing over the sparkling lake with one man beside him and another smaller man sitting in his lap with flowers in his hair. He smiled at the smaller man while rubbing the side of his face with his finger.

"Well," said Dessi with a smirk while patting Jacob on the hand. "I know you don't like me flirting with other men, but I must admit. I'm fairly interested in watching you flirt with other men."

"You can't be serious," replied Jacob, gazing back between Henry on the bench and Dessi by his side. "There's no way."

"What? You're just as cute as those men are. I imagine if we put some flowers in your hair and a little makeup on those cheeks, I dare say you'd pretty up real nice," teased Dessi with a sly smirk on her face.

"I think you're enjoying this a little too much."

"Oh, come on, I've seduced other women before. Surely asking you to play the dominator to one of the same sex can't be asking too much. One touch of your magic, and you're done. That's a great amount easier than the work I would have to do."

"It's far too much to ask," Jacob sighed. "But, fine, let's get this over with."

"What? Seriously? I was just teasing. Are you really going to?"

"It's your plan; I'll try to play along. But you're the professional here, so tell me how I should go about this. I'm not exactly accustomed to picking up men."

"Oh... ah... well," Dessi fumbled her words before turning back to focus on Henry, "Well, you'll want to get him away from his men for a moment, I'd assume. How long to influence him to your liking?"

"Well, it's not making him forget about me, that simple enough. But making someone interested in me would take a little longer. Perhaps a strong handshake for around ten seconds would do."

"Humm, then you'll definitely need to get him away from those men. Although he does seem partial to that one on his lap. So maybe he's the dominating type."

"I'm not sure I'm built for the submissive role."

"I suppose not," said Dessi, looking up at him, "Well, you are larger than him. Perhaps you could intimidate him into a moment alone. Make it sound official-like."

"You think that'll work?"

"Well, unless you want to go and take a seat on his lap like that one over there, I'd guess that's our best option."

"I think I'll be going with intimidation then."

Dessi left Jacob's side and went over to sit down on a bench to watch as he walked over to the three men.

"Excuse me, sir," said Jacob, placing his hand behind his back and standing in military posture.

Henry ignored Jacob's words and continued to stroke the chin of the man in his lap.

"Henry Delik!" spoke Jacob in a tone so loud that it attracted the attention of numerous passersby. "I require your full attention at this time."

Henry shook in his seat, bouncing the small man in his lap, before turning his attention to Jacob. "What? Who dares address me in such... Oh my, you are a big fellow." Jacob looked down at Henry, narrowing his eyes. "Ah! I mean. How may I help you, Sir?"

"Your father has asked that I deliver a message to you."

Henry sighed, scratching his head, "Oh, father again, I think you've gotten the wrong son. Franklin is down by the barracks polishing his sword." He turned back to the man in his lap. "And I'd prefer it if you'd left me to do the same."

"No, sir, the message was meant specifically for you; Franklin is not to be involved."

"Oh, really," said Henry in surprise. "Father wants something of me specifically? Then tell me, what is it?"

"Sorry, Sir. What I have to say is for your ears only. While you may tell your companions what I'm to tell you, they shall not hear it from me."

Henry raised a brow, "Is that so?" He maneuvered the smaller man off his lap, placed his hands on his knees, and stood up. "Very well then, I suppose a walk around the lake is in order."

Jacob turned and led Henry on a walk around the sparkling water.

"So, what's this business with my father?"

"Lord Delik wishes for you to represent him at a meeting at the school of Sceana in the coming months."

"Me? And not Franklin, are you sure you don't have the wrong son?"

"Orders were precise. Henry Delik is to represent the Duke, Lord Delik, at a gathering of nobles in Sceana. Perhaps you think too little of the trust your father places in you."

"Perhaps you haven't known my father long enough."

"Perhaps. I have only just joined your father's employ recently."

"And what is your name, soldier?"

"Malcom... Malcolm Trisdale."

"Well, Mr. Trisdale, has my father informed you of his disgust in my attraction for my fellow man?"

"No, Sir. I imagine he didn't find the matter of much import to bring up during my briefing."

"No, I suppose he wouldn't," Henry stopped walking, "Tell me then, soldier, what do you yourself think of my preferred taste."

"It is not my place to say, Sir."

"Oh, no need to be shy now. I'm sure I've heard worse. Go on, tell me how an upstanding soldier like yourself feels about what he saw just a moment ago."

Jacob closed his eyes and slowly opened them again, staring straight into the brown eyes of Henry, "Permission to speak frankly then, Sir."

"Oh... Well, of course, permission granted," said Henry, taken aback by Jacob's formalness.

"I don't care."

"What?"

"I don't care whether you suck one or a thousand cocks. None of that is any concern of mine. All I care about is can you do the job that's been assigned to you."

"What? Of course I can; I'm not a simpleton."

"Then that's all that matters, but now you will answer a question of mine. Are you ashamed that you find men attractive?"

"Of course not. You saw me earlier. Does that look like I'm ashamed, as if I'm trying to hide?"

"Then why care what others think?"

"He's not any other. He's my bloody father. What son doesn't want to be accepted by their father?"

"I suppose you have a point there. I myself have also spent a large amount of my life trying to please my father as well."

"A large man like yourself, what could you have to live up to?"

"No matter how old we become, we always feel as if we are children compared to our parents."

Henry laughed, "You're a strange one."

"Are you seriously saying that to me?" asked Jacob, turning back and taking notice of the men on the bench.

"Ha! I guess I am not in any position to speak. But tell me, why do my actions not taint your sensibilities? Can't imagine that's a regular thing in the military."

"My best friend preferred the company of men. So, my outlook on the subject is somewhat tainted."

"What?"

"Is that such a surprise?"

"Of course, it is. You should have led off with that. My interest alone would have made me follow you."

"It was during my time as a mercenary; his father would not accept him also, so he found his way into being a sellsword."

"And what happened to this fellow?"

"Well, as you can imagine, mercenaries don't live that long. A blade to the back took him."

"Oh, I'm sorry."

"It's fine. I took his blade as my own and had his name engraved on it near the hilt."

"A very honorable gesture."

"He was an honorable man."

Henry stared up at Jacob for a moment. "Would...

would you like to meet up tomorrow? Nothing too personal, perhaps some sword training. I'm not as good as my brother, but I like to think Father's lessons made me capable enough. That is, if you aren't forced to head back after delivering your message."

"That will do fine. I am allowed some leisure time after delivering my message."

"Good, you can meet me on our manor grounds in the morning."

"That will do."

Jacob and Henry continued to walk around the lake until Jacob left his side, bidding him farewell and walking out of the park back into the city streets. Soon afterward, Dessi left her park bench and walked out of the park to see Jacob waiting for her over at a flower stand.

"I guess it didn't work out as planned," said Dessi, walking up to Jacob.

"No, I will be meeting him tomorrow for sword practice."

"Oh wow, I never saw you touch him."

"I never did, we just started talking, and he invited me to come to his father's manor for practice."

Dessi grabbed a flower from the stand, handing it to Jacob, "Well then, you might have a natural talent for seducing men."

"Then I'm afraid that's a talent that I will never get to fully explore."

CHAPTER 21

Nighttime fell over the city of Molask as Victor and Silk left the room headed downstairs. Silk covered herself in a dark hooded robe while Victor wore his regular clothes. Again, the owner of the tavern was still nowhere to be seen when they came downstairs.

There was a surprising amount of people still out in the streets at night. But most didn't seem to care about who else might be around: a man pulled a horse through the street, a woman carried two heavy-looking watering buckets up through some doors, splashing with each step. But still the two moved forward, heading back through the city. When they arrived near the old chapel, they both saw more robed people and a decent amount of the citizens standing by the building.

Strange time to be holding services. "Let's sneak around and—"

Silk tugged on his clothing, pulling him back down before he could move forward.

"What's wrong?" whispered Victor.

"A guard is coming; don't you hear him?"

Victor paused, not hearing anything, but it didn't take long before two soldiers walked past their dark corner. *Okay, seems everyone is just a master of stealth besides me. Well, at least this one makes sense.* Victor grabbed hold of Silk's cloak, pulling her up in front of him, "Okay master assassin," he whispered. "You take lead on this. Our objective is to investigate that building. We need to avoid being seen and try our best to not kill someone. Think you can help me pull that off?"

Silk crawled forward, peeking around the corner, surveying the surrounding area. "Lots of guards, but they have openings in their patrol. Just follow me."

Soon Victor found himself maneuvering through the shadows of nearby buildings and beside wagons until they reached the side of the old worship hall. Victor indeed found that The Kemlor he met earlier was holding some type of service. From a nearby broken window, he could hear them speak as he crept forward in the grass..

"I want you all to know that I appreciate you all coming here these last few nights. I know things have been difficult, but we have come a long way since we first started."

"Can you really help us?" asked a man with desperation clear in his voice.

"No, sadly, I am just a man of flesh and bone like all others here tonight. What I offer is not some miracle cure for the disease of depression that has brought rot to your city and your lives. All I can offer you is a chance to help yourselves. What you do after that is up to you. The sacrifice is yours to make."

"He's a very talented speaker," said Victor.

"What is the sacrifice he's talking about?"

"No idea, but I'm guessing it has something to do with those red jewels."

"I remember the king saying that."

"I will have my men inform you all of our next meeting," said The Kemlor. "There, I will show you the power of the goddess herself."

Silk and Victor watched the crowd leave out of the room as a soldier approached The Kemlor.

"You really do like giving those speeches of yours, don't you?"

"It is the words that the people need to hear. I am merely the deliverer. But tell me, will our guest be arriving soon?"

"Yeah, I received word that he was on his way. But I've been told that he's been suffering side effects of the transfer."

"That's to be expected. He was an early-round tester. Him surviving this long proves just how durable he is. We were blessed to find him when we did. I'm not sure my conscience could have handled another round of failures. Have they started another set of the treatments on him?"

"Yes, which seems to be slowing down the worst of the symptoms."

"Good, follow me. I wish to show you the progress we've made so far."

The Kemlor walked over to a wall, and to Victor's surprise, passed through it, followed by the soldier.

"More illusion magic," said Victor. "I wonder where it leads."

He crept around to the edge of the building, examining the corner walls with his fingers, while Silk kept lookout. Victor placed his back against the wall and crept forward, searching the area with his foot, trying to step softly. Only after he was confident that there was nothing there did he make his way back to Silk, who was still crouched down by the side of the window.

"The back of the house is solid. So, either there, in a tiny room, or wherever they went was beneath the ground. A basement of some sorts, perhaps."

"You want to go and take a look?"

"No, that's enough for tonight; we've gathered enough information. Plus, there are too many guards around. It's best to call it a night and try again when there's not so many people around."

"Okay, then. We can..."

"What's wro—" said Victor before he was pushed down to the ground by Silk as she removed her cloak and tossed it over him, before removing the tie from her ponytail and letting her long white hair hang freely. "What are--"

Soon two guards came running around the corner. "I'm telling you I saw something from the window and..." The guard saw Silk with her back turned to him. "Oh, what do we..."

"Hey... this one don't look right, Davey," spotting Silk's white hair and skin from behind in the torchlight.

Silk quickly turned around, revealing her face in the night as the lantern's light cast shadows on her visage.

"Oh shit. What in the goddess," said one of the men as she quickly jumped back. His partner had already turned around and began to yell as he dashed around the corner.

Silk raised her hands and leaped at the man who quickly turned around and began running, falling to the ground, and dropping his torch before crawling around the corner as fast as he could, following his companion.

Victor quickly hopped up from the grass with Silk's cloak, grabbing her by the arm and sprinting off into the darkness as far away as he could before more men could come back. After crossing a safe distance, they hid in the shadows and watched the building as more men with torches came back around. They could hear some of the men laughing as one of the frightened guards desperately tried to convince them about what he saw.

They stayed out in the darkness for a little while longer before navigating their way back to the tavern and up to their room. Both entered the room covered in dirt, mud, and grass as Victor closed the door behind them.

"Okay, that was a small adventure and quick thinking with scaring the guards. They're going to be talking about the ghost of the chapel for months now."

"I'm happy someone enjoyed it," said Silk with her back turned.

"You're upset about something."

"I was starting to think that I didn't look that bad anymore; I guess I had just gotten accustomed to how you treated me." She raised her wrists up, looking at the black marks and started scratching at them with her fingernails. "Ah, I'm sick of this. I'm tired of wearing myself. I just want to go back to being somebody else, anybody else."

"Hey, stop that!" said Victor, walking over to her and grabbing her by the wrists.

Silk struggled in his grasp, "Let... go!" She flailed her arms, hitting Victor in his chest. "I'm sick of all this." Victor pulled her close, wrapping his arms around her and squeezing her against his chest as she began crying. "I don't want... I don't... to look like this anymore... I want to be human... again."

"Shhh... shh... It's okay... It's gonna be okay..." said Victor in a soft voice as he began to sway back and forth with Silk held tightly in his arms.

And there they stood in the silence of the dark and dusty room, from one moment to the next. Victor not allowing Silk to leave his embrace. Her fingers clutched to the back of his jacket, breathing in the smell of the dirt and sweat that had soaked into the fabric on his shirt. She had grown accustomed to this smell, lying beside him on the road every night for over a month. His arms wrapped around her when she was cold. It seemed to be the only thing that felt right when everything else was so very wrong.

"You calmed down yet?"

Silk nodded, grazing her face against Victor's chest, not wanting to speak out of embarrassment.

"Come on, the night's over. Let's lay down. We're both tired." Victor led Silk over to the bed, laying down and continued to wrap her in his arms until she fell asleep.

The following morning, Victor awoke to the sound of splashing water. Even with his eyes closed, he felt the irritation of the sun shining in their room, signaling for him to wake. He yawned and rolled over, then realized Silk was not by his side anymore. He quickly opened his eyes and lifted himself on his elbows, gazing around the room, only to find Silk in a corner with her back exposed and washing herself.

"Ah, usually I wake before you. I must have been more tired than I thought."

"I didn't want to wake you."

"Are you feeling better this morning?" said Victor, rubbing his eyes.

"Ah... yes... sorry again about last night. It's... it's not easy being like this."

"It's fine. I made the decision to get you out of that dungeon. I accept what comes along with that. But what I was referring to specifically was, how is that head of yours doing. You helped me out a lot last night. So, how's the spell been affecting you?"

"Oh, it's not as bad now. I was able to sleep last night without waking up from the pain."

"That's good," said Victor, raising from the bed and scratching his head. "Well, I'll leave you to finish cleaning, and I'll—"

"No, you don't have to leave," said Silk, standing from

her stool and turning, holding her tunic in her arms but exposing her breasts to him.

Victor raised a brow at her, "I'm just going to get breakfast, then I'll return. But I'm curious, does being naked not mean the same to you that it means to regular women? I'd imagine most girls would be embarrassed being naked around another man."

"Why? Do you dislike looking at me?"

"No, just an observation of normal traits of the opposite sex."

"You are the only one who's seen me like this and hasn't either run away or tried to kill me. The only people I've ever even had a conversation with while wearing myself are either you or my sister."

"What about that Grigguk fella you mentioned before?"

"He doesn't allow us to wear ourselves around him. Not even when..." Silk's voice trailed off as she looked down at the floor.

"Well, I think we've come a long way from me holding alagon powder over your head in the captain's chamber of a ship."

"Yes, protecting you during that trip was a pain. Drayvon wanted to kill you after he lit the sleeping root. I had to stop him when he came back, before he made it to your room."

"I'm happy you did, or else we wouldn't be having this conversation now. And with me being such a happy fellow, I can't fathom who'd want me dead. It was just supposed to be a peace talk mission."

"Grigguk said it came from the Mari kin..." Silk's voice cut off in her throat. She dropped her tunic and clutched at the black marks on her neck before looking up at Victor, who smiled back at her.

"Well, now I know it's someone from my own kingdom that wants me dead. It doesn't narrow it down much, but it's a start," said Victor as he walked over, knelt, and picked up Silk's tunic from the floor, handing it back to her. "You go ahead and finish washing up, and I'll go and get us some breakfast."

CHAPTER 22

Isha lay in bed, moonlight shining down on her. She spent the last few hours half asleep, falling in and out of consciousness. Something felt different, as if her body was hot. She turned, and as her hand flopped over, she felt only soft pillows where her sister should have been. Instantly her eyes opened as she sat up and began looking around the dark room, and out of the shadows she saw them. Both of her sisters, sitting down on the floor beside one another with their legs crossed. The pale moonlight barely showed their features in the outlines of their bodies. But she didn't need the light; in those silhouettes, there was the unmistakable glow of their golden eyes staring back at her. The golden glow poured out as the trails of magic that hovered around their bodies before fading away.

"Ah… Jacinta, Makeba… what's wrong," said Isha as she nervously looked around the room.

"Nothing wrong, sister. You go back to bed," said Jacinta in a calm voice.

"But… but your eyes. You're using them. I thought you said you only use them when you go hunting."

"That is true, sister," said Makeba. "You disappear for two days. We hunt for you, but could not find. We will not make that mistake again. From now on, we will remember our sister. And we find her when she lost again. We promise we will find you."

Isha swallowed nervously at the words of her sister, "Okay. I'm sorry. I left you two alone. I really am. But can you stop that for now? It's scaring me a little."

The two Sakari girls looked at each other. And soon, their golden eyes faded back into the shadows as they stood and walked back into the moonlight.

"We not want to scare sister. We just need to be sure that we find sister if she ever lost again."

"I understand. But can we go back to bed now?" asked Isha as she reached her hands out for her sisters to join her.

Makeba and Jacinta both climb back into bed with Isha, lying down on each side, wrapping their arms around her.

Isha took a deep breath as she felt the warmth of her sisters around her. *I really don't know what I'm doing anymore.*

Hours later, Isha awoke with her head on Makeba's chest, looking over into Jacinta's sleeping face. Slowly crawling out of bed, trying not to wake them, she left the room, making her way downstairs. Below, she saw Leo passed out on the couch with his head in Elena's lap while she read a book.

"Oh, good morning. Did you three make up last night?"

"Yes, I think they've forgiven me now."

"That's good to hear. Are you hungry? Would you like me to fix something for breakfast?"

"No, that's fine. I'm not hungry right now."

"Well, come take a seat then."

Isha sat down on the couch watching Leo sleep. "Did he have to work last night?"

"You can say that," said Elena with a smile, "While you were sleeping, he snuck in and started healing that leg of yours again."

"Oh, I didn't know." Isha looked down at her leg and began rubbing her knee. "It does feel a lot better than yesterday."

"You know, it's never going to get better if you keep over-exerting it like that. It's going to need a proper amount of time without you putting crazy pressure on it."

"I know. I keep making mistakes. Is he okay?"

"Who? Leo? Oh, he's fine, just tired is all. He'd be a good man if he wasn't such an idiot," said Elena as she ran her thumb across his face, brushing his hair to the side, "But, I'm afraid it's too late to change who he is at this point. He's destined for a life of stupidity and healing."

"Are... are you two a couple?"

"Us? Perhaps we are, although it's hard to whink of us that way while he keeps going on about that harem business. But we do keep each other company, and that's enough for now. Leo's like having a puppy that you feel compelled to help and look after. If he's left alone, well, he mostly just wallows, sulks, and probably breaks things. But if you tell him you need him, he will usually act and set out on his purpose." Elena giggled. "You are proof of that, considering how he dotes over you and that leg."

"Oh... well, ah... what's it like?"

"Humm? What's what like?"

"You know. Having a boyfriend and stuff."

"It's not like he's a foreign animal from some distant land. He's just Leo. A stupid, sometimes inconsiderate, kind hearted Leo." Elena continued stroking the side of Leo's face, before she looked back up at Isha. "Have you found someone that you like yet?"

"No, I… I don't have anyone like that," said Isha, shaking her head.

"Well, don't worry about it too much. The heart will go looking for what it wants on its own. You don't have to make it. Just don't run from it when it does show up."

"I'll go and get dressed. I want to see Soulden today." Isha stood back up from the chair.

"Oh, there's no class today. Is something wrong?"

"No, it's nothing important," said Isha as she walked back upstairs to change clothes to get ready. Inside the room, Jacinta and Makeba were still asleep on the bed. Making her way over to a trunk, Isha grabbed a set of clothing and began to change.

"Where sister going?" asked Jacinta, stirring from her slumber.

"Oh, sorry, I woke you. I'm just going for a walk, I'll be back soon."

"Okay, Jacinta… come too," she said with a yawn.

"No, stay in bed. I'll be back soon, okay."

"You no stay gone two days like last time?"

Isha smiled back at Jacinta, "I promise, I won't disappear again. Go back to sleep, okay."

Jacinta snuggled back together with Makeba as Isha finished getting dressed, headed downstairs, and out of the door. The streets of the floating city still had a few students out and about, but most were still in their dorms sleeping in. Isha made her way through the city until she finally reached the school. Opening the doors, she wandered inside. Her steps once again echoing in the empty hallway as she made her way forward and up the steps to the second-floor classrooms. She arrived at Soulden's office, but no one was inside.

Not here. I don't know where she lives. I guess I could wait until someone arrives and ask them where she is. It shouldn't be too... Isha's mind paused as she once again saw the orange light dancing within the roots sticking out of the wall. *Oh no, not again. I don't wanna go back in there.* But after watching the orange glow a moment and not feeling herself sink into the floor or the walls, she decided to step closer to the orange glow which once again moved away as if signaling for her to follow. *Okay, I'll follow, but I'm not going up any platforms or through walls, or anything else like that.*

The orange glow led her down back downstairs and towards the back of the school where she had once been brought through when she first arrived. It stopped at the door before vanishing into the walls. *Okay, so something is out here?* Isha put her hands on the large doors and slowly pushed them forward, peeking out into the garden. It was there that she saw Soulden sitting down at a table with Miss Huffles, having tea with each other, surrounded by the shrubbery of the moving hedges.

"Oh, it seems we have a guest," said Soulden as she noticed Isha coming out of the door.

"Who's that?" asked Miss Huffles as she turned around. "Well, if it isn't little Isha. Have your classes been going well?"

"Ah, yes, ma'am."

"What brings you out here so early, child? Surely you don't miss school so much as to show up on your off day."

"No ma'am, I ah, came to see Miss Soulden."

"Me? Well, that's a first. Usually, I'm the one who has to hunt down troublesome students."

"Troublesome? Soulden, now that's hardly a thing to say to the girl."

"Says the one who hasn't had to explain her recent fights at this school. Really, it's a blessing for you that I'm headmaster here. Anyone else and I dare say you'd have been expelled months ago," said Soulden, waving her hand and causing a chair from another table to fly over and land beside them. "Well, come over and have a seat then. You're here now."

Isha made her way over, sitting down in the chair.

"So, what's this you have to say to me then."

Isha began to speak, but glanced over at Miss Huffles, unsure of what to say.

"Don't worry, Miss Huffles won't repeat anything she hears here. You can trust her as you would me. What's been on your mind that you'd show up here on a day with no classes?"

"I... I think someone is going to attack the school."

"Oh?" said Soulden with a brow raised. "And what makes you think that?"

"A few days ago, I saw Pavel talking to someone. A lady, I think. They were saying that the attack was coming soon."

"Pavel? Are you sure?" asked Miss Huffles. "Isn't he that gifted child that some of the nobles believe in because of that prophecy about him?"

"Prophecy?"

"Yes, his little cult believes that he's supposed to stab his sword through the heart of the shadow king or something like that. I've never believed in such things, but it's good prestige for the school to have him here. The boy has a talent for magic. There's no denying that."

"The shadow king. I think I remember someone talking about that."

"Just a myth from hundreds of years ago. Nothing we here in reality need to be concerned about. Let the nightmares stay in your dreams, child."

"But what about the attack?"

"Oh, now that, I will most certainly look into. But notice where we are, child."

Isha looked around the garden, confused at Soulden's statement.

"No, not here," Soulden laughed, "I mean the school itself. We are in the sky, far away from those who could attack us, and even then, they'd need to get airships, which are few and far between; plus we have more than enough mages to blow anything out of the sky that dares to come near the school without permission. I assure you, not many places in all the kingdoms are as secure as the floating city."

"Oh, okay," said Isha, looking unsure.

"Can I ask you a question, child?"

"Huh, ah yes, ma'am."

"How did you manage to get involved with that bastard Oscar?"

"He, ah… rescued me from some nobles that were trying to take me away."

"With Oscar, I'm not sure rescue is the right word. Did you know he once tried to pawn off that boy of his here long ago? A boy he found that had mind magic, which in itself is a rare thing. But I sent him away because the boy's magical core had already settled. There was nothing we could do for him at that point."

"Oh, I didn't know that."

"No, I imagine not, but it leads one to wonder. How does Oscar manage to keep finding you little oddities? A mind mage is a rare thing, and we still don't know what you are exactly. The test showed that you're a healer mage. If anyone other than that bastard had given you to me, then I'd think no more of it. But with Oscar, nothing is ever that simple."

"Do you and father not get along?"

"Not get along? Ha!" She placed down her tea. "My dear, I quite simply hate the man. You yourself said you haven't been around him long. But don't worry, you'll see. Never has a man even been birthed who would go to such ridiculous lengths to get what he wants. Whether it's threatening to burn down a building with women and children inside, or instigating his own wars. The man is treacherous down to his very core. I curse the day he ever joined us."

"But he rescued me from the nobles."

"That he may have done, but whenever Oscar does anything, always stop and ask yourself why. Because if you don't, you'll wake up one morning and find yourself a part of one of a dozen schemes the man has. Even hiding up in the sky, I wasn't able to escape him. You yourself are firm proof of that."

"Oh, I didn't—" Isha's words were cut off by the sounds of the school's bells ringing at their usual time. "I… I should be going. I told my sisters that I would be back soon."

"Go on then, child. Miss Huffles and I will stay here a bit longer and enjoy the morning sun along with some tea. Be assured that I will look into the matter we discussed. But when you're around Pavel, just act normal. In case you might be onto something."

"Yes ma'am," said Isha as she made her way back into the school.

Inside, she saw the same orange light as before as it danced between the roots on the ceiling. *What are you? Why does no one else see this light?* She watched the orange light disappear back into the ceiling. *I guess I'm not going to get an answer now.*

Isha left the school and eventually made her way home.

"Welcome back," said Rima up in the window with a book in her hand.

"Hello, Miss Rima. Is everyone still home?"

"Yeah, they're still here. Where'd you run off to this morning?"

"Nowhere, just into school for a bit."

"Well, come on in. Nothing much is happening today."

Isha then opened the door to see Elena cooking, and Chloe was at the kitchen table being treated by Leo.

"Welcome back," said Leo. "You were gone a while. How was your leg during your outing? Did it start hurting at all?"

"No, it felt okay," said Isha as Leo continued to heal Chloe. "Am I going to be able to heal like that too?"

"Yeah, you'll start specialty training in your second year here," said Elena. "The first year is just the basics of magic, to ensure that your core doesn't get settled into one thing. It's the reason why Leo and I can use fire and soil magic even though our core is primarily settled on healing magic. I mean, we're not as strong as people whose cores have a natural affinity for those types. But it still comes in handy."

"Does that mean others can use healing magic too?"

"No, ours is an oddity magic that you're not able to tap into unless your core naturally picks it. The three basic magics are air, soil, and fire. Anything outside of that is a specialty type of magic or what people call oddities. For example, Chloe, what did the test say about your magic?"

"They said it was air or soil magic. I only have the partial test because I came late."

"Oh, wasn't one of your sisters supposed to be a soil mage?"

"Yes, Jacinta, maybe Makeba too since I've seen them both do the same spells. But the tests don't work on her. What does specialty magic mean?"

"It pretty much means that we can tap into their magic, but they can't tap into ours," said Leo. "But if you ever got into a firefight with a mage whose core was fire, you'd probably lose, just because their core has a stronger affinity than yours. So, they'll be stronger. But don't worry, as healers, we're protected under the Sunlight Accords."

"What's that?"

"It pretty much just means that people pay a high price for attacking us. You'll learn all this when Elena and I start teaching you this stuff next year."

"Elena is a teacher too?"

"Humm, in a way. But she's more like my assistant."

"But I've never seen you go to class before."

"Ha," Leo laughed, shaking his head. "Where do you think you're standing now?"

Isha looked around, scratching her head, "Downstairs?"

"Yes, and this whole house is our classroom. Haven't you even paid attention that Rima and Elena are always reading their textbooks here? We get maybe only one healer a year; last year, we didn't get any, and this year the only healer was you, and with the way your magic looks, I can't even be sure of that. What's the point of a whole classroom when I could just hold class here."

"Oh, I guess that makes sense."

"I hope so. I'd hate teaching in those stuffy old classrooms."

The next day, Makeba, Jacinta, and Isha were all back in combat class.

"Is everyone actually here today?" asked Mr. Higgins as he looked around the room. "Well, it seems like you all are. It must be a special day for me when my students actually show up for class." He waved out his arm. "Alright, you little miscreants, form up on the floor with your partners."

The classroom now had troughs spread all over the floor that were filled with a pink liquid. Isha walked over to her station and stood in front of the trough with Pavel, who smiled at her. She noticed that Mr. Higgins had placed Chloe farther away from her than he had before. Now she was over near a corner with Marlene and one other girl in a triangle formation.

"I'm glad to see you're okay," said Pavel. "Where did you disappear to?"

"Ah, I don't know. I just woke up and came home, and then everyone kept saying it was two days later."

"Oh, you don't think someone had you under a sleep spell or something, do you? The upperclassmen have been known to play pranks like that."

"I... I don't—"

"Okay, boys and girls, let's get to practicing," said Mr.

Higgins, shouting over the class. "I need to see you learning that magical padding this week. For those of you who weren't here for whatever reason, over the last few days, magical padding is when you focus your shield to cushion the impact of falling. Your shield protects you from magically infused objects, and padding protects the ground from the magically infused person that you are. Thus, cushioning the blow from a high fall or being thrown against a wall."

I think I understand. So it's just a different way to use the shield, thought Isha as she tried to follow along with Mr. Higgins instructions.

"And that's why I have brought in these long tubs of pink liquid that you all have been eyeing suspiciously since you arrived. The liquid is highly infused and will stick to anything that has magical power inside of it. If you focus your shields to push outward constantly, you should be able to place your arms inside the liquid and pull it out and not have any left on you. Let's not waste any time. On the side of the troughs in front of you are pins for you to pin up your sleeves if you have them. Now, get pinned up and dunk your arms in. It's going to get messy for the next few days."

Isha and Pavel knelt down beside the trough as instructed. She placed a finger above the pink liquid, and it seemed to respond to her as ripples swayed beneath her, following her movement.

"It's likely not going to be easy, but I think we'll manage," said Pavel as he placed a finger inside the liquid, trying to force the pink liquid off of his skin and failing. "Oh, it really feels weird. You try."

"Ah, okay," replied Isha as she dipped her fingers inside of the liquid. It did indeed feel weird to her; the way it coated over and stuck to her skin.

"Okay, now focus your shield on your finger and push outward," said Pavel, raising his pink finger over the liquid. "Try having your shield right over the surface of your skin and push outward." And falling freely, the pink liquid dripped from Pavel's finger back into the trough like a raindrop. "Now you try."

Isha focused on her finger and tried to keep her shield as close to her as possible before pushing it out. She succeeded partially as the pink liquid would move from one part of her finger to the next, sometimes even clumping together but never leaving her body.

"It's harder than it looks," said Isha as she concentrated and continued to watch the pink liquid move around her finger. But after several tries, she managed to free herself from it as she watched it fall back down into the tub with the rest of it.

"There you go. You think you can do that with both your arms dunked in at the same time."

"Oh no, is that what we have to do?" asked Isha, who was already feeling a little tired from having to focus so hard to remove it from her finger.

"I asked the second year's, and they said that we'll have to submerge half our bodies in this stuff to pass the class."

"That sounds impossible."

"Yeah, but if they did it, that means we can too," said Pavel with a chuckle.

Isha glanced over at the rest of the class as they all played in the goo. Some had dipped their whole arms inside without realizing they needed to take it slowly and were paying the price as they struggled to remove the pink goo. She turned to see Jacinta and Makeba, poking at it with a stick that they must have picked up somewhere.

Isha turned and saw Chloe over in the corner, squatting away from Marlene and the other girl. She seemed to be able to remove the goo fine. But as class went on, she noticed that as the others swapped hands, Chloe would only ever use her left hand and never the scarred one.

At the end of class, many students left the room with their arms covered in the pink goo. When the class was nearly empty, Isha walked over to her sisters who were already joined by Freedo, Marlene, and Serpene.

"Did sister Isha get all the pink stuff off?" asked Makeba.

"Yeah, but I only did a few fingers today. But your hands are covered in it," said Isha, looking at Jacinta.

"It really hard to get off, I clean off later. I tired now. But Makeba did really good. She got all off from whole hands."

"Wow, really?" asked Isha, turning to Makeba.

"Yeah," said Freedo, "How'd you do that. Show me. And stop looking at me with that smug look."

"Weak, kingdom boy," said Makeba, patting Freedo on the head.

"Hey, stop that. Why you always gotta show me up?" asked Freedo, pouting, "You're lucky I can't touch you right now, or you'd get it."

"But still," said Marlene, "You're probably the best in the class, Makeba. You really must tell us how you did it."

"Okay, I shall teach," said Makeba with a smile. "It kinda hard at first, but after focus, then I can remove a lot of it. But I'm tired now and wish to return home. I teach everyone there. Will sister Isha join?"

"Ah, yes, I'm tired too. Let's go."

And together, the group left the room with Freedo asking more questions to Makeba. On her way out Isha stopped by the door, looking back in to see Chloe was still over by the trough with her injured hand hovering over the liquid.

"Sister, come," said Jacinta.

"I'm coming," said Isha as she hurried to catch up.

CHAPTER 23

Dessi and Jacob were walking down the street together in the city of Orlana's shopping marts.

"Are we meeting back here tonight?" asked Jacob.

"Not unless you fancy a night of passion with that Henry boy. In which case, would you mind if I watch? A few of the girls at camp have talked about such things, but I've yet to see it. And I must admit, I'm curious."

"I'm afraid I have no intention of submitting myself to that fantasy of yours."

"So, that means my other fantasies are okay then?" asked Dessi, giving Jacob a sly smile.

"Depends, but what about you then? You going to pursue a deeper seduction of Franklin?"

"If I can help it, no. He's not my type. Besides, after last night, I'd say I'm pretty satisfied for a little while at least," said Dessi as she walked up, placing a finger on Jacob's lips. "Although when we get some time, I'd much prefer the other part of you." She lowered her hand from his lips, patting him on the crotch. "Try not to have too much fun with your boyfriend today." She then walked past Jacob and off into the crowd.

Jacob watched her leave before heading off through the city towards the Duke's manor. After a few stops for proper directions, he arrived at the gates.

"Who's there?" asked a guard.

"Malcolm Trisdale, I believe Henry is expecting me."

"Now there's an understatement. The master's been pacing around the back courtyard for over an hour, waiting for your arrival. I reckon he quite fancies you."

"I'm happy to have his approval."

"Oh, you have his approval, but I'm sure that's not all he wants to give you," the man said with a chuckle. "But judging how big you are, perhaps you'll be the one giving."

"I see Henry employs quite the carefree guards men."

"Ah, don't mind us. Me and the boys back there; we've been knowing the master's taste ever since he could wield a sword. The one in his hand, not the one in his pants. We raz 'em about it from time to time, but I promise ya, he gives as good as he gets."

Jacob and the guard made their way around the manor to find Henry standing beside a sword rack inspecting the blades.

"Hey Henry, your new boyfriends come to visit ya," said the guard.

Henry turned around with pursed lips and an embarrassed look on his face before walking over. "Dammit, Evan, must you embarrass me every time?"

"Who, me? No, of course not? It's *Us* who must embarrass you every time, "said Evan as he looked to the other guards behind Henry. "Isn't that right, boys?"

The men behind Henry laughed in agreement.

"I swear, you all are lucky I enjoy the company of men. Because given how gossipy you all are, I swear your wives could use a night with a real man."

"Ha, that's the spirit, my royal man-lover of a lord. Nothing better than embarrassing ya early in the morning to get the blood going. Speaking of which, ya ever noticed that the word embarrassed sounds a lot like *Him-Bare-Assed* when ya speak it slow? Which I'm guessing with how big this fella is, will be you later on tonight."

Henry's lips pursed to the point where Jacob could only see the skin above them as the man's cheeks flushed so red, he thought he was going to pop.

"Oh, piss on the lot of you," said Henry as he went over to the sword rack to grab a pair of blades.

Evan looked to Jacob, "Take it easy on our lad; he's not the best swordsman. Try to give 'em a bit of confidence, aye." Then he walked off to where the rest of the guards were sitting down, waiting on the show. "Give 'em hell, Master Henry. We want to see you knock that big lad down."

"I don't need your half-hearted cheers. I'm aware of my talents," said Henry as he handed Jacob a sword and stepped back.

Jacob took the sword and noticed that the blade's end was dulled so that it wouldn't cut. He smirked as he watched Henry take a fighting pose that seemed pretty decent. *His legs are a little wide for his height, but his form's not bad.* Jacob placed his sword in front of him in a defensive stance.

"Let's go; you waiting on an invitation?"

"On you then," said Henry as he came at Jacob with an overhead swing. His blade clashed against Jacob's as he blocked the attack.

That was pretty heavy. He might actually have some muscle

under that doublet. But foot work is important.

Jacob pushed Henry off with his blade that sent the man stumbling back off balance. "Plant your feet when you attack, establish your territory. Now come again."

Henry charged at Jacob again, swinging at his side. It was blocked. Then at his leg. Blocked again. He then drew back, placing the sword at eye level, and made a quick thrust at Jacob's chest. Jacob parried the attack, sending it sailing past before stepping towards him and slicing upwards, stopping the blade at Henry's neck.

"My goodness. Father certainly knew what he was doing when he brought you on."

"I have a lot of experience, but you're not bad. You still need some training, but I can tell you've put the work in."

"Despite their crass nature, these bastards you see before you here were quite dedicated to my training."

Jacob planted his practice blade into the soil and unbuttoned his shirt before tossing it to the side, revealing his muscular and scarred body to the men.

"Looks like you might want to take this seriously, Young Master," said Evan as he whistled at the sight of Jacob's war-torn body. "You don't get scars like that with practice blades."

"Huh? Oh… ah, yes," said Henry as he stared at Jacob's body. He then took off his own doublet.

"Well then, now that you seem ready, we can't leave your men with such a showing as that. Let's go again, and we'll see if we can't further your training along a fair amount today."

"Agreed," said Henry as he stepped back, gripped his sword, and came at Jacob again. Their swords clanged in the air as Jacob used his size to lean into Henry, forcing him back. Henry tried to plant his feet, but his tumbling was making it hard against Jacobs' charge. The young man placed his hand on the back of his blade for leverage and shifted his weight allowing Jacob's momentum to send him forward, exposing his back as Henry stepped to the side. Spinning around, Henry brought the sword around to Jacob's shoulder blades only to have Jacob twist and place his blade on his shoulder and block the blow. With his other hand he grabbed Henry's sword by the hilt while trapping one of his hands and sweeping his feet at Henry's legs. The young master hit the ground with a thud and quickly found Jacob's knee in his chest and his sword at his neck.

"Yield... I yield," He muttered out, gasping for air.

Jacob pulled his knee out of Henry's chest and lifted him back up to his feet.

"That... that was an impressive move."

"I get a lot of practice."

"Of that... I have... no doubt," replied Henry, trying to catch his breath.

"Who taught you that parry move? I doubt that's taught in the fancy courts of Orlana.

"Yeah, that'd be me," said Evan, "Showed it to 'em when he was younger as a way to pound Franklin during training. Meant to be a way to get his brother to stop whipping his ass in practice. Worked well enough the first few times. But you blocked it on the first. Just how many battles you been in?"

"Enough to last a lifetime," said Jacob as he glanced over, noticing that a woman and child had appeared at some time during their training.

"Evan might be a bastard, but he's a good teacher and always stays with me until I learn what I need to know."

"Oh, Henry, you sweet talker you. You get me drunk and I might just open my legs for you."

"Shut it, Evan, you whoreson," said Henry sighing and shaking his head.

Jacob laughed, "You've got a good group of men here. But who are the woman and child there?"

"What?" asked Henry as he turned around. "Oh, that's my sister Jolene and her son. Surely father mentioned them."

"No, my orders were simply to inform you of your assignment. The only reason I knew of your brother is because your father didn't want any confusion."

"Well, she did marry some years ago. But knowing father, perhaps he wouldn't have brought her up."

"Henry, what are you doing out here?" asked Jolene as she walked up with her son.

"Just training, sister. Ah. Where are my manners? This here is Malcom Trisdale, a soldier under Father's employ."

"Greetings, Sir, Malcom. Are you here to give my brother a hard time?" she said with a smile.

"Hardly, ma`am. Just a bit of training is all."

"And look at you, Henry, you've gotten dirt all over your face," said Jolene as she pulled out a handkerchief and began rubbing at the sweat across Henry's face.

"Ah, stop that sister, you're embarrassing me."

"Well, look at that, boys," said Evan patting his knee, "It seems the young master does know how to submit to a woman."

Jolene turned back to Evan, frowning, "And what of you three lounging around over there? Don't you have something better to do?"

"Hey, don't come shaking them tits over here. We're working."

"How dare you say that in front of my son?"

"I'd plow ya in front of your son if you'd let me."

"Why you limp dick ninnyhammer shortsighted milksop troglodyte, how dare you."

"I don't know what half those words meant. But fuck you too, you spoiled princess bitch," said Evan standing up from his seat.

"Wow, are they always like that?" asked Jacob as he watched the two verbally accost each other back and forth.

"Sadly yes," said Henry, shaking his head. "They used to be okay with one another. But then one day they just started fighting all the time."

"Perchance, was this around the time she got married?"

Henry thought back, "Yes, I suppose so. But you don't think the two of them... I mean she's a Duke's daughter, and he's... well, he's Evan."

Jacob watched the two argue and then looked down at the boy who was staring back up at him. His dark hair and light green eyes. And then to Evan and his dark hair and dark green eyes. *The boy's face is still pudgey with youth now, but he'll probably grow to resemble him thoroughly. It's going to get bad if he's still around then.* He watched Evan shaking his head as the woman berated him. *I wonder if those two have even realized. Perhaps her husband also has similar features.* "Perhaps not, but we all make strange bedfellows at least once in our lives. You can't really expect a Duke's daughter and guard to end up together, I suppose."

"I mean, for a little over a decade, he's watched over me since I was a lad. Evan may be the cunt that he is, but he's loyal to a fault," said Henry as he watched his sister storm off with her son in hand. Leaving Evan flush-faced and angry as he walked over to them.

"Are you and my sister done verbally assaulting one another?"

"Aye, we are, but now I'm all riled up, and I see just the big lad to take out my pent-up aggression on. So, what ya say? Don't suppose you'd wanna go around with someone a little more experienced?" asked Evan, walking over to the sword rack, placing his own blade down and grabbing a dulled one. "I don't get the chance to fight honestly these days."

"I don't see why not. And you seem as if you're going to do something stupid if I don't."

"You're mostly right. I don't think the bottom of a bottle can fix what I'm feeling right now."

"Now wait... a moment," pleaded Henry in protest.

"Go catch your breath, my humble lord. Sometimes watching is a better learning experience than doing," said

Evan as he never took his narrowed eyes off Jacob.

"Come on over here, Henry. We got a good seat waiting for you," spoke another one of his guards.

Henry frowned, but decided to leave and follow Evan's instructions and watch, "Fine, but don't you lose either, Evan, I see no need for both of us to get our asses kicked today."

"Oh, don't worry about that, my dear Henry. You just go and knock that dirt off. I'll plant this fucker in the dirt for ya."

Well, it seems he doesn't like to see his master getting beat. I must have opened an old wound alongside the ex-lover. Jacob planted his feet solidly into the ground, lowering himself into a defensive stance. "Ready when you are."

"Oh, having me make the first move. How generous of you," said Evan before dashing in swinging his sword in a sideswipe.

Jacob blocked the attack with his blade, parried the blow downward while turning to his side to let Evan pass. Evan's blade hit the ground as Jacob brought his sword back upward, only to find Evan's hand planted firmly on his face. Evan gripped Jacob's head and lunged forward, thrusting his arm, sending Jacob rolling across the ground. Catching his grip in the soil, Jacob stabilized himself on his knees, just in time to see Evan following behind him with his sword above him, bringing it down toward Jacob's head.

Jacob brought his sword up over his head just in time to block the blow with both his hands, one hand on the hilt, the other hand on the back of the sword to take the impact. He lowered his head and neck, allowing the back of his blade to take the blow to his shoulder blades and send most of the impact force into his knees and down into the soil. Jacob gritted his teeth, lunged forward, lifted the blade up and planted his shoulder into Evan's mid-section. The soldier's momentum sent him tumbling over Jacob, hitting the ground himself. Jacob dropped back to one knee twisting his waist and brought the sword around in a hard swinging motion with a yell.

Evan planted his blade into the ground to prevent himself from losing control and dropped to his knees. Jacob's blade clashed with his own as he then ripped it out of the ground, guiding Jacob's blow upwards over his head and sending his own blade flying off into the air. Evan then pushed himself forward on his knees and turned around, hitting Jacob's chest with his back, before wrapping his hands around Jacob's wrists. He twisted, forcing Jacob to drop his sword as he trapped his arms over his shoulder. Evan grunted, and he stood with all his might, thrust his hips into Jacob's waist, and leaned forward, sending Jacob flying over his head.

Jacob soon found himself in the air over Evan's head. In that second, as he was about to be flipped over, he tried to grab the man's trouser belt for leverage but missed and instead grabbed the fabric of his sir coat, pulling the material with him. It caught on Evan's ribs as Jacob was halfway into the air, the tension slowing his trajectory, sending both men crashing to the ground in the dirt with Jacob on top of Evan.

Evan grunted, letting go of Jacob's hand and reached over to Jacobs's nearby blade that he dropped. He grabbed the sword's hilt at the same time as Jacob grasped it in his own hand. The two men stared at each other for a moment before Jacob reached forward, grabbing the collar of Evan's surcoat, and as Evan himself drew his fist back to strike.

"Stop this instant," shouted Henry, "Are you two trying to kill each other?"

Both men snapped out of their daze and turned to Henry with faces half-covered in dirt.

"This was just supposed to be training. Not some type of personal war."

Jacob released Evan's collar and stood up, wiping dirt off of himself.

"Ah, why'd ya have to go and spoil the fun?" asked Evan, standing back up to his feet. "I ain't had a good time like that in forever."

"Fun? You two were trying to kill each other."

"Nah, just a bit of roughhousing is all," said Evan as he placed his hand on his neck, leaned and twisted his head, making an audible cracking sound. "But I give ya this. Ya brought someone worth a damn around this time. The big lad can put on a show, that's for sure."

"You're not too bad yourself. I didn't realize the cushy job of a manor guard required such skill."

"The boy's father picked me up in prison and offered me the job. I managed to kill a good amount of people before I was brought down. He got my release and stuck me here. Ain't so bad, but ya kinda miss that feeling of real combat. Here it's just your average mugger and the sorts. What about you? Where'd you pick up the trade?"

"Used to be a mercenary. Henry's father picked me up after hiring me for a skirmish."

"Makes sense. Kid's father seems to have a knack for finding people who have a talent with the blade."

"You got a decent man here," said Jacob, turning his attention to Henry. "He came to defend your honor?"

"He did what?" asked Henry, looking at Evan.

"I guess you got tired of seeing me beat on him."

"Yeah, well, let's just say I've had to put Franklin down a few times for doing what you were doing. But you're not a sadistic bastard as much as you are just a competent fighter. I can see that for myself now." Evan handed Henry the practice blade, "I guess that's enough from me then. I got out a good amount of the rage I had in me. I'll be over with the boys for the rest of the show. I softened his ass up for ya, Henry. I'm sure you know what to do next."

"Oh, enough from you and your mockery," said Henry, swinging his hand at Evan, who skipped away laughing. "I swear I'm going to arrange for one of those whore houses you frequent to give you a lady with a special surprise between her legs."

"Only if it's you dressed in drag. I'd gladly welcome it then."

Henry sighed, turning back to Jacob, "I'm sorry you had to be here to witness this foolishness."

"No, this is quite pleasant; my friend and I used to go back and forth constantly. But it grew way worse over time. Once to get back at me, after a battle he went around chopping the cocks off corpses. Then tied them together with a string and placed them around my neck while I slept. He then invited the whores around camp to pay me a visit that same night."

"What?" asked Henry with eyes wide.

"Needless to say, I was a lonely man for the rest of that campaign. And got the handy nickname of 'Malcolm, the Cock Chopper' for the next few months."

Evan grabbed his stomach in laughter, "Oh! Oh my, I... I... think I shall be glad that our ribbings have never gotten that bad. At worst, they've only sent women to my bedchambers after I've gotten drunk. And I thought that was bad."

"We used to pull pranks on each other constantly. So just be thankful you've got someone who looks after you," said Jacob, smiling.

"I... I... shall take... your advice to heart," said Evan, catching his breath and standing back up looking over to his men. "Although I would prefer if they did ease up a little on the teasing. But trying to change Evan is like trying to reverse the tide. He's been that way ever since Father brought him home with him. I still wonder why he assigned him to me and not Franklin."

"You never tried to ask why?"

"Oh, sure, but only to never get a straight answer out of him."

"He does seem like the type to make a joke of everything."

"Unfortunately, that is the case, but other than that he's

been a good friend to me these last eleven years."

"How old are you, anyway?"

"Seventeen, will be eighteen in the coming months. And what of you?"

"Twenty-four," said Jacob, rotating his arm. "Oh, well, I've rested enough. You ready to continue your training?"

"Of course, it's not like my ass hasn't taken enough of a pounding today." Henry closed his eyes and dropped his head, instantly regretting his words.

Jacob raised a brow at the turn of phrase.

"Don't... don't tell Evan I said that," said Henry with a small blush.

Jacob shook his head with a smirk on his face before he and Henry resumed their training with the clash of swords sounding throughout the back courtyard.

Dessi was walking through the city streets of Orlana with her arm linked with Franklin's.

"My men and I fought off a horde of bandits that day," said Franklin.

"Weren't you scared? I mean, you said it was only three of you there and five bandits," asked Dessi.

"I mean, of course there's always some danger. But being a mage gives me the upper hand against the mundane. Are you magically inclined, my dear?"

"Sadly not, I never got the talent. Oh! But my brother is. Father even managed to get him some training."

"Ah, so it was your brother then?"

"What's that?"

"Huh, oh, nothing. Is this brother of yours in the city?"

"Oh, yes, Father has him watching over me while he's away. When I told him where I was going, he wanted to follow along. But I told him to stop treating me like a child. Why? Would you like to meet him?"

"Oh, perhaps one day."

"What of you Franklin, do you have any siblings?"

"Me? Yes, an older sister who's been married off and a questionable younger brother."

"Questionable?"

"If you ever meet him, you'd understand. It's best to say that we do not share the same interests. But for today, I'm happy just to spend some time alone with you."

"Me too. It has been nice to get out and experience the city with someone other than my brother."

"Would you like to go to the art gallery with me? I've been meaning to stop by there since I had a piece commissioned."

"Of course, if you like. I'm quite enjoying your company today."

"I'm happy that I am to your liking. Tell me, how much longer will you be in this city?"

"Not much longer. Father is finishing up his business this week. He has to head out to the surrounding towns, but he promised he would return soon."

"Well then, my dear. Let's try and make the most of the time we have," said Franklin as he ran his hand across the back of Dessi's waist.

"I... I... think I'd like that," responded Dessi, looking down at the ground away from Franklin's smile with rosy cheeks. *It's not going to be that easy. You may like 'em stupid, but you're going to spoil me a little more first.* "What type of piece did you commission at the art gallery?"

"We'll have to go inside and find out. I can't ruin the surprise," said Franklin as they reached the building.

"Oh, you're a tease." *Odds are it's a picture of himself in some shameless pose.*

They both entered the building and began wandering around. There were many pieces of beautiful art. Some even glowed with magic the moment they approached them.

"Oh, why does it sparkle like that?"

"The paint is magically infused. I'm not exactly sure

how it works precisely, but I've heard that it responds like that anytime anyone of magical talent approaches. Watch." Franklin stepped back, away from Dessi, and she watched as the sparkles from the painting faded away.

"Oh, you're right, the lights have gone away."

"So they have," said Franklin, coming back to Dessi's side.

"I always wished I had magic like my mother and brother, but it never came to me."

"Perhaps your children will have it one day. As long as you pick a mate who has the talent. I'd imagine the chances are high for your offspring to have it."

"Well, I'm sure papa would like that. He's been trying to marry me off for the past year or so."

"Really? I can't imagine a woman of your beauty having any issues finding a partner."

"No, father finds good men for me. I'm sure," said Dessi as she twiddled her fingers together, "But I just never felt a passion for them. Like when you're a girl and your mother tells you the fairytales of how people fall in love."

"I'm afraid I wouldn't know much about being a young girl, but I suppose I can sympathize with being a romantic. We are in the hall of romanticism right now."

"We are?"

"Of course, what is art if not the purest form of love. To painfully stake away at your craft until you are satisfied with it. In hope of one day, someone will come along and appreciate you for the hard work you've done." Franklin turned to Dessi, cupping her chin in his hand, looking into her eyes. "Could the same not be said for a love you pine over in hopes that they would notice you?"

"Oh, that was beautiful," said Dessi as she allowed Franklin to lift her chin. "Who taught you that?" *Not bad, Franklin. Do you make the ladies in town swoon with that one?*

"I merely thought of it after looking at your beautiful face," said Franklin as he leaned in, pressing his lips against

376

hers. Dessi tilted her head up just a small amount to share in the kiss.

Oh well, a little bait is needed to catch the prize. I can always just wash the taste away with Jacob later. Dessi slowly pulled her lips away from Franklin, placing her hand over her mouth and batting her eyelashes at him.

"Oh, I... I... didn't expect that."

Franklin smiled down at her. "I hope to keep surprising you as we continue to spend more time together."

"I think I'd like that," said Dessi as she reached down and held Franklin's hand.

They continued through the art gallery as Franklin, and she talked about pieces and whether the art was to their liking. The gallery varied from pieces with flowers in pots to those that had portraits of animals along with their masters. Many of them were magically infused and sparkled when they approached. Eventually, they made their way to the end of the gallery and turned a corner.

"And this here is the piece I had commissioned for myself."

Oh, sweet goddess above us. "I... I... Oh my, that certainly is... impressive."

"Yes, I had it specially made as to give off a startling image."

"It... I mean... Do you really have so many muscles under your doublet? And what is that animal that you're atop of? I don't think I've ever seen it before."

"That animal only resides in the Sakari Wilds. The natives there call it a Prinlag. It's a vicious beast that, even with my magic, took some time to bring down. An agile beast if there ever was one."

"You killed it?"

"Of course, I even have it stuffed as a mount back at my home. Perhaps one day soon, I will take you there if you would ever like to see."

"I... I mean... you're naked. Did you fight the beast like

that?" *Oh, goddess, save me.*

"No," laughed Franklin, "It's merely a small dramatization for effect."

Small? Your cock's as big as your sword? Which one did you impale the beast with? "It certainly does give off an effect." *I can't run away fast enough.*

"I'm happy you approve. Come, I want to show you something."

"Ah... okay," *Oh no, not another one, I'm not sure I can handle another painting like that.*

Franklin led a grateful Dessi away from the painting and back out of the art gallery into the streets.

"Where are we headed?"

"It's a surprise. Don't worry, it's not so far away."

"Okay."

The two continued through the city, stopping once every while to admire its beauty as Franklin would answer some questions for Dessi. Eventually, they arrived at a temple of the goddess, where several white-robed figures were wandering around the area, cleaning the grounds and praying with some of the public.

"Ah hello, Mr. Franklin, how may I help you?" asked one of the robed men.

"Hello there Anders, I would just like the use of the grounds for the moment if you don't mind."

"Of course not, go on in."

"Thank you. Follow me, my lady."

"Ah... Okay," said Dessi hesitantly, as she allowed herself to be guided into the temple. *Now what, an impromptu marriage? I hope one of these bastards wasn't at Nyril a few months ago. It won't do to get spotted now.*

They made their way inside the temple as Dessi glanced around at all the murals of the goddess and candles lit throughout the building. They soon arrived at the end of the temple, where she was taken up a large flight of stairs through the innards of the structure and up into the tower.

There, beneath a gated awning in the temple tower, sat a small table with two chairs overlooking the city. Dessi stepped forward with her hand shakily on the tower's wall and gazed over the horizon.

"Oh, it's lovely. I can see everything up here," said Dessi as she turned around to see Franklin smiling at her. "Do you come here often?"

"Only when I need time to think."

"Oh," said Dessi as she placed her hands behind her back and leaned forward. "And what have you been thinking about lately?"

"This city for the most part," said Franklin as he walked over to Dessi, wrapping his arms around her waist, "But other things, of course."

As he held her in his arms, they both gazed out at the city of Orlana, with its hundreds of magical streetlamps that began to illuminate the streets of the city as the sun lowered itself on the horizon. Each part of the city glowed different colors as magic seemed to flow through the air.

"It looks like a dream."

"It is a dream. My dream. One day I will become Duke and take on the task of leading this city into the next generation of prosperity. Such as my father did and his father before him. And with hope, my sons will do it for me after my time has passed."

"I'm sure you'll be a wonderful Duke." *I should just kill him now, with this city's dream in his eyes. Might be more merciful that way.* "You seem to care for this city quite a bit."

"Of course, I've been here all my life. Father has groomed me for the role. He's getting older now and seeks to retire. He's expecting more grandkids soon to spoil and give him something to look forward to in his old age," said Franklin, looking down at Dessi.

Oh, well, aren't you the dutiful son? Willing to plow me for your father's sake. I guess one excuse is as good as another for men. "I'm... I'm not sure—" Suddenly, a popping sound could be heard as Dessi turned around to see little blue lights spark and explode over in the distance into wonderful colors over by the park where she and Jacob had met Henry. "Oh, my, what's happening?"

"Ah, that happens from time to time. The school of Sceana often teaches the children here small magic tricks. That's one of them. During the nighttime, their parents allow them to shoot magic into the sky to create colors like that. It really is a lovely image from here."

"It sure is," said Dessi honestly as the sparkles of light reflected off her eyes. She stared at the sight with Franklin for a moment before she turned back to him. "Oh, no, I forgot that I was supposed to be back with brother before sundown. Can… can you escort me back down?"

"Oh… ah, of course. I suppose it is getting rather late."

"Father should be back tomorrow. I must make myself ready for his return."

"Would you mind introducing me to your father? I would much like to meet the man," said Franklin as he escorted Dessi back down the stairs.

"I… I… I'm not sure you would like my family, especially my stepmother. They aren't exactly what people expect."

"Ha," laughed Franklin, "My dear, I think everyone thinks that way about their family. But please do consider it. There's to be a ball a few days from now, and I offer my invitation to your family to join me there as my guests. If you must leave with your father on his travels, at least try to stay for that gathering."

They reached the temple floor, walking back through the candle lit room and out into the darkening city streets. Dessi grabbed Franklin's hands.

"I shall try to convince Father to attend the gathering. I'm sure he will see reason. I can be quite stubborn if I need to."

"I have full faith in your abilities," said Franklin with a smile.

Dessi let go of Franklin, giving him a small kiss and a smile before hurrying back through the sparkling city streets as a colorful green and yellow night sky glittered above her head. Eventually, she made her way back to the hotel and up to her room. Upon entering the room, she saw Jacob sitting down at a desk reading a book.

"Oh, welcome back. How was your evening out with the target?" asked Jacob as he placed his thumb in the book to hold his page.

"Oh, it was a wonderful night. He invited us to the ball," said Dessi walking up behind Jacob wrapping her hands around his neck.

"Nice, I received the same invitation."

"Now, what's that you're reading?"

"A book Henry lent me about—"

Dessi placed her lips against Jacobs and breathed in deep, taking in his scent. She rubbed her face against his, taking in the feel of their noses as they touched. The cold night air between them contradicting the warmth of their skin. She savored the moment, pressing against Jacob with such force, as if she wanted to become a part of him. His chair leaned back with her force till it reached a tipping point, and they both fell to the floor with her arms pressed firmly against his chest..

Jacob wrapped his arms around her as their lips continued to embrace each other. His hands finding their way down her back and gripping the curvature of her underside beneath her bodice.

Dessi breathed in the pleasure of the feel of him touching her. His hands finding their home against her. She let her lips linger on him as his fingers explored her and found their way back up, gently caressing the side of her face.

"Now, what was all that about?"

"I needed to remember why I don't run off and become a princess in a castle, and to wash off the taste of the hopeful Duke Franklin."

"Oh, is that all?" asked Jacob with a brow raised.

"Just a kiss this time, not that he isn't interested. I'm quite the catch, after all. He even proposed us having babies to further his magical line of boy dukes."

"A tempting offer if I've ever heard one. How could you possibly refuse?"

"Well, while being someone's broodmare does have its prospects. I find myself quite comfortable where I am. But what of you? Did the sultry Henry manage to lure you away from me."

"No, but his teenage boy charms have grown on me. Also, I think your target sent some men to try and follow me today. I lost them easily enough, but he may have been watching us."

"I figured as much; he's the cautious type. I told him that you were my brother and that you were very protective of me."

"There is truth in that last part; I am deeply protective."

"Also, that Oscar was my father, and I may have hinted that Gregga was my stepmother."

"Oh, now I can't wait to see how this plays itself out," said Jacob with a chuckle. "Have you informed the old man of these recent decisions of yours?"

"Now, where's the fun in that? I figured I'd let it be a surprise, since Franklin insisted that I bring them to the ball."

"I'm sure he's going to be overjoyed."

CHAPTER 24

Victor was out in the streets, watching people go in and out of the old temple. *Just what type of wonders are you hiding down there? Only one way in and one way out. How the hell am I going to pull this off?* Victor turned around and walked away. *I guess something will come to me if I puzzle over it long enough. But first, let's get back to the murder princess.*

He made his way through the city until he saw the bell tower of the new temple in the distance. *Or perhaps I should take him up on that offer to visit a service.* Victor turned toward the bell tower and made his way there. *I hope you're still asleep. This might be a little longer than anticipated.* Outside of the temple, he saw more people praying alongside the white clergy members.

Real or fake, the man is certainly charismatic. Victor watched as The Kemlor prayed over the people who had come to his impromptu outdoor service. There were at least two dozen people out in the street receiving the goddess's blessing this time. A noticeable improvement from the previous six the day before. Victor placed his back against the wall of a building and respectfully waited for The Kemlor to finish the service, giving him a nod when he caught his attention.

Around half an hour later, he finished his prayers.

"Thank you for coming to today's service. In the coming days, I shall open the new temple and we all shall be able to hold a proper service. My men are working hard to fix the structural damage that comes from this place being in disrepair. So please be patient with us."

The crowd dispersed and wandered off in every direction to attend to their business as Victor saw The Kemlor walking towards him.

"So, you did manage to make it to our service."

"Well, I must admit that I was curious how you were going to save this town from its depressing nature. But judging from the turnout today, you are well on your way. You seem to be a man that can rally the people. You ever thought of being a public speaker for some high lord? I hear the pay's good."

"Oh, now wouldn't that be a sight. But sadly, the goddess has claimed my service. Perhaps in another life, I shall live in wealth and fortune for my services in this one. Walk with me Amadeus, I must attend to some business inside."

"You sure? Isn't that place off limits?"

"Merely to the masses, for fear of the place collapsing in on dozens of people's heads. I'd not want people to have even more reason to think that the goddess has abandoned them than they already have."

"But on our heads, it's perfectly fine?" chuckled Victor.

"Think of it as becoming a martyr for the people of this city. You died, so that they wouldn't have to. They may even build a statue of us in our honor."

"Ha, who knew a man of the goddess would have a sarcastic sense of humor. You're much different from the previous leaders of the goddess I've met. Usually every word out of their mouth is trying to enforce some type of personal message or agenda they have."

"Yes, well, I do admit that some of my brothers can be a little rigid. But I assure you they mean well."

"And if intentions translated into actions, then perhaps the world would not need the blessings of the goddess," spoke Victor as he entered the temple to see planks of wood along with hammers and nails scattered along the floors and walls.

"Very well said. Our sermons, our devotion, even our white robes serve as a reminder to those that see us that perhaps there is another way. And through that, perhaps we can influence them to do a little more good in the world than they were doing before."

"A slow and gradual approach. Do you not worry that a new belief or religion will appear before your grand goals appear?" Victor stopped at a half-painted picture of the goddess and began inspecting it. "While the history of the goddess dates back a thousand years, I believe your sect, The Will of the Goddess, has only been around for the last fifty or so. You're not afraid of any new competition."

"Tell me something, Amadeus," said The Kemlor as he picked up a board, placing it against the wall, and grabbed a hammer and nails. "What do you think is the difference between influence and indoctrination? Where is the line between the two?"

"I think you might be asking an impossible question of me."

"Perhaps, but a knowledgeable skeptic such as yourself

seems to be the only one I can voice my own doubts too. Can you hand me another nail, please?"

"Wait, shouldn't I be confessing my sins to you? Not the other way around," said Victor as he handed him a nail.

"Perhaps we shall confess to each other. Like any other man, I am not perfect. I feel angry. I'm tempted by women; I have the same hunger for depravity as others. I can accept these flaws within myself. But the one thing that grates on me is if I'm having a negative influence on others."

"How noble."

"I influence the adults who come to visit, but their brains are already developed and they can make their own choices. But if those same adults were to pass down these teachings to their children, then with each generation after the initial influence, does it then become stronger levels of indoctrination?" The Kemlor reached his hand back, "Another nail please."

"So, you're saying you want to influence, but not control." Victor handed him two more nails. "I'm not sure you can have it both ways. The moment you became a leader, it became your role. People will always look for someone to guide them. Children are led by their parents. Communities are led by their town leaders or elders. Large cities have dukes, and kingdoms have queens and kings. It might be more apt to say that you're a king without a kingdom."

"Well then, my friend. Would you hand me another nail? It seems I have a long way to go before I finish building this castle."

Victor reached into the pale to grab another nail. "You sound more like a philosopher than a religious man."

"I imagine so. But I wasn't always a servant of the goddess. In my past, I was a researcher of sorts, but I found my calling here with—"

"Sir, you have a visitor." said a robed man at the door.

Victor and The Kemlor turned to see a sickly-looking man in the door with dark hair. He was a fair amount larger
386

than the robed men, but Victor could see in his eyes that he was not in the best of shape.

"Oh! Sullivan, you've made it. Although your travels seem to have taken a toll on you."

"The carriage ride was a pain in the ass. I was never good with horses or wagons," said the large man.

"Amadeus, if you will excuse us. It seems I will have to tend to my friend here. He doesn't have the best constitution and has always been a sickly fellow."

"Oh, of course. It was a pleasure talking to you. I did enjoy our conversation. I will be in town a few days longer if you wish to continue."

"I'd like that. Please stop by again. I look forward to continuing this discussion."

Victor nodded to the men and left out of the temple, heading down the street before doubling back, and watching the doors from around a corner. *I'm already bad at being stealthy, and here I am, trying to do it in broad daylight, no less.* Soon he saw the Kemlor and the big man leave the temple and head down the street in the direction of the old temple. He followed them for just a few minutes but then ventured off. *No need to follow them all the way. Best to just assume that I'm right and that the temple is indeed their destination. For now, I'd better head back.*

Soon he arrived back at the tavern and actually saw the old man sitting at the desk again. "You're finally back. I had assumed you'd gone off and died somewhere."

"No such luck, I'm afraid. I'm old, and sometimes it doesn't do to keep myself held up in here for too long."

"Can't fault your logic there," said Victor as he looked around the depressing tavern. "I can actually hear the dust gathering."

"Humph," the old man chuckled, "Surprised you're still here, figured out you'd be gone by now with your little mistress up there."

"That's what I'd thought too, but she says she likes it

here. It reminds her of home."

"Then what a sorry life that girl must have lived. Try to at least give her a better one, since you're dragging her around with you."

"I'll do my best old man, but women aren't always the easiest to please," said Victor as he headed up the steps.

"Maybe, but it's a far sight better than pleasing yourself."

Victor smirked at the old man's comments as he walked over and entered their room to find Silk sitting up on the bed with her eyes closed and her legs folded under her. He noticed that she was back wearing her tunic again.

"Good morning, you're looking a little better. Those dark spots under your eyes have cleared up a bit."

"You were gone again; why didn't you wake me?"

"You seemed tired and I wanted you to rest. I'm your caretaker, remember. Figured I'd go out and get you some breakfast," He held the food up for her to see. "I want you to have the energy for it. We can head out again tonight."

"So... you're not going to leave me behind again?" asked Silk as she left the bed, walking over to grab the food.

"Of course not, especially now that we might know why your powers still haven't come back yet," said Victor as he watched the pouting assassin munch of her breakfast. *Goddess, help me. It's like having a pet. She even pouts like a child. Oh well, it's cute in its own way, I guess.* "Tell me, what do you think we should do next?"

"Humm? Yooo asking moooo?"

"Yes, you. And don't talk with your mouth full. You're the infiltration master. How are we going to find out what's behind that magical door they have in that old temple?"

"Wool."

Victor raised a brow at her, and she swallowed her food.

"Well, if I was still able to transform, I'd just kill a guard and take his clothes."

"But since you can't transform and I'd like to avoid killing when possible, what's the alternative?"

"I've been practicing my magic since I've been awake. I think I can manage simple sleep spells or illusion magic and such. If the guard is light one night, it should be enough to get us in."

"What is your magical core, anyway?"

"What do you mean?"

"I mean. most mages' cores settle for fire or something, what did yours settle on?"

"I don't know," said Silk, looking at Victor curiously. "I mean, Grigguk brought people in to train us, but they never mentioned anything about cores."

"Hmm," Victor closed his eyes, folded his arms, and leaned against a wall. "I don't have the talent, so I don't know how to describe it. Which magic is the easiest for you to perform?"

"Usually transforming is easy, unless I switch from one person to another. Then it's become harder, and I get a headache. Sometimes I'll get sick and pass out if I change too much."

"That's called magic sickness. It happens when you burn through too much magic in a small amount of time. Did you not know that?"

"No, I just knew that I couldn't change too much without getting sick."

"It's a sad day when I know more about magic than the mage," said Victor, shaking his head. "Well, still, we will go with your plan and try to sneak in and see what's behind that door on a night where there aren't many guards."

"Dammit, this sucks. These things won't go away," said Silk as she rubbed at the black marks on her wrists again. "What if I'm never able to transform again? I don't want to be stuck like this forever."

"I'm sure you'll heal up over time. How's the head now? Everything's still cloudy in there?"

"No, it's better than it was, and I can focus more on my magic now without feeling like I want to pass out."

"So, we just keep working on you, and I'm sure you'll be able to transform soon enough. Although I must admit, I've grown kinda fond of your ghostly appearance over the last month."

"How funny," said Silk, frowning at Victor. "Tell me something?"

"What's that?"

"What will you do after you've completed your mission?"

"Go and hide in a cave."

"What?"

"I've been trying to retire and go live in the countryside for the last half-year or so, but shit keeps happening. First, there was Clarissa and her mission, then the girl, then the chase, and when everything was finally set for me to run away. I find you locked in a dungeon, and now, here I am."

"Do you regret it now? Saving me, I mean," said Silk, lowering her head.

"Depends, What are you going to do after all this is over? Go back to being an assassin for Grigguk?"

"What do you expect me to do? They're all I have. I can't just retire in the countryside like you," said Silk in a tone of frustration. "My sister is there. I don't have anyone else. You can go and play the hero, and people love you. People see me, and I'm just the monster that they scream at."

Victor sighed, "Not all chains are physical."

"What?"

"Nothing. Just something an old bastard told me once," said Victor, shaking his head and walking over to the bed and taking a seat. "So then tell me, why have you and your sister never run away? Seems like you're plenty strong enough. And it's not like he'll find you with the whole transforming thing."

"And then what? Eventually, he'd get a tracer to find us. And then just lock us back in cages again."

"And what if you were in a place where he couldn't get you?"

"Ha! And where's that? He has people everywhere."

"You said it yourself; you know my history with the queen. You two could become my bodyguards. If anything, my current situation proves I need one. Especially with me not having magic and all. And I doubt that Grigguk fella would dare try to steal you away then." *Oh! Sweet goddess, what am I saying?*

"Ha, you've lost your mind. That can't happen."

"Why not? It's a position of power and nobility. You both might even be able to walk around in your own skin as a specially recognized guard." *Why can't I ever just let things go? Dammit Victor, just leave the nice assassin alone and go home and retire.*

Silk crawled on the bed, looking at Victor with narrowed eyes, "You'd do that for us? Why? What's in it for you?"

Nothing but pain and misery. Victor, don't look at her. You're about to ruin your whole life with this decision. "I'm stupid, remember. And who knows, maybe I'm falling for your murderous charms?" *I give up. If I'm going to be this dumb, then I might as well follow through with it.*

"You won't throw us away?"

"Sakari bonding ritual, remember," said Victor pointing to his chest. "I think that's fairly impossible now." *Well, old man, just because some chains aren't physical, that doesn't mean that I still can't break them.*

CHAPTER 25

Jacinta, Isha, and Makeba were sitting in the kitchen of Heart House as Elena finished making them breakfast, and Rima sat in a chair reading a book.

"Where Elena learn to cook?" asked Jacinta, "Food taste better than in camp."

"I suppose I learned like most girls; in the kitchen bothering my mother. I remember tugging on her apron when I was younger. She used to hoist me up on a chair while we made cakes."

"We never see Rima cook. She always in window when we come back."

"And you never will," laughed Rima, closing her book and wagging her finger. "I've never been one for the domestic chores. Back at home, I have cooks and maids who handle such things. I'll help out the more magic skills, not the mundane ones."

"Is Rima rich lady?"

"You could say that," said Rima, "My family name is Pintercrest and my family manages a large amount of trade. All my mothers children are given ships to captain, but I didn't much like the idea of smelling like fish all day. So when my power came to me, I jumped at the chance to run away."

"Like how you run away from learning how to cook?" joked Elena. "She's a high and mighty lady, indeed."

"Hey now, I'm not as pompous about it as my brothers. I just never enjoyed cooking. And I figure why not let Elena handle it since you seem to like it so much."

"I appreciate you allowing me to serve you, my lady," said Elena in a sarcastic tone.

"You can teach Sister Isha to cook, then she cook for us," said Jacinta, "That will make her happy."

"Hey, don't just decide that I'm going to cook for you."

"No, you caretaker sister. That means you are cooking sister. It is the Sakari way."

"What? No, it's not. That sounds like a lie. I've never heard of a cooking sister before."

"That because you need to learn more about Sakari," said Jacinta with a mischievous smile. "But do not worry, I shall teach you."

"Oh, no, you won't. I'm on to your game."

"It must be nice to have sisters," said Elena while laughing at the girls.

"You not have sisters?" asked Makeba as she tossed a piece of fruit in her mouth.

"Nope, just me and three younger brothers. So, I suppose I was the cooking sister at my house. My mother was quite sad when the healers came for me."

"Could you not stay home and not be healer?"

"I could have; the circle doesn't make anyone become a healer. But they offer a lot of money for children that are healers. And we were poor from a poor village. It wasn't so bad; they allowed me to go back home to visit twice a year."

"I miss home too. I wonder what momma doing," said Makeba.

"Well, in three months, you all can go back since the school sends everyone back home on the Blessed Day for two weeks."

"What is blessed day?"

"It's the day the goddess brought us to this land, according to the chapel. She opened a door and brought us here from a dying world. That's why we thank her during that time of year."

"That sounds like Ryland the conqueror," said Makeba.

"Who?"

"Ryland, he one of the—"

A knock came on the door, interrupting their conversation.

"Who is it?" asked Elena, walking over to the door.

"It's me, Caudbell. And I've brought Tannor along with me. I hope I'm not interrupting," he said with his voice muffled through the door.

"Oh, welcome back, Mr. Caudbell," said Elena, opening the door. "I hope everything is okay."

"Yes, of course, may we come in?"

"Yes, please do come in."

Caudbell stepped inside with Tannor following behind.

"Oh good," said Caudbell, spotting the girls. "I hoped I wouldn't be too late. I brought another test for the Sakari girls, if they wouldn't mind."

"Mr. Caudbell, you're still wearing that healing patch," said Elena, looking at the blonde-haired man's face. "Has it not properly healed yet? You really should just let us take a look at it."

"You're wasting your breath, Miss Elena," said Tannor with a chuckle. "He's going to be researching that till he finds that the goddess herself is inside the wound."

"It's fine; I've actually gathered some wonderful research on the topic. A piece of the shard embedded into my skin. It actually took a bit of work to get out. I have a piece in my lab to analyze later."

Elena grimaced at the thought of it. "Ah… okay, as long as you're alright, I guess."

"What blonde man bring us this time?" asked Makeba as her sisters walked over to Caudbell.

"Probably another thing for sister to break," said Jacinta.

"Oh, you think so, do you?" asked Caudbell with a smile as he reached in his pocket and pulled out a large round crystal about the size of an apple. The object had smooth ripples all over it, and inside they could see a brown object.

"Oh, what is it? It's pretty."

"I'm not sure, actually. It's one of the relics from when the school was first founded. I stumbled upon it while researching and came upon some discoveries. Elena, hold this, please."

Elena twisted her lips in suspicion. "It's not going to explode, is it?"

"No, I assure you that it's safe. I ran a multitude of tests before I thought to bring it here. It would have killed me long ago if that were the case."

Elena took the crystal-looking orb from Caudbell in her hand. "Okay, now what?"

"Just channel your magic into it and watch what happens."

Elena began channeling her magic into the crystal, but nothing happened; no color change or movement, the crystal just stayed still. "It's not doing anything."

"Exactly," said Caudbell, "It doesn't seem to react to any magic we've thrown at it; it's like it either just eats magic or negates it. We thought it was like an earlier version of the alagon stone. But coming into contact with it doesn't stop mages from using their power." Caudbell pointed to the other girls, "Let's have you three try your hand at it, shall we?"

Jacinta took the orb and began channeling her powers into it, but nothing happened. She then passed it to Isha, who tried, and once again, nothing happened. Isha passed it to Makeba and she channeled her magic into it, but nothing happened. Then suddenly, the crystal began to glow purple as the magic began to swirl around inside of the crystal ball before being sucked into the seed inside the crystal.

"Oh, it didn't break this time," said Makeba.

Caudbell clapped his hands with a smile on his face, "Yes, I was hoping that you would get a reaction."

"Well, damn. One of your crazy ideas actually worked," said Tannor as he poked at the jewel.

"But what does it mean?" asked Elena.

"I have no idea," said Caudbell, taking the crystal back from Makeba and holding it up to gaze at it. "But it most certainly means something. And as long as it means something, that means I have a lot more research to do."

"You mean we have more research to do," said Tannor. "I'm not letting you hog all the fun on this one."

Isha heard the sounds coming from outside the house and noticed that Elena had left the door open. Through it, she could see other students making their way to the school.

"Oh, that's right; we have class. We have to go," said Isha as she headed for the door. "Bye Elena, see you later."

The girls then left home and headed toward Mr. Higgins' class. On the way, Isha glanced around the trees through the city in an effort to see if the orange glowing light was following her again.

"Is sister Isha okay? She looking around funny," said Makeba.

"Huh, oh, sorry. I was just looking at the trees, is all."

"Trees, why trees?" asked Makeba as she glanced around. "Does sister want to learn tree magic?"

"No… I mean, is there such a thing? I've never heard of tree magic before?"

Suddenly the sound of something rumbled through the air. The girls turned around, along with many other students to see a huge airship closing in on the city. It flew over their heads. The force of the large vessel shook the trees beneath it as the ship passed over the city. The enormity of the vessel was a sight to behold. It seemed less of a ship and more of a flying building as it made its way to the castle.

"I think that's the High Mother's ship," a student near them chimed in.

"Who is High Mother?" asked Jacinta.

"I don't know," said Isha as she watched the ship disappear behind the castle. "But come on, we don't want to be late for class."

"Yes, I like big man's class. We get to throw balls at each other, like when sister was hit in face."

"Stop bringing that up," said Isha, frowning at Jacinta. "But it's shield training now. And I'm not good at it yet. Come on, let's just go."

The girls were soon in combat class with their sleeves pinned up, and their hands in the pink goo, trying to prevent it from sticking to their skin. The students were making progress, with many of them being able to keep their hands clean. Isha squatted next to Pavel as he dunked his arm into the liquid and watched as it came out clean.

"It's not so hard after you get used to it. The trick for me is to think of the shield as if it's a blanket you might sleep under; how it's always near the skin, or at least that's how it works for me."

"I still can only do my hands. Maybe a little bit of my arm if I try hard enough. But after that, I can't keep my focus," said Isha.

"Sister, sister, look what I can do now," said Makeba as

she made her way over with Freedo.

"Have you learned how to keep your hands clean?"

"Oh, it's more than that," added Freedo with a smile across his face. "Look."

"Watch," said Makeba as she slid off her shoes and hoisted up the hem of her robes. Isha caught Pavel staring at her legs a little more closely than needed. Makeba grabbed Freedo's hands to stabilize herself as she stepped into the trough, splashing the pink liquid out onto Pavel and Isha.

"Hey, don't get that on me," said Isha.

"And what do we have here?" asked Mr. Higgins, walking over to see Makeba stepping about in the goo. "I didn't realize my class was meant for bath time. I think you're going to have a hard time getting that off, young lady."

"No, I have learned the feet spell now."

"Then show me your feet spell."

Makeba stepped out of the trough and onto the floor, and they all watched as the pink goo effortlessly slid off her body down to the floor.

"Well, that's a surprise." Mr. Higgins rubbed his chin in contemplation. "Can you do your arms yet?"

"Yes, only up to here." Makeba pointed to her wrists. "Legs much easier."

"That's the most backward thing I've ever seen. How in the goddess's name have you perfected your feet and legs faster than your arms?"

"Makeba will do whole body soon. Just need to find out trick."

"I have no doubt," said Mr. Higgins as he glanced over at Jacinta, "What about that other one over there? Can she do it too?"

"Sister Jacinta, not as good as me. But I will teach her. We learn together."

"It's good to have family teach you, I guess. Well, you have my praise, little Sakari girl. You've done a good job."

Makeba gave a large smile at Mr. Higgins before running

back over to Jacinta with Freedo as they tried to pull her into the goo.

"Alright, you little bastards," said Mr. Higgins to the class. "I'm sure you all just saw what that Sakari girl did. So I'm going to need all of you to pick up the pace. We can't have someone who can barely speak our tongue, mastering our magic before we do. I expect to see you all knee deep in goo by the end of the class."

An audible moaning echoed throughout the classroom as many of the students voiced their frustrations.

"Seems your sister has made sure the rest of the class will get no rest today," said Pavel with a chuckle.

"Good. Better than them doing it to only me all the time."

"Ha, come on then. No need to waste time when we already know the outcome." Pavel stood up, grabbed some pins and tied his robe around the knees, then stepped into the pink goo. "Well, what are you waiting for?" he asked as he extended his hand to Isha.

"Fine." sighed Isha as she grabbed some pins and followed suit. Soon they both were knee-deep in the trough holding hands and raising their legs, trying to make the pink goo slide off.

At the end of class, a significant amount of the students left the room with their bottom half covered in pink goo.

"I think... I think I'm done for a while," said Pavel as he stretched out on the floor with a large amount of the pink goo still on his right leg. "The level of concentration needed to do it for the legs is beyond me today."

"You shouldn't try to keep up with Jacinta and Makeba. They have always been like that," said Isha as she sat on the floor with two pink legs.

"And here, people claim that I'm the prodigy. Clearly, your sister deserves that title," said Pavel as he rolled over, standing to his feet. "I shall go and take a rest in Leo's office. It is around the time for my inspection, anyway."

"Why do you have to get check-ups so often? Are you

sick?"

"I just have a weak constitution for as much magic as I have. It causes me to become tired quite fast. So, I have to visit Leo to ensure that the magical poisoning hasn't affected me too badly. I try to be careful, but you never know."

"Oh, okay. I guess that—"

"Sister Isha, we go eat, come join," spoke Jacinta with a small amount of the pink goo on her cheek and nose.

"It seems your sisters are calling you," said Pavel as he headed out of the classroom. "See you all next class."

"Okay, I'm getting up." Isha stood to her feet and walked over to her sisters. She reached the door, turning to leave with them, but again saw Chloe in the back of the classroom sitting down behind the tub with pink goo on the side of her face. As Jacinta and Makeba reached the door, Isha called to them. "You two go ahead. I want to stay behind a moment."

Jacinta and Makeba turned around, confused, but then noticed Chloe at the end of the class.

"Yes, you should go apologize to Chloe," said Makeba in a self-assured tone.

"Apologize? But I haven't done anything."

"Sister Isha always make people cry. You need be good girl and apologize like you did us," said Jacinta, following her sister's lead and nodding to herself.

"Yes, sister made us cry a lot and then run away to make us feel bad."

"But... that's not... It's not like I.... argh fine. Whatever; both of you just go away," said Isha as she turned around and headed towards Chloe to the sounds of Jacinta and Makeba's giggles behind her ear as they left the classroom.

She soon arrived at the trough where Chloe was.

"Ah... Chloe... are you okay? I can help you if you..." said Isha as she turned past the trough and saw Chloe's burned arm covered in the goo up to her elbow.

"It won't come off," replied Chloe as she reached across herself and rubbed her elbow with her other arm. "No matter what I do, it won't come off."

Isha knelt on the floor beside her. "My legs are still covered, so it's okay. Can I take a look? I promise I won't try to hurt you if you promise not to hurt me."

There was a moment of silence between the two girls that lasted a while before Chloe raised her burned hand to Isha while still keeping her head turned away. Isha slowly reached out taking hold of her goo-covered arm and began rubbing at the goo that had latched onto her scarred skin.

"Why... Why are you being nice to me?"

"I don't want to be mean to you," said Isha as she tried to move her own magical shield over the goo. "I want everyone to be happy, but I keep messing up all the time."

"Do you... do you remember anything about Passala?"

Isha's eyes shot open as she stared at Chloe, "Passala, were you in Passala too? Is that why you're mad at me? Did I do something wrong in Passala? Oh, are you one of Maggie's friends? Is she okay?" Before Isha realized it, her face was inches away from Chloe's face with hope in her eyes. "Are they safe?"

Chloe pushed Isha back, making her trip to the side, almost losing balance.

"Stop it. You're too close."

Isha let go of Chloe's arm and caught herself before she hit the floor.

"Oh, I'm sorry, I didn't mean to push you that hard."

"No, no, it's my fault," said Isha as she balanced herself and held out her hand for Chloe to return her arm to her. "I guess, I got a little too excited." Isha smiled.

"How can you wear that stupid smile all the time," said Chloe as she gave Isha back her hand.

"It's not like I'm happy all the time, but I do want for us to try to be friends. Oh, but I think I figured out how to get the goo off of your hand."

"How?"

"Well, I'm not skilled enough to remove it with my

shields. But Mr. Higgins said the goo responds to strong magic. I should just need to make my magic stronger than yours." Isha focused her magic into her hands as she held Chloe's arm, and slowly the goo began to wiggle and started crawling from Chloe's arm up Isha's fingers. "Oh, look, it's working," said Isha with a smile. After removing a small amount from Chloe's arms to her fingers, Isha placed her arm over the trough and dropped the goo back into the tub. "See, and we'll get you cleaned up real soon." Isha held Chloe's arm again, sending magic into her hand again to repeat the process.

"It's warm, your fingers," said Chloe.

Isha looked up from Chloe's arm, "Oh sorry, should I... your eyes, how do they do that?"

"Do what? "

"They're changing from blue to white, like flickering. Is that a spell?"

"What? My eyes are just blue. What are you talking about?"

Suddenly white lights began to appear behind Chloe as her eyes continued to change from blue to white.

"They're so pretty; what is that?" said Isha as she once again began leaning in towards Chloe.

"Hey, watch out. Stop. Stop!"

"Huh! What?" asked Isha as she snapped out of her daze only to see Chloe point at her face. Instantly the white light behind Chloe vanished along with the white of her eyes, turning back blue.

"The goo, it was making its way up your face."

"Huh?" asked Isha as she realized the goo had made its way up her arm and was on her neck. "What happened?" she asked as she started looking around the room in confusion.

"That's what I want to know. What were you doing? What if the goo had gotten in your eye or your mouth?"

"Oh, I'm sorry."

"Stop apologizing," said Chloe, becoming more

frustrated. "You were like this last time. Always apologizing. Just stop it."

"I'm sorry, let me finish with your hand."

"Don't worry about my hand. Get it off your face. Leo's gonna blame me again if something happens to you."

Isha began slowly moving the goo off her face. "Can I ask you a question, Chloe?"

"What?"

"Are we friends?"

"What?"

"I don't want to fight you anymore. I don't even know why we were fighting. And Papa always said—"

"Papa," shouted Chloe as she raised her fist to hit Isha.

"Ahh, I'm sorry. Please don't hit me," said Isha as she closed her eyes and raised her hands to protect her face and head. But soon, Isha realized the blow never came. She lowered her arms and looked up to see Chloe standing above with her fist balled up.

"What... what about my Papa, Fairline? Where's my papa?" said Chloe as she looked down at Isha with tears in her eyes. "It's not fair... none of this is fair," she muttered between her tears and ran out of the room, leaving Isha in complete shock.

I don't understand what's happening anymore. She thought back to Makeba's words before she left the room. *Maybe I do make people cry all the time.* Isha stood up and headed out of the classroom, wondering why Chloe had gotten mad at her. But her body quickly froze in place as she paused with the realization of what Chloe had called her. *Fairline, she called me Fairline. But I never told her my name. Did Jacinta or Makeba tell her? Wait, she said Passala, so maybe Maggie told her? Oh, I hope she doesn't tell anyone else. I might be in trouble.*

Isha headed back home to the Heart House dorm with thoughts of everything that had happened running through her mind. It didn't take her long, but she made it there and opened the door to find Leo and Elena sitting at a table with a brown-haired woman.

"Hey Isha," said Leo. You've got a visit… Hey, why do you have that goo on your face." Leo stood up and walked over to Isha, who started poking at her face.

"Oh, I forgot that I still had it on me."

"Well, don't forget that from now on," said Leo as he placed his hands on her face. "If that stuff gets over your mouth and nose, you could die." He channeled magic in his hands, and instantly the pink goo jumped from Isha's face to his hand and some of his wrist. "There, that's better. Be careful next time. I can heal a lot of stuff, but I can't heal the dead."

"Yes, Sir. I'm sorry."

"And don't call me, Sir."

"Yes, Leo."

"Goddess, you can be a handful sometimes," said Leo, turning to the woman at the desk. "As I was saying before, you have a visitor."

"Me?" asked Isha as she looked over at the woman.

"Hello there, little one. I've come a long way to meet you."

"You have?" asked Isha as she walked over to the table standing next to Elena.

"Yes, I was one of the statues in that room that Soulden brought you to when you first arrived here."

"Oh, I remember the talking statues."

"That's right. But I also know your father. Oscar Highland, we've known each other for a long time."

"Really? You know father? But you… you…"

"I'm not as old as your father?"

"Well… yes," said Isha, dropping her head.

The woman laughed, "Well, you're right. There's certainly a difference in our ages." She leaned down and placed a finger on Isha's nose. "I'm far older."

"What? Really?" asked Isha as she looked the woman up

and down who looked to be a lot younger than her father.

Leo laughed, "Isha, allow me to introduce you to the leader of the Healing Circle. This is the High Mother, Marie Heylorn. Oh, and she's an immortal."

"Immortal? Doesn't that mean you can't die?"

"Oh no, that's a common misconception people have," said the High Mother as she patted Isha on the head, "I'm sure I can die. Chop off my head, and I probably won't survive that. It just means that I don't age." She extended her arm, gliding a finger across her skin. "Beauty everlasting is what I shall have until they throw me into a volcano, like they used to do the mages of old."

"They used to throw people in volcanos?"

"Oh, yes. You live in a wondrous time, dear. In the past, they used to hunt down people with magic and kill them. We used to hide in caves for years, hoping they wouldn't find us."

"But why?"

"For any reason they could think of, really. Bad crops, cheating husbands, that one happened a lot, plagues, famines, you name it, and it was the fault of magic users. Granted, back then, magic wasn't as refined as it is now." She turned around and walked back to the table. "But that's all in the past now. I've actually traveled a long way to meet you," she said as she sat back down into a chair, waving her arm for Isha to join her.

"Really? Why?" asked Isha as she walked over, sitting at the table with the High Mother.

"Because of that special power you seem to have. And you're a healer, to boot. You might end up being an immortal like me, or grow wings and fly away. There's really no telling with oddities."

"Oddities? I think Leo told me about that."

"It just means people whose magic doesn't necessarily fit into the fire, soil, water triangle that the school touts around with. Every now and then, the magic core in someone's body mutates into something unique, which in some cases allows them to use a special magic that no one else has. In my case, it's my immortality. But I've heard of cases with people turning into animals or transforming their whole bodies into fire. Why, I even heard of a case where someone was able to make a tree uproot itself and start walking around."

"That sounds impossible."

"All magic should be impossible, but nonetheless, here we are. But if you don't mind, I'd like to have a peek inside and see what all the fuss is with your magic. Will you allow me to do that?"

"Ahh, okay. Will it hurt?"

"No, not at all. I can just use my eyes to see, but I want to actually feel what's got that little baby Soulden to request that you be admitted into the school. Now let me see your hand and try to focus your magic on your fingers. That will help me find it."

"Yes ma'am."

"Oh, just call me High Mother; you're a healer now. Soon you'll join the Healing Circle like Leo and Elena."

"Okay, High Mother," said Isha as she placed her hand in the High Mother's palm and began to channel her powers into her fingers as requested.

The High Mother moaned as Isha focused on her hand, and soon tears began to run out of her closed eyes.

Oh, she's crying. Why am I always making people cry?

"It's beautiful, like a constantly flowing river," said the High Mother. "But there's something else. Let's try going deeper. Oh, There's an affinity spell inside. I wonder who put that there. No, it's not like a river. That's only the first part, but there's another. Humm, I can't reach it. The farther I go, it's like it moves away from me." After a few moments the High Mother opened her eyes again. "Oh my, have I started crying? Everything's all blurry."

"I'm sorry."

"For what, dear?" asked the High Mother, wiping at her tears.

"I mean, I made you cry."

"Oh, you sweet baby child," said the High Mother as she wrapped her arms around Isha and pulled her into her bosom, stroking her head. "Don't you worry about me. I just get a little emotional, is all. It happens from time to time."

"Wes Hoo Mothooo," muttered Isha, her words muddled into the woman's breasts.

The High Mother let go of Isha and stood from the table. "Oh, it's wonderful that you are a healer. I can't wait to see what your talent develops into. Perhaps a new type of healing will emerge. So many mages spend their lives destroying things. It's always good to have those who specialize in putting things back together."

"Will you be staying long, High Mother?" asked Elena.

"Only for a little while. The five kingdoms have many magical schools, and I must ensure that each of them has adequate teaching and facilities for training healers. You'd be surprised how some schools are just not properly equipped to train in the ways of healing." She gazed around the room. "Would you mind if I spent my nights here again? I much prefer it over the stuffy dwellings they try to arrange for me."

"No, of course not," said Leo in a hurry. "You're always welcome here, High Mother. And there are plenty of extra rooms."

"Wonderful, I'll have a few of my things brought from the ship."

The door to Heart House opened and inside walked Jacinta and Makeba. They spotted Isha over by the elegantly dressed woman and walked over.

"Hello, sister, Isha. Who new lady?" said Jacinta.

"Oh, my word, it's true. They even have Sakari babies. I haven't seen them in ages. And they even called you sister. How cute."

Before Makeba and Jacinta knew what happened, they were swallowed up in the High Mother's embrace as she wrapped her arms around them and began smushing her face against theirs. Jacinta and Makeba tried to worm themselves free, but the High Mother had them in a stranglehold of giggles and cuddles.

"So soft and adorable."

"New lady free us," said Jacinta.

Leo chuckled as he walked up, standing beside Isha, "The name High Mother seems appropriate, doesn't it? Her students gave her that name because she always acts like this. But in truth, she's probably more child-like than anyone here." He shook his head at Jacinta and Makeba, squirming to get loose.

"Ha! I'm free," said Makeba as she popped out of the High Mother's embrace. Which only caused the High Mother to hold Jacinta tighter.

"No sister, don't leave me," pleaded Jacinta as the High Mother continued to hug her.

"Well, on the bright side," said Leo, trying to hold back his laughter, "I think you may have found someone who's more of a force of nature than your sisters are."

Isha watched as the High Mother's love descended upon the two Sakari girls. Eventually, over time things finally calmed down as Elena and Leo were cooking dinner, and the High Mother sat on the couch with Makeba in her lap, twisting her hair while Jacinta sat on the floor watching.

"Why you good at twisting Sakari hair? We try to teach sister Isha, but she bad at it," said Jacinta.

"Hey, I'm still learning; it's not like I haven't gotten better," said Isha, sitting at the table reading over her class notes.

"Oh, this?" asked the High Mother as she separated another section of Makeba's hair with a comb, braiding it down, close to the scalp. "I lived in the Sakari Wilds for about thirty years. Maybe forty or fifty, I'm not sure anymore. I even got married there. During that time, they taught me a lot, including how to handle you girl's hair. It's done much the same as normal hair braiding, except that you integrate more hair as you go along. Although I must admit when I first learned, it was an absolute terror on my fingers." The High Mother giggled. "All the Sakari women would come to get their hair braided by the pale skin wife of Montilla and Ma'gono. For the longests time, they believed that I was some type of tree spirit that had descended upon them."

"You lived in Sakar? Where?" asked Makeba.

"I think it was near Mulaway, but that was so long ago that it might not even be called that anymore."

"Humm, me never hear of Mulaway."

"Tell me, do they still have those Jakane creatures there? Or what about the Delkani?"

"Oh yes, Jakane is the beast that took mother's eye and put scar on Uncle Funnyman's chest," said Makeba. "Delkani move around too much; we only see them once in year."

"Well, that part is the same, I guess."

"You get married in Sakar, then you have Sakari babies?" asked Jacinta.

"No, sadly not," sighed the High Mother, "One of the drawbacks to having this immortal body is that I am not able to have children. My body never accepts the child. So, I've never been able to give birth."

"That's sad. Babies are big part of Sakar," said Makeba.

"It's fine; my wife and husband both gifted me a boy and a girl."

"Oh! That like sister Isha. Uncle Funnyman gave sister Isha to mother. Now she is care-sister for us."

"Oh, that is an honor," said the High Mother turning back to look at Isha. "Congratulations. That means you'll be picking a mate for the three of you. I hope you pick well, or he won't last very long."

Isha narrowed her eyes at them, "I have been told. Many times."

"Have you two found any man you like yet?"

"No, sister Isha doesn't want to pick yet. But she spends time with pretty girly-boy in class. And they say he strong," said Makeba.

"Pavel, his name is Pavel. At least start using his name. And no, I don't like him."

"Hey, what are you talking about over there?" asked Leo, "Don't you go trying to steal my harem away."

"You, weak man," said Jacinta with a smile. "You never have Sakari wife."

"Just you little rascals wait. You'll fall for my charms one day. Owe," said Leo as Elena whacked him with a wooden spoon on his head.

The door to the Heart House opened once again, and inside stepped Soulden Fegmont. She spotted the High Mother with Makeba in her lap and sighed.

"Oh, hello, Soulden. I wondered when you'd get here."

"Of course, you did," sighed Soulden. "There are protocols, High Mother. You can't just have that behemoth of a ship you have hover over the city dropping you off at your leisure. What if we had taken you for a threat and blown you out of the sky?"

"Little Soulden, please, my ship is hardly unrecognizable. Your people knew it was me from the moment I appeared in their skies."

"Little Soulden?" asked Makeba.

"Yes, I've known Soulden since she was known as the child prodigy of Miristal who still wet her bed."

"High Mother, please."

"Oh, hush you. Now come over here and sit down with us."

"Do not try to dodge the conversation High Mo—"

"Okay, children, shall I tell you the tale of when Soulden had a crush on the baker's boy of Freeland. Oh, she was so cute, the way she used to pine over him."

"Well, perhaps, I could stay for a moment," said Soulden

as she hurriedly came over and sat down in a chair beside Makeba.

"It's like watching the goddess herself make children of us all," said Leo under his breath to Elena.

"I don't think I've ever seen Soulden submit to anyone before," added Elena with a chuckle.

The High Mother patted Makeba on her head, easing her onto her lap. "Little baby Soulden was actually quite the adept mage, even when she was your age. But then she had always already mastered being a ship's pilot."

"Must you call me that in front of the students? It's bad enough you do it at all."

"You used to fly big sky ships?" asked Makeba, looking up at Soulden.

"Yes, but that was long ago."

"Soulden's just being modest. I'm sure you girl saw my ship when I arrived. Well, Soulden was actually my pilot for ten years. She wanted to see the world and used to drag me all over the five kingdoms and even over the seas because of her adventures. It was always, 'Let's go here Mother, or let's go there Mother' with her."

"You make it sound as if I took you to those places by force. A lot of those missions were your acts of philanthropy."

"I would like Soulden to teach me how to fly ships?" asked Makeba.

"Are you sure?" said Soulden with a smile. "That shielding technique isn't easily mastered. Many people quit after just trying to learn it."

"I sure, me want you to teach?"

"Okay, I will try to set up a time for you to start. We will test to see if you have the aptitude for it. But first you will need to master the basics of shielding."

"Oh, Makeba good at shield stuff. Even Mr. Teacher praised her for doing good."

"Really? If you got that brute Higgins to give any sort of praise, then you must have done an exceptional job.

Typically, all he seems capable of doing is scaring the children and using swear words. Well, after you master full body shielding, I'll have Higgins send you to me for advanced shield training."

"See, now we're all making friends," said the High Mother, letting the Sakari girl down from her lap. "Now since we have so many people here. What say I make us some dinner? Soulden, do you still prefer those Jalley cakes I used to make for you?"

"Oh, I love Jalley cakes. My father used to make those for me," said Isha.

"They're the favorite of a lot of children in the kingdoms."

The High Mother walked over, commandeering the kitchen. "Elena, be a dear and help me won't you."

"Yes, High Mother."

And soon, both Elena and the High Mother were in the kitchen cooking for everyone as she shared stories of the lives she lived.

CHAPTER 26

The next morning, Isha awoke to the smell of sweet meats. She rolled out of bed, leaving her sister's side, and made her way downstairs. She found the High Mother back in the kitchen cooking, except this time she was in a slightly revealing nightgown.

"Oh, Good morning. Did you sleep well?"

"Yes, Ma'am... I mean, High Mother."

"Well, go on and take a seat at the table. Breakfast is almost ready."

Isha walked over to the table and sat down. *This really is like she's my mother. I wonder what my real mother's doing now. She only came to visit once every year or two. So she probably doesn't even know I'm not there anymore. Or that the house is gone. Or where father is.*

"What's got you looking so down?"

"Huh," said Isha, glancing up to see the High Mother peering down at her while holding a plate in her hand. "Oh, it's nothing, just tired."

The High Mother frowned, "Okay, tell me about it when you're ready."

"No, really, its—"

"Should have known you'd be up this early," said Leo, yawning and scratching his head before taking a look at the High Mother in her nightgown. "Oh wow, you're still as beautiful as ever. You ever thought about dating a younger man before?" He gave the High Mother a smile before walking over to the table sitting down by Isha.

"Define younger," replied the High Mother, "You might be hard-pressed to find someone older."

"You know what I mean. Think about it. You could spoil me and take me around the five kingdoms in that giant airship you have. Trust me, I am not averse to being a kept man."

"Now there's a thought. I haven't taken a lover your age in a while. But I think I much prefer your brother at this stage in my life."

"What, Nahtalli? That bastard's never cared about women as long as he's been alive. He might as well have become a unic for as much as I know of his love life."

"You have a brother?" asked Isha.

"Yeah. What? Have I never mentioned that?"

"No."

"Well, we don't see each other that much. But he's a healer too."

The High Mother wrapped her arms around Isha, "He may not look it, but he and his brother are special. It's rare enough for boys to be mages. But both he and his brother

414

turned out to be powerful healers. Nahtalli is even a Grand Healer and Leo will become one too after he takes his test next year. Those two are such an oddity that I even considered paying their parents to just start popping out babies. Two Grand Healers from one couple, surely it's in the blood."

"Yeah, well. Same magic, sure, but our personalities couldn't be more different. And mother said she'd throw herself off a bridge before she'd let father make another one of us."

"Huh? Why's that?"

"Well, healing magic also gives us a lot of energy, because our muscles tire at a much slower rate than normal mages. I think mother had had enough of us bouncing around the house."

"Hoho," laughed the High Mother, "You should have seen the way she threw those boys at me when I came to pick them up. It was like she had found a new religion and was desperate to be rid of the old." She reached over and pinched Leo's face, "But they turned out to be such good boys, didn't they?" she said in a childish tone.

The door to Heart House opened once again, and in walked Chloe.

"Oh wow, this place really is busy compared to last year," said the High Mother. "Who's this one, then? Another healer? I hadn't heard of another."

"No, this one's a patient," replied Leo, "Come on over here, and we can get... what... What's that on your hand? Why do you have that pink goo on it?"

"I... I couldn't get it off," said Chloe, walking over and avoiding looking at Isha.

"Oh, for the goddess's sake, give me that hand," demanded Leo, "I can't believe you slept like this. You should have just come over." He placed his hand over hers and channeled his magic. The pink goo jumped from Chloe's hand to his, revealing the scarred skin beneath.

"Oh my," said the High Mother. "It looked bad from afar,

but that is some nasty work. What happened?”

“I... I... it got burned.”

“Well, I can see that, dear child; what I mean is how.”

“My house caught fire.”

“Yes, well, we’d best take care of it then.”

“Leo has been helping; he said it will take a year to heal.”

“A year?” asked the High Mother in surprise. “That? But why—”

“That’s right, High Mother, a year. It’s burned really bad,” said Leo, narrowing his eyes at the High Mother in a stern tone.

“Ahem, I mean, yes... It... It does seem to be burned to somewhat of a troublesome degree. A year isn’t that long, and I can see that you’ve already regained control of your fingers.” said the High Mother narrowing her eyes back at Leo, “It’s nice to see that at least that much has been done.”

“Anyway, I’ll go ahead and get rid of this,” said Leo as he forced the pink goo to roll into a ball in his hand and walked over, throwing it in the trash. “Okay, now let’s go ahead and start your session.” He came back to the table and had Chloe sit down in a chair in front of him as he began to heal her hand. He soon became annoyed as he noticed the High Mother peering down at what he was doing. “A little professional courtesy, High Mother.”

“Okay, okay,” said the High Mother, throwing up her hands in submission. “I trust your judgment.” She then looked over to Chloe, “How old are you girls now, anyway?”

“I think we’re all thirteen, but maybe my birthday is coming soon,” said Isha.

“No, you’re twelve. I’m thirteen,” corrected Chole.

“Huh? What do you mean? I’m thirteen.”

Chloe looked at Isha with tired eyes and shook her head, “Whatever.”

“Don’t whatever, me. Why do you always pick on me?”

“Now, now, girls. No need to fight. What about them Sakari girls then? Are they thirteen also?”

"I think so, maybe fourteen. I'm not sure. They never talk about it if you don't ask them."

The High Mother narrowed her eyes at Isha, "Are you sure you're not twelve? You're kinda small for your age."

"Not you too. I know I'm small. Why does everyone keep telling me?"

"Oh, honey, don't worry about that. Men like small girls. It makes them feel like they must protect you. Isn't that right, Leo?"

"Of course. I have to protect everyone."

"Okay, maybe Leo's not the best example. But you'll see, that sweet innocent look you have along with that affinity spell, will attract the men like honey."

"You said that last time. What's an affinity spell?" asked Isha.

"It just means it makes people like you. Or like you more. It mostly works on people who don't have magic. It doesn't really affect other mages. So, you'll have more men approach you when you get older. Some will try to make you their wives, and others will try to protect you. But keep in mind that all it does is enhance feelings that are already there. If someone hates you, then they may hate you with a little more passion."

Isha turned to look at Chloe, "Is that why you hate me? Did I do something bad to you in Passala or maybe Maggie did?"

"Oh, do you two not like each other?" asked the High Mother.

Chloe turned to Isha with eyes that seemed to look right past her, "I don't hate you anymore. Now... I'm just tired of you." She pulled her arm away from Leo. "I'll come back later," and walked through the house and out of the door.

"Well, that one is certainly the angry type. Just what happened between you two?" asked the High Mother.

Isha shook her head, "I don't know. I really don't."

Makeba and Jacinta came downstairs, dressed for class,

and looked over at Isha.

"Sister gonna be late for class again," said Makeba.

"Oh no, not again," said Isha with eyes wide as she jumped up from her seat and took off up the stairs.

"That one's not going to have an easy life, is she?" asked the High Mother shaking her head.

"Nope," said Leo as he plunked some meat from Isha's leftover food.

Isha quickly got changed and headed off to her Magical Theory class, where she was late.

"Welcome to class, Miss Highland. So glad to see you could join us," announced Ms. Webblebottom while shaking her head. "Well, go on up and join your sisters then."

"Yes ma'am." Isha made her way up the stairs sitting by Jacinta and Makeba.

"Okay class, let's continue." Miss Webblebottom open a book on her desk. "Magic is a part of everything we know. The rocks, the trees, even the air we breathe. So technically, when you breathe, you're breathing in magic. But as you all know, not everyone can use magic. So that means that something must be preventing the vast majority of people from accessing the magic that is all around us. Who here has any idea what that is?"

"They're too stupid to know how," said a boy in a smug tone.

"We were told it's because of babies," said Marlene, "So does that mean all new babies have magic?"

"If the brain filters magic, then does that mean their brains don't know how to use it," asked Serpene.

"All excellent theories. In truth, we still don't have any solid information on this phenomenon. We've had numerous academics looking into the matter over the last hundred years or so, but none have come close to finding an answer to this question. Perhaps if King Nevander's father were still alive, he might have been able to solve it. But alas, he passed away some time ago along with his knowledge."

"Wasn't he the previous king of Burlus?" asked Freedo.

"That's correct, but academia does not care where you are from. Certainly this school operates in Latrusa, but our students come from all over the five kingdoms and now apparently, even from the Sakari Wilds. Education has no sex, race, or skin color. Education is only information and information can be shared by all."

"Do you think we will ever find out why only some control magic?" asked a girl up front.

"Why, of course, everything will be revealed in time as long as we are vigilant enough. As I said, we still have numerous people researching on the topic and even some scattered across the five kingdoms performing field tests? No mystery stays a mystery forever. One of our researchers named Retallia was once on the verge of a breakthrough, but sadly it didn't pan out. So perhaps one of you will solve the mystery. But let's move on and talk about—"

The door to the classroom was pulled open as a blonde hair woman stepped inside.

"Where is she?" asked the blonde-haired woman in a demanding voice as two ladies in robes tried to hold her back. "I know she's here. Isha Highland; I know you're in this class. Come here this moment."

"What in the world?" said Miss Webblebottom. "Who are you, and what business do you have with one of my students?"

"I knew it. She is here. Which one is she? You're going to pay for what you've done," said the woman as she was dragged out of the door and Soulden Fegmont entered.

"I'm terribly sorry about the disturbance, Miss Webblebottom. We're having trouble calming Lady Evengale down, it seems." Soulden turned to Isha, "Isha, dear. You and those Sakari girls visit my office after you've finished classes today if you will."

"Ah… ah… yes ma'am."

"Good, now if you all will excuse me. It seems I must calm down Lady Evengale."

"Unhand me at once," came Lady Evengale's voice from outside the classroom. "I did not travel the five kingdoms with that insufferable healing woman just to be halted now. Unhand me, I said."

The entire class glanced up at Isha as she sat there in complete bewilderment.

"You really do have a way of just getting to everyone, don't you?" asked Pavel. "Who was that woman?"

"How am I supposed to know?" replied Isha.

"You sure? I mean, she did seem pretty mad at you."

"Sister always make people cry. This normal now," said Jacinta with a smile.

"Pay attention, class. There will be plenty of time to find out what Miss Isha has gotten herself into after we've finished up our discussion for today," said Miss Webblebottom, waving her wand around. "Now, can anyone tell me how illusion magic works?"

"We use the moisture in the air around us to reflect an image that we desire."

"Very good, Miss Humfield, that is correct. Keep in mind this magic does not work well in places with extreme heat or lack of moisture. While there can be a lot of moisture in a heated environment, the actual heat itself warps the image we try to create."

Miss Webblebottom walked in front of her desk. With magic channeling around her fingers, she raised her hand in the air and above her palm appeared a small wooden-looking house.

"Now, keep in mind that doing this is very difficult. Out of this entire class, maybe only ten of you will have the magic and the mind to properly construct anything. And out of those ten, maybe only one or two of you will be adept enough to construct anything complicated. I myself am not even that skilled. This little house took years for me to complete."

"Why it so hard?" asked Makeba with her hand raised.

"As I'm sure someone wise once said, 'It is far easier to destroy than it is to create.' Think about anything you do, whether it's making clothing or building a house. It takes a while, right? Lots of effort involved." Suddenly the image of the little house in her hand burst into flames.

"And now think about how fast that thing you build can be lost. A house that took a group of people months to build, can be lost to fire in a matter of an hour. The same applies for any magic that implies creation. Creating the illusion is much like being an architect. You must understand so much about what you're creating, that the process becomes such a labor in recreating every detail of something, that most never even attempt it."

That sounds a little too hard for me.

"Despite the mundane's belief that we wield absurd amounts of power with reckless abandon. The higher the skill level of a mage, then more than likely, the more absurd they were in perfecting their craft. You will all understand this after passing your basic classes. The world of magic is far vaster than any of you think." Miss Webblebottom allowed the illusion of the burning house to fade. "Who here would like to give it a go and attempt to learn some illusion magic?"

Seven female students raised their hands, including Makeba, to Isha and Jacinta's surprise. And after Makeba raised her hand, so too did Freedo.

"Sister like this new magic?" asked Jacinta.

"It looks fun; I would like to try," said Makeba. "Does sister Isha not want to try?"

"No thanks, I'd just find another way to get in trouble doing it. I'd rather just do the basic stuff for a while."

"Makeba understands, sister will make the illusions cry.

She really good at that. What about pretty girly-boy? You not try new magic."

"I've tried it in the past," said Pavel. "But I'm not good at it. It's really hard trying to keep an image in your head all the time. It's not just making the image, it's maintaining the image constantly. It wears you out quickly depending on how large and detailed the image is."

"Well, it seems we have a few volunteers. That's good. No other boys besides Freedo then? Well, that's not surprising since there's only four of you."

The class went on as Miss Webblebottom continued to talk about the magic theories until once again, the magical bell appeared in the air above the class and everyone was excused. Isha, Jacinta, and Makeba all headed off to Soulden's office together.

"Have fun with Soulden," said Pavel with a smile on his face.

I'm happy someone finds this funny. Because I sure don't. Thought Isha as she made her way up the stairs and noticed the little orange ball of light following her through the roots in the wall again. *What are you looking at?* The ball seemed to jump up and down joyously. Eventually, they all made their way to Soulden's office, and Isha shook her head and sighed before knocking on the door.

"Come in," said Soulden's voice from inside.

The girls entered the room to see Soulden sitting at her desk alongside the blonde-haired woman who was raving earlier. She was standing with her back against the wall with her arms folded and the heel of her foot impatiently tapping against the floor. And beside her was the girl whose arm Makeba had broken when they first arrived.

"Hello, children. Sorry about the outburst earlier. It seems Miss Evengale has been a little upset with you."

"A little? Those little savages broke my daughter's arm."

"Merely a misunderstanding, I assure you. And her arm has been fully healed now by our people here. I believe she herself told you that she was fine now."

"We both know that that was something you told her to say the moment I arrived. And yes, the physical pain has been healed, but what about the emotional trauma my sweet baby received at the hands of those Sakari savages over there? I should have you three thrown from the edge of the school grounds for what you've done," said Miss Evengale, whose face was reddening the more her words increased.

"Yes, yes, I'm sure these girls are very sorry, aren't you girls? Would you please apologize to Miss Evengale?"

"I'm sorry," said Isha.

"Ala-go ha ma neway," said Jacinta and Makeba.

"There, you see, they apologized."

"What? That was barely an apology, and I didn't even understand what those two Sakari girls said."

"It's how they apologize in Sakari. It's a big honor for them to apologize in their native tongue. It shows how much they respect you."

"Well, I don't trust them. They're just savages who have no training. They have no reason being in a school this prestigious. Why couldn't they be shipped off to Salana or Fedna's magical school? I'm sure they would be better suited to handle these uncivilized types," said Miss Evengale, frowning at the girls and looking down her nose at them.

"You know as well as I do that no other school in the five kingdoms has gotten magical Sakari. Do you really think you would be able to convince the rest of the council to allow them to be trained elsewhere?"

"Those idiots and their hunger for prestige almost got my daughter killed. Surely, that's enough reason to--"

"Since she did not get killed, it is not," interrupted Soulden in a frustrated tone. "You girls can go. I still have matters to discuss with Miss Evengale on how to properly teach her and her daughter what happens to bullies in our school."

"Yes Ma'am," said the girls as they left the room.

"Ahh! See, those little miscreants speak kingdom tongue," said Miss Evengale as they closed the door behind them and headed off back down the hall to see Pavel waiting for them.

"How'd it go?"

"Okay, I guess. She was the mother of the girl whose arm Makeba broke."

"Oh yeah, I forgot about that. That's when the whole Sakari Justice legend went spreading around school."

"Did people really say that?"

"Goodness, yes. The second years even performed a play about it. With magical dolls and everything."

CHAPTER 27

"Let me understand this correctly," said Oscar, looking over at Dessi and Jacob in their hotel room. "I'm your supposed rich merchant father, Gregga is my Sakari trophy wife, and your stepmother."

"And I'm her brother," added Jacob.

"Of course you are," said Oscar, annoyed.

"This be fun," said Gregga with a chuckle, "so many stories remind me of Jasper."

"Yeah, the part of Jasper that I never had the patience to deal with. Him and his damned stories." Oscar shook his head, "Fine, the ball's tomorrow night; we will wait until then."

"You men can wait," replied Dessi. "Us girls are going to head out and buy new outfits for the ball. You can't expect us to just show up in the filth we have on."

"And once again, I assume I'm paying for this shopping spree."

"Oh, does Oscar not wish to spoil his Sakari trophy wife?"

"I'm starting to wish I'd have never taken on this job, considering how much gold it's starting to cost me."

Oscar handed Gregga a sack of gold.

"Thank you, fake husband. Jasper would be proud of you."

"I'm flattered, but that—"

A knock came at the door as Oscar signaled for one of his guards to open it, and in walked a well-dressed man with almond brown hair and brown eyes. Oscar gestured for him to take a seat as he was provided a chair.

"I assume everything is going according to plan?" asked the man as he sat down before Oscar.

"We were just discussing the final details. But they both will be dead during the night of the ball. Currently, the plan is to make it look like a double suicide."

"Currently?"

"You're asking for an assassination of two high-profile targets that will both be surrounded by guards. Plans change depending on the situation. But rest assured, they both will be dead by the end of that night."

"If everything has been settled, then I'd ask you gentlemen to excuse us. Us ladies have some shopping to do if we wish to execute this plan," said Dessi as she and Gregga left the room together and headed down into the city of Orlana.

Finding a clothing shop was not difficult, as the city streets were littered with fine apparel stores that catered from evening gowns to royal ceremonies.

"Which should we pick? I rarely do the shopping for

clothing," said Gregga as she walked alongside Dessi, noticing more and more people looking at her as they walked together. "The kingdom people here very much seem to gaze at me."

"Sakari are a rare thing in the kingdom. Did Jasper never take you to any of the major cities?"

"Oh, he did on occasion, but mostly I stay in camp to lead my people."

"Is it normal for a Sakari woman to be a leader? Usually here, the only way a woman has any power is if she has magic."

"Sakari only care about the capable. I was not always the leader. I was a warrior. Then I survive battle, so I become the leader of a small group. I survive more, and then I was named leader of clan. Some men did not like the decision, but so did not some women. And some of them challenge me. And some of them I kill in combat."

"Do Sakari women really kill the mates they deem unworthy of them?"

"Yes, it happens. But your understanding is not clear. Perhaps a mate wounded in battle. Then they ask mate to send them along for the sake of clan. Then it is honor as a mate to grant final request of those we love. Or sometimes partner is wrong and worthless to their lover. Then it falls to lover to free themselves. They must take responsibility for choice they made. But to do that would make future mates question them. So still, it makes mating harder for those that do."

"That sounds far more complicated than I had assumed. The rumor just says that Sakari women just like to kill men."

"Perhaps we do. I must admit that I enjoy it. As long as it is not my man."

"Maybe, I am your daughter after all," joked Dessi as they both walked into an apparel shop.

"Hello there," said a female store clerk. "And how may I help you la... Oh my, a Sakari, this certainly is a first."

"Yes, my mother and I."

"Mother," replied the woman in shock before catching herself. "I mean, but she looks so young."

"My father remarried. Anyway, I was invited to the ball tomorrow night, and we need something to wear."

"That's so soon," said the woman examining the two. "But you ladies are in such good shape; perhaps we could look through some of our pre-mades or display models and see if we can't tailor something to your proportions." The woman clapped her hands, and two other young girls popped out of the back of the store. "Girls, we've got us a project. These ladies need dresses for tomorrow evening. And I'll be damned if I miss the chance to highlight a Sakari in front of the whole city's elite in one of my dresses." She rubbed her hands together. "I do assume you ladies have the coin for this."

"Oh, don't worry about that. Papa gave us plenty of coin to work through," said Dessi as Gregga pulled out the coin bag and jingled it in her hand.

"Well then, let's get started, shall we?"

The women ushered Dessi and Gregga to the back of the store and began having them try on a multitude of dresses, both long and short hemmed. Some that exposed their legs, others that exposed the backs. Some had ribbons, where the wrappings crossed their bodies in odd patterns, while others cupped their breasts while squeezing against their rib cages.

"Oh, how uncomfortable? I never understand why Jasper would bring me clothes like these," said Gregga with a smile on her face. "Perhaps he liked to watch me suffer. How can I fight in such a thing?"

"You won't be fighting. You should only be dancing. And did Jasper really bring you clothes like these?"

"Oh, yes. He would bring clothes for me, Jomo and Momo. All types of weird outfits every time he return from his assignments. Sometimes he help me try them on; other times, he enjoyed taking them off of me. He was a man of contradicting ideals, I think." said Gregga as she ran a finger over the bodice.

"I don't understand how marriage worked for you. I mean, he also had Prinja and Keltre. Were you okay sharing him with them?"

"For the Sakari, mating and marriage are two very different things. If I bring another man into my bed, it is purely to satisfy a need. And for Jasper, he merely satisfied a debt to those girls. A debt that I recognize as legitimate. Would it surprise you to know that I have had those two share my bed even without the company of Jasper?"

"I... I... didn't know that."

"Tell me, is it not the same for you? You sleep with different men when on mission, correct?"

"Well yes, but—"

"And has not Jacob slept with the woman that Oscar has sold him to? How many children do you think he has now? Three, four, perhaps? Maybe more for such a big man."

"I see your point," said Dessi as she sighed and looked down at the floor.

"You judge yourself only by your own standards. I chose to love Jasper, and he chose to love me. And it is through accepting that as truth were we truly happy. We were one and through our time together, he never lie to me. Even when I held a blade to his neck, with his blood dripping across my fingers. That fool never lie." Gregga rubbed her hands over her belly with a smile. "I once thought there was a promise he could never keep, that perhaps that was a lie. But it seems I was wrong about that too, and now I wait for his promise to return to me."

"You mean Rana, I mean Isha."

"She is our daughter, the child that he promised me. It was once prophesied that I would have three children that would travel across the world." Gregga chuckled, "Silly me for thinking that meant that I would birth them."

"Do you really see Rana as a daughter?"

"Of course. Not all bonds are made in blood. The same as I chose Jasper, and he chose me. I did not seek out any of my daughters. They all found their way to me. Whether through honor or through battle, each one stood before me and asked that I be their mother. And just as Jasper and I chose each other, so did I and my daughters. To refuse them would be to refuse Jasper, and I would burn this whole world down before I would do such a terrible thing," said Gregga as her eyes showed a hint of water around their corners.

"Gregga," said Dessi as she took a deep breath, "I... I... have to tell you something I think you should know."

"Oh." Gregga turned her attention to Dessi. "And what is that?"

"I... I'm the reason Jasper died."

A moment of silence hung in the air a long while as Dessi lowered her head and Gregga narrowed her eyes at her.

"Okay, I have the fabric we need, and..." said the store clerk, pausing as if she could see the tension in the room.

"Ma`am," said Gregga to the store clerk.

"Ah, yes?" asked the clerk nervously.

"I am having a very important talk with my daughter. Please leave us till I call for your return."

"Oh yes, of course," said the woman as she quickly and happily left the room.

"Now tell me, why is it you think you killed my husband?" asked Gregga in a measured tone that sent chills down Dessi's spine.

"The arrow that went through his neck... the only reason he got hit was because he pushed me out of the way."

Another moment of silence passed as Gregga just stared at Dessi before stepping down from her wooden block, letting the hem of the dress drag slowly on the ground as she approached and stood before Dessi.

"Look at me," said Gregga.

Dessi felt as if she were a child about to get scrowled by her mother. She raised her head, looking into Gregga's gray eyes. She realized how tall the woman was. Even on the block, Gregga still looked directly into her eyes.

"You stand before me, admitting that you are the reason that my husband was stolen from me," said Gregga as another round of silence filled the room. "Well, answer me, Girl," shouted Gregga.

"Yes, I'm sorry. I'm so sor—" said Dessi before a hot fiery pain shot across the side of her face that instantly made her eyes water.

"You dumb girl, you will not stand before me and claim my man's sacrifice as your own curse."

"But, he—" said Dessi, grabbing the side of her face.

"But what? My daughter was with you, yes? What if he took arrow for her instead? Would you then say it would be Rana's fault he died? Would then blame her?"

Dessi stood there quiet, not knowing what to say.

"Of course, you would not. The person who killed my man was the man with the arrow. And he is dead, along with every other guard in that damned city. You were just there when he died. Which I wish I had been. Jasper Flannigan died because he was Jasper Flannigan. He died doing what Jasper Flannigan would do. Protecting people he loved. And for you to say that you killed him, to me of all people, is as great'ah insult as you could give to us."

Gregga placed her hand on Dessi's red cheek and lifted her head to look her in the eyes. "I would hurt you more, but I know you would find justice in it. So, I will not. Instead you will live, knowing that a great man protected you. Because that is what great men do."

"Ah…" said the store clerk peeking back into the room, "I'm not trying to be rude here and spoil the mother-daughter moment. But we really are short on time. I'd like to resume the measurements if it is all the same to you."

"Yes, please resume," said Gregga as she turned away

from Dessi and stepped back onto the wooden block for the lady. "And ensure that my daughter here is properly suited for ball. She is trying to impress a man that she likes."

CHAPTER 28

"Okay, so this is quite impossible," said Victor as he sat in the shadows with Silk, watching as white-robed figures went back and forth into the old temple. "That is a large amount of people for a place that's supposed to be in disrepair."

"Why do you think there are so many?" asked Silk.

"Any number of reasons. But there doesn't seem to be much of a guard. Just those two up front. The rest of them just seem to be moving stuff out and taking it somewhere."

"Who is that one?" said Silk, pointing to a large man who came out giving orders to the others. "He seems different from the rest."

"That's the fella who visited the Kemlor when I was at the main chapel in the city. Although, then, he looked like he was half dead."

"Well, he sure seems healthy now," said Silk as she watched the man walk outside of the temple and begin peering off into the darkness.

The man gazed around before his attention seemed to stop on where they were located.

"Okay, time to go." Victor grabbed Silk by the hand and pulled her back around the corner, walking off down the street.

"What? Why?" asked Silk in protest as she allowed Victor to lead her away.

"I know when something's not right, and the way his attention instantly turned to our location the moment he came outside. He may not know who where are, but he most certainly knew he was being watched."

"You can't be serious; it's pitch dark, and he was so far away."

"We live in a world where you can transform, people can cast fire from their hands, and you're having trouble believing that someone might be able to see in the dark?"

"Okay, fine. Then what are we supposed to do? We don't really have that many options."

"We'll try to figure it out, but tonight is over. We're headed back to the inn."

"I think you're just being paranoid. There's no way he could have..." said Silk before quieting herself as she listened to the sounds in the night. She dug her heels into the ground, stopping Victor from pulling her, and yanked on his arm.

"What's wr—"

Silk pulled on Victor's arm, darting into an alley with him, just before five men in robes appeared from around a corner.

"Are you sure they went this way?" asked one man.

"How am I supposed to know? I didn't see them. He just said they went this way."

"Who is that guy, anyway? I ain't never seen him before yesterday."

"The Kemlor says he's here to help, and that's good enough for me. Things have gotten much better here since that guy arrived."

"Yeah, well, I just want to eat a decent meal for once. I don't want to get involved in nobody's damn personal war. Whether that be the goddess or who the fuck ever," said a darkhaired man as he waved around his torch in the night, looking for signs of anyone. "And didn't one of ya say you saw someone snooping around a day or so ago?"

"That was Amson; bastard claims he saw the ghost of a woman around the temple."

"This whole thing stinks. First that Kemlor shows up, someone starts seeing ghosts, and now that new fella just appears and starts giving us orders. I'm telling ya, something ain't right."

Victor watched the men bicker from the shadows while he wrapped his black cloak around himself and Silk, blending in with the darkness.

"Well, you wanna be the one to bring it up with the Kemlor then? Go ahead."

"Bring it up, my ass. I'm thinking about high tailing out of this city before all of this goddess crap blows up in my face. This town's always had bad luck. What makes you think that Kemlor just ain't gonna make it worse?"

"Hey!" shouted an old woman from a window. "Who's down there keeping up that noise this late at night?"

"Ah, keep your mouth shut, Agne. We're going."

"Is that you, Vaben? What you doing down there?"

"None of ya damn business, go back to sleep," said the man before turning back to the other men. "Alright, come on then, let's get this search over with. They all headed down the dirt road between the houses and off into the night.

Silk tried to move, but Victor held her tightly under his cloak.

"No, we wait. We wait until we are sure," said Victor in a low tone. "Impatience will only get us caught or killed."

They both waited in the silence of the chilled night, beside the wall of a building for over another hour before they removed themselves and headed back to the tavern for where they were staying. Once again, the tavern owner was gone, so they both headed up to their room, closing the door.

"Well, tonight's been a fun night. How about we don't try that again?" asked Victor as he took off his cloak.

"How did he see us? It was completely dark, and we were hidden."

"I'm sure it involved some type of magic. But I haven't a clue what type."

"How did you know he saw us?"

"I've been on recon missions before with my troops. On more than a few occasions, we were spotted, and every time, they always had that same look on their face. A sort of realization. Their bodies freeze for a small moment as their brain considers what to do. I may not know what magic he used to see us, but I was sure that he did, in fact, see us."

"And I would have gotten us caught, if you didn't pull me away."

"Yeah, well, your hearing's a lot better than mine. How did you know that group was coming?"

"Remember, I told you that Grigguk used to keep me and my sister locked in a dark place. Well, over time, since we couldn't see anything, we got really good at hearing. At first, it was small, like the sound of a rat off in some corner. But eventually, we started noticing things through the walls, like the sound people's feet made when they walked. Or the vibrations on the floors when something fell."

"Seems to me that we make a good pair then," said

Victor as he sat down on the bed removing his boots. "The real question though, is what's the plan to sneak inside now. We obviously can't do it at night anymore with Mr. Cat Eyes on the prowl. I guess that means we go during the daytime."

"Won't that be dangerous?"

"And you're going to tell me what we just went through wasn't dangerous. Either way, I'd rather not deal with that bastard. There's something off about him. I'm a magnet for unnecessary shit happening to me. And I can promise that bastard is giving off all kinds of stay-the-fuck-away vibes. I'd rather march through half their little cult before I deal with whatever the hell he is."

"You don't think you're being paranoid? He's probably a mage with a weird skill."

"And I'm a mundane with terrible luck," said Victor as he stretched out on the bed. "And that's more than enough reason for me to try and steer myself as far away from him as possible. The real question is, how am I going to get you into that old temple in broad daylight?"

"You still intend to take me with you?"

"Of course. Your headaches have finally stopped, haven't they? And I have no intention of restarting that process over again. I may go out from time to time to restock on supplies or gather intel, but if I'm going to do something as foolish as invade that old temple, then you can rest assured that you will be nearby. Half a magical shape shifter is better than not having you at all."

Silk walked over, removing her black cloak, and laid down on the bed beside Victor.

"Fine, so what do we do until then, my caretaker?" she said as she rested her head on his chest.

"We do what people are supposed to do in the dead of night. Get some damn sleep. In the morning I'll go out and get us something to eat."

They both closed their eyes and were soon fast asleep.

Hours later, Victor awoke to the sounds of the city as

it once again began to move for its daily tasks. Silk stayed asleep with her head resting on his chest as he took in his environment and began thinking.

Right, well, let's get this started then.

Slowly, he slid himself out from under Silk and rested her head on the pillow, before putting on his boots and heading out of the door. Downstairs, he saw the old man at the desk.

"Headed out again, I see."

"Yeah, going to pick up some breakfast for myself and my friend upstairs."

"Off with ya then. Be careful in this city, though. I swear ever since those goddess folk showed up, people been acting strange."

"You're not the only one who thinks so, but people will always find hope where they can. Who are we to judge?"

"The people who have to suffer through their hope are the perfect ones to judge."

"Now that's an interesting way to look at it," said Victor with a smirk. Then he looked over at the old man for a moment.

"What ya got in that head of yours, boy? You giving me a look like you want to know something."

"This might sound like an odd question, but I don't suppose you'd have a mask or two around here."

"What, you mean like for your face?" said the old man, giving Victor a suspicious look before sitting up from his seat. "Alright, wait your ass there." He wandered into the back of the tavern and soon came back out with two dusty wooden smiling masks that were painted in spiraling colors, placing them on the desktop. "Here, I won't ask what ya need em for, but I'll charge ya one gold for em."

"Done," said Victor as he picked one of the masks, inspecting it. "What's up with the spiral color pattern?"

"People 'round here celebrate the night of mystery once a year. I sometimes hand out those masks to the children when they show up here during that time."

"Night of Mystery? That sounds like a fun time. What's that about?"

"Nothing really, I'm sure it used to mean something long ago, but now it's just a night for children to fool around in the streets while their parents fuck around for a while."

"What a wholesome tradition," replied Victor with a chuckle as he reached to his side and pulled out a gold coin and placed it on the table.

"Appreciate your patronage." The old man as he grabbed the coin, rubbing it between his fingers.

"I have a few more gold coins for you, if you don't mind doing a job for me."

The old man looked at the coin in his hand and then back to Victor. "I'm listening."

A few minutes later, Victor headed out of the door and back down the street into the muddy city. He once again was sure to pass by the old chapel on his way. There were only two people standing guard outside now as people filled the street. Many of the white-robed people were going on about their business throughout the city, and as he passed the bell tower, he once again saw The Kemlor preaching to the people who had come to hear him. He scanned over the crowd, seeing some of the men who were looking for him and Silk the night before.

There you are. He thought as he noticed the man who the woman in the window called Vaben. *For as much as you complained, I see you still arrived for the morning lecture.* Victor walked over and bought some bread and waited for the morning service to end, which took some time as The Kemlor seemed heavy with breath this morning. But eventually, the crowd parted and went their separate ways. Victor followed the man a few blocks before approaching him near a blacksmith's shop.

"Excuse me, sir, you there?"

"Huh, you talking to me?" asked Vaben.

"Yes, Sir. I was wondering if you could help me."

"I don't got no money; just leave me alone."

"Oh no, it's not that. You see, I'm and traveling wine merchant, and I—"

"Wait, I've seen you before."

Shit, I thought he'd be the dumb type. He must have seen my face.

"You're that guy that was with the Kemlor when we escorted that supposed sick fucker into the bell tower. What ya want from me?"

Okay, change of plan. "Ah, yes. I'm a friend of the Kemlor."

"Then what do ya want with me."

"I simply wanted your opinion."

"My opinion on what?"

"On the type of wine to be at the grand opening of the bell tower of the goddess's new temple."

"The what? What the hell you talkin' 'bout?"

"The Kemlor wishes to throw a celebration on the day when everyone would be invited inside to worship. And with you being a stout man, I figured you'd be willing to assist me."

"Well, ya figured wrong. Be on your way; I got work to do."

"Not even if I wanted you to become my wine taster?"

"What?" asked the man, turning back to Victor.

"I did just say I was a wine merchant, didn't I? So, I need a tester, and when I saw you in that crowd as the Kemlor spoke earlier. I said to myself; Now that's a man who knows how to hold his drink. Or do you think I was perhaps mistaken?"

"The fuck? You think I can't hold my drink?"

"That's the question, isn't it? Will you be my tester, or must I search for a man who has a stronger constitution?"

"All right, you fucker," said the man, stepping up to Victor. "Lead the way, I'll outdrink this whole damn city till the waterways are filled with piss."

"Spoken like a true connoisseur if I ever heard one," said Victor as he led the man to the nearest wine house and began ordering drinks. True to his word, the man could most certainly handle his liquor as he was done with a full bottle before the signs of the alcohol began to show about him.

Hours later, Victor left the wine house and went around to stores picking up breakfast and supplies before heading back to the tavern. He entered the room to find Silk sitting back up on the bed waiting for him.

"You always do that," said Silk in a frustrated tone.

"Do what?"

"Leave when I'm asleep."

"Best time to leave," responded Victor, dropping a bag down on the floor before closing the door. "You're acting as if you miss me when I'm gone." He chuckled while reaching into the bag.

"I do. I miss you a lot."

Victor paused with his hand in the bag. "I really think we need to have a talk about what type of relationship we have. What do you expect from me? I thought I was supposed to be a caretaker till we got you sorted."

Silk turned to the side of the bed and lowered her feet to the floor as she gazed out the window. "In the entire world, you and my sister are the only people who I have never lied to. The only people who speak to me when I'm wearing myself. I... I don't want to lose that."

"That could change, people just—"

"It won't."

"I don't think you give people enough credit. Everyone can—"

"You're a smart man, Victor. But I have seen this world through the eyes of hundreds of people. That prince said he wanted to keep me as a pet. The same way Grigguk does. Everyone who saw me down in that dungeon, everyone who has ever seen me, looks at me with disgust. Except you."

"I think you might be forgetting the ship when we first met."

"No, I remember everything," said Silk as she stood and walked over in front of Victor looking down at him still crouched over with his hand in the bag. "When I revealed myself, the captain's face turned to disgust. But not yours; you just looked at me with curious eyes. Even when you were angry at me for bringing up the Queen. You called me an oddity, the name used for all magic users who have a special talent. When I fell from the ship, I saw your hand reach for me. I remember that look on your face; you looked sad."

"Well, your memories are better than mine, it seems. But I don't think you're understanding your own emotions. What you feel isn't love. You've just grown attached because of how I treat you. I've seen it happen to both women and men in war after they find somewhere safe. You're looking for comfort. After being with me awhile, it'll pass."

"You're the one who doesn't understand, Victor. These are my thoughts and my feelings. And you're right. I do feel safe around you. But is that so wrong? Because I can promise you, these feelings that I'm developing for you are feelings far better than the feelings I feel for Grigguk."

"So, you know what's happening and you're still allowing yourself to feel this way? That sounds like a dangerous way to live. What if I'm secretly as bad as Grigguk? Surely you must be aware of the things I've done in the war's I've been involved in."

"Victor Krill, The Demon of Flowers," said Silk as she looked up to the ceiling and closed her eyes as if thinking to herself for a moment. Then after a few seconds, she opened her eyes and stared down at Victor as if making up her mind. "No, if I can't trust my own feelings, then I can't trust anything, and throughout this whole trip, you have never called me anything other than my name. You have cared for me as you would anyone else."

"I think I might have used the term, 'murder princess' once or twice."

"Victor," said Silk with a smile.

"Yes"

"Shut up."

"Is that an order?"

Silk placed her hand on his shoulders. "Call it a strong suggestion." She then pushed Victor forward, causing him to lose balance and land with his back on the floor.

"Hey," he said, hitting his back against the floor as Silk climbed on top of him, straddling his waist.

Before he could utter another word, Silk grabbed him by his collar, pulled herself down to him, and placed her lips on his. She arched her back, grinding her waist on top of him as she tasted his lips upon hers. His skin felt warm and smelled of sweet wine and dirt. Her hands found their way up to his face and into his hair. She gripped the strands between her fingers, pulled her lips just slightly away from him in order to breathe him in and exhale, feeling the heat rise up from within herself, before plunging her face down again to embrace him with as much force as she had.

Just let me have this, you bastard. Haven't I suffered enough without you pitying me? Just touch me, just let me feel that I'm not...

But then came the feeling of his hands on her tunic, the rough fabric grazing against her skin as his hands began to feel their way across her body. The feeling inside burned in passion, in need, in want. After a moment of satisfaction, his hands finally made their way to her bottom, and she felt as he gripped her ass. Satisfaction coursed through her veins and her spirit as if a weight had finally been lifted from her. The feeling of freedom overtook her as she pulled her lips away from his and sat up on Victor with her hands planted firmly on his chest as she looked down at him.

And this is the result of my meddling. Making out with a murderous assassin on the floor of a dirty tavern, thought Victor as he felt Silk's lips pressed against his. *Just let her have what she wants, Victor. You got yourself into this mess and there's no way in the goddess's name you're going to finish this mission if she becomes spiteful of you.*

"Victor," said Silk with a smile looking down into Victor's eyes. "Aren't you going to say anything?"

"That… that was interesting. Are you sated now?"

"For now, yes. But I need you to understand something."

"And, what's that?" asked Victor as he swallowed and caught his breath. *Please don't confess your undying love for me. I can't imagine the tales of this questionably romantic outing being sung by the bards in my historic tales.*

"When my powers return. I will come to your bedside. And you will take me, or I will take you."

"Wait, are… are you threatening me with sex?"

"Yes, yes I am," said Silk as she laid herself down on Victor's chest. "I don't know if you want me, Victor. Or why you are really helping me, but I have decided that I need you, and now that I have decided, I will never let you go."

Oh, my goodness, she's another Frenka. Whatever happened to the meek and shy girls? Wasn't the plan to find myself one of those? Why am I the victim of the aggressive types? "Is there a choice in the matter? I mean, you have the Sakari bond control, you could just make—"

"No, I won't do that. I… I… I need you to want me. If I did that, then I would be no better than the people who give me orders. I can't make you do anything. But you can't make me not follow you. That is my choice."

"I'm not sure everything you said made sense." *I'm so royally fucked; I just know it.*

"Doesn't matter; that's how I feel."

"That's the most womanly statement I've heard you say... Oof" coughed Victor as Silk playfully punched him in the stomach with a decent amount of force. *Violent... okay, she's aggressive and violent.*

"I am a woman, and you should know better than to say things like that."

"Agreed," muttered Victor, grabbing his stomach with a smile on his face. "You win, you win. But I think you're forgetting about a certain dark-haired woman from the capitol who has also apparently claimed me. I doubt there's room for another."

"Then I'll convince her to give you to me."

"Okay, so now I'm just property."

"I want you. Does that make you property?"

"I'm not sure Frenka will just let me go."

"I'll just tell her that I'll haunt her forever. It'll be the first time I can think of that looking like this will come in handy. I'll just scare her into letting you go."

"Okay, you win; I give up. I'll let you and Frenka handle this. But you are not, I repeat, are not allowed to kill her."

Silk sat up, looking offended at the statement, "I wouldn't do that. You care about her."

"Just making sure. It's better to be sure than for me to just assume and wake up with a dead mountain woman's blood on my hands," said Victor as he patted Silk on the leg. "Now can you get off me? I have something to discuss with you."

"What?" asked Silk, dismounting Victor and sitting to the side of him as he sat up.

"You may want to slide back just a little bit farther away," said Victor, reaching into his bag, pulling out something wrapped in a bundle of cloth.

"Why, what's that?"

"Something I asked for from the capitol before we left. Can you hand me that hammer and grinding bowl I brought back earlier?"

Silk lifted herself back up to her feet and retrieved the item from a table, bringing them back to Victor.

"Thank you," said Victor as he pulled out a long white cube.

"Where'd you get that?" asked Silk, jumping back to keep her distance.

"It was something I asked Dekol for before we left the capitol. I didn't have time to resupply, so I figured I'd ask him for this instead. And he obliged."

"You," said Silk with a hurt tone in her voice. "Did you think you would need that for me?"

"What's that? Are you doubting me already?"

"What? No... I mean... then why would you want it?"

"I'm on a mission as a mundane against goddess knows what, but it's probably something magical. Why wouldn't I need it?"

"I... I'm sorry. I shouldn't have just assumed it was for me."

"Considering how we met. I think your assumptions are justified."

"Wait, how do we know that's not what was making me sick?"

"That's what I thought too. During the first night I figured it might have an adverse effect on you. So, I kept it on the horse, and it's been there ever since. Unless this cube can affect you from twenty feet away, then it wasn't the cause of your problems," said Victor as he spread out his cloak onto the floor.

"What do you plan to do with it then? We don't even know if they have mages."

"I operate under the assumption that everyone's a mage. And since the little block isn't enough to throw at everyone, I plan to grind it up and lace my cloak with it. You mages have your shields. Well, this will be my own mundane mage shield."

446

"Does that even work?"

"On occasion, it has, but not for long. But I don't need long; I just need long enough."

"Fine, I understand. Just… Just keep that stuff away from me," said Silk looking worriedly down at Victor as he crushed the stone with his hammer. "What did you want to talk about?"

"Oh, well, it just so happens that I came across a wonderful conversation with a very drunk man, and it turns out that I may know at what time we might want to try our luck at that chapel."

CHAPTER 29

Isha stood in her room, throwing her blades against the board that Jacob and Dessi had given her. She was getting more of them to stick into the wood with every morning practice. Most still bounced off the board, laning on the floor, but she felt she was getting the hang of it.

I still need to practice more. I wish Dessi were here to show me what I'm doing wrong.

Below, she could hear the sounds of her sisters downstairs. And after a few more throws and taking the time to pick up her blades, she made her way down stairs. There she found her sisters sitting at the table being served breakfast by the High Mother, who was still in her revealing nightgown.

"Sister come eat before class," said Makeba.

"Good morning, little lady, come on down and get yourself some breakfast," said the High Mother as she set another plate at the table.

Isha blinked and rubbed at her eyes, trying to focus, before making her way over and sitting down at the table.

"Now, which class do you girls have today?" asked the High Mother.

"We learn more magic today," said Jacinta.

Isha bit into a piece of meat before noticing the same orange glow from the castle now on the wall behind the High Mother. She dropped her food in surprise as it hit the floor.

"Oh my. Honey, what's wrong?"

"Huh, oh," she reached down to try and pick up the food, but didn't pay attention and spilled her drink across the table where most of it landed in Jacinta's lap.

"Ah," yelped Jacinta. "Sister splash me."

"Oh no, I'm sorry. I didn't mean to."

"Is sister okay? She not often clumsy like this."

"Yes, I'm sorry. I'm just tired, is all. I wasn't paying attention," she said as she watched the orange glowing light begin to dance around the lower floor before it went upstairs.

Why does no one else see it? It was right there in front of them.

"It's okay. We all make mistakes," said the High Mother as she came over with a cloth and began wiping off the table. "Come on, Jacinta, let's go and get you cleaned up before school. We can't have you in class being all sticky, now can we." The High Mother turned Jacinta's chair and escorted her into the bathing room.

"Is sister alright? She been acting funny," said Makeba, looking worriedly at Isha.

"I'm fine... I think," said Isha as she popped a few of the meats into her mouth. "Come on, we should get dressed, and we can bring Jacinta's clothes back down with us."

After getting dressed, the girls headed back off through the city, and along the way Isha watched as the orange glow appeared through the trees of the city as it followed her to the school.

What do you want? Why are you following me? Is something wrong?

The orange ball of light just bobbled between the trees following them.

Of course, you're not speaking.

"Sister, look, funny people," said Jacinta pointing across the school grounds.

Isha looked ahead to see men and women dressed in golden uniforms carrying cases into one of the other dorms.

They saw Pavel over by the uniformed people talking to one of them, before walking ahead into one of the buildings.

"That's the servants of Evengale house. They arrived today. Looks like they brought a lot of stuff with them," said one of the students walking by. "I guess they're going to be staying here for a while."

"Oh, that mother of girl whose arm I broke," said Makeba. "She has lots of people."

"Yeah, come on. Let's not be late for class," said Isha as they hurried through the streets and into the school's castle. They soon reached Mrs. Webblebottom's class and took their seats.

"Now that everyone's here, let's continue where we left off, shall we? Who here can tell me what channeling is? Yes, Miss Hengles," said Miss Webblebottom, spotting a girl with her hand raised.

"That's when you make magic tools. My uncle has a magic sword that he uses. He said he channels his magic into it."

"Good. That is correct. But more can be done than

just making magical weapons. Magic can be infused into almost anything, and with it you can substantially change its properties. You all should be a decent way along in Mr. Higgins' class. Has he brought out the tub of pink gooey stuff yet?"

"Yes ma'am." said Freedo, "We're getting really good at it too."

"Good, then that's a perfect example. That pink goo was originally just water and honey mixed together. But after some tampering, it has become what you all have seen before you. That is one of the key things about magic and where a lot of our less imaginative students fall short," said Miss Webblebottom as she began pacing in front of the class. "Does anyone know why channeling magic is so important?"

"It's not because of weapons?" asked a male student.

"Weapons are a part of it, Mr. Patchkins. Anyone else has an answer?"

"Don't we also use it to build castles?" asked another female student.

"While that is true, Miss Elise, that is not the main reason why channeling magic is so important," said Miss Webblebottom with a smirk. "You see, unlike typical elemental magic, where a person's brain limits the amount of magic they can cast, channeling has no limit. You can splash about in that pink gooey liquid all day, and it will never turn back into water and honey, unless the spell is cast to do so. A magic wheel meant to sharpen swords will do so until it breaks completely, and even then traces of magic will still remain in it."

"So, the things we channel our magic into, don't have limits?" asked Patchkins.

"Exactly, Mr. Patchkins, exactly. Whether it's jewels, clothing, or even this floating city itself. The moment we channel our magic into anything in order for it to accomplish a goal. Then that goal becomes a natural part of that item's identity. Trees provide us with oxygen; it's a natural occurrence. And channeling, if you're skilled enough can rewrite the personal identity of an item to whatever you so desire. It is a fantastic magic with unlimited possibilities."

"Then why don't more people use it?" asked Marlene. "If it helps so much."

"Because, Miss Hunker. Channeling was only discovered a little less than a hundred years ago. Or perhaps that's wrong. Maybe it's better to say that the potential for channeling was only discovered around a hundred years ago. And to be quite frank, most mages aren't that good at it. Even now, only a few here can even attempt the process without passing out. Each tub of pink goo that you all splash around in took over a dozen mages two years to make."

"What? That's crazy. Why even attempt such a thing if it costs so much time," said a male student in the back row of the class.

"Because it is how we will advance as mages. I admit that the time investment is long and for any reasonable gain, it may take a lifetime. But without the sacrifice of others, we would not have this floating city or the use of airships. Both of these are the result of channeling. Whereas casting flames from your hands and lifting up the soil is fancy, it's a very selfish magic. But channeling magic," she raised a finger and pointed it over the class. "That will advance the culture of us as mages."

"It still sounds like a pain in the butt," said Mr. Patchkins, shaking his head as the class laughed.

"That, it may be," responded Miss Webblebottom with a smile. "But the road less traveled is often the road that leads to making a mark on history. And I, for one, would like to be remembered for what I left behind, not just what I did while I was here."

The class continued until once again the magic bell appeared in the air above them rang out, the sound filling their ears.

"Okay, everyone, that's it for today. Try to think about what we discussed. We will pick up this topic once again next time."

As the students left the class, Isha knelt down, placing her hands on the large root where the orange light seemed to be inside. It felt warm, but she didn't feel anything odd.

"What is it you want? Why is it that only I can see you?" murmured Isha to herself.

"What sister doing?" asked Jacinta, kneeling down beside Isha. "Does she like big trees now?

"Huh? Oh ah, no. It's just... ah.... It's nothing, I thought I dropped something."

"Sister has been acting weird. Maybe she is sick. Should have Leo take a look."

"No, I'm fine. Really. Come on, let's go."

Isha walked with the girls through campus back to the dorm.

That night the High Mother was not there, and the girls went to bed as usual. But after everyone had gone to sleep. Isha crept out of the bed and made her way back to the school in the middle of the night. She followed the orange light once again into the darkness of the school, back towards the platform that she had taken before. She looked around for anyone, but the school was completely quiet. She stepped onto the platform where the orange light hovered beside and turned around.

"What sister doing?"

"Ah! Goddess help me," said Isha in surprise as she turned around and stood face to face with Jacinta. "What... what are you doing here?"

"Sister acting funny, so we follow you."

"We?"

"Sister Jacinta wanted to follow you, so I decided to follow as well," said Makeba, stepping out of the shadows and standing on the platform."

"You two shouldn't be here; it's dangerous."

"If dangerous, then sister Isha should not be here either. And why you here in dark when no one around? You learn how to go up?"

"Ah! Well," Isha looked up the shaft, "I'm not too sure about that. Last time, the orange light made it go up, I think?"

"What orange light?"

"You can't see it, but it's right there in the roots that go through the wall."

Both Makeba and Jacinta looked up, but didn't notice anything.

"I no see it," said Jacinta. "But if sister says it is there, then it is there. How we make it move?"

"I don't know the last time. I think the light did it."

"So, we ask light." Jacinta looked up into darkness. "Orange light person, can you make thingy go up?"

The platform stayed still.

"Maybe we ask together," said Jacinta.

Suddenly the platform began to light up and shift before the orb in the center glowed. Then, to their surprise, the platform lifted into the air, and once again, Isha watched the world beneath her shrink as they were taken into the upper levels of the castle. But this time, the platform did not reach as high as before; instead, it stopped some levels below. And in front of Isha once again was a pathway covered in roots and veins.

"So many tree parts. We go through, yes?" said Jacinta with a smile on her face. She reached forward and touched the entrance's roots and they moved aside, revealing the dimly lit passageway ahead. "Oh, this is fun."

Well, at least someone is having fun, thought Isha as she followed behind her sisters as they ventured forth into the dark corridor. But unlike before, there were no rooms off to the side with people performing odd magic. Instead, it was just a long dark hallway with an orange glow at the end. After the long walk, they made their way into the light and

Makeba and Jacinta were stunned by what they saw. Once again, Isha was back in the room with the giant tree with the orange glowing leaves. But this time it was different; all the smaller surrounding trees also had orange glowing leaves instead of the green leaves from before and throughout the domed room, leaves were scattered all over the floor.

The Sakari girls ran inside, gazing around at the wondrous sight.

"Sister, there are so many; even Sakar not have trees with these colors," said Makeba.

Suddenly a strong gust of wind entered the room from somewhere, picking up the small orange leaves, sending them spiraling around the room and the girls. The leaves flew around them and up into the air at the top of the dome.

"Oh, so pretty," said Jacinta. "How sister Isha know about this place?"

Isha walked through the smaller trees as the leaves came falling down, landing in their hair.

"I don't know; I just ended up here one day."

"Sister should tell us when she finds fun places, then we come visit."

"I didn't know how to return here. I'm not even sure where here is," said Isha as she walked up to the large tree in the center of the room once again. She placed her hands on the trunk, and once again, it felt warm. As if she could feel something inside of it.

Teurm blec, mona ah gols jun said a voice into Isha's mind.

"What are you saying? I don't understand?"

"What sister doing? You talk to big tree?" asked Jacinta.

"I... I don't know. I think I can hear it. But I don't know what it's saying."

"It magic tree, so maybe it speaking magic?"

Isha just stared at her sister for a moment after giving such a simple explanation.

"Well. I guess it's worth a try," said Isha as she turned back to the tree, and just like in class, she began to channel her magic inside of it.

She could feel her magic enter, but nothing else happened. She tried hard and allowed her shield magic to make its way over a small part of the tree.

You are me. She heard the tree speak into her mind. *You are us.*

Isha's eyes opened wide, "Us? Who is us?"

You are me. You finally understand. You finally hear.

"No, I don't understand. I hear, but I don't understand."

"Sister talk to tree now?"

"Yes, I hear it... ahh you two try to. Push your magic into the tree."

Jacinta and Makeba placed their palms on the tree and forced their magic inside.

No, that is not how they hear. Spoke the tree into Isha's mind.

Isha looked at her sisters as they both shook their heads. She then dropped her head and began to think. *Why doesn't it work? They are doing the same as me. And they both have better magic than me. It should work. Wait. Me! Maybe it's...*

"Jacinta, instead of forcing your magic into the tree, try pushing it into me."

"Won't that hurt sister?" asked Makeba.

"Of course not, I'm supposed to be a healer, remember? That means I can accept other people's magic." *Oh, goddess, I hope that's true. I mean, I can put my magic into other people, right? So why can't they put theirs into me?*

Makeba and Jacinta looked at each other, unsure.

"If sister Isha says so, then we will try," said Makeba. "But we not use too much, okay."

"Okay," *Oh, I have no idea what I'm doing. Why am I doing this?* Isha felt her sisters place their hands on her back before she heard the sound of cloth ripping. She looked back, "What are you doing," and saw that the Sakari girls had ripped open the back of her robe, exposing her skin.

"Clothes in way. No use much magic, only little," said

Jacinta as she and Makeba placed their hands on Isha's shoulder blades. "Okay, sister. We try now."

Suddenly Isha felt pressure against her back as power rippled inside her, causing her whole body to shake. It felt as if someone rattled her skeleton. The force blew into her stomach and into her chest. The pain took her breath away as she tasted blood in her mouth. And suddenly everything went white as the world around her seemed to melt away.

Isha awoke alone in a white room. There was no one around. No window, no door, not anything, just white.

"Hello?" she called out. "Makeba, Jacinta, can you hear me?"

There was no return sound, only silence.

"Where am I?" asked Isha, sitting down on the ground. "What was I thinking asking them to do that? I'm not that pink goo stuff. I'm not even a healer yet. Ah! I'm such an idiot." Isha laid down on the floor, closing her eyes. "What do I even do now."

"What do you want to do?" asked a soft voice.

Isha opened her eyes to see a small, brown-skinned girl bent over, looking down at her. She reminded her of her sisters.

"Hello."

"Ah!" Isha yelled, startled as she raised up, not thinking of her position, and cracked her head against the brown-skinned girl's head. They both screamed and grabbed their foreheads as they went rolling around on the floor.

"Ow, that hurt; why did you do that?" asked the girl, as she covered her face with her hands and planted her forehead into the floor.

"Ah, why... I didn't... you just appeared," replied Isha as she rolled around on the floor in pain.

"Oh, we found sister and she with other girl. Oh, look sister, another Sakari." said Jacinta's voice.

Isha squinted, her watering eyes trying to block out the pain, and looked ahead. A little way in front of her she could see images of Makeba and Jacinta, but they were transparent and would vanish and come back.

"Where we at?" asked Jacinta. "And why can I see through sister?"

"Don't ask me; I don't know what happened. And I can see through you too," said Isha, still rubbing at her forehead.

The three girls all turned to the new Sakari girl who had sat with her legs crossed, still rubbing at her recently hit forehead with a frown on her face.

"Hey, who you?" asked Jacinta. "When another Sakari get here?"

"Ala-Kiyo mun hayla," said the girl.

"Mun wala gri-pala un," replied Makeba.

"Un-tep?" said the girl.

"Mun hela Isha Fun pala," replied Makeba.

Isha narrowed her eyes at the girls and listened, trying to remember the Sakari words Makeba and Jacinta had been teaching her.

"Mun wala un nu-na," said the girl.

I... from... what does nu-na mean?

"Fola un ma-way un nola, cap a noy que" said Jacinta.

Fola? Ahh... taken... nola... tree... a noy... clan. "Ah! I can't keep up. What 's going on. What tree clan?" asked Isha in an annoyed tone.

The three Sakari girls turned toward Isha in surprise.

"Oh, she understand Sakari?" asked the new girl.

"She not understand much yet, but we are teaching her," said Makeba as she turned towards Isha. "You did good to understand, sister. I very proud of you."

"It's *I am very proud of you,*" said Isha, frowning and standing to her feet, "What is going on? What happened?"

"Oh, I don't know. You're the first people I have been able to talk to in a very long time." said the new girl with a bright smile.

"Huh," responded Isha with slumped shoulders and her mouth wide. "What do you mean? What about the orange light always following me places? Or the dark hallway, or the being pulled into the walls."

"No idea; I'm always watching the people here. That's how I learned to talk. But you are the first person to see me. I started following you, hoping that you would talk to me. And now you are here."

"But where is here?" asked Isha, waving her hands around.

"Here is inside me; you all are outside and inside. Look, see what I see," said the girl as she waved her hands, and instantly all around them, images of the school and its students appeared. In one image, there were a few students outside looking up at the stars. Another image had a student sitting at a desk with a candle while reading a book.

"Oh, sister look," said Jacinta pointing upwards.

Isha looked upward to see an image of Mr. Higgins naked on top of Miss. Webblebottom, taking her on top of the stands in a classroom. He thrust hard into her as she moaned in pleasure. And just as quickly, he flipped her over on the stand and raised her legs into the air before reaching forward, cupping her breasts, plunging his face down towards her vagina. His tongue and lips sucking at the mound between her legs.

"Oh, no, stop, stop," said Isha as she waved her arms in the air as the images faded away.

"Awe... I want see more. I want know what do when Isha finds us mate."

"I think he was using magic in her soft space with his tongue," said Makeba.

"Oh, goddess help me," said Isha, covering her face with her hands, letting them slide down in frustration. She then turned to the new Sakari girl and realized she didn't know her name.

"What is your name?"

"Lonta'Mar," said the girl.

"Lonta'Mar, where are we? Can you show us where we

are in this place?”

Lonta’Mar looked upward where a new image appeared, and inside the girls saw an image of themselves.

“Oh, it is us,” said Jacinta.

The image showed Makeba and Jacinta with their hands still on Isha’s back. But after looking closer, Isha could see the blood on the floor beneath her. She looked above and noticed blood leaking from her mouth.

“What’s happening to me?” asked Isha.

“Why sister bleeding? We not casting magic here,” said Jacinta, looking at her hands.

“I don’t know,” said Lonta’Mar, “No one has ever come inside tree before. It is...” Lonta’Mar waved her hand and another image popped up. “More people come to room.”

Isha looked up at the image and saw the uniforms of the people who were talking to Pavel earlier walking in and, along with them, the face of the blonde man who almost caught them last time. They were once again in the midst of the tree, slowly making their way towards the center. The blonde man stopped and pointed at one of the smaller trees and began explaining something to the golden uniformed men behind him.

“Oh, that not good. I break girl’s arm, so they not like me,” said Makeba as she watched the uniformed men look around the room, slowly coming closer to them.

“I don’t think they see us yet,” said Isha, turning to Lonta’Mar. “Can you get us out of here? We have to go.”

“But... but... will you come back?” asked Lonta’Mar with a panicked face.

“Yes, I promise... But... but if those men find us. We might never come back.”

“Oh... then I kill them, then?”

“What? No? That... that would be bad... I think,” said Isha, looking at the image. “Can you just let us out? I promise I will come back as soon as I can. But now we really have to go.”

Lonta'Mar frowned, "Okay, I let you go."

And in a flash of light, everything before Isha vanished. As soon as the white light disappeared, her vision returned to her as she stared at the ridges between the tree's bark. But something was wrong. Her body would not move as she wanted. As her senses came back, her neck snapped back as she coughed a large amount of blood on the bark of the tree before falling to the floor, convulsing. Her body spasmed in between the roots of the tree as Jacinta and Makeba tried to hold her still.

"Sister... sister, what is wrong?" asked Jacinta.

"Who's over there?" asked the voice of one of the men in uniform.

"Oh! They coming. What we do now?" asked Jacinta.

"Sister say not to kill, so not sure?" said Makeba.

"Maybe run away then?"

"How? Sister too heavy to run with."

Seconds later, the man came around the tree. "Who's there?" But all he saw were bloodstains on the bark of the tree and roots below.

Moments later, the girls found themselves floating in a sea of blackness. Their bodies were moved back and forth as if being guided through the darkness. To them, time seemed to stand still as their bodies were pulled in all directions before Isha opened her eyes and once again found herself on the floor of the school. Her body still not moving; all she could do was watch as her sisters frantically spoke to each other.

She didn't understand them anymore. They continued to panic. Their speech switched back to their Sakari tongue, and she was too tired to try and translate. She saw them pointing to a room, then her sisters grabbed her by the arms and dragged her inside, before Jacinta ran back out of the door and down the dark corridor. Her body still refused to listen to her as Makeba pulled her close and rested Isha's head on her lap.

"It going be okay Sister," said Makeba.

Isha looked ahead to see the setting sun through the window of the classroom.

Oh, that's right. That happened last time, too. I wonder how many days we were inside. I always... Isha felt something wet and cold hit her by the eye and roll down her cheek. She looked up to see Makeba crying above her. She was saying more things, but she couldn't hear her anymore. *Oh, no! I'm sorry... I made you cry again.* Suddenly the world above her began to turn blurry as tears began to form in her own eyes. *I really am a terrible sister, aren't I?*

CHAPTER 30

Through the darkness, Isha began to hear the sounds of someone singing. Her hearing was coming and going. One moment it was clear; the next, it was muffled. *Someone's singing. Who is it? I think I know that song; I remember it. It's so nice. Wait, where am I?* Isha tried to open her eyes, but only saw darkness. *There's something on my face. I can't see.* She tried to move her arms, but they didn't respond. There was something warm against her arm. A person. She could feel their breathing against her skin. The way the hair brushed over her wrists, swaying back and forth felt odd.

Isha tried to move her legs, but still, they didn't respond.

Her body felt so wrong to her. *What's happening? Why can't I move? What's wrong with me?* She began to panic, eyes darting back and forth in the darkness. Frantically she searched through her body for any limb, any finger, any muscle that would respond to the demands she was placing on her body. She heard the sound of a moan leave her mouth as she struggled, and instantly the singing stopped.

"Oh goddess, you're awake," came Chloe's voice. "Leo, Elena, wake up; she's awake."

The sound of Leo yawning was heard.

"Humm? What?" said Elena's voice as Isha felt the warm feeling leave her arm as hair brushed over her skin. "Is she okay?" Isha felt a warm hand rub against the side of her face. "Oh, poor baby. We were so worried about you."

"I'll go get the High Mother," said Chloe's voice as Isha heard her footsteps leaving, heading off somewhere unseen.

What's going on? Am I back home? Elena, is that you?

"Welcome back, little lady," came Leo's voice that was immediately followed up with a yawn.

Isha felt the object over her face move as it was lifted away, and she saw Leo and Elena's face smiling back at her.

"Ah...Ah..." she tried to speak, but no words would come out.

"No, no, not yet," said Elena, and she placed her hands on Isha's forehead.

"Yeah, you probably won't be speaking for a day or two. Your insides were all messed up," said Leo before he narrowed his eyes at Isha, looking serious. "Your sisters told me what you tried to do. Me and you are going to have a proper talk when you get fixed up."

Fixed up? I heard that. Does that mean I'm going to be okay?

"Don't be so harsh with her. She didn't know any better," said Elena as she frowned back up at Leo.

"Yeah, well, that doesn't make it any less reckless, now does it?" asked Leo, shaking his head. "If you're worried about your sisters, they're over there passed out. Between

Jacinta running at full speed from the school to come and get me to the frantic crying, they were doing when I brought you back. The High Mother felt it best to cast a sleep spell on them to calm them down. They will be fine after about a half-day or so."

"Is she really okay?" asked the High Mother entering the room with Chloe behind her as they made their way over to her bed. "Well, hello there. Welcome back, sweetheart. I'm happy to see you've woken up."

Isha's eyes looked up at the High Mother and blinked.

"Don't worry, now that you're awake, we're gonna get you fixed up. You really put your body through the worst though, didn't you? Your nervous system's just completely shut down. No motor function, no nothing. It's like your whole body just panicked and turned off. Even I've never seen anything like it. I mean maybe an arm or a leg, but the whole body. Never." The High Mother ran her hand across Isha's arm and sat down beside her. "Luckily, you have some really good healers with you. So we'll get you fixed up." The High Mother turned to Elena and Leo, "You two ready?"

Elena stepped forward, sitting to the left side of the bed, grabbing Isha's hand. Leo followed to the right, taking the other hand, and the High Mother walked above Isha and placed her hands on her head, wrapping her fingers under her chin.

"Okay, everyone, focus on your respective body parts, and let's fix my poor baby as best we can."

Leo and Elena closed their eyes as Isha felt a coldness come over her body. The coldness flowed in from her arms and head and began to consume her as the feeling circulated inside. This chill was deeper than when Leo or Aukube would fix her leg. They all stayed with Isha for hours and continued the healing process. During which time, Isha would often fade in and out of consciousness.

Every time Isha would come back to the world, she would see the three of them still healing her. But one thing became clear quickly. Elena was having a harder time keeping up with the other two. While the High Mother and Leo were as still as stone. Isha could see beads of sweat beginning to show on Elena's face as her breathing started to become labored.

Isha faded out of consciousness once more and came back to them again to see Elena struggling even more.

"Okay, everyone, let's rest for now. Five hours is a bit much to ask from any of us."

Hours? I think they said something about hours. How many has it been? Isha looked up and saw that the sun had indeed come up and was shining into the room. The lantern lights had gone out.

"I'm sorry, I'm slowing you down," said Elena as she tried to control her breathing, with Leo reaching over to wipe the sweat off of her face with a cloth.

"Oh baby, you're doing fine," replied The High Mother as she walked over and wrapped her arms around Elena. "Just the sheer fact that you kept your magical output matched with ours as long as you did is really an impressive feat. If Leo and I have the talent to heal, then I think your hard work will make you a great healer. And you haven't even finished your schooling yet. I can't wait to see how good you become." The High Mother turned to Leo, "You've done a good job training this one, Leo."

"Of course, I have. Can't have any half-assed healers in my harem."

"Oh wow," said the High Mother. "You really would be a good man if only you didn't say things like that."

"That's... that's what I always tell him," said Elena with a laugh.

Leo frowned at the two, "As the only male in this house, I simply feel that I have a responsibility to ensure the happiness of all the women here."

"Are you sure that responsibility isn't coming from your pants?" asked the High Mother with a raised brow.

"Pleasing so many women is a sacrifice that I'm willing to make. I shall go down in history as a martyr."

"What about Darla then? Is she part of this harem plan of yours?" asked Elena.

"Fuck Darla. I'm half tempted to believe she's a man in a woman's body. For my own sanity, she doesn't count."

"I really hoped that I could raise you better than this," said the High Mother shaking her head.

"So, he really has always been like this?" asked Elena.

"Sadly, yes. He would constantly hide under our skirts when we first brought him and his brother with us. Giving those poor girls such problems as they tried to handle their studies." The High Mother sighed. "Some things are just in the blood, I suppose."

"Ah... Ah..." murmured Isha as her eyes darted between the three as they stood above her.

"Now you hush down there," said the High Mother, frowning at Isha. "You're going to be out for the rest of the day with the damage you've done to yourself. But with the three of us here, we'll get you up in a day or so. And you should be talking by the end of the day. Rattled vocal cords are not so hard to heal as all of the rest of the damage you've done." The High Mother gave Isha a hard pat on the top of her head, which made her flinch. "Has she always been this reckless?"

"Not just her," said Leo, thrusting his thumb at Chloe. "That one over there is just as bad. Between that scarred hand and the constant fights between her and Isha. I'm amazed we have time to heal anyone else at the school."

"That's not fair. I..." blurted out Chloe before closing her mouth.

"What's that? Couldn't think of a good excuse for all the worry you two put me through?" asked Leo, staring at Chloe.

Chloe looked down at the floor. "I'm... I'm sorry."

Leo walked over, placing his hand on her head and ruffling her hair. "Well, at least things seem better now.

What's that song you were singing earlier? I never heard it before?"

"You heard that?"

"Of course, I did. It was probably the most peaceful, relaxing thing I've heard in years. I'm pretty sure it calmed Isha down too."

"Water's Grace, it's a song one of the... I mean, someone taught it to me a long time ago."

"Yes, it was very beautiful," said Elena. "Can you teach it to me one day?"

"Yes... if you want, I can."

"Well, we are all a bit tired and would like a rest, at least for an hour or so. And that little lady back there won't be going anywhere anytime soon. Chloe, would you mind staying with her again as we head downstairs to eat and rest for a while?"

"No, I... I will stay."

"Thank you. And obviously no fighting. Seeing as she can't defend herself and all."

"I know that," said Chloe, frowning and puffing up her cheeks.

Leo chuckled, "Just making sure. Let's go all and leave the girls alone."

"Did they really fight each other?" asked the High Mother.

"Oh yeah, you should have seen the scratch marks on their faces," said Leo as his voice trailed off as he left the room with Elena and the High Mother.

Chloe slowly walked over and sat down beside Isha, "How do we always end up like this?"

Isha's eyes just gazed back up at the brown-haired girl.

"I hated you," said Chloe looking down at Isha. "You're so stupid. You were like that before. Asking all those dumb questions. How many rooms are here? How big is it? How many fish are inside? Can't you catch them with your hands?" Chloe sighed and slumped her shoulders, "I'm tired. I'm tired of all of it. I'm tired of this school, I'm tired of fighting, I'm tired of hating you. And I don't know what I'm going to do when I leave here. Where am I supposed to go? I'm the only one left."

Isha watched Chloe continue to ramble on about things she couldn't hear. The ringing in her ears just sounded like a whistling sound where only pieces of information would slip through between the moments. But she knew Chloe looked to be in pain by the expression on her face. Her eyes were puffy. Her lips trembled, and the lines above her head crinkled the more she spoke.

I'm sorry. I wish I could hear you. But I can only hear a little bit at a time. What fish? Were the fish fighting? Is that something at this school?

But none of that would matter as Chloe dropped her head on the bed beside Isha and slowly fell asleep with her brown hair covering Isha's hand.

Isha looked down at the girl's head, feeling the softness of her hair as it slid over her fingers. The sun shone down on them both through a glass window as the golden light filled the room with tiny sparkling pieces of dust that glittered all around them.

CHAPTER 31

Hidden in the shadows of nearby buildings, Victor and Silk crouched low while watching as the last of the guards left the old chapel. It was still somewhat dark, but the sky was showing a small hint of blue as the light from an approaching sun slowly crept over the horizon.

"If we're going, it will have to be now," said Silk. "I don't sense anyone else around."

"I guess we go then."

They both crossed the roadway into the tall grass. The greenery was wet from the moisture of the night, sticking to their clothing as they made their way towards the side of the building. Once they made it to the chapel's wall, Victor peered into the broken window, scanning the room.

"No one's inside."

"What about the guard up front? Do we kill him?"

"A distraction will do fine."

"Killing him and dragging his body inside would be easier."

"I'd prefer to not get messy if I can help it. Are you sure you don't like killing?"

"It's not about liking; it's about convenience. But fine, we'll try it your way."

The two crept forward toward the entrance to the old chapel.

"We gotta be quick before people start to come out of their homes."

Victor tossed a rock over the man's head that landed nearby. But the man didn't budge from his position. Victor frowned, found another larger rock and once again tossed it over the man's head. It landed with a thud even closer to the guard. But again, the man didn't move.

"What is he, oblivious? Even I heard that."

"Oh, fuck it, we don't have time for this."

"Hey, wait."

Silk crept up to the man with a blade in her hand, then she stopped, shook her head and stood up before walking past the man and slowly opening the door behind him. Victor's face twisted in confusion as he crept up the guard, only to find the man sound asleep on his feet. He stared at the man for a moment in wonderment before following Silk's example and shook his head before tip-toeing in the temple with Silk slowly closing the door behind him.

Inside the chapel, everything was mostly as desolate as it seemed from the outside. Broken chairs and benches were piled in a corner, but on the dusty floor were wet footprints that led to the fake image of the wall. Victor stepped forward, placing his hands on the fake wall, and watched as his fingers pierced the illusion.

"Ready?" asked Victor as he turned back to Silk.

"The faster we get it done, the faster we are both free from all of this."

"Well said," and with that Victor stepped forward, penetrating the mirage. Once inside, he was greeted to the sight of a stairwell leading down into a cave.

"Are you going in, or just going to stand there?" asked Silk as she walked past Victor, stepping down into the darkness. She walked forward into the blackness, her feet splashing into a puddle as she disappeared. "I found a torch. Should I light it?"

"Seems we don't really have a choice," said Victor, making his way down. "I can't really see in the dark. Do you sense anyone nearby?"

"Not yet, but I'm still having issues controlling my magic. I could hold your hand and guide you if you want?"

Victor looked into the darkness and sighed, "Yeah, let's go with that."

"What? Really?"

"Yeah, if we're trying to be cautious, it makes the most sense. Keep the torch, though. Just in case."

Victor stepped down to the cave's soil as Silk walked back out of the shadows, reaching out, grabbing his hand before leading him back into the darkness. The ground was wet with moisture as they entered the cave. The dripping of water for the ceiling could be heard from several locations as the drips echoed off the walls at different volumes.

"For once, I must admit that being a mage has its uses. Seeing in the dark would come in handy right now."

"Yeah, well, I'm not using magic. I'm just used to the dark. Watch your feet; there's a big rock sticking out of the ground."

Victor felt the large rock graze his boot as he slowly stepped forward, following Silk's guidance. Up ahead, he began to see glimmers of light coming from several locations in the cave. Each seeming to lead in a different direction in the catacomb area.

"That can't be good."

"Stay here. I'll go check."

Silk glided ahead into the shadows like a cat prowling the night. Her nimbleness was surprising as she silently stepped forward.

How do I always find myself in these stealthy situations? Clearly, I'm the only one in the world not qualified for the skill. Victor watched Silk peak into the rooms with the light sources before making her way back to him.

"Bodies? Not sure if they're asleep or dead. Wanna have a look?"

"Sadly, we don't have a choice. The more information we have, the better."

Victor made his way to one of the rooms and peeked inside to see shirtless women and men laid out on tables. *What in the goddess?* He looked around before turning to Silk. "Stand guard." He then stepped inside. Immediately he noticed the red crystals that were embedded into the flesh of the people on the tables. *Okay, that's a big, objective complete. I don't know what they are doing, but I can confirm they are doing something.*

Victor leaned down towards a man's body and felt the man's breath glide over his face. *Okay, so they're alive. Asleep but still alive. What the hell are these things?* The Jewels were embedded across different body parts in each of the bodies: one man had a jewel above his heart, a woman, one between her breasts, while another two had jewels in each of their shoulders. Victor stepped around the room, inspecting the bodies till he came across one that had a jewel embedded in his head. It wasn't as big as the others but still was a sizable shard. He leaned down close, noticing that unlike the others in the room, this man was dead. *Wonder what killed him.*

"Anything out there?" asked Victor as he left the room.

"Quiet, and I hope it stays that way. Find anything out?"

"I can confirm that the goddesses' people are doing it. But I have no idea what they're doing."

"Are we done?"

"Not yet; there's still a lot of questions. And since we're here. Let's see what else they might have down..." Victor's words trailed off as he and Silk both heard the sound of several footsteps coming from where the stairs were.

Soon the light of a lantern began to glow from around a corner. Victor and Silk stepped into another room with bodies on tables and waited for whoever was coming to pass.

"Alright, just grab another bag, and this should be the last one."

"I hope so; I'm tired."

"What? You gonna fall asleep like Heppen did?"

"Hey, the guy just had twins. I'd like to see you stay awake after a night with those tiny terrors."

"No thanks," The man grunted. "I prefer my kids unknown and far away."

"Ha! When are we supposed to get the bodies out of here?"

"Hell, If I know. I'd rather just leave them down here with that creepy bastard. Now that's another person I wish to be unknown and far away."

"I agree with ya there. Come one, let's get this shit outta here."

The sounds of wet feet on the ground passed through the cave along with the lantern light that was slowly fading away, leaving Victor and Silk back inside a dimmed darkness. They both waited to make sure no one else was heard coming down the stairs. Feeling confident about not getting caught, Victor walked over and began examining more of the bodies that were laid across the tables.

"What are you doing? asked Silk, turning back at him.

"Just checking these since we're here," said Victor as he ran his finger over the jewel embedded in a man's neck.

"This one's dead; what about those two beside you?"

"Seriously," said Silk, frowning before turning back to the bodies and inspecting them. "These two are still alive."

"Where are the crystals on their bodies?"

"One has a set on the ribs, the other on his chest. How do you plan to get out of here now? That sleepy guard is probably awake, and we don't know who else is up there."

"I have a few ideas. But nothing concrete yet. Either way, making a break for it and hightailing it out of town might be the best option."

"Okay then, so we look for another way out."

"And gather more information on the way."

The two continued deeper into the cave, finding even more rooms with bodies in them.

"Goddess, how many people are down here? Surely, not all of them are from this town. Someone would have noticed," said Victor.

"This is too many people for a sleep spell. You think they signed up for this?"

"Probably, that Kemlor fellow is pretty charismatic. The crowds for his sermons get bigger every morning. And when people are desperate, they'll often turn to anyone who offers them help."

"You mean like I did with you."

A moment of silence hung in the air between them.

"Do you regret it?"

"No."

"Good, then let's keep moving."

The two continued deeper into the cave until they reached a room where a brighter light was shining.

"Well there's the end of it all, be prepared for whatever happens."

"You think it's trapped?"

"I think that certain moments in my life always tend to end a certain way. And I'm starting to get a feeling that this is one of those moments."

"We can always turn around and take our chances with the guards that are probably waiting upstairs."

Victor frowned, "A lovely thought, but no. Let's see what they're hiding in there."

The two entered the room to see the large man, who was sick days before, lying down on a table. Over in the corner were two baskets of the red jewels that were embedded into the bodies they had just seen.

"Only one body," said Silk.

Victor crept up to the man and saw the five jewels embedded across his chest.

"More than the rest," whispered Victor, turning to Silk. "You see another way out?"

"Not unless you can walk through walls." Silk picked up one of the red crystals from the basket, inspecting it. "I wonder what's so special about these things that all those people put them into their bodies."

"I'm sure they're not just cosmetic. Not even the craziest jewel aficionado would cut open their own body for fashion," said Victor before spotting some parchment on the floor. Walking over, picking it up, he examined it. But the ink had long since washed away. Flipping the parchment over, he noticed that above the smudges of old ink was something very clear. The sigil of the Magical School of Latrusa.

What the hell does Sceana have to do with any of this? Are they performing experiments on people? If so, why do it here. Why not in their giant fortress in the sky? No, something's not adding up.

"What's that?" asked Silk, coming over to see the parchment he was holding.

"Not sure, yet. But something's not right. It might be that a school of magic is involved with this mess."

"Is that surprising? Don't they do experiments and stuff at those magic schools?"

"Exactly, they do it up there. Then why are they doing it down here? Doesn't seem worth the risk to just—"

476

"You really shouldn't have come here," said a voice from behind them.

Victor and Silk turned around to see the man who was on the table asleep, now standing between them and the doorway.

"And of course he wakes up," said Victor as he raised his hands in submission. "Don't suppose you're willing to just let us go and keep quiet about this?"

"No, you've seen it. So, you're going to die down here."

"And what have I seen? What are you doing to these people down here?"

"Oh, we're making—" The man thrust his hand forward sending a wave of force at Victor and Silk as they both leapt out of the way towards different parts of the room. "There's no need to talk to dead people."

Of course, he's a fucking mage. Thought Victor as he watched Silk dash across the room and wave her arm, sending out a wave of force that sent the man sliding back on his feet as he raised his hands to shield himself. *Oh, that's right. I have a mage with me this time. This might balance things out a bit.* Victor pulled out a dagger from his side as he noticed small rocks and dust falling from the roof of the cavern to the floor. *Either that or they'll bury us all alive down here.*

Victor dashed at the mage who had managed to grab hold of Silk's garb and held her in the air. She kicked at the man's chest, which seemed to do no good as the man took the blows and brought down a heavy arm at Victor. Victor brought his blade up and pierced the man's arm. But the impact of the blow dropped Victor to his knees, stopping him in his tracks. He grimaced as he felt his bones and muscles rattle from the blow.

Damn mage strength.

The man kicked Victor in the side, which he blocked with his arms. But the force still sent Victor rolling across the ground, hitting the wall on the other side of the room.

Gritting his teeth on the impact, he shook his head, trying to block out the pain. Looking back over to the man, he saw Silk blast some type of magic into his face before he reached back and tossed Silk through the air as she came crashing into Victor, knocking the wind out of him even more. *Fuck! We're getting our asses—* Victor looked up to see the man gathering energy that seemed to crackle in his hand. The man looked at them with a snarl and thrust his hand forward, sending out a wave of flames. Victor quickly brought in his legs and wrapped Silk in his arms as he covered them with his cloak.

The sound of the flames crackling around them could be heard outside as orange and red light pierced through the darkness of the cloak as they huddled beneath it. Victor looked down to see green light forming in Silk's hands. When the flames stopped, Silk burst out of Victor's cloak as the man was in the process of ripping Victor's blade out from his arms. He saw Silk coming and swung his arm down at her; she rolled over still with the magic cradled in her hands and raised up, placing the magic in the man's chest. Suddenly Victor felt a large gust of wind as he saw the man lifted up into the air, crashing against the ceiling of the cave before falling back down to the wet floor where Silk kicked him in the face before bringing out her own blade and stabbing it at the man's head.

He rolled over, grabbing Silk by the leg, snatching her off of her feet and climbing on top of her. She kicked at him with her other leg, but once again, it didn't seem to do any good. He grabbed the side of her masked face.

"Burn," said the man as Victor saw his hands begin to glow over Silk's mask as she squirmed beneath him.

Victor struggled to get up and ran forward, picking his knife up off the ground as Silk began to scream in pain as her face was devoured by a wave of flames that spewed forth from the man's hand and across the floor. Victor raised his hand as he rushed the man, only to feel himself lifted off the ground and slammed back down.

"I've had enough of both of you," said the man as he looked at Victor on the ground and noticed he didn't have his blade.

He looked down only to see Silk drive Victor's dagger into his side. The man grabbed the blade at his side as his grip loosened on Silk's now half-burned face.

Silk released the knife and began punching the man in the face over and over until he stumbled backward, placing his back against the wall and watched as Silk and Victor picked themselves up off the floor.

"Another monster," said the man, looking at Silk's face.

Silk gritted her teeth as she peeled what was left of the burned mask from her face, revealing what was left of her ashen skin. One of her eyes was closed as the left side of her face showed the hideous damage. The skin was melted onto itself, and fresh spots of blood began running down the side of her face, dripping off of her cheek.

"Even if you manage to kill me, you won't make it out of here."

"First things first, let's get on with the killing you part. We'll think of the rest after," said Victor as he grabbed a broken piece of wood from the floor.

"Humph, I won't make it easy for you." The man ripped out the blade from his side and thrust another wave of magic at Victor, who dodged out of the way as the force crashed against the wall. The cave's room shook as dust and rocks fell from the ceiling around them.

Silk rushed forward as the man slashed Victor's blade at her neck. She ducked under, kicking the man in the side where the blade had pierced him and punched him in the face. His head bounced back, hitting the wall, but as Silk tried to punch him again, he dodged, grabbing Silk by the back of the head slamming her face-first into the wall as he pulled himself forward. Then he twisted himself around and kicked Silk in the back, slamming her into the wall again.

She gasped as she fell to her knees with her hand on the wall, trying to keep herself from falling over.

Victor brought down the piece of wood on top of the man's head. The blow dropped him to his knees, hovering over Silk. Victor then slid the stick in front of the man's face, placing it against his throat before reaching around with his other hand, grabbing the other end. He then pulled back as hard as he could, wrenching the man away from Silk as he began gasping for breath.

Doesn't matter how strong you are if you can't fucking breathe.

The man began flailing as the wood slid across his neck, embedding splinters into his skin. Victor pulled back as hard as he could, but the wood was brittle from all the time in the moist cave and it shattered from his force. The sudden release from the broken wood sent both men spiraling in opposite directions. Victor stumbled back, falling over and banging his head against a wall, while the man tumbled forward crashing into the baskets of red crystals, which sent them rolling through the floor of the cave room.

Victor's vision turned blurry after cracking his head against the wall. The sound of flowing water passed through his mind as he shook his head and squinted, trying to once again focus on the man who was beginning to pull himself up. *He just refuses to die.* Victor lifted up from the floor. *Fine. Do I have anything that can bring this guy down? No more alagon stone. Out of sparks and the rest are just healing materials.*

The man stood up, grabbing at his side, which Victor noticed had been burned and was now just charred skin. *Dammit, he cauterized the wound. Argh. Fucking goddess. Why is nothing ever easy?* Victor stood up and made his way over to the man, bending over and grabbing two of the red shards off the floor. *I gotta stop this bastard before he has the chance to cast more of that damn magic.* He looked over to see

Silk still face down on the floor. *You did well. Now, let's see if I can get us out of this.* Victor approached the man as he looked down at him in anger.

"What's wrong? Don't feel like dying yet? Well, let me fix that for you."

"We'll see how smart you are with your head caved in," said the man as he swung a fist at Victor.

Yeah, that's right, get angry. The angrier you are, hopefully the less magic you cast. Victor dodged the attack and hit the man under the chin. Then ducked another blow, punching him in the side where the burn wound was. "What's... wrong... finding it hard to focus, you big fucker?"

The man screamed and continued swinging his arms wildly at Victor, who continued to dodge. He caught hold of Victor's cloak, and Victor, quickly turned, bringing down his elbow onto the man's wrist before he could get a solid grip, then backhanded him in the face before headbutting him in the nose which sent the big man reeling backward before Victor kicked him in the balls which brought him to his knees. *Let's see if this kills you.* Victor flipped the shard in his hand and drove it towards the man's head. But he leaned sideways, and it instead pierced his shoulder. Victor tried to snatch it out, but the man grabbed his hand, covering the shard. He trapped Victor's hand in his ever-tightening grip. Victor grimaced as he felt the shard crack beneath his own fingers as fragments of it began embedding into the flesh of his hands.

"Got you now," said the man with a bloody smile on his face.

He squeezed Victor's hand with more force than the red crystal could handle, and it shattered in his hands as Victor gave out a scream as he felt his fingers break in the man's grasp. And with his other hand, the man drove his fist into the side of Victor's face while keeping hold of his mangled hand. Over and over he smashed the side of his face until he shattered the side of the mask with his knuckles and ripped the mask off Victor's face, revealing his green eyes. Victor's body hung limp in the man's grasp as he smiled.

"I told you you'd die down—" said the large figure.

The man gasped; his neck stretched back with his mouth agape in pain as he felt Silk's teeth bite into the side of his neck as she landed on his back, grabbing hold of his shoulders. His hands twitched in pain, his eyes wide as he screamed as Silk sunk her teeth deeper into his flesh as blood spurted onto Victor's now exposed face. The man quickly let go of Victor and reached behind his back, trying to grab hold of Silk. He flailed wildly as Silk stayed latched on to him. Victor looked around for anything, grabbing another red crystal from the floor. He then lunged upward with as much force as he could, driving the crimson jewel into the man's neck. The man froze for a moment as it pierced his body, blood leaking from the wound down onto Victor's hands. The man dropped to his knees as Silk bounced off of him and rolled across the ground.

Victor stepped back as the man fell forward and rolled over onto his back with the crystal sticking upward into the air from his neck. Exhausted, he then limped himself over to where Silk was on the floor coughing up blood.

"Hey... you okay?" asked Victor and knelt in front of her.

"No," she coughed up more blood onto the floor. "I'm not." She looked up at Victor with a smile, but to Victor she was a harrowing sight. Blood was splattered across her burned and ashen face, along with a large amount of blood at the sides of her mouth, pooling over her chin, and covering her teeth.

"Come on, let's get the fuck out of here. We're done," said Victor, shaking off the haunting visage.

Victor reached down and picked Silk up off the floor, holding her up with his arms under her shoulders. Together they headed towards the door and entered back into the cave, only to hear the sounds of multiple footsteps.

"Okay, search all the rooms, make sure we don't miss

anything," echoed a voice down through the cave.

"Oh, seriously, fuck me," said Victor as he heard the sounds.

"Got... any plans?" asked Silk.

"I'm thinking, you think you--" said Victor before they both felt a gust of wind flow from behind them inside the room.

They both turned around to see a crimson mist begin swirling in the air around the body of the dead man. Small red particles were coming up from the crystals that were scattered around him.

"What the fuck..." said Victor as his face twisted into pure non-understanding as he watched the dead man's hand slowly rise up and take hold of the crystal in his neck. He quickly turned to Silk, "Can you still cast magic?"

Silk just stared at the man as the mist floated above him and began to spiral.

"Silk, Silk," said Victor in a desperate attempt to bring her back to reality. She finally snapped out of her gaze and looked back at Victor. "Can you still cast magic?"

"Ah... yes, I think so, but it's hard to focus on—"

"I just need you to use that push magic you used earlier," said Victor as he brought her back into the cave room and sat her down in the corner. "Here, I want you to use as much of that force magic as you can into the floor in this spot.

Silk sat on the floor and watched as the man ripped the crystals out of his neck and let the bloody crystal fall to the floor. They then watched as the red swirling mist flowed down into the crystals inside of the man's chest. Victor turned back to Silk, grabbing her face and looking her in the eyes.

"Don't watch him, just focus on the magic. Okay. Just focus on the magic."

Silk looked into Victor's green eyes, then nodded her head as she began to control her breathing.

Victor turned back to the man who was now starting

to rise up from the floor. He noticed that some of the red crystals near him had now turned entirely black. The man stood up and looked around the room as if confused. He raised his hands up in front of his face and began wiggling his fingers.

"Sun-sa Mah RemSha," said the man as he continued to look around the room, and to the crystals on the floor. He knelt down and picked up a now black crystal, placing it to his nose and sniffed, before tossing it back down. He then turned around, finally spotting Victor and Silk huddled over in the corner. "Unja mal fu-lik," he spoke with a smile across his face that sent a chill down Victor's spine.

"Silk, I need you to cast that magic quick," said Victor as he watched the hole in the man's neck heal itself as he took a step towards them.

Silk screamed as she sent as much power as she could into the ground. The sound of cracking could be heard as the ground gave way beneath them, and they fell through the floor down into the icy water below.

The water carried them forward only a few feet before they stopped. Victor quickly grabbed hold of Silk, lifting her up, and standing in the small running water. It was dark inside, where the only light was that that shone from the hole up above where they had crashed in.

"Can you see up ahead? There must be a way out?"

Silk shook her head, trying to focus with her one eye, and peered into the darkness up ahead. "I... see."

"Hey Fratton, what's going on? What happened in here?" came the voice of a man up above. "Did you make that hole? Hey, what are you doing? Stop, stop!" Soon the sounds of men screaming in pain pierced through the sound of running water below as Victor watched the body of one of the white garbed men fall through the hole and crash into the water behind them.

"Okay, time to go. Just keep moving," he said as he stumbled forward with Silk's arm over his shoulder into the darkness with the sounds of men and women's screams echoing in the background.

Victor stumbled through the darkness as Silk guided him until the water came up to her chest. They waded into it a little farther until finally stopping at a wall.

"Water exits here," said Victor, grabbing a hold of Silk. "Hold your breath and dive under."

They both submerged themselves under the water and swam forward. The moment they submerged they both could see the sunlight shining ahead and swam for it, eventually emerging out of the other side at a small lake that was a decent trip away from the city. Crawling up back on to land, they both coughed as they laid down beside each other with water still covering their legs. Breathing heavily, their bodies both mangled, smashed, and burned, they laid there for a short moment before Victor took a deep breath and once again picked up Silk.

"Come on; we can't afford to get caught now. Hopefully, they're still dealing with whatever that was instead of coming to look for us. We gotta make as much space as we can, before they get it under control."

Victor climbed to the top of the lake with Silk and looked around the area, seeing the town below. He looked up in the sky and then town before moving his hand in front of him and turned to the left.

"Okay, we gotta go this way." And he and Silk walked over into the woods. They wandered through the woods for what seemed like dozens of minutes.

"Where we headed?" asked Silk in a meek voice.

"I didn't think we'd be staying in town long after we left the tavern. So, I tried to arrange... there it is."

Ahead of them, Victor saw their horse and carriage tied in an opening in the woods with the old man from the tavern sleeping in the passenger's seat with his hands crossed over his chest and the morning sun shining on his face.

"What? Why?" asked Silk.

"We hit it off, so I took a gamble and offered to pay him to sleep out here and catch some morning sun." Victor led Silk to the back of the wagon and helped lift her up with his one good hand before walking up to the front and shook the man on the shoulder.

"Huh! What?"

"Wake up, old man; your shift has ended. Time to go home."

"Oh, it's you. Wow, you look like you got the shit kicked out of you."

"I did," said Victor as he reached into one of his pouches and pulled out a small bag, handing it to the man. "And here's the other ten gold, as promised."

The old man smiled, taking the gold. The sound of ruffling in the hay then caught his attention as he turned back to look inside the wagon as Silk wormed her way beneath the blanket covering herself. "I take it you and your little girly there won't be coming back here anytime soon." He stood up and slowly stepped down from the wagon, grabbing his back and stretching.

"Not even if the goddess tried to make us."

"Ha," the old man chuckled, "Well, best be on your way then; the roads just past them trees. I should start my own walk back if I intend to make it back to my bed before the sun's fully up."

"Thanks for your help,"

The old man waved off his thanks as he walked off into the woods, "Thanks for the coin."

Victor then snapped the reins on the horses and headed off into the trees and back onto the road.

CHAPTER 32

Isha awoke to see Makeba and Jacinta asleep in their bed with her as the morning sun shone down into the room. She tried twiddling her fingers, and to her surprise, they moved, if not sluggishly. She tried the same with her toes and took a breath of relief when she felt the same.

"Well, good morning there; happy to see that you're awake."

Isha turned her head to see the High Mother sitting down in a chair with a book in her hand, smiling at her.

"I... I... can move," said Isha with a sore throat.

"Of course, you can. We all worked on you pretty hard.

But can you speak? You haven't had a drink of water in a whole day." The High Mother reached down, grabbing a flagon of water from the floor and walking over to Isha, placing the tip against her lips.

Isha drank slowly as the cool water pierced her throat, and with it a relief she didn't realize she needed.

"You've been passing in and out of consciousness these last two days. It's good to see that head of yours not bobbing around this time."

"Will I be alright?"

"Of course, your body's just weirded out from not being able to move these last few days. We just gotta get you up and moving around. But it's going to be a terrible feeling at first. I hope you're ready for it."

"Oh, she's awake," said Elena, walking into the room holding a tray of meat and bread in her hand. "I was wondering when she would come around. Well, I brought food just in case."

"Good, you're just in time; help me get her away from her sister's and onto the floor. We're going to have to force her to get those motor functions going again."

Elena put down the food tray as the High Mother roused Jacinta and Makeba from their sleep.

"Alright, up you two. Breakfast is ready. Get on up; we have to work on your sister."

The Sakari girls slid out of bed and stood to the side, both rubbing at their eyes as Elena and the High Mother grabbed Isha under her arms and lifted her out of bed. Her feet dangling in the air.

Instantly, Isha grit her teeth as her whole body tried to wake itself up. It reminded her of the feeling of her leg falling asleep. Those hundreds of tiny prickles were now all over her body, making her lips tremble as she tried to endure the feeling.

"Bear with it, honey. That's the feeling of your body waking up from a long sleep. It's going to be a lot of weird pain."

Isha bit her lip and nodded her head, not wanting to even try to speak because she knew she would cry out if she allowed any sounds to slip from her mouth. They helped her place one foot forward. Pain shot up her leg as she closed her eyes, trying to endure the return from numbness. They placed her other foot forward, allowing her weight to shift, and another surge of pain coursed through her body as her back convulsed and her hands twitched.

"What are you two doing?" asked Leo as he walked inside the room to see the two women helping Isha walk.

"We're doing therapy; what does it look like?" asked Elena.

"Oh, for the goddess' sake, her body is just asleep. It's not broken. You're only prolonging her suffering like this," said Leo as he walked over to the three women and knelt down in front of Isha with his head at her waist. "You gotta do it all at once and jump-start the nervous system."

"Wha... what are you going—" muttered Isha, but before she could finish her sentence, Leo had wrapped his arms around her waist and lifted her into the air with a big hug, giving her a powerful squeeze.

Her arms and legs flailed in the air as she felt her and Leo's bodies smush against each other. Her whole body turned to prickly fire as every muscle turned into a hyper-sensitive chaos of sensations. She let out a massive scream as tears ran down her face as her head bobbed around in the air. Leo bounced Isha's body up and down in his arms a few times, before her body limply laid across him with her head resting on his shoulder as if she were an infant child.

"There we go," said Leo in a cooing voice. "There we go, it's going to be all better now. That's the worst of it. Just gotta give your body time to adjust." He held Isha in his arms like a giant baby, patting her on the back. Her head still limped over his shoulder.

"That's such a horrible way to do that," said the High Mother shaking her head.

"He never did understand other people's pain," added Elena, shaking her head, "I imagine that is the difference between male and female healers.

"Yes, Nahtalli could also be a bit forceful in his healing."

"Oh shush, both of you, " said Leo, frowning at the ladies. "You're both just babies. Doing it your way would have taken half the day. I've done this same thing multiple times for the boys who get knocked out in combat class. Besides, you don't see her sisters complaining, do you?" He said as he smiled, looking over at Jacinta and Makeba, who were munching on the sweet meats and bread that Elena had brought in.

"Leo, good man, he does what's best for sister," said Jacinta as she popped another piece of meat into her mouth.

"There, you see. I have the approval from her own next of kin."

"Your bedside manner is just horrible," said Elena.

Isha watched the world in a daze as she bounced up and down in Leo's arms. Outside of the immense pain that had paralyzed her body, the feeling of being held like this reminded her of when her father used to hold her when she was a child. Or when she had thrown herself into the arms of Uncle Jasper after he rescued her from the wagon. Then sat her atop his horse before taking her off into the woods. She remembered waking up on top of him, her face on his chest. He had those weird claw marks from some type of beast and began to wonder where he'd gotten them. All stories he had promised to tell her, and now he'd never get the chance.

Around an hour later, Isha was downstairs in the common area on wobbly legs, making her way back and forth to each side of the room to an awaiting Jacinta and Makeba who were there to catch her if she fell.

"There you go, look at those little legs work," said Leo,

coming back down the stairs with a smile on his face.

Isha stumbled but kept her balance as she narrowed her eyes at him.

"Hey, what's with that look?"

"That really hurt, what you did."

"Of course, it did, but it worked. Look at you, already walking around. If I'd have let Elena and the High Mother have their way, you'd still be struggling to sit up on your own. Sometimes a little brute force is needed."

Isha watched the big dumb smile on Leo's face as he finished coming down the stairs. *When I'm able to move my arms again, I'm going to punch you.* She tripped and fell into Makeba's arms.

"Sister doing good. Are you feeling better now?"

"A little, my body just feels a bit weak, is all. Just let me rest for a moment."

Makeba sat Isha on the floor to catch her breath as Leo sat down at the table.

"Now, perhaps you could tell me why in the goddess's name you asked your sisters to push their magic into your system for so long, let alone at all?"

"I just thought since healers can force their magic into other people's bodies, then it must be possible for us to accept other people's magic into our own."

"And you thought correctly; it's certainly possible. But there's just never been any reason to actually do it, except for some weird research they do from time to time. Once someone thought they could transfer magical energy into healers and have them convert it into their own. The problem with that was that your mind would still be filtering it, so you'd just burn out twice as fast. But if you want to learn it, I can teach it to you. It's a fairly simple technique."

"Really?"

"Yeah, but only after you've fully recovered and only in hopes that you never do that to your body again. I'm not sure I can handle Jacinta and Makeba crying around me again as I rush what's left of you back home."

"Oh," Isha dropped her head, feeling embarrassed. "I never thanked you for that. For coming to get me, I mean."

"You can thank me by not being so reckless again anytime soon. But with your track record, you'd end up breaking that promise before the day is over. So how about this? Instead of worrying me and Elena half to death. If you're ever curious about how our powers work. How about you ask us first, rather than just doing something that could have killed you?"

"I'm sorry."

"Don't be sorry, just be careful. We're all here to teach and protect you. I'll give everything I have to keep you girls safe. Just be careful, okay."

"Okay," said Isha, sulking in self-shame.

"Come one, don't be like that," said Leo as he left his seat, walking over to her. He reached under her arms and lifted her up to her feet. "Come on, let's go another round, shall we?"

Isha allowed herself to be picked up by Leo as he guided her throughout the lower levels of the house. Occasionally she would stumble into his arms, which she realized didn't feel so bad.

The next day Isha was back up and moving around and about to head off for class. She soon noticed the orange light hovering inside one of the nearby trees and decided to walk up to it. The orange light danced in front of her. *Surely, just doing this much isn't me being reckless.* She placed her hand on the tree and pushed her magic into it.

Hello? Can you hear me?

There was a moment of silence before she heard it.

Hello. How are you? I watched man take you off. Are you better now.? Can you come visit?

492

Not yet. It hurts me to visit you. I need to learn how to do it properly. But I think it's okay to talk to you like this.

Oh, okay then. Talking is fine. I like to talk. Are you coming to school today?

Yes, I'm on my way now. I will talk to you then. Okay.

Yes, okay, we talk when you get to school.

Isha removed her hands from the tree and turned around to see Jacinta and Makeba staring at her.

"Sister, talk to Sakari tree girl?" asked Jacinta.

"Yes, I did. We can go to class now." They headed off towards the school. "Are there glowing trees in Sakar, like the orange one inside?"

"No," said Makeba. "We never saw tree like that before or girl who lives in tree. It is very weird tree."

"I wonder how she got in there," said Isha as they made their way into the castle and toward their magical theory classes where Miss Webblebottom was standing in front of her desk. Instantly Isha remembered the sight of her naked body bent over the table with Mr. Higgins on top of her, and she blushed a little.

"Teacher, teacher," said Jacinta as she waltzed over with a smile on her face.

Oh no. Isha tried making her way through the class to catch up to Jacinta.

"Yes, dear," said Miss Webblebottom.

"Can you teach us tongue trick?"

"Tongue trick? You mean with magic? I mean, I guess it's possible to cast magic with your tongue."

"No, we saw man face in your—"

"No!, No, no, no. Let's go, Jacinta," said Isha, grabbing her sister by the arm and dragging her up the steps.

"But what about tongue trick?"

"We don't need to know that right now. Let's just go and take a seat."

Miss Webblebottom raised a brow at the girls but shrugged and started the class. "Okay, class, Jacinta

Highland has brought up a theory of, are we able to cast magic with our tongues. Which sounds like an interesting idea."

Instantly, Isha dropped her head into her hands in embarrassment and her mind brought back images of the two teachers embracing each other. Soon she felt something rub against her leg as the class went on with the discussion of the best way to use their tongues. Isha turned to her side to see a root had broken away from the larger one beside her and was rubbing against her leg. She reached her hand down and the root coiled over her finger and into her palm.

The people are back again?

What people?

People you told me not to kill, they back, walking around me. I am not liking them.

Have they hurt you?

No, they just walk around me, and the man with golden hair is saying things. It only two of them.

Okay, I don't think they are supposed to be there. I will tell Soulden about it after class. Please tell me if they try to hurt you.

I will tell you so if they do. Can we talk now?

I guess so, but I need to also pay attention to class. What would you like to talk about?

Why are there no more Sakari here? Those two only Sakari I see since I come here.

Oh, well, you're not in Sakar. You are in the five kingdoms. Do you not remember how you got here?

Five kingdoms? I know that this is school, and this is Sceana. Did not know it was also Five Kingdoms. I not remember much since the airship that took us away.

Airship?

Yes, they promised to teach us their magics. But on ship, we all felt sleepy. That's when I woke up inside tree.

Wait? How long have you been here?

I not know. But many people have come and gone. You are the first that I am able to talk to. It was nice to talk to Sakari

494

again. But they not see me anymore.

We are working on that. I need to train more, but I think we can all come visit you after I learn how to do it properly.

That would be good. Talking is nice, but visiting would be better.

Perhaps you could teach me more Sakari tongue. With everything that has been happening, I have been falling behind on my lessons.

Oh yes, I like that. I teach you to speak more Sakari.

Isha's attention went back and forth between Miss Webblebottom's lessons and chatting with Lonta'Mar in her mind as the class went on. Soon the magical bell appeared in the air above them and began to ring.

Okay, I have to go. I'll talk to you again later.

The wooden piece uncoiled itself from around her fingers and from her hand and went back into the large root beside her. Isha then stood up and walked down the stairs and out of the classroom with her sisters.

"We go home now?"

"No, I need to go and visit Soulden."

"Oh, do we come?"

"Yes, you both should come along as well. I'm not sure how much trouble we're going to be in after telling her all this."

The three girls made their way up the stairs and over to Soulden's office. They knocked on her door.

"Come in."

Opening the door, they saw Soulden sitting at her desk, going through pieces of parchment with a bottle of wine beside her.

"Oh well, this is a surprise. Come in, tell me what mischief you've found yourselves in this time. So that I may have an excuse to finish the bottle of wine that was given to me."

Isha looked at Soulden with a downtrodden face as they took a seat.

"Well, you see--" said Isha.

"Oh goodness you have, haven't you? Goddess protect me from the children of Oscar Highland." Soulden poured herself another drink. "Well go on, continue telling me of your rousing adventures in my school."

Isha opened her mouth and couldn't hold back her need to speak, "We found the big orange tree, and there was a girl inside, but then the golden men showed up, and I think they wanted to hurt the girl inside the tree. But I'm not sure."

Soulden just stared at the girls for a few seconds in utter confusion. "Okay, let's start from the beginning. First, what orange tree?"

"The one in top of castle, with all the little trees," said Jacinta with a smile.

Soulden narrowed her eyes at the girls until realization of what the Sakari girl said came in, then she quickly stood from her desk spilling the wine to the floor. "How... how did you get in there? That area isn't accessible to students."

"We don't know; we just followed the light and—"

"What light?"

"Sister Isha can see funny lights; it take us to orange tree," said Makeba.

Soulden stared at the girls before sitting back down into her chair and placing her hands on the side of her face. "Children listen. That area is off-limits. You're not allowed to go back... Wait. You said there was a girl in the tree. Was someone else there with you?"

"Yes, the golden men came? And man with golden hair."

"What golden men? What golden hair?"

"The ones loading things into buildings," said Makeba.

"Loading things... Wait, you mean Miss Evengale's men? The mother of the girl whose arm you broke?"

"Yes, I think so. They were led by another teacher, I think. The man with the golden hair with the two bandages above his eye." said Isha.

"That's Mr. Caudbell. Why the hell was he there with

them?"

"They chase us, but we escape," said Jacinta, folding her arms in front of her. "They not good people."

"What… but… why?" Soulden tapped her fingers against the top of her desk. "Are you girls sure you saw this?"

"Of course, we sure. We take floaty circle up in air, go into dark place and then see orange tree. And golden men come after us," said Jacinta, frowning and becoming annoyed at Soulden.

"Fine, I guess there's no way you could make all that up if you haven't been there. But now that you've told me. You girls stay out of that room with the orange tree. I will go have a visit with Miss Evengale and Mr. Caudbell. Even if she's a council member and he's a teacher, having her subordinates break protocol is a serious breach of the rules."

"So… we're not in trouble then?"

Soulden sighed, looking at the girls, "No, I suppose not. In fact, you've done me a favor by informing me of this. You three go on home for the day. Rest assured that I will be looking into this immediately."

"Yes, ma'am," said Isha as she stood up from the chair and left the room with her sisters.

"What we do now?"

"I don't know, we told Soulden so—"

"We go see Leo then. He should know about the orange tree too," said Makeba.

"Oh, okay," said Isha, and they walked down the corridor to Leo's office, placing her hand on the door.

"You don't have much longer, Pavel," said Leo's voice from inside. "You're going to have to make a decision sooner or later."

"I know, just… just give me a little more time," came Pavel's voice.

Isha opened the door to see the bare skin of Pavel's back and shoulders as his robe was pulled down around his arms as Leo sat in front of him.

"Oh! Hello there," said Leo as he stood up and patted Pavel on the shoulders, "We're done for today, I guess." Pavel pulled up his robe, as Leo came over to greet them. "What brings you three here?"

"We come to tell you secret. Why pretty boy here? He hurt?"

"Happily, no," said Pavel as he came over with a smile. "I need to get regular check-ups because of how my magic works."

"Pavel here is kind of an oddity because his magic doesn't exactly work like everyone else's."

"Leo has to give me check-up's to make sure I don't get sick."

"You know, kinda like what I have to do with Isha since breaking her body is her favorite hobby."

"Yes, sister, need healing a lot too."

Isha sighed as her sisters and Leo laughed at her expense. Pavel then placed his hands on her shoulders.

"Seems we both need healing, a lot." He said while smiling and turning back to Leo. "Well, classes are done today, so I'm going to head back. I'll see you next time, Doctor."

"Yeah, that's fine," replied Leo. "But remember Pavel. It'll happen soon."

"I know. I'll make a decision by then," agreed Pavel before he left the room.

"Now, what can I do for you girls?" asked Leo, turning back to the three.

Isha's words froze in her mouth as she thought about what Leo told Pavel. *He said it would happen soon. What's going to happen?*

"We saw big orange tree up in castle and golden men chased us," said Jacinta without a care in the world.

"What?" asked Leo as his eyes opened in recognition. "That thing's in the center of the castle. How'd you three get in there?"

Well, can't hide it now. But Leo's taken good care of us. Telling him can't be wrong, can it?

"Orange light take us there, and we meet another Sakari girl that lives inside the tree."

"You what? Another Sakari?" Wait... wait... stop, just... just let me have a seat first," said Leo as he sat down in his chair and began listening as the two Sakari girls began to tell him the tales of how everything happened before they came to him the night Isha passed out. And Leo sat there the whole time and listened. Only interrupting to gain clarification on situations he didn't quite understand.

"All this really happened? It's not just some fever dream? Including falling through the building?"

"Yes, Sir," replied Isha.

"Oh wow, you're calling me, Sir again. It really must be true," said Leo as he slapped his palms against his face in an attempt to wake himself up. "Okay, I had to make sure I wasn't dreaming." He stood up, "Well, you told Soulden, and that was the most important thing. Let's head home and warn the others."

"You believe us?" asked Isha.

"Of course, you haven't lied to me yet. Why shouldn't I believe you?" asked Leo as he patted Jacinta and Makeba on the back, leading them out of his office. "Also, this explains why you wanted to learn how to take in others' magic. We'll start that training tonight. Maybe then I can meet the Sakari girl in the tree."

They went down the steps and out of the school, headed towards their home while Jacinta and Makeba continued to tell Leo of their harrowing adventures. Some stories not even Isha knew, which surprised her considering how much time they spent together.

Eventually, they made their way back home to find Elena and the High Mother sitting down having a cup of tea. It didn't take long before the stories of the girls' adventures became the topic of conversation in their home.

"And to think I invited her on my ship, and this is what she does," said the High Mother in an annoyed tone. "Well, first thing in the morning, I'm going to go have a discussion with her about this. But this is certainly the first I've heard of a Sakari girl living in that tree. And keep in mind that the Trialage Tree was planted over five hundred years ago."

"Five hundred?" said Elena in surprise.

"Oh yes, it was one of the new ideas brought up by one of the old researchers here. I forget his name, but he is one of the statues you see when on your way to class, right outside the castle steps." The High Mother then looked at Isha, "So you think learning to perform intake magic will allow you to speak with the Sakari girl inside the tree?"

"Yes, I think so," said Isha.

"Well, as a healer, you're certainly capable of that type of magic. But it can be quite taxing on the mind, filtering your own as well as someone else's magic."

"I go get clothes," said Jacinta as she went upstairs.

"Elena, you understand the principles of the technique. Why don't you show her?"

"Yes, ma'am," said Elena as she left Leo's side. "It's really simple. The same way we push our magic into others, it'll be the same as you trying to push magic from your right hand into your left hand." She took Isha's hand and placed them over each other. "Okay, now just try to circulate your magic from one hand to the other."

"Sister, I bring clothes." Jacinta brought down a set of their Sakari clothing which exposed their backs. "This way, we not have to tear clothing."

"So that's what happened to your other set of robes," spoke Leo from the kitchen, "Elena and I were trying to figure that out for days. I suggested that you had sprouted wings and started flying."

Elena, frowning back at Leo. "And I told you how stupid that was."

Isha took the clothing from Jacinta and placed them

beside her as she began to take off her robe. But was stopped by the High Mother.

"Hold on dear," said the High Mother, turning her attention toward the kitchen. "Leo dear, don't you think you should step out for a moment."

"Why? She's not old enough to properly get me excited."

"Leo, out... This instant," demanded Elena in an authoritative tone while pointing her finger at the door.

"Fine... fine..." replied Leo as he left the room. "I swear you ladies have no idea how inconvenient it is to be the only male in this house."

"Now, go ahead and change Isha and we can continue," said Elena.

Isha changed clothes to her Sakari outfit, and Elena continued to teach her the technique as Jacinta, Makeba, and the High Mother watched.

It took over an hour, but eventually Isha began to understand how to properly intake magic from different sources. The moment she felt the magic against her body, she had to treat it as if it was her own. Which became easier the more she practiced with Jacinta and Makeba.

"There you go, " said the High Mother, looking at the girls on the floor. "I can see the magic flowing inside you. See, it wasn't that hard, now was it? Just don't go around trying to absorb fire balls or other mage attacks. That's a whole other issue. Hostile magic given form is different from pure magical essence like what your sisters are doing."

Jacinta and Makeba stopped pushing in their magic, and Isha gasped before falling over on the floor, breathing heavily.

Elena pulled Isha over and rested her head on her lap, "You did well. We probably went a little longer than we should have for someone who isn't used to this yet." She then looked to Jacinta and Makeba. "And you two have to control how much magic you push into your sister. Don't push in so much. Just a small amount is good enough for training."

Jacinta and Makeba looked at each other for a moment.

"We practice more," said Jacinta.

"We not want to hurt sister, so we will get better," said Makeba.

CHAPTER 33

In a peaceful appearing manor surrounded by trees overlooking the countryside of Burlus, Prince Saffron sat naked in a chair at a desk, staring out the window. The room was filled with ornate furniture atop a wooden floor as long white curtains hung from the window overlooking the grounds. From the window he could see the surrounding forestry and hear the singing of the morning birds.

Joining the birds sound was the morning moans of his wife as she rolled over in the white bedsheets amongst an assortment of pillows.

"Good morning, Prince Saffron," said Laura, rubbing

at her eyes and trying to blink away the morning sun. "Is everything okay?"

"Yes, of course dear Laura. Why? Do you think there is much cause for concern?" asked Saffron with a smile on his face. "After our events in that dreadful place, I'd think you've had enough excitement. Are you perhaps the thrill seeking type?"

"What? No," said Laura, sitting up on the bed, nervously clutching the sheets in her hand, covering her chest as she slid over to the side of the bed. She placed her feet over the edge, allowing her toes to touch the cool floor. "I mean, unless that is what my husband desires. I want to try and please you."

Saffron sighed, before reaching out his hand to Laura, "Come here wife?"

Laura fully placed her feet on the floor wrapping the sheets around her body and took a step towards Saffron.

"Laura Montavia, you are my wife. I sit here before you as naked as the day I was born. Am I not allowed to ask to see you in the same? Or do you wish to hide your body from your husband?"

"Huh, no... I mean," Laura took a breath before releasing the sheets, allowing them to drop to the floor and stood before Saffron, revealing her body to him.

"Good, now come to me, wife," said Saffron as he turned his chair towards her and outstretched his arms. Laura stepped forward towards her husband, allowing Saffron to wrap his arms around her and pull her down into his lap as he lay his head against her breast, placing a kiss against her nipple. "There, is this not better for the both of us?"

"Yes, husband," said Laura as she sighed, wrapping her arms over Saffron's head. "I just wish to be worthy of you husband."

Saffron chuckled, "Me? I think it will be I who will be living a life asking for your forgiveness."

"Why? Is that because you love Miss Frenka?"

Saffron eyes went wide as he pulled his head back away from Laura's embrace, staring back up as her. But Laura's expression seemed to just look down at him as if she had just stated the nature of the weather outside their room.

"What? I mean," said Saffron trying to find his own words. "How did—"

"Mova told me the night she came to inform father that we were to be engaged. She said that she wanted me to know what I would be in for, should we be married."

"Of course, she did," said Saffron, dropping his head. "And what of you, do you not think it strange that your husband covets another woman."

"At first, I was... not understanding. But I suppose that is just how men are. The other girls talk about you being with women around the capitol. And my mother deals with father even though he has three other children that she pretends that she doesn't know about. But she sends them money from time to time."

"Your father? If there was ever one for infidelity I'd never expect him. He's such a rigid fellow," said Saffron, shaking his head in disbelief.

"Mostly she puts on a brave face, because she wants to keep it a secret. She said that a wife mustn't shame her husband and act as if she knows all he does."

"Putting on a brave face. Truthfully she's not wrong. Soon, when we start dealing with the nobles, we will be forced to smile at people we dislike or even despise. So I suppose you should practice at that. Deals with shady merchants to broker trade routes that supply materials for the king. Things like that. Our kingdom has a lot of secret dealings or the sort."

"I want to be a good wife to you. And I will keep your secrets for you if need be and put on the faces you ask of me."

Saffron looked into her eyes, seeing the pure honesty in her words. *And I'll be the bastard of a husband that forces you to do so.* He thought with a sigh, before regaining himself and patting his wife on the bum. "Well, you know my secret, although I guess it's not really much of a secret. So then tell me, what is your secret?"

"Mine?" asked Laura looking confused, I don't really..."

"Please, you spent your life as part of the nobility. A court of jackals and high minded thieves. It's impossible to come out completely unscathed. So what have you wished to do, that no one knows about." Saffron smiled as her eyes focused on him as her mind began to ponder. "Come dear wife, now is the time to show trust in your husband. Or are we doomed to have a hopelessly loveless marriage, like the ones that plague the nobility around us."

"I... I know it's silly," said Laura lowering her eyes, and looking away to the floor. "But, I would really like to go on an adventure."

"A what?"

"You know, like in the fairy tales. I'd travel the land, beating up the bad people and saving the good people and become a hero.

And it seems my wife is a hopeless romantic. And quite the strange one at that, thought Saffron as he stared up and Laura, his face not hiding his confusion.

"You see, I knew you'd find it weird," said Laura, folding her arms in front of her. "Everyone always did make fun of me for it."

"No, I'm just surprised is all. Typically you'd expect a princess to want to stay in a castle and have her servants attend to her. Not roughing it out in the countryside sleeping in the bushes and fighting off bandits."

"Well, I like camping. Father would take me sometimes, I can even make a fire without magic," said Laura with a sigh, "But whats it matter, its just a stupid dream anyway."

Saffron drummed his fingers across the side of her waist. "I'm not so sure," He then turned and watched the early morning sunlight reflect off the black crystal. I think I
506

may have just the adventure in mind for you."

"What do you mean?"

"Nothing just yet," said Saffron with a smile, "But give your husband a little time and I think I'll be able to give you a fantastic wedding present."

"Really? Just what kind of—"

Suddenly a knock came from their door, interrupting their conversation.

"Who's there?" said Saffron as Laura hopped off his lap, jumping back into bed. The door swung open and Dekol appeared with two of Laura's attendants peeking out from behind him. "Ah, Dekol, what brings you here so early in the morning.

"Just wishing to update you on the day's activities, he said with a smile and nodding to Laura who had her head peeking out over the bed sheets. "But If I've come at a bad time..."

"No, of course not. Me and my lady wife were just having a conversation on having an adventure. Something you and I should know a little something about."

"You mean us almost dying every time you drag us somewhere?" asked Dekol walking into the room.

"Rightfully so," said Saffron, turning to his wife. "Laura, I'm not sure you've been properly introduced to Dekol."

"Not formally, but you two are always together. So we have spoken once or twice."

"Well, this man is essentially my better half. Been together since we were children. I would like for you to treat his words as my own. Because outside of myself no one will fight harder to keep you safe and protected. And even then he may have me beat. So I ask that you grow accustomed to being around him. Although he may not listen to any orders you give him. Goddess knows he rarely ever listens to mine.

"My job is to protect you. Not listen to you."

"And thus my point is proven," said Saffron with a chuckle.

"If that is what my husband desires, then I shall try to do so," said Laura easing out of bed with the sheets wrapped around her. "I shall go and wash up and prepare for the day."

"Do you also not wish to cover yourself," said Dekol, nodding to Saffron's nakedness as he sat in his chair.

"Oh please, they're her attendees. There are going to be plenty of times where they will find us naked. Might as well have them grow accustomed to it now, rather than some awkward misunderstanding later on.

"And will it be a misunderstanding?" asked Dekol with a raised brow.

"I'd like to think so," said Saffron as he watched his wife exit the room and one of her servants shut the door behind them. "Although I do admit that no change is sudden, I'd like to think I've done well enough as a bachelor to leave most of those ways behind. And she already knows and seems to have accepted my one affliction. So I think all is well."

"Then you are a lucky man."

"Indeed, I am. But enough on that. You said you wanted to talk about the on-goings. So were we able to find out any information on that dreadful manor?"

"Unfortunately not," said Dekol as he walked past Saffron, sliding his hand through a curtain to look outside. "We sent out a tracer, but they weren't able to find anything. Just another black crystal in one of the mannequins there."

"Of course, they couldn't, that would make things too easy," said Saffron, turning back to his desk and lifting the black crystal back into the light. The sun reflecting across his face as he twirled it across his fingers. "I don't know about anything right now. Between my father and whatever he's up to, I'm starting to wonder who I can... "Saffron felt the cold steel of a blade across his throat. "Trust."

"Hello, Prince Saffron. It's nice to finally meet you," said Dekol.

"And... who... are you," said Saffron, trying to keep his composure as he slowly rotated the crystal in his palm to see the image of his close friend smiling back at him in its reflection.

"What do you mean?" said Dekol, "Do you not see for yourself, I am your guard and apparent best friend."

"A lie, I would never believe? What do you want? You must want something since that blade is at my throat instead of inside it."

"I like a man who gets to the point," said the imposter Dekol. "Keep looking, your highness, and tell me if you recognize this face."

Saffron stared in amazement as he saw in the reflection of the crystal, the face of his friend morphing into something different. The pink of his skin fading into a creamy white. The slight sound of fabric shifting and bones making a popping sound as Dekol's image was replaced with the face that had already pierced its way into his mind. The ruby and sapphire eyes once again staring back at him inside of ashen skin.

"You... again? I should have known Father's spell would not have worked?"

"Not quite sweet prince, then one you speak of is my sister?"

"Sister? There are more of you monst—" his words froze in his mouth as the blade pressed against his throat even harder.

"Careful now, princey. We are quite temperamental about that word." The ashen skinned assassin rubbed its head against Saffron while closing its eyes and taking a deep breath. "You do smell nice. It makes me want to gobble you up right here. "But family first, what have you done to my sister?"

"I answer that and you kill me. That's what your sister tried to do—"

"No, your sisters mess to clean up. But it is my job to get her back. But if you don't answer my questions. Then I will most certainly kill you, along with everyone else in this place, until I find someone who is willing to give me the answer I want. I imagine that princess of yours would be quite sad to find herself being killed by her new husband. Oh, I get excited just imagining the sight of it." The creature bit its lip as a grin of pure glee took over its face.

"My father..." said Saffron as a look of disgust overtook him as he watched the creature's face become filled with excitement. "He gave her to an emissary from Mari in exchange for his services. She's with him now, would be my guess."

"Mari? Humm... And what would be this emissary's name, prey tell."

"Victor... Victor Krill."

"Oh, really. Now that certainly is interesting. His name shows up again. I wonder if this is some type of fate."

"You've gotten what you wanted. So what now?"

"Now? Well now I go and have myself a word with that Krill fellow. You've done well little prince," said the ashen skinned assassin as it leaned over, licking the side of Saffron's face, sending a shiver down his spine. "But now, I think it's time for you to take a nap."

And with a squeeze of the hair on his head, Saffron felt as his head was quickly jerked back and then sent forward. The last thing he saw was the desk as his face plummeted into it.

"Your highness, your highness," came a female's voice sometime later.

"Huh?... What?" asked Saffron as he was awoken from the floor after being shaken by one of Laura's servants. "What happened?"

"You were on the floor, my lord. Did you fall and bump your head?"

"I... I... what?" asked Saffron before his eyes opened

wide and he began looking around the room. "Where is it? I mean he."

"Who, your highness?"

"The monste... no," said Saffron, regaining his senses. "They would be gone, wouldn't they. How long have I been out?"

"I don't know, your highness. I was just told to come and retrieve you when Master Dekol arrived."

"Dekol?"

"Yes, your highness, he and the men should now be coming in through the gate. I saw them from up the hill."

Saffron allowed the servant to help him to his feet; stepping on shaky legs over to the window where he leaned against the wall, pulling back the curtain. And sure enough there was Dekol, dismounting his horse. *Are you the real one? Or is this another trick?* He shifted his eyes back toward the servant girl who helped him up. *Or are you that creature also in disguise?* Saffron shook his head. *No. If I started doubting the people around me. The paranoia alone would drive me mad. I just need to be more cautious is all.* He pushed himself off the wall, heading for the door. "Thank you, I'll go see him now."

"Your highness, wait. Please."

"Yes, what is it?" asked Saffron, stopping midway to the door.

"Your clothes, you highness," said the servant girl as she hurriedly went about picking items from the floor. "Don't you think it wise to get properly dressed before you greet them?"

Saffron looked down, finally noticing that he was still naked and smiled. "I suppose you're right. I certainly can't go out looking like this now, can I?" He then turned around, walking back to the servant, holding out his arms for his clothing.

The door to the room opened as Laura and her servant girls stepped into the room.

"Husband, Dekol has come through the gate, but wasn't he just..." Laura stood there in shock as her naked husband stood holding the hand of one of her servant girls, who was down on her knees in front of him.

"Well, that is quite terrible timing," said Saffron, looking between himself, the servant girl before him and his wife. "Ah, honey, remember earlier, when I said that the servants would need to get accustomed to us being naked. Well, this isn't exactly what I meant."

Laura's eyes went wide for a moment as she took a breath, squeezing the front of her dress into her palms before calming herself and stepping forward into the room. "Girls, please help my lord husband get dressed." She walked over to Saffron.

Oh. Well that was unexpected. She made a decision. I wonder what it was, Thought Saffron as the girls entered the room.

"My lady, it's not as it appears. I... I... was only picking his clothing off the floor," said the servant looking nervously between Laura and Saffron.

"I believe you Madeline. My husband already promised to try and restrain himself around other women, and I doubt he would break such a promise so early into our marriage. And you don't seem as if he's accosted you in any way. Your hair is still in preem condition."

Aren't I the true bastard here. Already asking you to throw on a mask. Thought Saffron as he noticed her trembling hands still clenched to her dress. *Perhaps there is more to you, Laura. Or are you just playing the role of the dutiful wife. Is this how your mother acts, even knowing her husband has sired bastards?* "It is so nice to have a wife who understands that not everything is what it seems. I'm starting to think that being my wife demands such a thing.

"Then I want to prove to you dear husband, that you chose wisely."

"I think you already have," said Saffron as he leaned over and kissed his wife.

CHAPTER 34

Oscar, Gregga, and Jacob arrived by carriage at the manor where the ball was to be held, along with dozens of the city's most elite upper wealthy patrons. The large manor had been erected near the center of a large lake, and there was a substantial bridge that led up to it. They exited the wagon as it stopped at the head of the household, stepping out onto a giant red carpet into the cool night air. Jacob had elected to wear a full dark blue uniformed garb with golden tassels covering his right shoulder. His blonde hair was pulled back and matched the golden belt that was strapped across the side of his chest that held up a similarly matched hilted sword at his side.

"It seems we are right on time, Father," said Jacob.

"Considering how much all this cost me, we'd damn well better be," replied Oscar, stepping out in a fully black attire with doublet and pants set, with a gray under-shirt to match the salt and pepper of his beard. As he stepped down to the ground, Oscar turned back inside the wagon, reaching his hand inside. "Is my lady wife ready to make her grand entrance?"

"Of course, my second husband," said Gregga as she stepped out of the wagon wearing a beautiful white dress, where at the waist were a set of ribbons tied around the back, that allowed for orange, green, and red strings to hang down the back of the dress. Atop, she held the fur of one of the Sakar animals, a deeply black fur that hung around her shoulders, but wrapped around the shoulder of her left arm. Her hair was still in the long black ponytail that she preferred, adorned with golden trinkets that wrapped around her neck. The scar over her eye was highlighted by a golden floral ornament that clipped to the side of her hair.

"You look wonderful tonight, Gregga," said Jacob. "I'm sure someone certainly watches over you quite jealously."

"The kingdom people must really enjoy their bright lights," said Gregga as she stepped out of the wagon onto the red carpet, overlooking the scenery. The water around the manor glowed with a neon blue light that reflected off the sides of the castle. The flowing water painted a picture of a web of liquid over the stone surface of the building. "This building... it looks much like a tiny castle than just a home."

"That's usually the taste that the rich go for. Apparently, they all want to live in castles. Giant elegant tombs to bury their next of kin inside," said Oscar as he escorted Gregga towards the entrance.

"Will this be the way Oscar shall pass? Encased inside his tomb of high walls and pretty colors?"

"No, I imagine it will be with a sword in my back like the

rest of the people around me."

"That is not so bad. Be sure to die face up looking at the sky rather than face down looking at the ground. A person's last sight should be of something beautiful, looking at something they love."

"How very poetic of you."

"It is what Jasper used to tell me. While it may be a lot of effort for dying in that manner. I do believe it is worth it."

"Have you mourned him yet?"

"No, not fully. But I will when my daughters have returned to me. We shall mourn together."

"I'm surprised you allowed them to go so easily. I assumed you'd stab me again. Or require another type of payment."

"A mother must do what is best for her children. And that place you mentioned will teach my girls to be better than what they are. I miss them, but I do what's best for them. Is it not the same for you? You send your daughter away."

"More or less, but it's not your camp that she was at risk of burning down had she continued to be left untrained."

"And so that goddess of yours has brought us here."

"So it seems," said Oscar as they both approached the door to the manor.

"Greetings. We've been expecting you tonight," spoke a man at the door holding a book in his hand.

"You know who we are already?" asked Jacob.

"Yes, we've been informed of your coming by the Duke's son Franklin. And I don't imagine any other Sakari will be showing up tonight. Come, come, this way. I'm to person-ally escort you to the ballroom." The man stepped ahead, signaling for them to follow.

"Wow, it seems Dessi has done her job well."

"She always had a knack for these types of plays," acknowledged Oscar. "Addison always did claim that she was a natural at lying and manipulation."

"And here I thought that was a skill that all you kingdom people practiced."

"Considering how good your late husband was at it, it's no wonder you would get that impression."

"Here you three are," said the man as he handed the group three masks.

"Oh, what's this?" asked Gregga.

"Tonight's host, Berlan Fritnoland, decided to change it to a masked event at the final hour. It seems he had hundreds of these silk eyepieces made up as a surprise for our guests. Please pick any color that you desire." He held out a tray with several silk face masks that covered the eyes but left the nose, mouth and cheeks uncovered. "Although I don't think they will do much to hide your beauty, madam."

"Oh, a charmer you are," said Gregga with a smile as she took the mask and placed it against the skin of her face. "And how will it... oh." The moment the mask neared Gregga's skin, it conformed to the structure of her face on its own, forming a perfect seal.

"Magically activated, madam, for ease of use."

"I see."

"Just think, the words; "For the glory of Sceana, three times in succession and the mask will remove itself."

"A convenient trick, the toys of nobles are always fun trinkets," said Oscar. "But why Sceana. Are they such a large donor to this city now?"

"Why yes, the Duke formed an agreement with them that they would get trade support from the city in exchange for some of their non-threatening magical advances."

"A fair trade, I suppose. You give them a playground to test their theories and in exchange become known as a city of magical splendor."

"Very astute of you, Sir. That is the way of it, "said their escort." And here are your magical trinkets, gentlemen. A collection of half masks. Either one will cover the half of the face, the top half, or just the side. I would not suggest
516

the bottom half as a number of our guests have expressed restricted breathing during tonight's more exhilarating events."

"Thanks for the warning," said Oscar as both he and Jacob both grabbed masks that covered half the sides of their faces. They both wore fox masks that seemed to have been a set, with Jacob choosing the right and Oscar choosing the left side.

"And now to have you three join the rest of tonight's guests. I do so hope that you three will enjoy yourselves tonight," said their escort as he placed his hand on the dual door's golden handles and opened the way to the ballroom.

The golden embroidered doors swung open, granting a vision of a hundred men and women in their finest dresses and doublets spread throughout a large marble floor in a checkered design.

A blue light reflected off the floor; the same blue lights that seemed to illuminate the water below and glowed above them across silver accented chandeliers.

The three stepped forward into the room, and instantly, Gregga caught the room's attention as the contrasts of the white dress against her dark skin drew the night's patrons like moths to a flame. Quickly, they were surrounded by the ladies of the evening as well as their escorts.

"Oh my, so Franklin was telling the truth. A Sakari would be gracing us with her presence tonight. I must say I've never seen one before," said a woman.

"And that ornament above her eye, what of the scar beneath? I must know the story behind it," spoke another lady to their side.

"You're the center of attention again, Gregga." Oscar smirked.

"It would seem so. But I will indulge your kingdom people tonight. I am to play the role of a mother after all," whispered Gregga in a low tone before smiling at the crowd that had gathered. "Hello everyone, I am Jola and this is my husband, Monlaty; we would like to thank Mr. Franklin for inviting us here tonight."

"Husband? Oh my, a Sakari wife, how bold," came a woman's voice from the crowd.

"Okay, okay, enough gawking," said Franklin, walking through the crowd with two of his guards and Dessi at his side. He wore a standard black and red uniform of the city's military guard with a sword at his waist. "Greetings." he turned to Oscar and Gregga, "I do so hope you two will enjoy yourselves tonight. Your daughter has told me many things about you."

"Has she now?" asked Oscar, raising an eyebrow at Dessi, who was wearing a red dress with white floral designs scattered loosely throughout the garment to match her partner for the evening.

"Hello, father, mother," she turned to Jacob. "Brother," she said as she intentionally clung closer to Franklin's arm.

"Hello, sister," replied Jacob. "I do hope tonight finds you in good company."

"It does, and I'm sure it will only get better as the night draws on."

"I am pleased to hear it."

"I see you also carry a sword," said Franklin. "Perhaps we will get the chance to test our mettle against each other."

"If the opportunity presents itself in the future, then I would be honored."

The two stout men stared at each other for a moment longer than necessary, before Dessi patted Franklin on the chest.

"Come Franklin, you can continue to show me around this marvelous place. Didn't you say you wanted to introduce me to some people?"

"Yes, my dear. I just wanted to introduce myself to your parents first, is all," said Franklin, turning back to Oscar and Gregga. "Enjoy your evening here tonight."

"You do the same," replied Gregga as she looked at Dessi.

"Do take care of our daughter. She can be quite foolish sometimes."

"Oh, I intend to." Franklin chuckled. "I seem to have grown quite fond of her over this last week." Then both he and Dessi disappeared back into a crowd of half-covered faces and colorful dresses.

"Well, doesn't she seem to be enjoying herself," said Gregga.

"She should; it's her plan after all," said Oscar.

"Who is that woman dancing with the men, there?" asked Gregga as she watched a woman dancing between four different men as she elegantly swayed from one man to another. Each man waited to catch her, then spinning her around, and extending their arm, sending her off towards another man who was waiting for her arrival.

"Oh, that is Lady Estrola," said a woman near Gregga. "Each one of those men are her husbands."

"She has four different husbands?" asked Gregga. "How wonderful for her; I did not know such a custom existed in your kingdoms. Jasper had his girls, but I was his only wife."

"Typically, not in Latrusa, no. But it does in the kingdom of Dresha, where lady Estrola is from. Even the queen there has three husbands herself, and I heard she plans to take another in the coming year."

"One or two occasional lovers, I can see, but four husbands seems like an exhausting situation to be in." Gregga watched as the woman effortlessly glided between the four men to the rhythm of the music.

"Excuse me," said Jacob. "I must begin my search of this wonderful event in search of my own prey."

"Enjoy your hunt, young man. Your father and I will continue to entertain the kingdom people."

Jacob smirked back at Gregga and began to make his way through the crowd as the onlookers watched as guests danced to the music being played by artists with silver instruments on a stage at the head of the room. But try as he may, he did not see the young man anywhere in the area. Soon, that did rectify itself as the ballroom door opened once again and through the door came in the young duke's son with his entourage of equally dressed men. Instantly the music stopped, and ladies and gentlemen cleared the floor.

Henry and the three men behind him all wore black and pink star button-up doublets along with black trousers that had pink shirts tucked inside. The three men behind him wore pink bird masks to match their shirts with feathers on the opposite sides that covered half their faces, while the one in the back wore one that covered the top of his face. Whereas Henry wore a pink owl's mask that covered the top right of his face and the bottom left of his mouth and jaw in a checkered design that matched the floor's appearance.

Instantly, he and his men garnered the attention of the room as they walked into the ballroom dance floor. Henry slowly pushed his men away one by one until another man stepped out of the crowd wearing a pink tiger mask and began dancing with Henry in time with the music. They swayed together in a dance as the magical lights cascaded down over them.

Now that's a nice trick, thought Jacob as he watched a few of the lights above them change color from a soft blue to a pale pink. Henry and his partner's dance continued in a flawless display of poise, but this was offset with the two men switching between the male and female lead positions interchangeably throughout their dance. One tipping the other over, only to then have the other take control and repeat the action to their partner.

Henry stepped forward, forcing his partner back, who then swirled around him, grabbing him by the waist and holding him tight, not allowing him to move. Henry moved his hips in tune with the music in an attempt to escape his partner's grasp, but his partner placed his legs between Henry's legs, not allowing him to move. Trying to control the space, Henry then jumped into the air, pushing his partner down to the floor as he slid a few feet away, waving his hands in flow to the music, before standing back up.

The other man wiped his hand across his chest, then took hard exaggerated steps back towards Henry. He grabbed at Henry's hands, only for him to slap them down. He reached in once again, and once again.

Henry slapped them down and reached out grabbing the man's face and stepping forward, invading his territory, forcing the man back.

The man then tripped and was about to fall as the crowd gasped, but Henry reached down, holding the man's arms as he hung vertically in the air. The crowd clapped as Henry pulled the man back up to him, placing his hands around the man's waist for only a moment to stare into his eyes. He then quickly stepped back and pulled the man forward before whipping his arm and spinning the man across the floor before he came to a halt and fell to his knees with his hands outstretched to the crowd while spinning. The magical blue lights focused on him as he circled around.

It seemed to Jacob as more of a battle for dominance than an enjoyable ballad. Which man is the more qualified to lead their dance?

More twirls and holds followed until the music finally stopped, and each man stood with their legs out, and their fingers pointed at each other as sweat poured down their faces.

The crowd surrounding them clapped and whistled at the performance of the two men as they both turned and bowed in every direction to receive their applause.

"The young master does have a flair for the dramatic, now doesn't he?" said Evan as he walked up behind Jacob. "He and Yanis over there have been practicing that for about two weeks now."

"Seems it's paid off; if I were to judge by the crowd's reaction. Did you get in on their practice?"

"Thankfully, no. I'm good at fighting, not so much dancing. Mum always did say I was born with two dead feet."

"Isn't the expression two left feet?"

"Yeah, but mum must have figured I was even worse than that."

Jacob smirked at the response as he watched Henry go around the crowd and give his greetings before the young man spotted him and began making his way over.

"Oh, seems the young Master's caught sight of you," said Evan. "I'll be on my way then. It's time for me to play my part. You both enjoy the show tonight." And he vanished back into the crowd.

Your part?

"I was wondering if you'd show tonight," said Henry.

"Of course, I gave my word. I'm more surprised that you did."

"Yes, well… It's best to find the courage and face destiny head on, I suppose."

"Speaking of destiny. Are you sure yours isn't in someone's dance hall? That was quite a show you put on."

"I'm glad I have your acceptance of it. I put forth a decent amount of effort to learn it."

"I heard. But are you sure the people here aren't accepting of your choices? They seem to praise you readily enough."

"You would think so, wouldn't you?" asked Henry, turning around facing the crowd. "But I'm the Duke's son; what else would you expect them to do? Granted, there are those here who I can count as friends and some ladies who have had the wonderfully scandalous nature to whisper in my ears how they would like to join me and a male counterpart of mine in one of our evening romps. But that is more of a frivolous nature than one of true genuine respect and friendship."

"Seems you've put a lot of thought into this."

"It is my life; how can I not put a lot of thought into it?"

"Clearly, you need to experience the world more. I promise there are many out there who live life without putting much thought into it at all."

"Yes, well, after tonight. Perhaps all that will change."

Suddenly the room went dark as the light above the chandelier went out. Even the blue light that glimmered in the waters outside that pierced the windows of the room had left. The crowd gasped at the sudden lack of vision as their whispers filtered out through the darkness.

"I am the terror of the five kingdoms, and I have finally made my way here," said an ominously deep voice that carried heavily through the room.

More gasps from the crowd.

"Who is it, who has done this?" said a male voice in the darkness."

"I am Queen's Bane."

The crowd gasped again.

"And I have come for your head... Son of Duke Delik."

The lights came back on. And in the center of the room stood a single man dressed in all black with a black monster's mask over his face and a sword at his side.

More whispers from the crowd at the sudden appearance of the dark man in the center of the checkered ballroom. Quickly the dancers near him spaced themselves out, joining into the crowds.

"Come and face your demise. Franklin Delik, or are you as much of a coward as your father?"

More gasps from the crowd at the insult.

"If you dare challenge me, you fiend of the night, then I shall answer with my steel," said Franklin as he stepped out of the crowd and onto the checkered floor to stand facing the man calling himself Queen's Bane. "And I promise, you will pay for besmirching my family's name with your life."

"Then let us see, just how capable the son of a duke truly is," said Queen's Bane as he drew his sword.

Franklin rushed at Queen's Bane, thrusting his sword forward; the latter shifted his weight to his side, guiding the blade away as he planted his feet and thrust his shoulder into Franklin's chest, which sent him stumbling back, holding his chest and gasping for air.

"Oh no, dear Franklin. I have waited for this day for a long time. And I'm afraid for you, that it will not be over so easily. Now come at me again if you are as brave as you claimed."

Franklin rubbed the side of his mouth with his fist as his hair hung down over his face, looking a bit disheveled.

"Fine, I'm not sure what your game is, but I shall not shrink from a challenge."

Franklin adopted a different fighting posture than before, slowly spacing his feet apart and inching closer to Queen's Bane.

"Your brother also seems to have a flair for the dramatic to arrange such a thing as this," said Jacob, noticing that the men were using blunted blades.

"He wishes to gain the favor of the nobles in town, for when father declares him Duke. This is one of the many entertainments he's planned in anticipation of the day."

When Franklin had reached a distance that agreed with him, he swung his sword left at Queen's Bane's chest. But it was parried downward as both men's swords hit the floor. Queen's Bane brought his blade back upwards towards Franklin's face, but the man dodged to the left and rushed forward with his own blade to turn to the side to slash across Queen's Bane's chest. Queen's Bane quickly jumped backward, allowing his blade momentum to fly over his head to his back while twisting in the air, turning himself around. As his feet hit the ground, he knelt with the blade at his back. Franklin's sword clashed with his as he went past, parrying his own blade into the air.

"Now, that was an impressive maneuver," said Jacob as the crowd clapped at the show of swordsmanship. "It seems as if your brother also knows his way around a sword."

"One of his few redeeming qualities, I can assure you," said Henry as the two men in front of them squared off once again.

"Who are you?" asked Franklin as he began circling the man clad in black. "You're not the swordsman I hired. What is your purpose here?"

"I have come to test your mettle in a true duel. That is all you need to know," said the fake Queen's Bane, as once again the men attacked and parried each other's moves. A jab at the leg, then at a shoulder, each man dueling back and forth, testing each other's strength.

"I could have my men take you now if I so choose."

"And look weak in front of all those you wish to impress? I think not," said Queen's Bane as he stepped forward, sliding his feet in between Franklin's legs, causing him to stumble back. He then followed behind with a thrust which hit Franklin in his side, sending him stumbling back even more until he was caught by men in the forefront of the crowd. "That is one hit for me; how will you respond?" asked Queen's Bane as he walked back to the center of the floor.

"Oh, he got you good that time Franklin, surely you won't let that go unpunished," said one of the noblemen who caught him.

Franklin narrowed his eyes at the fake Queen's Bane before stabilizing himself and turning back to the crowd. "Surely not, but I must admit, his tricks provide a formidable challenge, even for one of my skills. But let's try again, shall we?" The crowd cheered him on, and Franklin walked back to the center of the floor to meet his adversary, "You are skilled; I shall give you that, impostor. But I shall not be made a fool of so easily."

"Then shall we continue, your grace?"

"Whenever you're ready, imposter."

Queen's Bane jumped forward and swung his sword

diagonally towards the shoulders of Franklin who blocked with his blade, pushing him back, his feet sliding across the floor. Franklin then threw his sword at Queen's Bane, who easily dodged and rushed at Franklin. Right before Queen's Bane struck, he turned around with his sword in front of him, barely blocking Franklin's sword that had come back flying through the air.

Franklin then rushed forward, elbowing Queen's Bane in the back as he reached out, grabbing the hilt of his own sword and, with Queen's Bane off guard, spun around, bringing his blade at the man's waist as hard as he could. Queen's Bane blocked the strike, but while still unbalanced. The force of the blow sent him tumbling back over the floor to the shock of the crowd as they all clapped at the display of magic and swordsmanship.

"What's wrong, oh mighty Queen's Bane? Are you done so soon?"

The cloaked figure stood back up to his feet while holding his sword to the side, letting it drag along the floor. "You have done well to strike Queen's Bane; I give you credit. You do indeed possess a fair amount of skill with the blade. If not for the sight of your hand glowing with magic, I would not have foreseen the blade at my back."

"Am I to take it that you yield, then?" asked Franklin, dropping his fighting stance and raising back up to his full height.

"In a way, yes. I said that tonight I would slay the duke's son. And since you have proven much the talented fighter, and since Queen's Bane has never broken his word," said the cloaked figure as he dashed toward the crowd at a furious speed. The onlooking crowd split as he jumped towards them, only to watch as Queen's Bane's blade pierced the side of Henry's chest, lifting him off the ground and carrying him forward. They both crashed into the window, shattering it, only to go falling down into the watery depths below.

The last sounds heard, other than the gasps of the

crowd, were sounds of broken glass hitting the floor only to be followed up by a splash as their bodies hit the water.

"Don't just stand there! That man has attacked my brother. Quickly, outside. We must find them," said Franklin as he led his men back out through the gates of the ballroom.

Dessi watched in horror as the dark cladded man stabbed Henry and took him out of the window. *What the hell happened? I didn't plan for some lunatic appearing. It was supposed to look like the two brothers killed themselves. Now what am I supposed to do?* She turned and watched Franklin lead his men out of the door. *And there goes my target, off to be valiant. Goddess, what a waste of a good plan. I guess the night will go on.* She watched as the crowd began to whisper and mumble to each other about what just happened.

"So, was it an assassination?" said a male guest.

"Perhaps, it was still part of the play," said a female.

"Don't be foolish, he was run through the window. I've never seen a stage play go that far."

"Franklin must be at his wit's end. That was his brother."

Soon the whispers died down as guards began to escort the night's guests out of the ballroom and into the courtyard where their carriage drivers were arriving to take them all home.

Dessi stood outside of the manor in the moonlight. The magic of the evening faded away along with its watery glow, as the horses carrying the last carriage trotted off into the darkness.

"Excuse me, Miss," said one of the Manor's servants, "Are you waiting on someone? Would you like me to find you a carriage?"

"I suppose so." Dessi sighed. "The night does seem to be over, doesn't it?"

"No hold on, I shall escort the lady home," said Franklin

coming out of the shadows with his boots covered in mud. "Sorry, for my late return, my dear. You do understand, don't you? We needed to search as hard as we could to try and prevent an escape."

"Oh no, I fully understand. Did you find him?"

"Sadly no. We searched near and around the lake; I even had men dive in, in search for their bodies. But it is as if they disappeared."

"Could he have been kidnapped then, like the stories where they hold people for ransom?"

"A possibility, a Duke's son would make for a valuable trade. But that blade seemed to have run him through. Perhaps if they spirited him away, they would have a healer on hand," said Franklin as he looked at Dessi in her dress as she rubbed at her arms. "But if nothing else would come of all this tonight; allow me to escort you back."

"Are you sure? I wouldn't mind just going back alone if you need to continue your search."

"I appreciate the thought, but no. We've done all we can do here. A full investigation will be launched tomorrow." Franklin called for his driver to bring around his personal carriage. When it arrived, he escorted Dessi inside and entered himself as he told the driver to take off.

"Do you know who the masked man was?"

"No, I had arranged to have a gentleman dressed as he was to become a sparring partner for me tonight, as a way to entertain the audience. But something seems to have gone awry, and now I have a missing brother along with a lot of unanswered questions."

"Oh, I see," said Dessi as she glanced out of the carriage doors opening. "Where are we headed? I don't see the lights of the city anymore."

"To my home, I figured the night a bit too dangerous to send you home alone. I would ask that you stay the night with me, if only to ensure your safety," said Franklin as he took Dessi's hands into his. "That is if you do not mind, my dear."

"Oh, no. I don't mind. I mean, are you sure?" asked Dessi, looking down at the floor. *I guess I can kill him in his bed, but that just leaves this messy, and then what of the servants who see me enter the home. Everything has just gone wrong tonight, all because some bungling assassin couldn't wait one more damned day. We would have even done his job for him and saved him the trouble.*

"My dear, I would like nothing else," said Franklin, smiling in Dessi's face, before the carriage came to a crashing halt.

"Who goes there?" asked the driver. "Put your blades away. Do you know who this carriage belongs to?"

"What is happening out there?" said Franklin, lifting himself out of his seat only to have Dessi fall on him. "My dear, what's wrong? I assure you everything is—" Franklin's mouth gasped on his last words as he looked down to see a blade sticking out of his abdomen. With his mouth agape, he looked back up into Dessi's eyes. "Wha... why?"

"Sorry, it was supposed to be both brothers tonight. It can't be just one." And she brought down another blade from her other hand at the temple of Franklin's skull. The blade pierced easily into his brain. His eyes rolled into the back of his head as he slumped over in his seat. Dead before he realized it.

Dessi reached her bloody hand over, opened the carriage door, and peeked out to see Jacob staring back at her and sighed. "I figured it would be you. Did you arrange for that whole show back there?"

"No, that was someone else's idea. We just went along with it."

"Well, you could have told me. Instead, I stood there dumbfounded trying to figure out what to do next."

"You were with the hero all day. We were never able to contact you. Plus, for effect, it's best that you looked as out of the loop as possible. The surprise on your face clearly showed you had nothing to do with it."

"Great," said Dessi, looking toward the frightened driver of the carriage, "Then what do we do with him?"

"Oh please, don't kill me. I promise. I will never speak of this night. I promise."

"Yes, but on the contrary," said Jacob, walking over and grabbing the man's wrist as blue magic formed over his hand. "We need you to tell everyone about this night, about how Queen's Bane came and took Franklin away."

Two other men reached inside the carriage, pulled out Franklin's corpse, and threw it over the saddle of a horse.

"And the body?" asked Dessi.

"We'll dump it somewhere where no one will find it. For now; as far as the world will be concerned, the two sons of Duke Delik both disappeared tonight, never to be seen again."

"And where's Oscar and Gregga?"

"Both are already headed back. We'll join up with them later, after we dispose of prince charming there."

"Fine," said Dessi as she walked over and straddled a horse. "It was fun being a damsel in distress, at least for a while."

Jacob let go of the man's hand as he looked around confused and began mumbling about Queen's Bane before snapping the horse's reins and taking off into the night. Jacob then walked over and mounted his own horse.

"Have you decided that you wish to live the quiet life now? A few kids and baking sweets in the early morning."

"No, not with that one. He preferred his women to be more stupid and dependent on him. That's not a role I could keep up. It wouldn't have been long before I killed just out of my own self-respect."

"Sounds like you're going to be a handful for the man you eventually end up with."

"Oh, I will be. So, you best spend your nights thinking of ways to make me happy."

"I think I already spend most of my nights doing that."
"Good, but I still think you need more practice."

CHAPTER 35

Isha awoke tangled in the arms of her sisters. After freeing herself, she was greeted by the sight of a familiar orange glowing light dancing inside of a root that had found its way into the wall of their room. She yawned, setting herself down onto the floor. Wiping at her eyes, she made her way downstairs.

"Good morning," said Elena, sitting on the couch with a book in her hand. "You still have an hour or so before class; what's got you up so early?"

"Couldn't sleep," replied Isha, continuing to rub at her eyes and sitting down beside Elena. "What are you reading?"

"A book on healing through heavy infections. Sometimes, healing isn't enough. We have to employ the aid of herbs to fight off certain diseases, infections, and poisons. Otherwise, all we are doing is prolonging their suffering."

"Is healing hard?"

"Not so much hard, as much as it requires a lot of concentration. It's why we wait until the second year to really start teaching it. It's best to spend the first year understanding how your magic works. Formula, shields, elemental magics, those extend out your magical core, which allows you to cast different types of magic."

"How long did it take you to learn it?"

"I'm still learning. The only ones who can say they're masters are the grand clerics and the High Mother, well, maybe Leo, but he still has to take his final test."

"Where are they?" asked Isha, looking around the room. "Are they still asleep?"

"Leo headed off to the school early this morning, and the High Mother went to have a talk with Miss Evengale, I think. So, it's just us here."

The door to the house opened and in walked the High Mother.

"Oh. Well, never mind then. Welcome back, High Mother. Did you finish your business already?"

"Hardly," said the High Mother looking frustrated. "It seems Soulden got to her before I could, and they've gone off somewhere." She walked in and sat down in the chair opposite the girls. "I suppose I'll just have to wait my turn. It is her school, after all."

Makeba and Jacinta made their way downstairs.

"Oh, look who's awake," said the High Mother. "And with their hair in dire need of a fresh setting. Come here, you two."

Isha noticed the orange glow following behind her sisters throughout the roots of the house before settling near her on a crack in the wall. Out of curiosity she stood and went over to it, placing her hand near where the light was.

Are you there, Lonta'Mar?

Yes, I am here. Hello.

Hello... ah... has anything weird happened today?

Weird?

Anything not normal?

No, the golden men came. But they gone now.

"Is sister talking to the tree Sakari? Can we talk to her?" asked Jacinta as she sat between the High Mother's legs, getting her hair pulled back into a puff ball.

"Oh, is that how you speak to her?" asked the High Mother. "By putting your hands on the plants?"

"She can do a lot," said Makeba. "She can find anyone in school and show pictures."

"Well, if that's the case, perhaps she can tell me where Soulden and Miss Evengale have gotten off to."

Isha turned back to the root and focused, *Do you know where Soulden or Miss Evengale are?*

Golden lady is on skyship with school master.

Skyship? "She says that they both are on a skyship."

"Who's sky ship? Not mine. If so, they're in for a surprise."

Lonta'Mar. Is it possible for you to show me a picture when we talk like this? LIke when I visited you?

I... I do not know. But I will try.

A blurry image partly entered Isha's mind, but she could barely make out the shapes. *There are multiple ships,* she thought. Focusing more of her magic into the root, the image in her mind slowly began to become clearer. She could see various ships, including the very large ship that the High Mother had arrived in. There were other ships, smaller ones.

Which ship is it? Can you take me inside? Oh, I hope this doesn't turn out like last time with Mr. Higgin's picture.

It is the black ship. I will try.

The moving hedge bush that the ships were near started swaying into each other, and Isha saw a root near the ship reach up out of the marble and grasp onto the hull on the vessel. Slowly it wound up the side of the ship before wedging itself between the wooden beams and inside. Suddenly Isha's vision changed from her looking over the shipyard to the hedge mage and into the soil beneath the marble and out again. It followed the root up the hull of the ship and inside.

It was dark inside, but there was enough light to make out most of the surroundings. She was in a ship's cargo bay. There were boxes and a woman in uniform walking forward and taking a seat behind a corner. Isha turned left of her and saw metal bars. It was a cage, and inside Isha saw Miss Evengale and her daughter. Next to them, also in the cage was Soulden Fegmont, holding a bloodied hand over her head as she stared out of the cage at the guard in front of her with a look on her face that would normally send chills down someone's spine. Isha pulled out of the dreamlike image which caused her to recoil as her mind came back to her.

"Are you okay, dear?" asked the High Mother after watching Isha fall back to the floor.

"Soulden… they have her in a cage."

"What? Who? Soulden? Where?"

"I saw her. She had blood on her hand as she covered her face. And she was guarded by one of those people in golden uniforms."

"Do you know where they are?"

"Yes, they are one the black ship next to the big gold one."

"The big gold one is my ship. The black ones were the ships that Miss Evengale sent to bring items for her daughter up to the school. Two of them, I think."

"What are we going to do?" asked Elena, turning to the High Mother, "We can't just leave them there."

There was a moment of silence while everyone looked at each other.

"Girls," said the High Mother, "Do you understand what you're asking? I will go to the school and try to get help, but things may not end happily. I don't know what's going on, but if Soulden is locked up somewhere hurt, then that means that more people will get hurt trying to get to her."

"Makeba and I can fight. We not afraid to kill people. Even sister Isha kill before."

"Is that true?" asked Elena looking at the girls in disbelief.

"Well, yes, but it's not like I wanted to."

"As much as you girls want to help, I think we should head to the school first," said the High Mother. "But everyone, be careful; none of us here are fighters except for the Sakari. And I doubt two small Sakari girls can fight off whatever's happening here. We're going to have to be smart about this. I'd rather not find ourselves locked up along with them."

The girls agreed as they went upstairs and came back down wearing their school clothes.

"Right, let's be on our way," said the High Mother as she approached the door. "Leo, you idiot, you certainly picked a fine time to be away."

The girls left the heart house and made their way through the streets toward the school. But it wasn't long before they realized that something was wrong. Outside of the school were all the students who had come for their morning classes. The teachers, along with the people in golden uniforms, had formed a perimeter around the main entrance to the school as green and grey smoke was seen coming out of the doorway.

"What's going on here?" asked the High Mother as they approached.

"Ah, High Mother, perhaps you could help us," said one of the second-year teachers. "It seems one of the experiments of the children got out of hand, and a bit of poison managed to escape. We have people inside trying to handle it, but a few of the closer students were affected by it before they could be evacuated."

"Has anyone died?"

"No ma'am, thank the goddess, but they are showing signs of the poison and are weak."

"Take me to them; we shall do what we can."

"Yes, right over here."

They were taken to the left side of the school in the courtyard, where more than two dozen students lay on the ground on blankets as people tended to them. All of them at this point were showing signs of poisoning as the veins of their bodies were showing through their skin in an odd green color.

"What type of poison is this?" asked the High Mother.

"We aren't sure. We just began rushing people out the moment the symptoms appeared."

"Okay," then let me see them," said the High Mother, walking over to one of the students and placing her hand on their head. "It's a serious poison, one that kills within a few hours." The High Mother looked over the courtyard at the more than two dozen people showing symptoms of the poison. "Oh my, how are we going to heal this many before someone dies?" She then turned to the man who had escorted her. "Do you have any Provillion seeds?"

"Ah... no, but the Spider house might. They deal with agricultural studies in their magic."

"Then please go and get me as many as you can as soon as possible, along with a grinding wheel, bowls, and buckets of water."

"Yes ma'am, right away, ma'am," said the young man before running off.

"Elena, you've had experience in treating poisons, haven't you?"

"Ah, yes, High Mother. Shouldn't we tell the teachers

about Soulden?"

"I don't know yet. You saw them. They were with Evengale's men. I'm not sure we won't end up locked away like Soulden if we did."

"So, what do we do now?"

"For now, I'm going to need your help here if we are going to have any chance of saving them," said the High Mother as blue and green magic swirled over her fingers and across the man's body. "We are going to need to stabilize as many as we can until he returns with the seeds."

"Yes, ma'am," replied Elena as she knelt down beside one of the sick students to apply healing magic.

"That's it. Hopefully, that fellow comes back quickly. Then I'll have him, and others begin stirring up a cure. We just need to keep as many as far away from death as we can." The High Mother looked up at Jacinta, Isha, and Makeba, who were just staring at her.

"What we do about Soulden?" asked Jacinta.

"Girls, I'm sorry." said The High Mother shaking her head. "I can't. If I leave them here unattended, they all will die."

"That fine, you stay," said Jacinta. "We go free, Soulden. We know she in black ship, we find new way around."

"No, that's not..." said the High Mother, but Jacinta and Makeba had already taken off towards the other side of the courtyard. She then turned to Isha who was about to follow them, "Child, you can't."

Isha turned back to the High Mother, "I... I can't let them go by themselves," before turning around and running off after her sisters who were over by a large hedge bush at the back of the courtyard.

"Sister, you ask tree Sakari to make us way through?"

"I can try, but..." suddenly the hedges in front of them began to shift, and a path to the other side began to open.

"Oh, it moved. She listens to us," said Jacinta, looking around. "Thank you, tree Sakari," She then dashed inside, followed by her sisters.

Once on the other side, the hedge closed behind them. And the girls realized they were now at the back of the school, where the pool was with all the roots that flowed into the water.

Above them, they could see the huge golden ship of the High Mother along with pieces of the smaller black ship alongside it. They even heard some soldiers ahead of them, beyond the hedge maze next to the huge chain that was wrapped amongst itself.

"What are we going to do now?" asked Isha.

"Sister Jacinta won right as war sister. She decide," said Makeba.

Jacinta thought for a moment, "Too many kingdom men for us three. Did sister Isha bring her spikes?"

"I did, but I haven't been able to practice that much."

"Good, me and Makeba brought blades," said Jacinta as she revealed a long curved blade from under her robe.

Where did they get those? I've never seen them before.

"But sister Isha still bad at fighting, so we sneak to ship."

"Thank you," said Isha, relieved that her sisters did not expect her to fight. "If we can get Soulden out, I'm sure she'll be able to do something."

"Makeba stay and hide; you help if something go wrong. Me and Sister Isha go on ship."

"Okay, I stay," said Makeba before then taking off into the side of the hedge maze.

"Sister, come with me now."

"Ah... okay," said Isha as she followed behind Jacinta.

The hedge maze opened up for the girls as they made their way forward until they reached the outermost wall of the small green labyrinth. A small window to see through opened in the brush for them to peek through. Inside they spotted a guard walking beside a ramp leading onto one of the black ships.

"Tree Sakari good to have on hunt," said Jacinta." Makes

hiding much easier."

I guess this would seem like a hunt to you two. "What do we do now?"

"We wait, guard moving slowly. When he turn, we go."

"Okay," responded Isha, her hands shaking as the situation she was in started to come down on her. *What am I even doing here? I woke up and everything was fine, now I'm trying to rescue someone.* She looked over at Jacinta who was peering out at the ship. Her sister twirled the blade around in her fingers as if she were just waiting to use it. *How are you so calm? Even if you are Sakari, you're still the same age as me.* Isha closed her eyes, trying to shake the nervousness from her mind. *No, don't think about that now. I rescued Dessi, Well, I kinda rescued her. I need to be brave. I can do this, and I have Jacinta with me. She knows what to do. I just need to not mess this up.*

They both continued to peek until the guard finally turned, heading to the side of the ship. The hedge opened for them and they dashed out, hiding behind some crates. Jacinta peeked out making sure the guard hadn't turned around, then swooped around and slowly started making her way up the plank with Isha following behind her.

"Ah!" Yelled a guard.

The girls froze.

"What's happened?" yelled another guard above on the ship.

"I tripped on some damned root on the ground. Almost broke my leg."

"Well, get up then. You had me worried there for a second."

The girls sighed, making their way onto the ship, but not before Isha caught a glimpse of Makeba fading back into the hedge bush with her blade in her hand. Her eyes had a vicious seriousness in them that she'd never seen before.

Aboard the ship, they quickly made their way downstairs, pausing at the bottom as Makeba peeked around the corner.

But no one was there. They crept forward in the small cabin.

"They should be around corner there," whispered Isha to Jacinta. "In the next room."

Jacinta nodded, and the two girls both eased their heads around the corner of a crate next to the wall. Ahead of them, they could see Soulden in the cage. But now there was a ripped piece of cloth over a portion of her face, covering one of her eyes. Beside her were Miss Evengale and her daughter.

Miss Evengale quickly spotted them and looked over to a place the girls couldn't see before tapping Soulden on the hand. Soulden looked up to Miss Evengale, who gestured her head toward the girls. Her one eye went wide as she saw the girls staring back at her. Soulden then herself gestured to a space behind a wall that the girls couldn't see. Jacinta flashed her blade at Soulden, trying to show her intentions. Soulden froze for a moment before nodding her head in an unsaid agreement.

Jacinta pulled Isha back and made her kneel beside her, "Sister, stay," and climbed atop the crate while gripping her blade in her hand. "When golden person fall, you catch so they no make sound," she whispered.

"Fall, what fall? What are you about to do?" she whispered back.

"You there, guard," said Soulden.

"Yeah, what do you want?" asked a woman's voice.

"I see those weapons you bought there. Why are you doing this?"

"That's none of your business."

"Then why capture us and not kill us?"

"Hostages in case things go wrong. I'd just as soon kill you, but they want you alive until we have that damned tree, then it'll be over with."

"Is that what that thing there is for? To collect the tree?"

"What thing?"

Soulden pointed her finger to the back of the cabin.

"That golden thing right there, that we passed coming. The one that glowed."

Footsteps were heard, "What thing?" asked the woman.

"On the other side, there. You must be more blind than me if you don't remember your own tools."

"Oh, shut up," said the woman stepping forward; "there's no—"

Jacinta plunged the blade into the woman's neck with such force that it pierced through to the other side, scratching the wooden hull of the ship as she bounced against the wall. Her knees gave out from under her as she went crashing down towards the floor. Isha stepped out with her arms open, trying to catch the woman as she fell. The weight of her descent brought Isha crashing to the floor with the woman on top of her, making a soft thudding sound.

"Oh, sister did good. I barely hear her die."

"Get... her... off," said Isha, being crushed by the woman's dead weight along with the large amount of blood that was spilling onto her.

Jacinta made her way down from the crate and rolled the dead woman off Isha to the floor. Isha sat up, trying to rub the woman's blood off the side of her face and neck, but only succeeded in getting her hands just as bloody. As she stared at the woman's blood covering her hands and arms, Isha felt her stomach heave as her breath left her mouth. Suddenly she dropped to her knees as she gasped for air. Her mind raced back to the night when she stabbed Molan in the neck; the way his blood pooled over her.

"Sister... sister..." said Jacinta in a low tone patting Isha on the back. "You must get up. We no have much time. "Sister Isha."

Isha heard her sister calling her name and clenched her hands into fists on top of the wooden beams of the ship. Gritting her teeth, she clenched her stomach muscles. Don't think about it. *Don't think about him. Think about something else. Anything else.* She thought to herself over and over

542

until the panic and anxiety began to leave her body and she stuffled back up to her feet and took a breath.

"Sister okay now?" asked Jacinta.

"Ye… yes," said Isha as she placed her hand on the hull of the ship to stabilize herself and forced herself to take a step forward towards Solden's cage.

"The keys, child, she has the keys on her belt."

Isha turned around and began rummaging into the woman's clothes, finding a ring with a key. She took it and hurried over to the cage, slipping the key into the lock. It clicked and Isha slid the door open."

"What do we do now?" asked Isha.

"Tell me, child, is it still morning outside?" asked Soulden.

"Yes, ma'am."

"Then remember that pool of water at the center of the hedge maze? Take me to it so that I may wash off this damned alagon powder. But don't touch us. I'd rather some of us keep the ability to use our powers."

"Come, we go now. Sister Makeba outside," said Jacinta as she walked ahead, ripping her blade free from the woman's neck as she passed her body. Isha watched how capable her sister truly was when she wanted to be. This was so very different from the Jacinta who wrestled with her when they were having fun. The look of playful joy that was usually on her face had been replaced with lowered eyelids, few words, and a seriousness that she'd never seen before.

We really are so different. She and Makeba seem so used to this.

Jacinta stuck her head out above the deck, peering around for anyone.

"Come, we must be quick."

They all headed upstairs behind Jacinta with Isha in the rear and made their way down the plank just in time for one of the male guards to come around the ship and spot them.

"Hey, how'd you get free? Stop!" said the man.

Instantly they all ran forward toward the opening in the hedge maze.

"They escaped!" yelled the man as he chased after them. The man was fast and managed to snatch young Miss Evengale up into the air. "I got you now. Hold still damn...." and before he could finish the words, Isha drove her metal spike into his ankles with as much force as she could as she ran up behind him, and they all went tumbling over the marble ground.

Isha then stood up, grabbing the young Miss Evengale by the arm, and lifted her up as they made a break for the hedge maze. When they passed the ship, she could see more guards coming towards them, a few tripping on the roots that seemed to sprout up through the marble.

They all made it into the other levels of the hedge maze and kept running as the guards closed in on them. Soulden and Jacinta reached the pool area first and turned back, waving for Isha and young Miss Evengale to come and hurry. The hedge maze quickly closed in behind them, locking in the guards. Both girls jumped at the final hedge as it closed in on them. They landed on the marble floor by the pool as the hedges closed in, trapping the arm of one of the guards that was reaching for them.

One of the guards trapped arms poked out of the hedge as he cursed profanities. The soldier even cast fire at the girls that burned the side of Miss Evengale's dress.

"Ah! Put it out, get it off," she said as she fanned at the flames.

Jacinta responded by bringing down her blade and hacking into the man's hand. He screamed in pain as the blade carved into his flesh. But he couldn't move it as he was locked into the brush. And with two more sickening hacks from Jacinta, the bloody appendage fell to the ground, only to be followed up by his continuous screams. Blood squirted from the wound to the marble beneath, leaking into the water of the pool. Then they heard a gurgling sound. Then nothing. Isha stepped forward as she parted the brush only a little to see the man's face inside. He had a look of agony in dead eyes with his mouth wide as small limbs from the brush seemed to go down into his throat.

Isha stepped back with a look of horror in her eyes.

"Come out. We know you're in there. Don't make us burn the place down."

"No chance of that," said Soulden, "Don't worry, girls, this place is magically protected. It'd take an inferno to even singe the trees here as long as that water is in the pool." Soulden ripped the cloth from her face, revealing the blood over her eye and the cut above it. She then grabbed at her robe and lifted it over her head, revealing her shift underneath. "But I need my damned magic back." Soulden then jumped into the water, and at the same time, Makeba came through the hedges.

"Sister, I see six of them in the maze. Do we kill them?"

"Yes, the hunt is not over until we are safe," said Jacinta, looking at Isha and reaching out her hand. "You come, sister. We finish this now."

The look in Jacinta's eyes told Isha she didn't have much of a choice in the matter. They were each other's responsibility and sending them off alone on this wasn't an option.

"You can't just leave us here," said Miss Evengale, clutching her daughter who looked just as frightened.

"We'll be back, don't worry." *I hope we'll be back.*

Isha and her sisters walked in the brush of the hedges as it opened up for them. Soon the three of them were outside, into the corridors of the hedge mage. The vines and leaves seemed so much more alive now as every leaf and twig swayed back and forth around them. Inside she could see the orange light of Lonta`Mar, moving up and down through it all.

"Sister Isha, you make them follow you. We do rest," said Jacinta.

"Ah... okay. Is that it? They just have to follow me."

"Yes, you no worry. We protect you."

Okay, I... I can do this, thought Isha before focusing on her sister and making a fist, "I can do this."

Her sisters faded slowly back into the brush, leaving Isha alone in the middle of the maze. *I can do this; I can do this.* She wandered her way through the maze, peeking around corners with one of her spikes in her hand. After a few turns of slowly peeking around corners, she found one of the golden uniformed men with his back turned, walking away from her location. She turned her back against the corner of the brush. *Okay... okay... I just need to get his attention.*

Isha took a deep breath and turned around the forestry and stood in the middle of the walkway. "Hey, ah. You there."

The man quickly turned around. "Well, there you are, come to give yourself up, have you?"

"No, you're going to give up," said Isha as she raised her hand, swung forward and launched the metal spike into the air. The man put up his magical shields only to have a metal spike pierce his thigh.

"Agrh," He screamed in pain, clutching at the metal spike in his leg.

Oh, it worked; it hit.

"You... little bitch," snarled the man as he hobbled forward toward Isha.

Oh no, ah... he's chasing me. What now? Ah. Magic. The push spell. Isha thrust her out in front of her. *Push, push, please push.* She saw Makeba come out of the brush behind the man right before he was about to grab her. *Push, dammit.* And a force of energy shot out of her hand that threw her to the ground and launched the man into the air, over Makeba's head and into the brush so hard that the brush folded around him.

"Dammit, that hurt, you... hey... what's happening... stop... let go," screamed the man as the small branches
546

from the brush began wrapping around his arms and legs, entangling him.

"Hey, what have you done?" asked a female guard appearing from a corner behind Isha. "Hold it right there, or I swear I'll burn you alive," said the woman as she slowly stepped forward with red magic hovering over her hand, directed at Isha. "Hey, I got two of them pinned down here," shouted the woman before looking at Isha. "Where's the rest of your group? I know there's more of you."

The hedges beneath the woman opened up and out dashed Jacinta, slashing the tendons of the woman's legs, sending her crashing to the ground on her back. She screamed in pain as she wormed on the ground, trying to lift herself, only to see Jacinta in the air above her as she drove the blade down into the woman's eye. The woman's body went slack as Jacinta landed on her, forcing her head down to the ground. She quickly ripped her blade free from the woman's eye socket, sending blood spattering across the leaves. Giving her sisters a single glance, she once again dashed back off into the opening in the hedges.

Isha stood there in shock as she just watched her sister appear, then break down someone, murder them, and vanish again in what seemed like seconds. She then felt Makeba grab her arms.

"Sister, we must go; others are coming."

"Ahh... right!" They dashed through the hedges together once again, only to be confronted by another set of guards.

They tried to turn back, but a man grabbed Makeba's arm, who turned around and began hitting him in the face until he reached out and grabbed her around the neck. But before he even had time to squeeze, Jacinta appeared from the brush again, plunging her blade into the side of the man's neck in front of Isha. She could see her sister's face and arms covered in blood as she rolled over on top of the man. Jacinta snatched her blade free from the now dead man's neck and vanished back into the brush once again.

The other guard paused at the sight of the girls, before taking a step back as two more guards came around the corner.

"Don't just stand there, you idiot. Get them," said one of the guards, and all three of the guards rushed Makeba and Isha at the same time. The hedge opened up for them to go inside, where they saw the pool. But they were too slow as two of the guards grabbed Isha on her way inside. Holding Isha tightly, they both made it into the pool area while the third guard grabbed Makeba by the arms, yanking her back to the other side as the hedges closed behind them.

"I have the Sakari girl," yelled the man on the other side of the brush. "Ow, the bitch bit me."

"That's fine. We found the rest here," said the guard holding Isha in the air with his hands around her neck. Miss Evengale and her daughter only watched over in a corner, huddled against each other as Isha struggled to free herself from the man's grasp. "Now you all are gonna give up or I'm going to wring this girl's neck, and then I'll do the same to you."

Suddenly the sound of the man screaming was heard from the other side of the bush.

"Hey, what's going on?" asked the guard holding Isha in his grasp. But there was no answer from the other side, only silence. "What the fuck is happening?" His voice becoming more frustrated as he turned to the other guard, "Fine, go grab that girl there; then we'll get out of here." But the other guard didn't move; his body just froze. "Hey, didn't you hear—"

"Can't... move..." said the man struggling to speak.

Suddenly Isha fell to the roots and marble beneath her. She quickly crawled away from the men, only to see Soulden soaking wet in her shift, casting some type of magic. The scar on her head was still leaking blood on the left side of her face over her eye. She swirled her fingers around, and the two men turned around to face her.

"I don't know who you people are, and I stopped caring right around the time I woke up in a cage covered in that damned powder. But you come to my school and attack my students. There is no way anyone you brought here with you will live to see the end of this day. But first, let's send a message to your friends."

Soulden twisted and balled her fists in her hand as Isha watched the men's bodies began to contort into directions that were unnaturally cruel: bones snapped like twigs, piercing and protruding from their bodies as their soon to be corpses hovered in the air.

Isha watched their necks stretch before one popped off. Soulden's magic-covered hand squeezed the air between her fingers harder as she grit her teeth. The fury of an angry mage dancing in her eyes as the bodies before her crumpled together like used parchment, to be tossed aside and thrown away like useless trash.

Makeba and Jacinta appeared out of the brush, only to watch the men twist and turn.

They weren't even given the mercy of screaming. Only the sounds of torn fabric and broken bones were made as pools of blood leaked out of the mass of meat that was left of them as it floated in the air. Soulden thrust her hands forward, launching the disfigured ball of human body parts over the entire maze. A large blood trail followed behind it as it crashed into the hull of one of the ships, landing on the ground with a wet, bloody thud.

"And now for the rest of them," said Soulden as she turned around, magic pouring from her hands like thick green. She began walking towards the school when Isha ran in front of her.

"No, you can't."

"Thank you for your help, child. But I must save my school."

"No, they've poisoned the inside of the school; if you go in, you will be poisoned too."

Isha watched the rage in Soulden's eyes grow as her face turned red. Her eyes widened as she bit her lips so hard till the point where blood flowed.

She then turned to the bush to the side of the school, "That hedge trick, can you do it here to let me pass?"

"I... I think so..." said Isha, looking around, "Did you hear that Lonta`Mar? Can you let us and Miss Soulden pass back through here?"

The hedge once again opened up, and Soulden walked through only to see The High Mother and Elena still nursing the poisoned students in the courtyard with two students using grinding wheels beside them.

Soulden walked forward as if in a daze as her school turned into chaos with people running in every direction. She spotted someone in a golden uniform watching over the sick children and reached out her hand, and they rose up in the air and began struggling to free themselves, their legs kicking and squirming. She snatched her hand down and they plummeted back down to the ground head first, instantly snapping his neck. She raised her hands again, bringing them up once more before casting her arm left, sending the now dead body crashing into the side of the school so hard that they cracked the marble wall as their bloody body stuck into the crevice.

The High Mother watched the display and turned back to see Soulden, wet, bloody, and in her shift.

"Soulden, are you okay?" asked the High Mother as she ran over to her, "You're bleeding, let me—"

"I'm fine," assured Soulden, pushing the High Mother aside. "Please... continue taking care of my students. Save as many as you can." Soulden's hands began to glow white with magic as she placed them over her mouth. "Attention Sceana Academy." Soulden's voice rang through the air so fierce that it echoed off every nearby structure. "This is your headmaster, Soulden Fegmont. I was held captive by those around you wearing golden uniforms. I have now been rescued by some of our brave students. Hear me, this is an absolute order for all those who call Sceana their home and work here under me. You are to execute anyone wearing those damned golden uniforms upon sight. Do not detain. Do not subdue. Do not accept surrender. They are hereby deemed unworthy of living and will be treated as such."

It didn't take long before the screams pierced the air as teachers and soldiers engaged in battle. Some of the more advanced and gifted students could also be seen joining in the fray as fire, and large pieces of the ground flew through the air. Isha turned around to see two large airships taking to the sky.

Isha saw a root pop out of the ground as the orange light of Lonta'Mar appeared again. She quickly reached down grabbing it and started channeling her magic.

Hello, is everything okay?

There are golden people here and they are taking the trees.

What? Are you hurt?

No, they only take parts of me, but I still here. I have less power now... and am getting... tired. Lonta' Mar's voice started to fade away in Isha's mind. *New people... are here...* and they fight. *They.... near.... wall now.* And then her voice was completely gone from Isha's mind as the orange light in the root disappeared.

"Miss Soulden, there are people upstairs in the room with the orange tree. They're taking the plants."

"What? How do you..."

Suddenly, an explosion erupted in the sky overhead at their side of the castle that sent tons of marble hurtling downward towards where the poisoned students were.

"Goddess, no," were the only words Soulden managed before witnessing the falling debris herding towards them. She quickly raised her hands shooting up waves of forced magic, deflecting as many of the huge rocks as she could, forcing them to crash around her and not near the students.

She managed to deflect most of the debris but collapsed

to her knees after another set of spells. Sweat began to pour from her as she tried to catch her breath, only to look up and see one final piece of huge marble break free head straight for her. Utterly exhausted, she looked back at her students and closed her eyes as the marble came down towards her.

But nothing happened, no impact. She opened her eyes again to see blades of grass spiraling around her and above, the massive piece of marble floating above her head. Soulden turned around to see the High Mother, with her palm outstretched, with beads of sweat running down her face.

"Can... you please... move, little Soulden? I'm afraid this is quite... heavy."

Soulden's eyes opened wide as she hurried from under the large piece of marble as the High Mother dropped to her knees, breathing heavily, letting the stone drop to the ground. Elena and Isha ran up to the High Mother as she fell over on her side after seeing Soulden was safe.

"High Mother, are you okay?"

"I'm fine. Treat Soulden, she won't be any good to anyone if that head wound doesn't stop bleeding."

Elena stepped forward, and started healing Soulden as they all looked up and watched the two ships in the air, one hovering over the opening that they made in the wall.

"I don't know. Everyone just seems so beat up. Is there any way to stop them?" asked Elena.

"I was told the lower levels of the school were poisoned. There's no other way up. I don't—" said Soulden.

The ships started pulling off as fire balls were seen being blasted at the vessels from inside the hole in the wall. Quickly the ships began to pull away and take to the sky's but not before one of the ships took a heavy hit from a large magic blast and started wobbling in the sky. The other ship pulled alongside, and they saw people jumping from one ship to the other, before the injured ship began to turn around.

"What are they doing now?" asked the High Mother.

The uninjured ship took off in one direction as the injured ship slowly turned back around.

"Are they trying to pick up others, even when..."

They all noticed the ship tilt downward in their direction.

"No... no... they wouldn't," said The High Mother. "After all this, they wouldn't dare."

The ship sped up and made its way toward them, and the injured students laid out on the ground. Quickly the few people around began to panic and run away. Isha and Elena watched the ship plummeting towards them as Soulden Fegmont released herself from their grasp. She took a few steps forward with her feet on the grass, watching as the vessel headed directly at them. Stretching out her hand, she began channeling her magic into her palm.

"Soulden, you can't shield everyone here from that," screamed the High Mother as the ship approached.

Soulden didn't say a word, just dug her toes into the ground beneath her feet and waited. Everyone was exhausted and could only watch and wait along with Soulden.

The smoking ship grew closer and closer, appearing larger and more ominous until finally, it was so close that it cast a shadow over parts of the courtyard. Soulden sent out a wave of magic that struck the ship. It didn't seem to affect the ship at all as it kept its course.

"Soulden, if you do this... you will die," said the High Mother as she watched Soulden throw her arms out and pushed her own magical barrier forward.

And seconds later, like the crackling sound of thunder came as the ship crashed into Soulden's barrier.

Isha watched as the ship folded in on itself, layer by layer. Steel and wood exploded against her barrier as flames burst out from the ship. Soulden stood there in her shift, forcing out every bit of magic she had. The white of her eyes filled with red with blood as the magical poisoning began to consume her. Her arms shook. Her fingers trembled. Her knees wobbled.

Isha ran forward placing her hands on Soulden's back trying to stop her from falling over.

Suddenly another explosion happened in the vessel and Isha watched as flames spread out in front of them and washed over Soulden's shield like a wave of orange and crimson, looking for a way in, scorching the ground and trees on the other side of the barrier.

Isha held on to Soulden as tightly as she could as the worn out mage dropped to her knees with her hands still held out and she exerted her magic. Isha's feet slid across the grass in front of Soulden as she wrapped her arms around her, doing all she could to hold up the exhausted mage as Soulden's head slumped down on Isha's shoulders.

Isha could only look on in horror as she saw the cost Soulden was paying. Blood poured from the side of her eyes and leaked out of her mouth. But still, her hands stayed up, casting the barrier that was weakening with each passing second. Flames pierced the veil of protection, scarring the ground around them as chunks of burning metal and wood were pushed through the shield and fell in front of them. Isha could feel the heat of the flames against the back of her neck, nipping at her skin.

She's going to die. It's going to happen again, just like with Uncle Jasper. There's nothing I can do, Nothing... Nothing... Nothing.

"Run... stupid... child," spoke Soulden's soft voice in her ear.

Around the courtyard, the fire roared in front of them. But inside, Jacinta, Makeba, and the High Mother noticed something odd. Small balls of white light seemed to appear around them.

"What is this?" asked the High Mother, looking around the courtyard. The white orbs hovered in the air and headed towards Isha and Soulden. Isha held Soulden tightly as the white orbs began spinning around the two, scorching the ground around them as Isha's hands began to glow white. Her small fingers burning through Soulden shift, searing the flesh on the woman's back. Soulden coughed up blood and grit her teeth from the pain as Isha's eyes began to glow.

The surrounding air heated up as Soulden and Isha's image began to morph as their clothing began to burn.

"What's happening?" screamed the High Mother.

"We not know," screamed Makeba back as she tried to shield their eyes from the brightening white lights that swirled around their sister.

As their clothing burned, Soulden's skin began to glow white along with Isha's. Suddenly both their eyes turned white as Soulden's shield solidified, appearing like a diamond wall in front of the whole courtyard.

"Oh goodness. What in all of Ellendor," said the High Mother as she gazed at the spectacle of shielding. The ship's flames were being pushed back as Soulden's shield continued to expand forward.

"High Mother, I brought help so... what in the goddess's name," said Leo as he appeared with students and teachers behind him. He quickly ran over to the High Mother who was still on her knees on the ground. "What's happening?"

"I don't know. Isha, she grabbed Soulden and then... I honestly don't know. The students, you need to help Elena; she's been..."

The final explosion of the ship sent the mass of metal and burned lumber crashing down to the ground as the shield continued to push it back against the wreckage, digging a trench in the ground along with it.

The barrier soon faded away as the naked bodies of Soulden and Isha fell down to the scorched ground beneath. And on the backside of Soulden, scarred across her shoulder blades, were two burn marks in the shape of Isha's small hands.

Makeba and Jacinta both ran over to their sister, screaming her name.

The High Mother just looked on in shock as the Sakari girls ran over to the crumpled bodies of the two with the burned ground beneath them.

"No, it won't end here!" said the voice of a man followed by a scream.

The High Mother turned to see a man with a blade against Elena's neck, his face and clothing half charred so bad that you could see the disfigured skin leaking blood.

"Stop, let her go," screamed the High Mother, "Haven't you done enough?"

"This is all your fault," said the man as he frantically looked around. "You all up here get everything you want while the rest of us suffer. Well, not anymore." The man reached to his side and ripped off what was left of his uniform, revealing a red jewel inside his chest. He whispered some words before plunging his own hand at it, clawing at the red jewel before ripping it free in a splatter of blood that sailed through the air, landing on the ground before the High Mother. "Now... now... you will suffer like we have suffered." He then plunged the jewel into the abdomen of Elena, forcing her to drop to her knees. The man smiled as he also dropped to his knees beside Elena and keeled over on the stone beside her. "Share... in... the suffering." were his final words.

Elena began breathing heavily and clutching at her side as blood seeped out of the wound. Leo quickly ran up to her, dropping to his knees. He ripped open the cloth of her uniform to see the spot where she had been pierced.

"Don't worry; I'll fix you right up. Okay... okay," said Leo, forcing Elena to meet his eyes.

"Ehmm,"

"Leo, something's wrong," said the High Mother. "Use your eyes."

Leo looked back at the High Mother in confusion as he turned back to Elena, using his talent to see the magic coursing inside of her.

"Your magic, it's changing," said Leo.

"I feel so hot," said Elena as a hint of steam flowed from her mouth.

"I'm going to pull it, okay?" said Leo.

Elena closed her eyes as Leo gripped the jewel in his hand, and with a quick motion, ripped it from her body, throwing it away on the grass. He looked Elena over once again, but her magic was still transforming inside her.

"No, dammit. Why won't it stop?" yelled Leo in a panic and tried forcing healing magic on the wound. But that only accelerated the change inside of Elena.

Elena raised her hand to Leo's face and smiled at him. "It's okay, Leo. It's going to be okay."

Immediately tears started to flow down Leo's face as he witnessed Elena accepting what was about to happen. "No... no... mama bear, please... don't go... don't leave me." He wrapped his arms around Elena, her head resting on his shoulders.

Elena rubbed her face against his, "I love you," and her body collapsed down on his.

Leo held Elena's limp body in his arms, pressing her tightly against his chest. She was showing the signs of an odd glow underneath her skin, so much so that Leo could see the veins beneath as it began to flicker inside of her as if a lightning storm was raging inside her body. The air around her and Leo began to swirl, with orange sparks appearing as magic crackled around the two.

"Leo, get away from her. Something's wrong. Her magic, its..."

And before the High Mother could finish her words, a ball of flame appeared around the couple, swallowing them whole, scorching the ground beneath them in a spiraling mass.

Isha awoke just in time to witness Leo and Elena become consumed in the fire as she lay on the ground unable to move. The revolving flame reflecting off the tears in her eyes as both Leo and Elena were swallowed by the flaming sphere. The spinning blaze sucked in the air around them like a vacuum. Leaves, grass, and pieces of marble were sucked into the small vortex. The fiery ball shrunk in size for only a moment before it exploded out again, sending waves of fire through the courtyard, singeing the High Mother's clothing along with some of the nearby poisoned students. Isha watched as the wave of flame dissipated before reaching her and Soulden, only reaching them as a wave of hot air.

Where Elena and Leo were now only sat two black husks. One holding the other in its arms. Their clothes were gone, skin was charred, and their hair was completely burned away.

"No, my goodness no," said The High Mother as she crawled forward to the burned bodies of her students.

Jacinta and Makeba just stared at the bodies that were once their friends with whom they had spent every morning for the last six months.

"Leo... Elena... please... take me to them," said Isha.

"But people, sister. You have no cloth. Lots of people."

"Please," pleaded Isha to her sisters.

The High Mother saw them and removed her top, tossing it over to the girls with it landing on the ground beside them as more people began to appear. Jacinta stepped forward grabbing the white garb from the ground and brought it back to Isha, draping it over Isha as Makeba and Jacinta lifted her up.

Her Sakari sisters then placed their shoulders under Isha's arms, lifting her up, and escorted her on shaking legs over to the burned bodies of Leo and Elena as the High Mother knelt before them on hands in knees beside them with her head down.

"Ah... are they... are they gone?" asked Isha, unable to control the shakiness in her voice.

"Oh, my baby Leo, I'm so sorry. I know you loved Elena,

but there was nothing you could do," said the High Mother.

Isha felt her feet give out from under her as she dropped back down to her knees in front of the charred statues that once had been her friends. Immediately thoughts of them together back at home flashed through her mind. Leo saying stupid things about his harem: all the times he would heal her leg, the hugs she started giving him every morning, how embarrassed she'd felt as he screamed he loved her as she went to school, Elena in the kitchen cooking for them, while scolding Leo, how she would try to teach them magic, how she felt like a mother, and that night where she found her crying in the corner, how she consoled her in her arms until she finally managed to stop shaking. The world in her mind grew darker as her breathing quickened. She clutched at her chest and grit her teeth as a flow of emotions overtook her mind.

She clenched a piece of broken marble in her hand so hard that it pierced the skin, dripping blood onto the blackened ground as her eyes began to water. But as she sat with her head down on hands and knees, she heard the sound of a crackle. She glanced forward and noticed a small movement in Leo's charred arm around Elena. Then another crackle as a piece of charred flesh fell from Leo's arm to the marble below. She looked back up to the spot where the piece had fallen from and she saw Leo's burned skin; it was healing.

Sounds of more crackling were heard as the charred flesh of Leo's skin continued to break apart and fall from his body. Suddenly, his burned head leaned back, the skin around his jaw ripping apart as his mouth opened, and out came a heartbreaking gurgled scream.

Leo's charred body fell over on the ground, twitching as Isha watched as his flesh attempted to heal itself, inch by inch.

CHAPTER 36

Victor rode back into the city of Burlus with Silk once again hidden into the back of the wagon. He was forced to grip the reins on the horses with only one hand as the other hand lay mangled in his lap. Poorly made splints were set across his four fingers to keep them in place. His face was disheveled and dirty as his body swayed with the motion of the carriage. The morning sun shone on him, revealing the bags under his eyes from severe lack of sleep. Stopping at a stable inside the gate, he spotted a boy sitting down on a haystack.

"Here, boy."

"Yes, Sir. Want me to feed your horses?"

"No, do you know the woman named Frenka? She works—"

"You mean the palace guard's lady, I sure do. Everyone knows her."

"Good lad, there's two pieces of gold in it for you if you can bring her here before the hour."

"Really?"

Victor flashed two shiny gold pieces in his good hand. And the boy took off running up the street. Victor waited for the boy, trying to stay awake as he watched the merchants of the city begin to set up their shops in the street.

Around half an hour later, Frenka appeared from around a corner.

"Why you send boy to find Frenka?"

"I'll explain, but would you mind if I went to your home?"

Frenka tilted her head to the side in suspicion, "I suppose not," she said as she climbed up into the wagon. "Go forward and turn right."

Victor snapped the reins with his left hand, and the carriage took off.

"Your eyes, you are not looking well."

"Trust me, I feel a lot worse than I look."

"You will sleep at Frenka's. Seems you need it."

"I shall take you up on that, but first, I must visit the king. Is Nahtalli still in the city?"

"Who, healer man? Yes, he still here. He trains the smaller healer for now."

"Good, I'll be needing a lot of work from him," said Victor, raising his right hand to show Frenka the splints on his fingers.

Frenka shook her head, "Perhaps you needed Frenka and Dekol with you on that mission as well."

"Perhaps, but what's done is done."

Frenka looked in the back of the wagon and saw someone moving under the blanket in the hay. "Is that old lady, you still travel with her?"

"Yeah," Victor chuckled. "You can say that. Would you mind her coming along too? She also needs healing."

"Frenka supposes not, but you will explain things to Frenka."

"Yes, I will explain everything. You may even be surprised. It was quite the adventure after all."

They rounded another corner and pulled alongside the small gate to Frenka's home. Frenka walked past the gate and opened the door to her home as Victor escorted Silk out of the wagon. She covered herself with a cloak so that no one would see her skin as Victor ushered her into the house with Frenka closing the door behind them.

"Now. Victor will explain?"

"Yes, but I must head to the castle soon."

A little girl walked into the room.

"This is Melana. She live with me."

Victor smiled at the girl, "Hello there, can you keep a secret, sweetheart?"

The girl smiled back at Victor. "I can. Are you Mr. Victor? Frenka said you wear glasses."

"That would be me. I am indeed Victor. What else has Frenka mentioned about me?"

"Hush, Melana," said Frenka to the girl before turning back to Victor. "What secret you show? Why old lady covered up?"

"Well, better to get it over with, Silk."

Silk showed her hands from the cloak revealing her ashen skin, and untied it from her neck, letting it fall to the floor, exposing her bandaged face.

Frenka gasped, "A Dula-hon?"

"A what?" asked Victor in confusion.

Frenka stepped closer to Silk, examining her face, "A Dula-hon, she one from stories father tell us when young. Dula-hon ride through the sky at night on pale horses. They have ashen skin and hair and weird magic weapons." She turned to Victor, "How you capture one?"

"That... I want to ask you a question about that, but I'm short on time at the moment. I need to report to the king. I'm sure he knows I'm in the city already. The short story is, she's not a Dula-Hon, or maybe she is. I don't know anymore. But she is injured, and she is no danger to you. Would it be alright if I left her here and asked Nahtalli to come heal her."

Frenka stared at Victor for a moment, "This important to you?"

"It is."

"Then it important to Frenka. You wait a moment," said Frenka as she walked over into the kitchen and grabbed a small corked jar, and came back to Victor. She reached in, pulling out a small amount of orange sand, and placed it under Victor's nose. "June dust keep you awake with king; you sound like you need it."

"Appreciate that."

"Now you go on. See king, and send healer man here. I will look after your Dula-hon."

"My name is Silk."

"Oh, she speaks?"

"You know she's female?"

"Of course, all Dula-hon are female."

Victor shook his head, "Anyway, I'm gone. Silk, stay here. I'll be back as soon as I finish with the king."

Victor then rushed out of the door jumping into the carriage, headed back into the city towards the castle. It didn't take him long before he arrived at the castle steps, and with luck, found Nahtalli and the smaller healer leaving through its doors.

"Hello, Victor," said Nahtalli. "You have returned."

"Hello Nahtalli," said Victor walking up the steps, "Might I ask a favor of you two?"

"I don't see why not, how may I... Oh my," said Nahtalli as Victor raised his mangled hand for him to see, "Let me have a look. I can get started right away."

He really is passionate about healing; he didn't even ask what happened. "Actually, I wish for your apprentice here to heal me. I actually have someone in much more serious condition that needs your attention."

"What? Who? Where?"

"She's at Miss Frenka's place; the person has burn marks over her face."

"Of course, I shall head there at once. I believe I know the location. I treated her little girl once before," said Nahtalli as he made his way down the steps.

"Hey, Nahtalli," yelled Victor.

"Yes?"

"When you get there, refer to what you see as a female. It will make things a lot easier for you."

Nahtalli looked confused for a moment but nodded and made his way down into the streets..

Victor turned towards Rayrah. "Would you mind holding off on the healing for a moment and follow me? I need to speak with the king."

"Ah... yes, Sir. If that is what you wish."

"Yes, and try not to mention anything about me sending the Nahtalli to Frenka's house. I'd like to avoid any misunderstandings."

"Oh, yes, sir. I am aware of the prince's desires."

"The prince's desires, huh... that sounds a lot better than stalking violent obsession."

Victor and Rayrah made their way back into the castle. After being informed of the King's whereabouts by the guards, they made their way up the stairs to the king's chambers where Victor knocked on the door.

"Enter," spoke the king's voice.

"Should I really be here?" asked Rayrah, looking nervously up at Victor.

"Don't worry; I need you with me for a moment."

Victor walked inside to see the King sitting down at his

desk. "Greetings, your highness. I hope things have been well." Victor walked in and sat down in the seat in front of the king without an invitation.

"Victor, I see you've made your way here quite quickly this time."

"I assume your people told you of my arrival in the city. After I restocked up on supplies, I figured why waste time? I did stumble upon one of the lovelier of your guards, though, before my visit."

"Stumbled upon is a strange way of saying, 'waited for'. And who you sleep with is of no import to me, but I suppose if you seek to gain even more ire of my son than you already have, then I suppose you're on the right track."

"Consider my time with her as repayment for this. Victor raised his mangled hand for the king to see."

"Looks like a nasty bit of work. Did you accomplish your task?"

"Rayrah, please begin healing my fingers," said Victor, extending out his arm for the girl.

"Ahh, yes, Sir." Rayrah reached out, gently grabbing Victor's hand, and began channeling her healing magic.

"I did," said Victor as he felt the cooling effects of her magic over his finger. "And I can confirm that it is a splinter group of the Church of the Goddess, that has been killing the townsfolk from small villages between kingdoms."

"So, they're really implanting the jewels into people?"

"Mr. Victor, the bones in your fingers weren't properly set; I'm going to have to reset them."

"I figured as much. Go on. Get on with it then."

"Yes, Sir."

"They were, in fact, embedding crystals in their bodies." Victor's finger made a loud cracking noise as Rayrah reset the first finger. Victor grit his teeth. "I'm…. I'm not sure why. But… I can tell you that I stabbed one of those jeweled bastards in the throat, and he fell to the floor dead. Then a few minutes later, he rose back up to his feet, chanting some strange language."

"You think they've managed to find the key to resurrection magic?" asked the king with a raised eyebrow as Rayrah reset another one of Victor's fingers to the sound of a loud crack.

"No... it's something different. His wounds healed after he got back up, but the odd thing was that he looked at his hands in a weird fashion. It was like he'd never seen them before."

"A form of possession then?"

"That would..." Rayrah set another one of Victor's fingers as he slightly bit his lip. "That... would likely be the case. But as for who possessed him, I have no idea."

"You seem to be having difficulties with your hand there. Why did you come here so soon instead of getting yourself tended to first?"

"I've had injured men report to me with their dying breath. I'd be doing them a disservice if I wouldn't follow their example. I just so happened to meet Miss Rayrah on the way here and figured I'd get both jobs done at once," said Victor as Rayrah shifted his final finger back into place with one final audible crack that sounded throughout the room.

"That was it, Sir. I shall heal the tears in the tendons now."

"How very noble of you," said the king with a chuckle. "But you've made your point. You take the mission seriously. I respect that." The king rubbed at his chin, "But tell me, whatever became of the white she-beast you made the bargain for, if you don't mind me asking."

"I had one of my associates break the mental bonding spell. I did allow the one about not hurting your family to stay intact. Then I sent her off back to Mari."

"You'd be better off dissecting it for study rather than trying to tame it."

"I convinced her to tell me her name, along with a few

other details. I think I can find a few other uses for her."

"Foolish sentimentalism that will get you killed. But as long as she poses no threat to my kingdom. Then I shall drop the matter."

"Then I'll be on my way then," said Victor as he stood up from the seat, pulling his hand away from Rayrah's healing efforts.

"Oh," said the King as Victor reached the door. "The Sakari bonding ritual, be sure to tell Clarissa I send my well wishes."

"I'm sure she'll be delighted to hear that," replied Victor with narrowed eyes. "But I think I shall visit Miss Frenka for a while and have her properly tend to my wounds."

"Ha," the king laughed. "Luckily for you, my son is not in the kingdom at the moment. He has been quite in the sour mood since your last encounter."

"Is he not accustomed to someone taking his toys away?"

"Perhaps not, but you should watch yourself in the future. Jealousy is quite an unpredictable beast."

"Jealousy perhaps is, but spoiled nobility tends to be quite predictable," said Victor as he left the room with Rayrah, closing the door behind him.

The moment the door closed, Victor leaned against the wall with his elbow and clenched his teeth in pain as his hand began shaking uncontrollably.

Rayrah began to speak, but Victor placed a finger over his mouth and quieted her as he removed himself from the wall, making his way slowly back down the steps.

"Do you think it is wise to antagonize him so?" asked Rayrah when they had gotten far enough away from the king's chambers.

"Perhaps not, but I'm always making stupid decisions. I figure there's no need to… stop that trend now."

Victor managed to stop his shaking from the pain in his hand before exiting the steps and made his way out the castle's front doors into the city streets.

"Thank you Rayrah, you can leave now if you wish."

"Oh no, Master Nahtalli would never let me hear the end of it if I left you without being fully healed."

"Well, I guess you're tagging along then. Try to not be surprised when we get there."

Victor purposely took a longer way through the city. Once he arrived at Frenka's home, he opened the door to see Frenka's little girl sitting in Silk's lap as Nahtalli tended to her wounds.

"And then the boy tried to grab me in the market, so I punched him in the face and he fell down."

"Did you now?" asked Silk to the little girl as Nahtalli's magic flowed from his hands over her eye. "Aren't you a brave little girl?"

"Well now," said Victor, closing the door behind him, "Don't you look comfy." He noticed Rayrah stunned in silence as she gazed upon Silk's ashen skin. "Hey now," said Victor, patting her on the back. "Go on, it's not nice to stare."

"Ah... right," replied Rayrah as she stepped forward. "Master Nahtalli, is everything alright."

"Huh... oh yes. The skin on her face was badly burned. And her tissue structure is different, but it didn't take long before I found the proper way to heal her. Come over here and try to heal her, and you will see for yourself. This will be a good experience for you."

"Ah... yes, Sir,"

"What's it like being a Dula-hon?" asked the girl in Silk's lap.

"I don't know. Why? Are you scared of me?"

"No, Frenka says you're okay. And that you're friends with Victor."

Silk looked at Victor, "Yes, we are friends."

Victor knew that wasn't the look that friends give each other as he stepped forward and placed his hand on the side of Silk's unburned face. "Your face, the skin looks disfig-ured, You probably won't be winning any beauty contests until we find someone to fix that."

"It's not like I never could anyway," said Silk, shaking her head. "To make the hideous even more of a monster than before. What's the point anymore."

"Hey, don't you act like that now. Not after what we've been through. I'm with you now. So at the very least, you will have someone who won't look at you that way." Victor reached out rubbing the small girl's hair in Silk's lap. "And you seem to have already found someone else who accepts you. "Isn't that right, dear."

"I like her, she has skin like milk," said Melana.

"See," said Victor with a smile. "Now you are the milky white Dola-hon of Victor Krill. What better life could you ask for."

Silk chuckled despite herself, "Thank you. This is the first time I've been around so many people wearing myself. I... I think I'd like to get used to it."

"Give me some time and I'll see if I can't make that happen." Victor then patted Silk on the shoulder, before turning to Nathalli. "How long until she's fully healed?"

"Give me another day to ensure the healing is permanent. Her biological structure is odd and healing her was more difficult than usual. I would like the time to ensure that I have done nothing wrong and that the healing methods used are correct."

"That's fine with me. I want her to be well taken care of. I don't suppose you have any creaming skills?"

"In fact, I do," said Nathalli with a smile. "While I'm not as proficient as a master of the trade, I like to think of myself as capable enough. Though it will take some time."

"Well, aren't we lucky to have you around. Okay, then, I shall leave her in your capable hands," said Victor as he turned and walked over into the other room where Frenka waited for him as Nathiall and Reyrah continued their healing of Silk.

"Are you satisfied, now that Frenka has taken care of

your Dula-hon?" asked Frenka as she placed a book back into a slot on the shelf.

"Yes. Thank you for this."

"Come, sit and talk. You explain now," said Frenka, walking over and grabbing Victor by the hand and sitting him down on a sofa.

"So, Dula-hon was old lady in back of cart?"

"Yeah."

"And did Dula-hon turn out to be good person?" asked Frenka as she sat down in Victor's lap.

Victor thought for a second. "More or less, I think so."

"Then, more or less, you did good thing to help her."

"Thank you, but I think I'd like to take a break for a while," said Silk's voice as she came around the corner, half her face covered in new bandages where the burn marks were. "Victor, I wanted to ask you if..." Her words caught in her throat as she saw Frenka sitting down on Victor's lap. "Oh, I'm sorry... I..."

"Will Frenka and Victor have babies now?" asked the girl running up to Frenka.

"What?" asked Victor.

"That's how we have babies; when a woman sits on a man's lap."

"I mean, you're not wrong, but—"

"I think Dula-hon wants to have babies too; she looks at Victor like Frenka does."

Oh, sweet goddess, how perceptive is this kid. "Now, little one, I'm sure—"

"Really?" asked Frenka, "Did you make Dula-hon love you?"

"What? No, that's not—"

"Yes, I love Victor."

Please stop; this is not helping.

"I... I mean... I think I do... and I want to stay with him."

Frenka sat up off Victor's lap and walked over to Silk, looking down into her green and red eyes. She turned back to Victor, "Do you claim the Dula-hon?"

"I'm not sure I have much of a choice anymore at this point," said Victor, shaking his head and giving up. "I'm pretty much stuck with her now."

"Then Frenka accepts."

"Accepts? Accepts wha…" Victor looked up to see Frenka's lips planted on Silk's.

Silk's red and green eyes went wide as Frenka kissed her. She stepped back, almost tripping, but Frenka caught her in her arms.

"I catch you," said Frenka as she pulled her lips away from Silks. "Are you okay?"

"Ahh… yes, what's happening?"

"What you mean? You will be sister wife, but Frenka was first; she will look after clan," said Frenka, who released a confused Silk and knelt to the girl, "Melana it is a good day. Today we will add a strong Dula-hon to the clan."

Victor dropped his head into his hands. *That's right, she's from the fucking clans. They take multiple lovers.* "Wait," he said, lifting his head, looking confused. "I thought you wanted out of the clan life. What about that dead husband of yours?"

Frenka turned back to Victor, "Gresham? He was bad man who beat wives. I do not think Victor is type who beat wives." She turned around, looking back up at Silk. "Has Victor beat you?"

"What? No."

"Then Frenka made the right choice. It would be shame to kill Victor after choosing him."

"Yes, that certainly would be a shame," said Victor as he tried to stretch out his still stiff fingers. "Am I to constantly have my life in danger now?"

"Your life always in danger, but that is because you stupid."

"Are you going to leave your prince's side and travel back to Mari with us? My so-called mountain wife."

"I will visit for new husband, but Frenka is prince's royal guard. Victor will live here when not on missions."

"The logistics of this relationship of yours might be a bit impossible."

"Husbands spend months away on hunts in clans. How this be different?"

"And you're not afraid of me getting snatched up by another clan while away?"

"True, Frenka thought about that. After all, Victor is stupid man. But now, with strong Dula-hon sister-wife, Frenka not worry so much." Frenka turned back to a stunned-faced Silk, "Dula-hon, you will protect Victor. He not as stupid as prince, but he will need to be watched. You will ensure he is not taken by other clan or killed."

Silk looked to Victor, "Say something about this."

Victor laid down on the couch, turning his back to the women while waving his hand in the air. "I give up. I only pray this damned June powder allows me to sleep."

"Victor!"

"You wanted to be my partner; that means you have to deal with her just the same as I do. It's going to be nice to have someone else suffer with me for once."

Nahtalli walked around the corner, "Congratulations Victor, I did not realize you practiced in the clan mating rituals."

"Yeah..." said Victor, in a yawn. "Funny thing about that. Neither did I."

CHAPTER 37

Oscar was back in his normal mercenary clothing as he sat in his tent, chipping away at a piece of wood when Amos entered.

"Sir, Jacob and Dessi have returned."

"Well, that took long enough," said Oscar as he raised from his seat and walked out of the tent. He looked downhill to see Jacob and Dessi followed by a few Black Jewels along with four other riders.

They both stopped their horses, unseated, and made their way over to Oscar.

"Hello, father. You enjoying your morning?"

"Hardly, and what of you, Dessi? I take it the task was completed."

"It was. Although changes had to be made since I wasn't kept up to date."

"Ya can blame my son for that; he made that decision."

"I thought you said it wasn't your idea?" asked Dessi, frowning at Jacob.

"I would like to thank you, Sir," said Henry, walking up behind Jacob. "If not for you, I'm not sure what would have happened to me."

"Oh, I have an idea. Go on then…" replied Oscar as he gestured to a lady and her child up ahead of them. "We'll decide what to do with you later. She's been waiting for you all morning."

"Ahh… yes sir," said Henry as he hurried over to greet his sister and nephew. She immediately embraced him in hugs and kisses on his cheeks.

Oscar watched the showering of affection with a smirk. "You think he'll find out his sister was the one who hired us to kill him."

"Hopefully not," said Jacob. "This way works out for them both. He gets to live, and her son gets to be Duke one day."

"And what do we get?" asked Oscar, "A whelp who's barely a swordsman. Seems a waste of a lot of time and gold."

"I've been thinking about that," said Dessi. "Why not pair him with Amos. Seems he'd be a good representative to send to nobles in search of work."

Oscar rubbed at his chin, "You hear that Amos, you got yourself a playmate. Train 'em well."

"What… me? Why?"

"Think of it this way. Train 'em well, and you'll cut your workload in half. Train 'em poorly, and he'll get both of ya killed. Ya wanted more responsibility and dangerous work. Now ya got it."

"That's not… fine," said Amos, looking at Henry, before

squinting his eyes off in the distance. "Hey, what's that?" he asked, pointing up into the sky.

"What's what?" asked Oscar, following Amos's finger. "That's an airship. The fuck one's doing way out here?"

"Looks to be headed this way, Sir," said Amos.

"You expecting company, father?"

"Not unless someone's coming to offer another job, but I ain't received word of one. Amos go tell the mages to blast that thing out of the sky if it starts acting hostile."

"Yes, sir," said Amos as he ran off through the camp.

"Well, it's certainly headed this way. That's for sure," said Dessi, watching as the ship got closer. "Wow, never seen an airship that big before."

"Ah, fuck. That ship belongs to that healing bitch of a High Mother," said Oscar.

"Isn't she the one that sent us of that suicide campaign where I almost got my head chopped off?"

"Yeah, that'd be her. The real question is, what's she doing out here?"

"Another mission, perhaps?"

"Then she can right well fuck off and find some other bastard to go get themselves killed."

"A mercenary group turning down work? said Dessi with a chuckle. "And here I thought you only cared about gold."

"Yeah, well, you weren't there for that campaign. The whole thing was a waste of good men."

The ship flew over the camp, stopping just outside, and hovering over the ground.

"Right, well, let's go and get this over with," said Oscar as he, Jacob, and Dessi walked over to the edge of the camp to see the High Mother standing aboard her ship looking down at them.

"We meet again, Oscar Highland," said the High Mother.

"Yes, we do. Now if you would be so kind as to leave and never come back. That would be great."

"Are you sure about that? I've come to return something

that belongs to you."

"Aye, and what's that then? I can't imagine you have anything that..." Oscar paused as he saw Jacinta, Makeba, and Isha appear beside the High Mother, followed up by another brown-haired girl.

"Ah... hello father," said Isha as Soulden walked up behind her.

"Do I have your permission to come down now, Oscar? Your men down there seem powerful and quite frightening," spoke the High Mother gazing out over the number of mages that had gathered before her ship.

Oscar shook his head, "Fine, meet me in my tent then, and bring along my daughter. I suppose there is a good reason for this set of events."

It didn't take long before the ship's platform lowered, and everyone was on the ground. Isha quickly found herself wrapped up in Dessi's arms.

"Welcome back, honey. Have you become a great and powerful mage yet?"

"Ah... not yet. But I'm learning."

Jacinta and Makeba found Gregga as she approached, ran over to her, and began telling her tales of their adventures.

"What's that one then?" asked Oscar, looking at the other brown-haired girl.

"Ahh... she's a friend of mine," said Isha, "Can she stay with us until we go back to school?"

Oscar took a second look at the girl, noticing her scarred hand. "Fine, I guess there's a story behind this. And it seems we're inviting people today, anyway." He glanced back over at Henry, who had taken a seat on a well-knit blanket alongside his sister, as his nephew seemed to annoy one nearby man about his sword. "Perhaps I should just start recruiting more child soldiers."

"Thank you, father," said Isha.

Oscar sighed, looking down at his daughter, "We'll come along then. We can discuss why you're here in my tent. I imagine it's something important if you found us all the way out here."

"It is," said Soulden as she and the High Mother made their way back through the camp with Oscar and into his tent.

"Have a seat, ladies," said Oscar as they entered.

The High Mother and Soulden both grabbed a chair, pulling it up to a shabby wooden desk as Oscar grabbed a flagon of wine and three cups.

"I see you are still playing at being a mercenary, Oscar," said the High Mother looking around the tent.

"And I see you're still wearing that ridiculous outfit and parading around as the Holy Bitch."

"It's nice to see someone disliking Oscar as much as I," said Soulden, taking the flagon of wine that Oscar placed on the table and pouring herself and the High Mother a serving.

"I don't hate Oscar; we simply have different opinions on things is all."

"Yeah, I want to live, and ya spent the better part of a year trying to get me and my men killed."

"You did accept the contract after all," said the High Mother, picking up her own glass of wine. "And if I remember correctly, the last time we met, you held a blade to my neck and threatened to cut my head off. It was quite the ordeal."

"Aye, a threat I should have followed through on. Surely the five kingdoms would be a better place without you in it," said Oscar, sitting down in front of the two women.

"Aren't you going to go inside?" asked Dessi, listening outside the tent alongside Isha and Jacob.

"Not unless you want to get involved in this mess. I think I'll stay out of it," said Jacob as he then gazed down at Isha.

"How did you meet the High Mother? You really do get into everything, don't you?"

Isha frowned back up at Jacob.

"Alright, tell me why you're here," said Oscar, his eyes glancing toward the three shadows outside of his tent.

"Two reasons," said Soulden, "There was an attack on the school, and four of our students along with two teachers were killed."

"One of whom belonged to me," said The High Mother in a disgusted tone.

"So, someone attacked Sceana and killed a healer? Bastards must have a death wish. Who was it?"

"We don't know for sure," replied Soulden. "Everything is still being considered. The attack was well planned and everyone they left committed suicide with some type of red crystals that engulfed their bodies in flames." Soulden pulled out a black gem and showed it to Oscar. "This one was pulled out of one of my students before she died in the same fashion."

"Yeah, I know it."

"You've seen the gem before?"

"Yeah, I got my hands on one some months back, only it was red, not black. But it was smaller, and it blew up, taking half my damn tent with it. But if you've come for information, that's pretty much all I've got. You can talk to Dessi if you want to know more. She's the one who threw herself at my daughter the moment you brought her back. She said she found 'em in dead bodies."

"Dead bodies? That's sort of the same with ours. Ours was ripped out of someone's body. But they died only after it was pulled out. Some type of experiments, you think?"

"Probably?"

"Well, we want to hire you to continue to look—"

"No."

"What?"

"No."

"And what reason do you have to deny this request? You're mercenaries. I thought all you cared about was coin."

"Normally, you'd be right, but this whole thing seems like another Broken Gate war. Perhaps if it was just ya who'd ask alone, but that one beside ya there. Nothing is ever as simple as it seems with her. For all I know, she'd have me facing their whole religion."

The room grew quiet for a moment as the three just looked at each other.

"Oscar," said the High Mother, "I'm sure you know how protective I am over my healers. To me, they are my children. Well, I brought you back your daughter. But the girl who I lost the day of that attack was one of your daughter's friends. I brought you back, what I lost. So, do us both a favor and take the damn job."

"Father, please find out who did this," said Isha as she entered the tent.

Oscar leaned back in his chair, "I told you once before to make a decision. Is this what you want?"

"Yes, Sir."

"Everything comes with a price, daughter; you should know that by now."

"I do."

"And are you willing to pay it?"

"Yes, Sir. I want to know who killed my friend."

"Fine," said Oscar, turning back to Soulden and the High Mother, "The price will be worked out between us later. But there's someone else who may know something about the gems. Victor Krill."

"Isn't he that Mari general?" asked Soulden.

"Aye, that'd be him. He was also there in the city when the gem was found. He might have looked more into it by now. No harm in asking what he might have found out. If

I'm going to get dragged into this, why not see if I can rope that bastard in as well?"

"I can head to Mari after this," said the High Mother.

"Alright then, if that's the first one, then what's the second thing you wanted? You said there were two."

"Right, well, the second involves your daughter. She has a different type of magic."

"So she's an oddity then. I figured that much. My son's an oddity. So what's it be, can she use mind magic, shadow magic, talk to animals or something?"

"She's an amplifier."

"A what?"

"In simpler terms, she makes other mages stronger. Any mage, and it's significantly stronger. Very significant."

Oscar looked down at Isha, "Well, I'm sure we'll find a use for it. She can still use other magics since her core's not settled, right?"

"Oscar, I don't think you understand what that means," said Soulden, leaning forward. "She makes any mage two, no, maybe even three times more powerful than they were. And that more than likely includes archmages. That means the King and Queens."

"Great, so how many people know about my daughter's little talent?"

"Wait, there's more. It doesn't seem like she pays the cost that all other mages pay."

"And that is?"

"The toxic nature of magic. We can only use magic for so long before our brains shut down to protect us and we pass out. Well, I can promise you that with the amount of magic your daughter pushed into me. I'd say that would normally have been enough magic to kill over a dozen mages. And yet, here I am. And add to that the fact that she used this power in full view of the most elite mages and children in all the five kingdoms. Then that means that every queen, king, and noble either knows about her now or will learn of her existence in the coming weeks."

"Guess that explains why Duke Richards had you," said Oscar, scratching his head, looking down at Isha.

"Oscar, with as little respect as I have for you, I would still expect for you to take this matter seriously. And yet, you don't seem too worried about this at all."

"You've been living in your sky city too long, Soulden. I'm the one down here doing the dirty work, and you don't do what I do without knowing the type of people who can make someone disappear. If I wanted, I could make it so that my daughter becomes nothing more than a myth if need be. You've taught her to keep that power under control; I take it. Then it shouldn't be an issue to hide her away till we get this sorted."

"Wait, before you do that. I would like to make a suggestion."

"And that is?" asked Oscar with a raised brow.

"Let her finish out her training in Sceana."

"After what you just told me about an attack at the school. You expect me to allow my daughter to go back there?"

"I assure you, that was under a very unusual circumstance of one of our council members bringing them there. I assure you that problem has been taken care of. Oscar, we don't like each other. I won't deny that. But you know my character and what it means when I give you my word. Allow your daughter to attend Sceana again; it will be the safest place for her, and she will get to continue her training."

"You say that, but you could have just kept her there. Why bring her back here and ask me for my permission?"

"As I said. You know my character. The school is now closed. We've arranged for everyone to go back to their families. Only after that did I even think to make this trip here."

Oscar sighed while tapping his hand on his knee and turned back to Isha, "What say you in this matter, daughter? It's your life we are talking about. I suspect you might have an opinion on the matter."

"I... I would like to go back, Father."

Oscar closed his eyes, taking a deep breath. "Well, that settles it then. How long before that school of yours opens back up?"

"It will be back open in around a month's time."

"And I'm supposed to expect every noble in the five kingdoms breathing down my neck in the coming weeks."

"Most likely, yes. Your daughter is a one of a kind at the moment, and I doubt another one of her type will be born within our lifetime."

"Fine, I'll start making arrangements then. If they're going to hunt me down, I might as well make it easy for them to find me till this whole thing gets under control."

"Is there anything else?"

"No, that will be everything. We will be heading back now," said Soulden, standing up along with the High Mother.

"I'll return you to the school, Soulden, and then I'll head off to Mari to try and get in touch with that Victor Krill fellow," said the High Mother.

"I look forward to seeing you again soon, child," said Soulden to Isha. "Take care until then. But I guess there's only so much you can do if Oscar is your father."

"Yes, ma'am."

The High Mother stepped over to Isha and knelt in front of her. "Oh, darling child. I do so wish you would have turned out to be a healer. But I still think of you as one of my own children. Please contact me if you ever need anything. I will do what I can to help you."

"Yes, High Mother. I... I'm going to miss you too."

The High Mother gave Isha a kiss on her forehead. Then standing, she and Soulden left the tent, headed down to her ship.

Oscar watched the ladies leave and then reached over, grabbing the flagon of wine, pouring himself a cup, and gulping it down.

"So how's it feel to be one of the most prized mages in the five kingdoms?"

"I don't know. I don't feel any different."

"Well, you're still young, and I can't really get any use out of ya. But I'll keep ya safe enough, that's for sure. But if what they're saying is true, then this might turn out to be a valuable learning experience for ya."

"Really? What am I going to learn?"

"Ya going to see why I'd rather be down here in the dirt, rather than up there with them nobles. But that's going to take some time. Until then, I'll have a tent set up for you and your little friend. You all can sleep together tonight, but tomorrow we're leaving. If Soulden found us, then it won't be long before others do. And I'd rather have you in a position where you can't be snatched away."

"I'm not helpless now. I know magic. I can fight."

"Yeah, then tell me. Soulden said there was a battle up there. How many mages did you see die up there?"

Isha was quiet.

"Yeah, it's a lot, ain't it, and they all were probably stronger than you. Magic doesn't make you invincible, child. It just makes you predictable and overconfident. Think about that night in the tent with that flying bastard. I betcha he felt mighty unstoppable before he was pinned to the ground with a blade in his neck."

"Then what should I do now?"

"Just let me worry about that for a while. It seems I have another month with ya, and I intend to use it to see that you're trained properly. So give your father a few days to make some plans. For now, just head out and play with your friends. I'm sure they're waiting on ya, especially that one with the scarred hand. She looked like a lost puppy the way she was staring around the camp. Go see that she's tended to. I told ya before those Sakari girls were your responsibility. Well, seems like you can add her to that list as well."

"Yes, Father," said Isha as she ran out of the tent.

Oscar watched his daughter leave out of the tent before he leaned back into his chair and closed his eyes. "I wonder just how much that damned spell is affecting me. Damn Jasper, you brought me one hell of a headache." He took a deep breath before standing up from his seat and walking out of the tent. Looking around, he spotted Amos still over beside Henry and his sister.

"Amos, come here."

"Yes, Sir," said Amos, jogging over.

"What's the nearest trade city from here?"

"Vontal, I believe."

"We can't go back to Vontal yet. What's the next one."

"Ahh, that'd be Faylon. It's by the sea and deals with a lot of commerce. It's only about a week away."

"Alright, tell everyone we leave for Faylon, first thing in the morning. And we need to make it there in five days, so we're going to be pushing it hard."

"Yes, Sir. Do we have a new job already?"

"No, I just gotta prepare for some guests it seems, and being caught out here in the middle of nowhere isn't a solid plan by any means."

"I will inform everyone now, Sir," said Amos as he ran off into the camp.

CHAPTER 38

A week later, Jacob was escorting a noble and his son through the streets of Faylon.

"We're almost there, Mr. Harrowhill," said Jacob to the man beside him as they walked through the street together.

"Tell me, how did you acquire the girl? I heard that she keeps two Sakari girls with her as her bodyguards at all times. Is that true?"

"Yes, for the most part. You must understand, she is quite the valuable prize," said Jacob as they entered a large three-story stone building. The lobby was packed with people in fine suits and dresses conversing with one another. They spotted Jacob, and a few men rushed at him spouting demands.

"Calm down, everyone, calm down. My father can only meet with one group at a time. I promise everyone here will get their chance to speak with him if you all will just be patient," said Jacob as he led Mr. Harrowhill and his son to the steps where four of the black jewels guards were blocking the entrance.

"Are all of them here for the girl?" asked Mr. Harrowhill as the guards allowed them to pass.

"Unfortunately, yes. Father has been entertaining guests all day. We had to buy out the entire second and third floors, just to ensure there would be no intrusions for the auction."

"I… I see," said Mr. Harrowhill.

"Father, do you think we'll be able to get her? I mean, there were so many."

"Don't worry, son, I'm sure we will do fine. We have a distinguished bloodline after all."

The inside of the building was lush with colorful silks hanging from the walls and planted foliage that sat in vases on the stairwell as they climbed up. "This way, gentlemen." Jacob led the men upstairs to the top floor and down a hall until they reached a door with two Sakari men standing outside with blades gripped in the hands.

"So, you do have more Sakari in their employ, not just the two girls then?"

"Employ is a strong word," said Jacob as he opened the door and escorted the man and his son inside.

"Gentlemen, allow me to introduce my father, Oscar Highland, and his partner Gregga Flannigan. And the Sakari over in the corner there is Aukube, she is our healer."

"Come in," said Oscar as he and Gregga stayed seated with a few chairs in front of them. "Have a seat and let's discuss business. The room was a mess, with clothing thrown about the room: open trucks with dresses spewed out, fancy silks hung from the ceilings, as well as an assortment of other items thrown about the floor. "Don't mind the mess, people have been bringing all kinds of gifts today and we simply ran out of space to put them all."

"I see," said the man as he took a seat in front of Gregga and Oscar.

"Now, Mr. Harrowhill, when I heard that you were coming. I had my men keep everyone else downstairs. A man with as prestigious a name as yours is a high-value client. I imagine your crest is on half the armor in Latrusa at this point."

"More than half actually, and we are moving our weapons and armor sales into Burlus now," said Mr. Harrowhill as he fidgeted with his collar nervously.

"I see, and as a mercenary group. I suppose you can see why I place your interests above others at the moment."

"Yes, I think our businesses are two sides of the same coin," said Mr. Harrowhill as he looked around the room. "The girl is she here?"

"Ah, no. I have her hidden away for the time being. I can't risk someone kidnapping her for their own gain. Which tends to be a tradition these days. Tell me, did that Starlight Queen ever find her stolen child?"

"No, and I see your point. Best to keep her hidden, I guess."

"It's good that you can understand my thinking."

"Well then, Mr. Highland and Ms. Flannigan, was it? No need to keep up the pleasantries. Let's get down to business. I imagine you'd not sell the girl since she is more valuable as a mother."

"Aye, you seem to have the way of it, yes. Why sell the girl when I can have her pump out kids for the next twenty years and profit from that."

"Then instead, I would like to buy the rights to her first child. My son here is fifteen, and if you would allow him to bed her, then I offer one-hundred thousand gold pieces, plus an extra thirty thousand gold if the girl is not yet deflowered."

"That's a decent offer, to be sure. And one I might be willing to consider. But you must understand that this day won't come for some time yet. The girl has only reached her thirteenth name day. And we both know that damaging a girl sexually at too early an age can lead to complications with birthing down the line. So, I plan for her to stay flowered until her sixteenth name day. Only then will I allow the boys to have their way with her."

"Oh yes, I understand. She is a one-of-a-kind. You can't risk damaging her."

"Also, to improve the chance of her having magical offspring. I need to ensure that she continues her magical training at Latrusa. Her core is still developing after all."

"Yes, that makes sense. We want the highest chance for the child to possess her powers. Tell me, have you seen her use them? Can she really increase a mage's power that much?"

"Oh yes, we have a couple mages in our camp. She was able to turn a mage who had no proper training, whose flame was as small as an apple, into a blast that covered the sky. That's one of the main reasons why she needs to continue her training. We can't have her killing herself in some unforeseen magical mishap."

"Is the girl pretty? I don't want to lay beside some filthy creature," said the young boy besides his father as he folded his arms in front of him.

"Shush boy. You'll do it for the family no matter what she looks like."

Oscar laughed, "Oh, not to worry, while she's not the prettiest thing under the sun, I'm sure she'll grow to be fair on the eyes."

"Then, I take it we have a deal, Mr. Highland?"

"Not a deal, but we have an understanding. A lot can happen between now and three years."

"What about one of those Sakari girls then?" asked the

son. "Can I buy one of them? I was told they have some."

"Oh, you would like a Sakari girl, then?" asked Greega with a smile. "You certainly are a brave little man, aren't you?"

"Shut up, boy. Sakari kill their mates."

"We not kill all of them. Some of them we turn into slaves for our pleasure." Gregga rubbed her fingers together in front of the boy. "Would you like to be a slave boy? I have met many men who start to like it after some time."

"No, that's quite alright," said Mr. Harrowhill as he stood up nervously, "Thank you for your time, Mr. Highland, Miss Flannigan. I hope to be hearing from you with updates on the girl, and please contact me if you need anything."

"We will do that," said Oscar as he turned to Jacob, who was standing by the door. "My son will see you out."

Oscar watched as Jacob left the room with Mr. Harrowhill and his son. He then stood up and stretched out his arms. "And another one down, another hundred to go."

"These kingdom people really want our daughter, I think," said Gregga with a smirk as she watched Oscar kick away some of the fine clothing in the room.

"So, it would seem," said Oscar as he made his way through the clothing over to a trunk with more clothing spewing out.

He knelt and began tossing aside silks and linens inside until none were left. He then reached in and lifted up a false shelf, tossing it aside, and revealing his daughter Isha huddled inside with tears in her eyes.

"Well, you look like you've been having fun," said Oscar with a smile on his face to his daughter as he then turned to Aukube. "Alright, healer, come over here and remove that paralysis spell."

Aukube made his way over and placed his hands on Isha's head as Magic began to swirl around his hands. Slowly Isha began to move, and Aukube held her up. Tears continued to run down Isha's face as she sniffed and rubbed at her nose.

"Why did you... lock me in there like that?" asked Isha, looking at Oscar.

"So that you would hear everything they said, and the spell was to make sure you didn't reveal yourself. I'm glad to see you kept those powers of yours under control this time."

"I don't want to do that again. I don't want to hear them say that about me anymore."

"Well, too bad. I asked ya before if ya were willing to pay the price. And that's one of the ways you're gonna pay it. Ya gonna stay locked in that box and listen to every single noble come up here and talk about fucking you till your damn ears start to bleed."

"Why... are you doing this to me?"

"To you? Yes, I guess it does seem that way," said Oscar as he walked over to the window. "But I'm doing it for you. Before I send you back off to that magic school with that bitch Soulden, you're gonna realize exactly how everyone sees you now. So, the next time anybody talks to you. You're always gonna know in the back of that head of yours, just what they might be after."

"This is a good lesson for you, daughter. I know it is hard to hear what the men say. But it's a lesson that you need to learn. Or even worse, things happen to you because you are blind to them. We will make you not blind. We do this because we love you."

"Now come over here daughter, I wish to show you something."

Isha made her over to Oscar by the window. And as she gazed out over the sea, her eyes witnessed the amazing sight of hundreds of airships filling the skies above the city and out over the sea; each ship painted a different color.

"So many," said Isha in shock.

"And each one has some little noble or some old man trying to fuck you for their own power. This is the life you're choosing for yourself. I hope you're prepared for this, daughter."

The door to the room opened as Jacob stuck his head inside.

"Father, Count Roanmill from Urjsun has arrived with his two sons. They're down stairs requesting to come up."

"Oh, two boys this time," said Oscar with a chuckle. "Fine, go down and bring them back up."

Jacob shook his head, closing the door.

Oscar then looked down at Isha, "Now will you go back in the box, or are you going to give up now? Because the only way I allow you to go back to that school and try to find out who killed your friend is in that box."

Isha narrowed her eyes at Oscar, glowering back up at him.

"That's a nice look on your face, but remember, I said that this choice of yours would come with a price. So, let me hear you say it. Because we are going to have dozens more visitors today, and then dozens more tomorrow, and the day after that."

"I... I... will go back in the box, Father." She said as she turned around and walked back over to the large trunk and stepped inside. She bundled herself back down as Aukube once again placed the paralysis spell on her, freezing her body in place.

Oscar walked back over, picking up the lid of the trunk's shelf, and smiled down at Isha. "Listen well to all you hear, daughter. Because this is how the world really is." He then took one last look at his daughter as tears began to slide out of her eyes and down her cheek before placing the lid back on top of Isha, trapping her back in the darkness and tossing silks and linens on top of her.

Soon came a knock on the door, and in the darkness of the trunk, Isha heard Oscar's voice.

"Gentlemen, hello. Come in, and please tell me what wonderful plans you have for the girl."

Thank you for reading

A Melody of Magic

For more information on books from the author
Teddy Baire.
Please visit
www.teddybarie.com
for updates on any future novels.

9 781734 951646